FALL OF CTHULHU

THE FUGUE

FALL OF CTHULHU: THE FUGUE — published by Boom! Studios. Fall of Cthulhu is copyright © Boom Entertainment, Inc. All Rights Reserved. Boom! Studios™ and the Boom! logo are trademarks of Boom Entertainment, Inc., registered in various countries and categories. All rights reserved. Office of publication: **6310 San Vicente Blvd Ste 404, Los Angeles CA 90048. www.BOOM-Studios.com**

FIRST PRINTING: April 2008
Collecting Fall of Cthulhu #0-5
10 9 8 7 6 5 4 3 2 1

PRINTED IN KOREA

ISBN-13: 978-1-934506-19-6
ISBN-10: 1-934506-19-2

51499

9 781934 506196

FALL OF CTHULHU
THE FUGUE

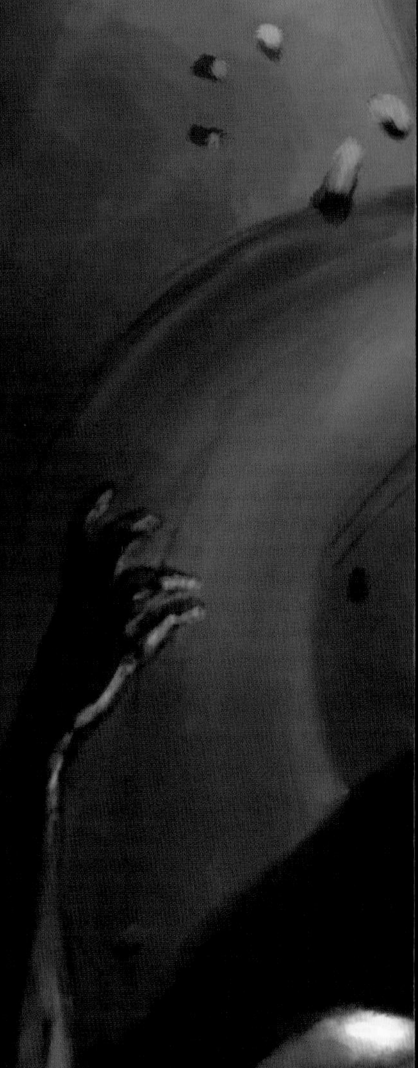

MICHAEL ALAN NELSON
story

JEAN DZIALOWSKI
art

IMAGINARY FRIENDS STUDIO
colors

ANDREW RITCHIE
dreamland sequences

TERRI DELGADO AND
MARSHALL DILLON
letters (intro story)

ED DUKESHIRE
letters (part one-five)

MARSHALL DILLON
managing editor

JOYCE EL HAYEK
assistant editor

VATCHE MAVLIAN
cover artist

TYLER WALPOLE
back cover artist

BOOM!
STUDIOS

ANDREW COSBY
ROSS RICHIE
founders

MARK WAID
editor-in-chief

TOM FASSBENDER
vice president,
publishing

ADAM FORTIER
vice president,
new business

CHIP MOSHER
marketing &
sales director

MICHAEL ALAN NELSON
associate editor

ED DUKESHIRE
designer

DANIEL VARGAS
publishing coordinator

GLOSSARY

THE NECRONOMICON
The "Al Azif" -- from Arabic for "that nocturnal sound (made by insects) supposed to be the howling of daemons". (One Arabic/English dictionary translates `Azi f as "whistling (of the wind); weird sound or noise") -- also known as the Necronomicon was written by Abdul Alhazred. Among other things, the work contains an account of the Old Ones, their history, and the means for summoning them.

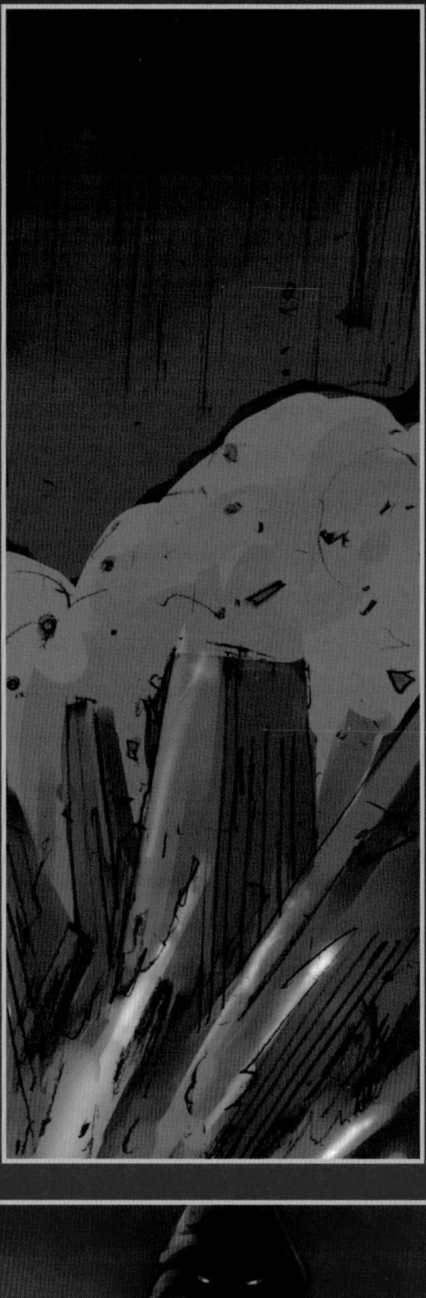

ABDUL ALHAZRED
is the so-called "Mad Arab" credited with authoring the occult book Kitab al-Azif (the Necronomicon). From Sanaa in Yemen, he visited the ruins of Babylon, the "subterranean secrets" of Memphis and the Empty Quarter of Arabia (where he discovered the "Nameless City" below Irem). In his last years, he lived in Damascus, where he wrote Al Azif before his sudden and mysterious death in 738.

THE DREAMLANDS
A vast, alternate dimension that can be entered through dreams, similar to astral projection. Experienced dreamers are among the most powerful inhabitants of the Dreamlands and may become its permanent residents after their physical deaths.

THE NAMELESS CITY
An ancient ruin located somewhere in the deserts of the Arabian Peninsula older than any human civilization. Their city was originally coastal, but when the seas receded it was left in the depths of a desert. This resulted in the decline and eventual ruin of the city.

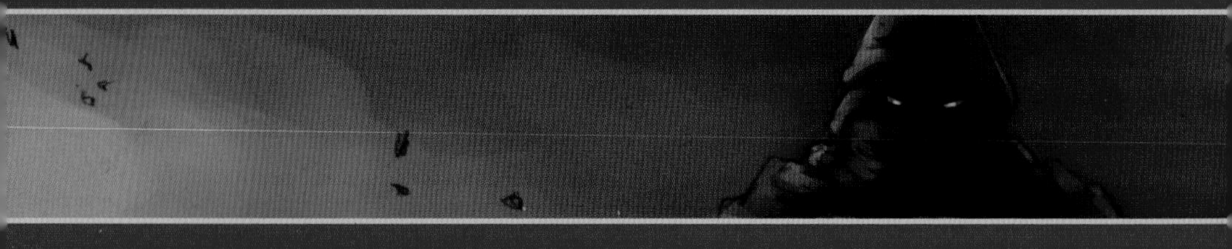

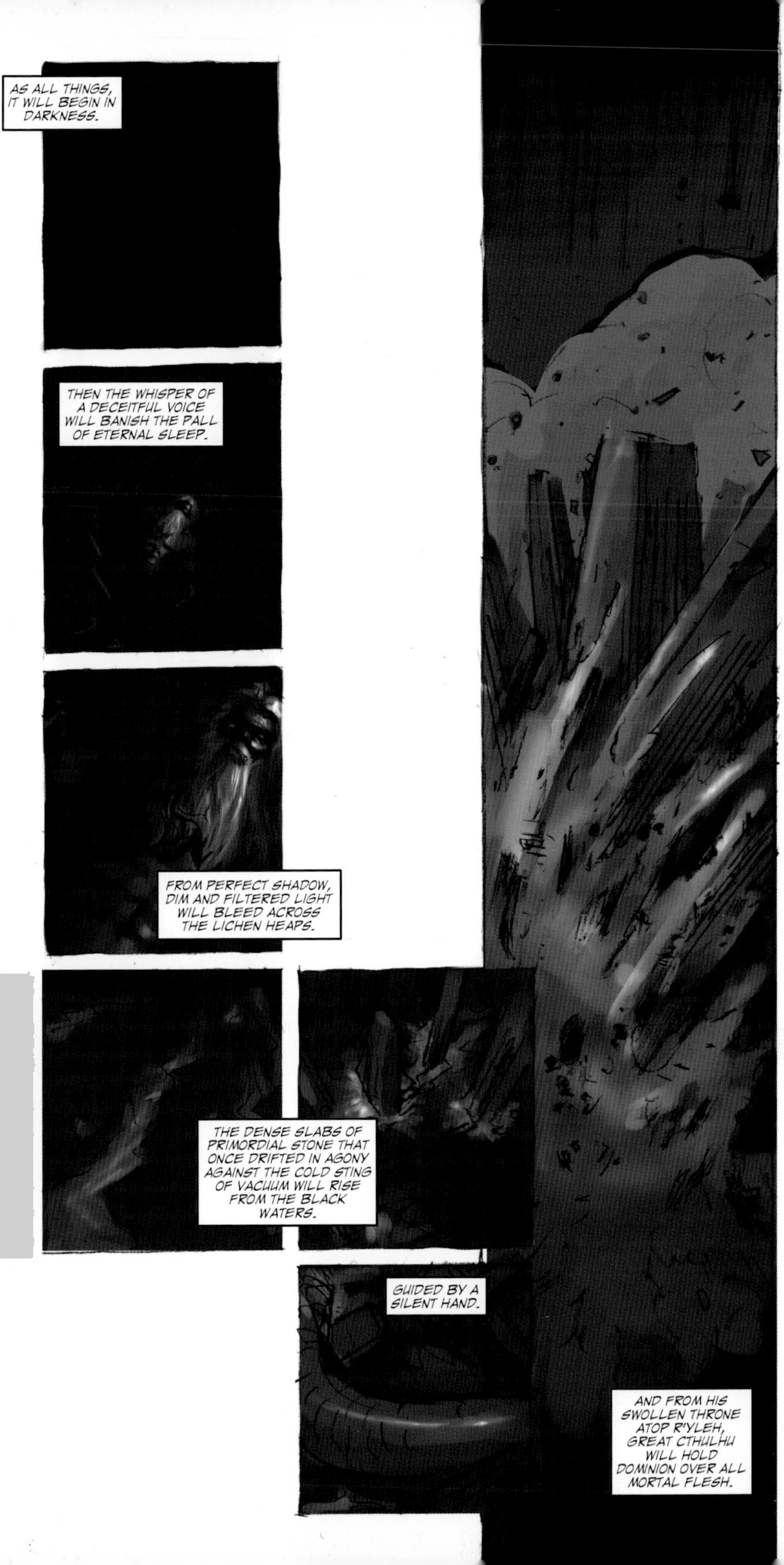
AS ALL THINGS, IT WILL BEGIN IN DARKNESS.
THEN THE WHISPER OF A DECEITFUL VOICE WILL BANISH THE PALL OF ETERNAL SLEEP.
FROM PERFECT SHADOW, DIM AND FILTERED LIGHT WILL BLEED ACROSS THE LICHEN HEAPS.
THE DENSE SLABS OF PRIMORDIAL STONE THAT ONCE DRIFTED IN AGONY AGAINST THE COLD STING OF VACUUM WILL RISE FROM THE BLACK WATERS.
GUIDED BY A SILENT HAND.
AND FROM HIS SWOLLEN THRONE ATOP R'YLEH, GREAT CTHULHU WILL HOLD DOMINION OVER ALL MORTAL FLESH.

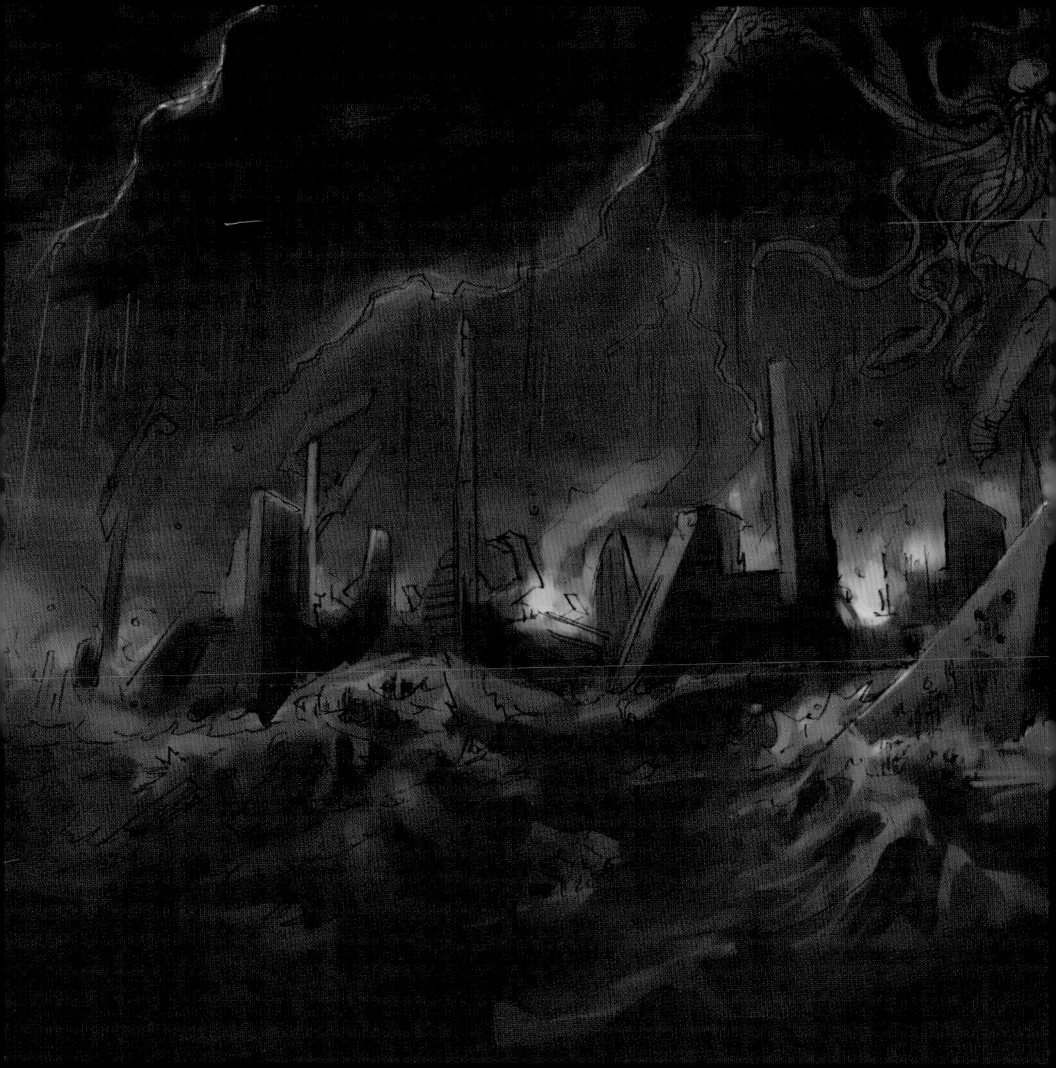

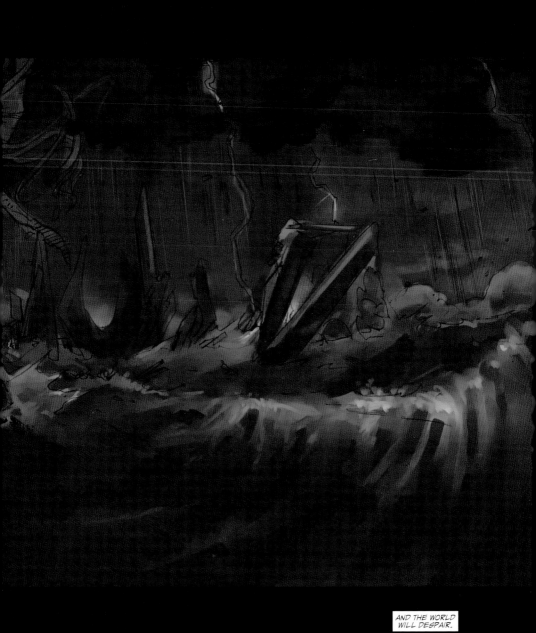

AND THE WORLD
WILL DESPAIR.

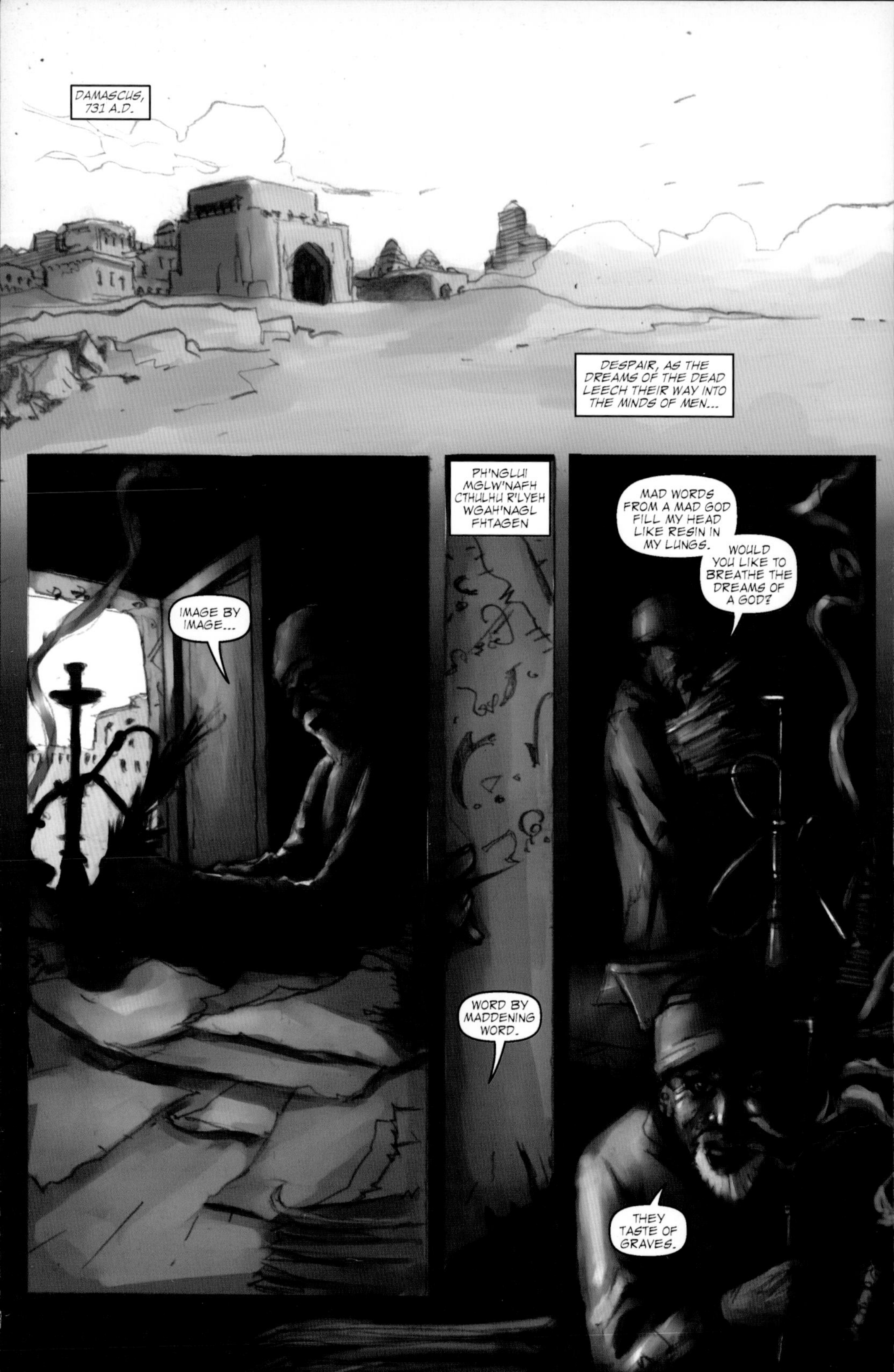
DAMASCUS, 731 A.D.
DESPAIR, AS THE DREAMS OF THE DEAD LEECH THEIR WAY INTO THE MINDS OF MEN...
IMAGE BY IMAGE...
PH'NGLUI MGLW'NAFH CTHULHU R'LYEH WGAH'NAGL FHTAGEN
WORD BY MADDENING WORD.
MAD WORDS FROM A MAD GOD FILL MY HEAD LIKE RESIN IN MY LUNGS.
WOULD YOU LIKE TO BREATHE THE DREAMS OF A GOD?
THEY TASTE OF GRAVES.

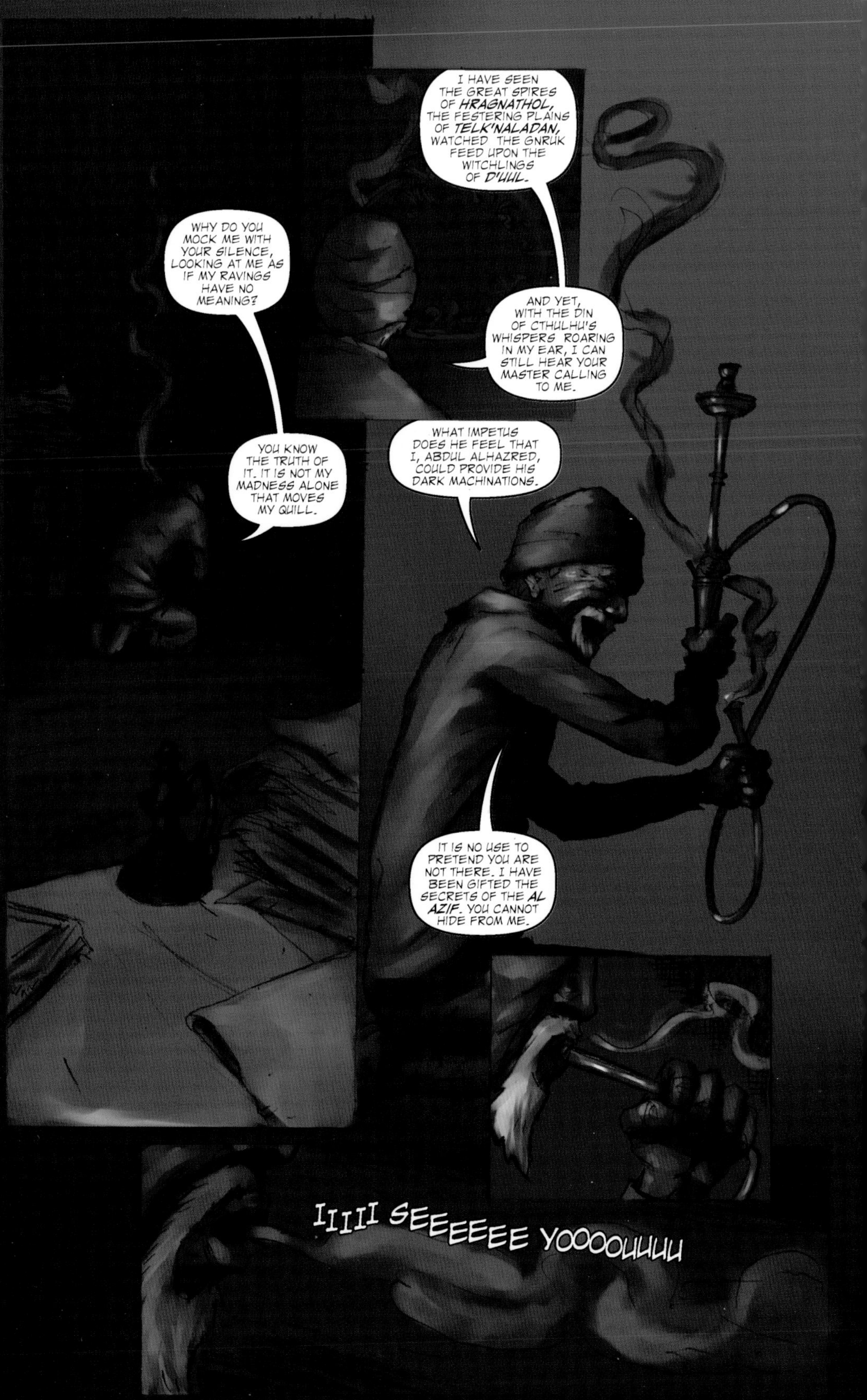
I HAVE SEEN THE GREAT SPIRES OF HRAGNATHOL, THE FESTERING PLAINS OF TELK'NALADAN, WATCHED THE GNRUK FEED UPON THE WITCHLINGS OF D'UUL.
WHY DO YOU MOCK ME WITH YOUR SILENCE, LOOKING AT ME AS IF MY RAVINGS HAVE NO MEANING?
AND YET, WITH THE DIN OF CTHULHU'S WHISPERS ROARING IN MY EAR, I CAN STILL HEAR YOUR MASTER CALLING TO ME.
YOU KNOW THE TRUTH OF IT. IT IS NOT MY MADNESS ALONE THAT MOVES MY QUILL.
WHAT IMPETUS DOES HE FEEL THAT I, ABDUL ALHAZRED, COULD PROVIDE HIS DARK MACHINATIONS.
IT IS NO USE TO PRETEND YOU ARE NOT THERE. I HAVE BEEN GIFTED THE SECRETS OF THE AL AZIF. YOU CANNOT HIDE FROM ME.
IIIII SEEEEEEE YOOOOUUUU

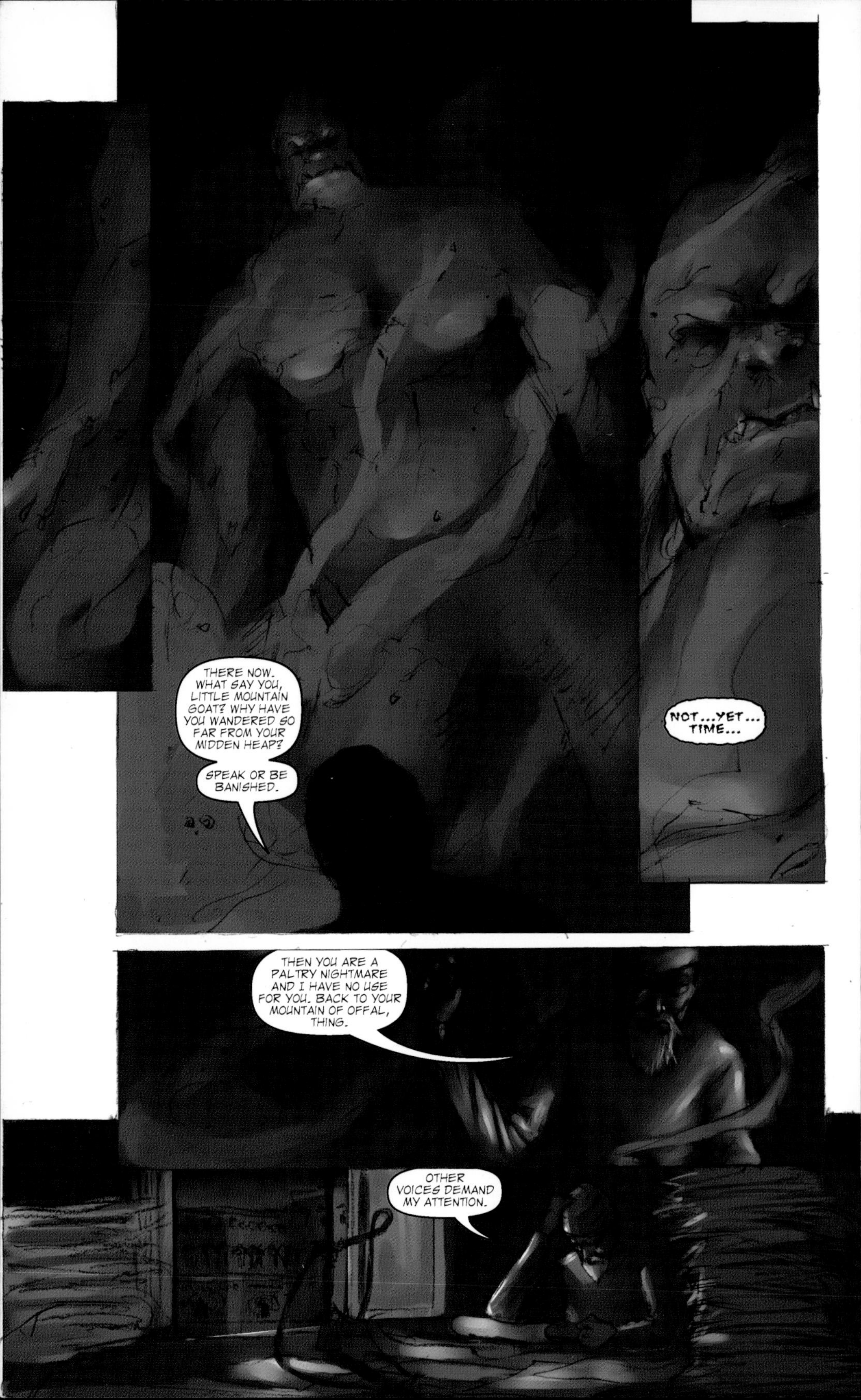
THERE NOW. WHAT SAY YOU, LITTLE MOUNTAIN GOAT? WHY HAVE YOU WANDERED SO FAR FROM YOUR MIDDEN HEAP?
SPEAK OR BE BANISHED.
NOT...YET... TIME...
THEN YOU ARE A PALTRY NIGHTMARE AND I HAVE NO USE FOR YOU. BACK TO YOUR MOUNTAIN OF OFFAL, THING.
OTHER VOICES DEMAND MY ATTENTION.

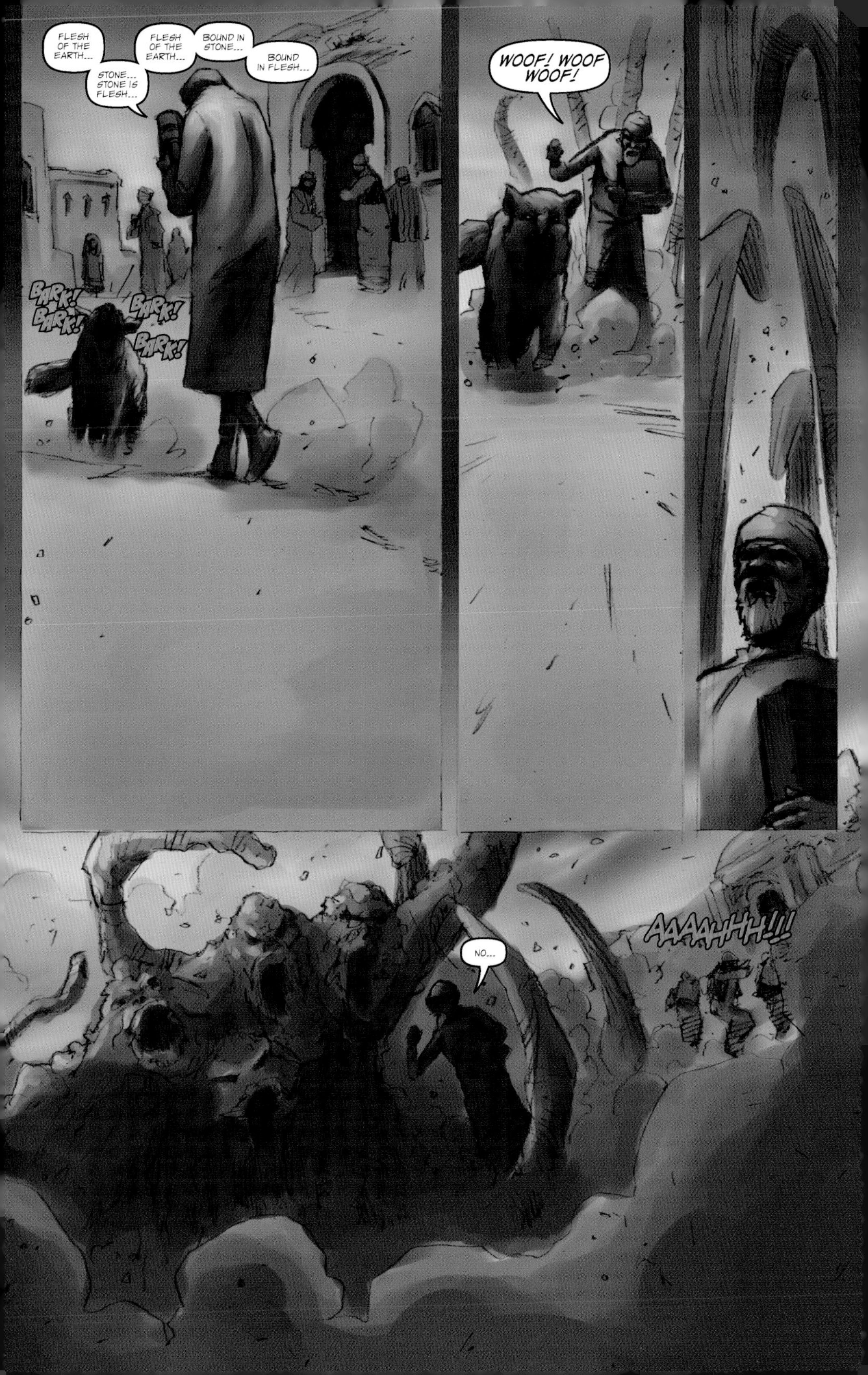
FLESH OF THE EARTH...
STONE... STONE IS FLESH...
FLESH OF THE EARTH...
BOUND IN STONE...
BOUND IN FLESH...
BARK! BARK!
BARK!
BARK!
WOOF! WOOF WOOF!
NO...
AAAAHHH!!!

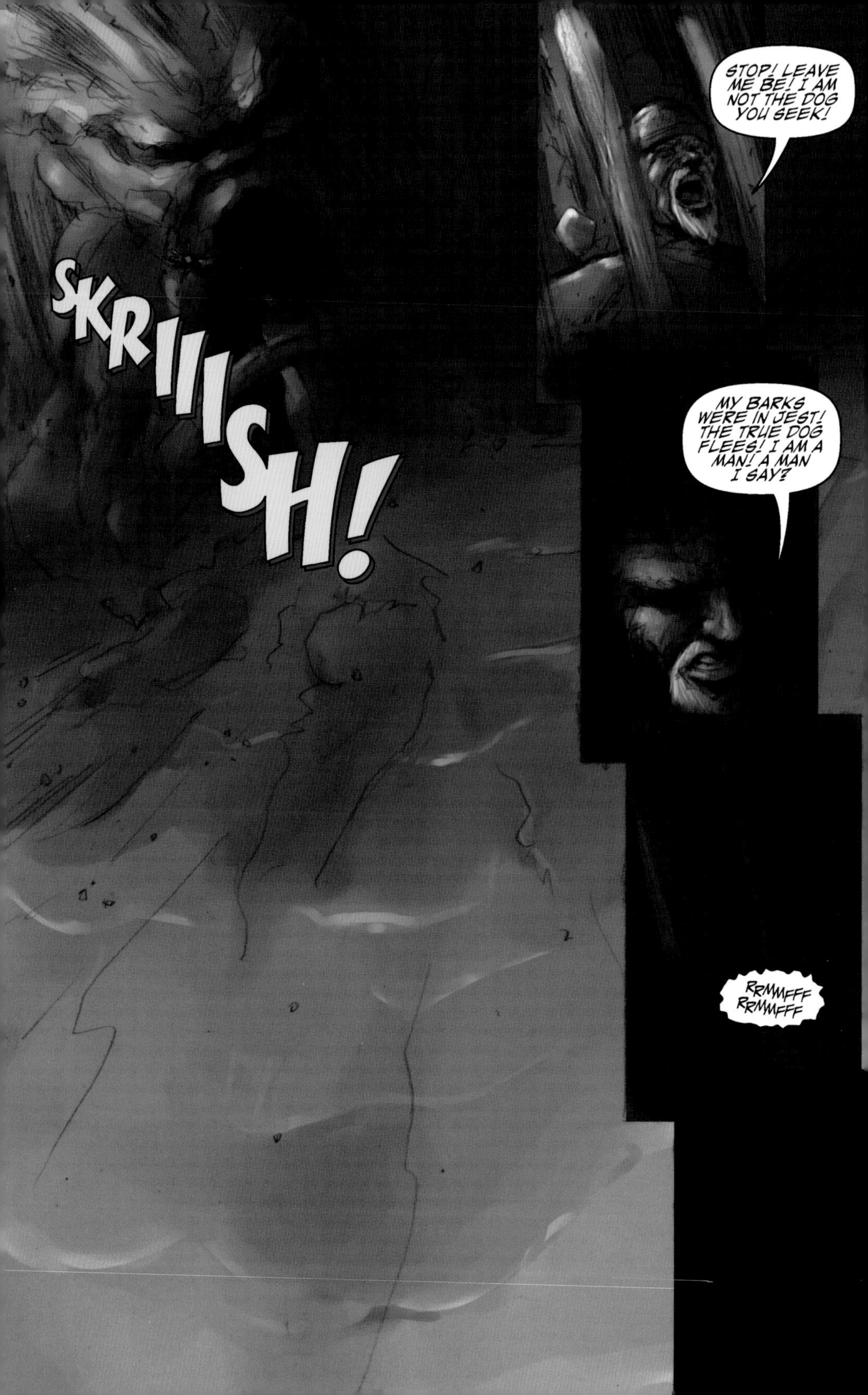
SKRIIIISH!
STOP! LEAVE ME BE! I AM NOT THE DOG YOU SEEK!
MY BARKS WERE IN JEST! THE TRUE DOG FLEES! I AM A MAN! A MAN I SAY?
RRMMFFF RRMMFFF

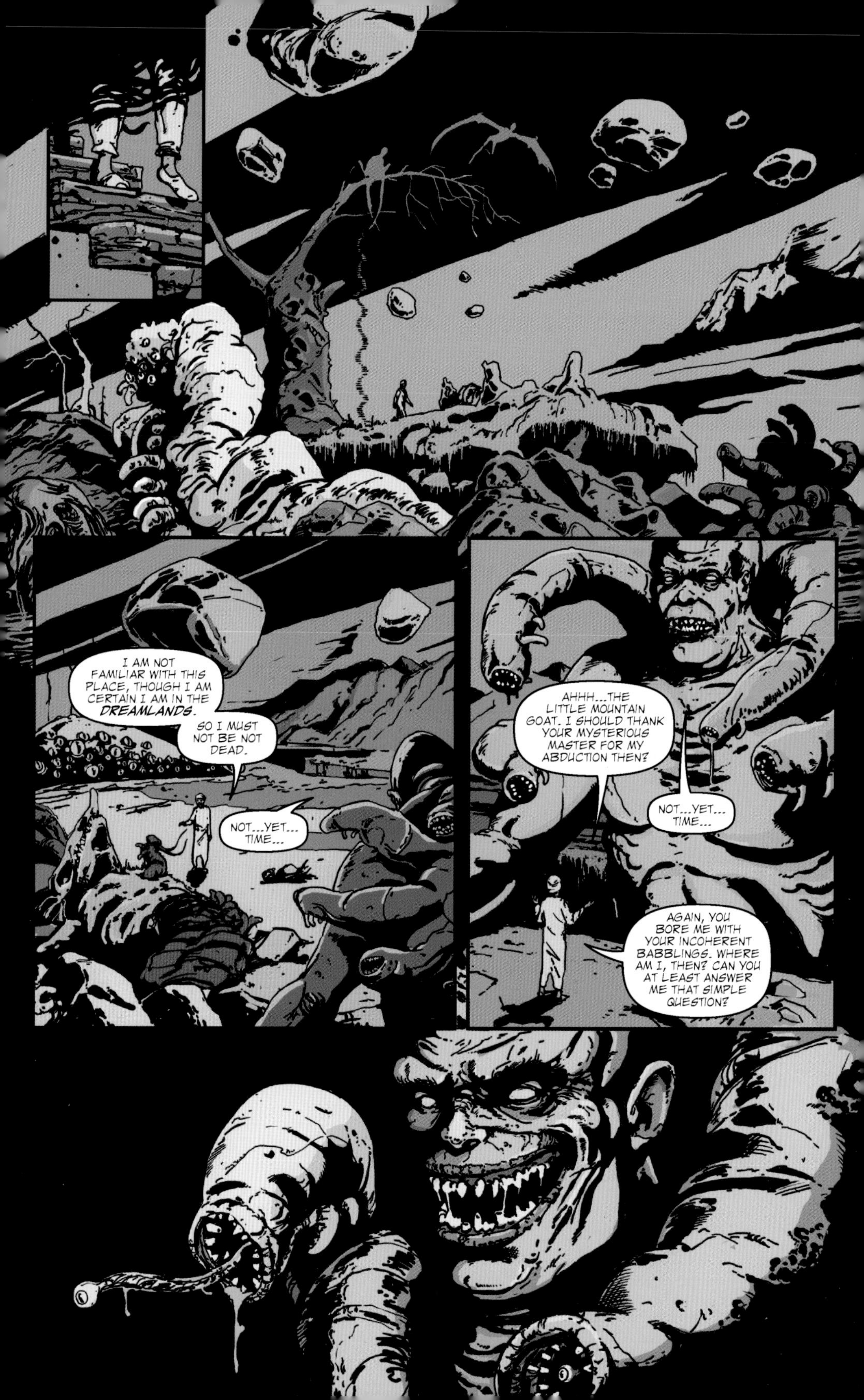
I AM NOT FAMILIAR WITH THIS PLACE, THOUGH I AM CERTAIN I AM IN THE DREAMLANDS.
SO I MUST NOT BE NOT DEAD.
NOT...YET... TIME...
AHHH...THE LITTLE MOUNTAIN GOAT. I SHOULD THANK YOUR MYSTERIOUS MASTER FOR MY ABDUCTION THEN?
NOT...YET... TIME...
AGAIN, YOU BORE ME WITH YOUR INCOHERENT BABBLINGS. WHERE AM I, THEN? CAN YOU AT LEAST ANSWER ME THAT SIMPLE QUESTION?

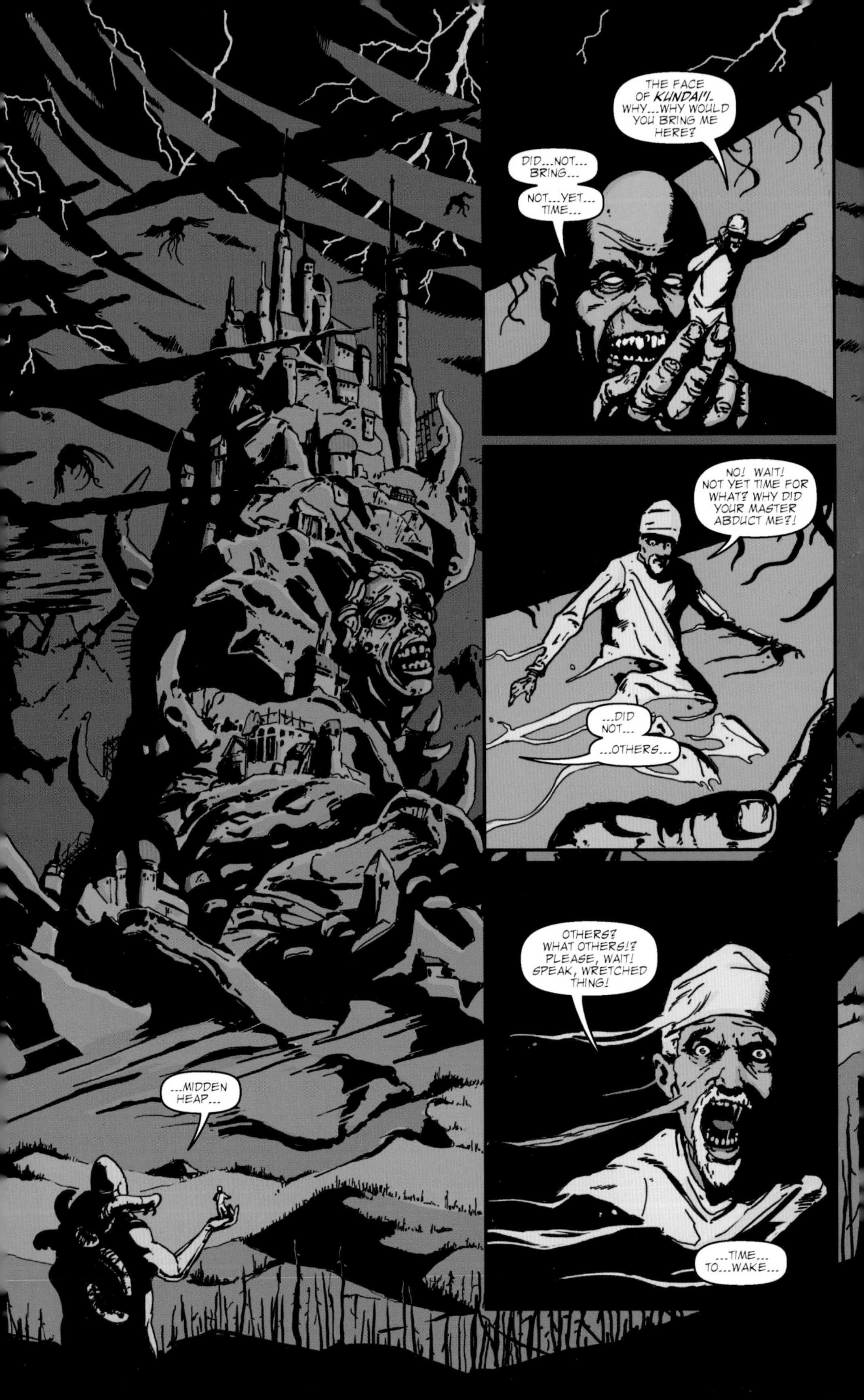
...MIDDEN HEAP...
THE FACE OF KUNDAI'I. WHY...WHY WOULD YOU BRING ME HERE?
DID...NOT... BRING...
NOT...YET... TIME...
NO! WAIT! NOT YET TIME FOR WHAT? WHY DID YOUR MASTER ABDUCT ME?!
...DID NOT...
...OTHERS...
OTHERS? WHAT OTHERS!? PLEASE, WAIT! SPEAK, WRETCHED THING!
...TIME... TO...WAKE...

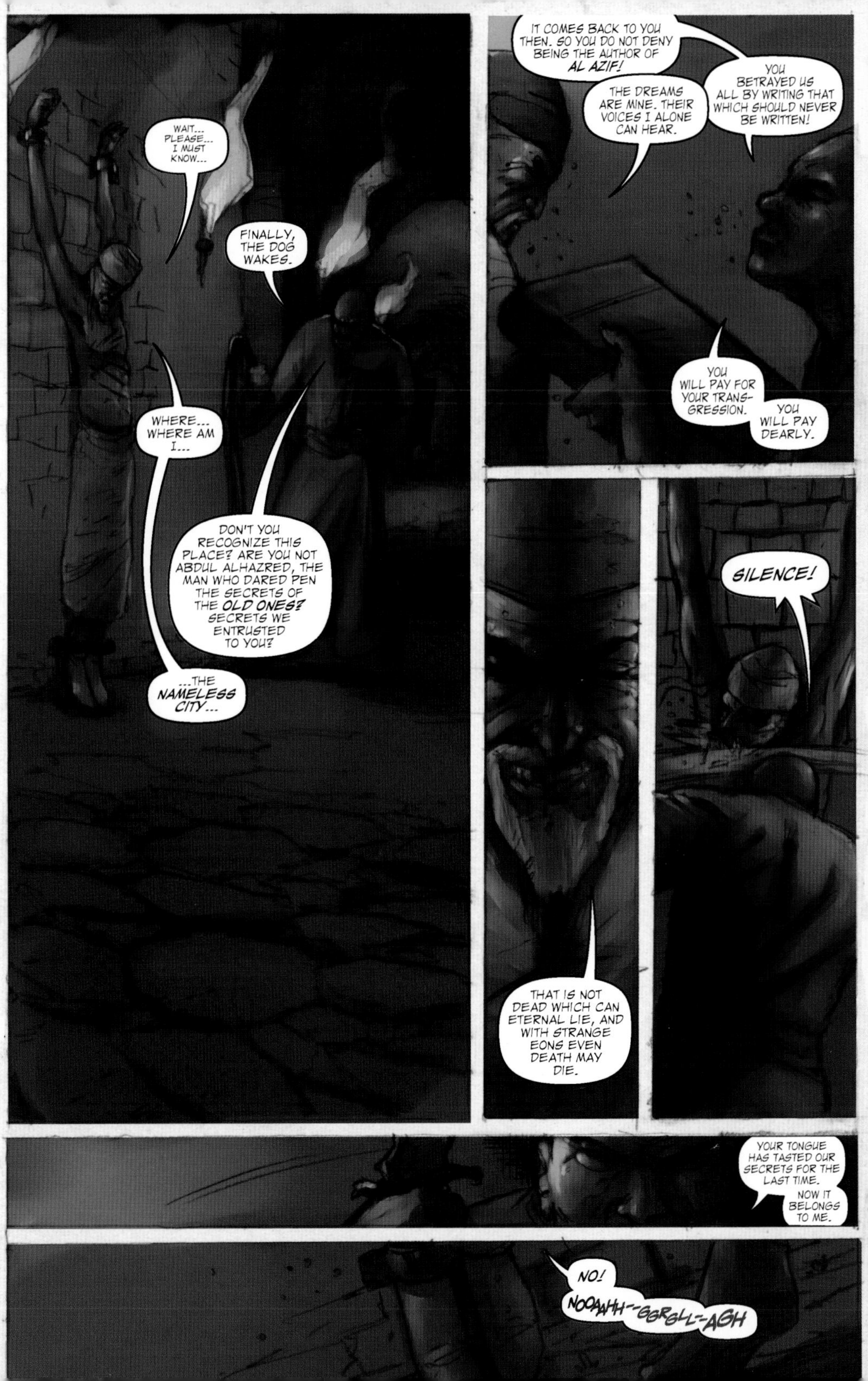
WAIT... PLEASE... I MUST KNOW...
FINALLY, THE DOG WAKES.
WHERE... WHERE AM I...
DON'T YOU RECOGNIZE THIS PLACE? ARE YOU NOT ABDUL ALHAZRED, THE MAN WHO DARED PEN THE SECRETS OF THE OLD ONES? SECRETS WE ENTRUSTED TO YOU?
...THE NAMELESS CITY...
IT COMES BACK TO YOU THEN. SO YOU DO NOT DENY BEING THE AUTHOR OF AL AZIF!
THE DREAMS ARE MINE. THEIR VOICES I ALONE CAN HEAR.
YOU BETRAYED US ALL BY WRITING THAT WHICH SHOULD NEVER BE WRITTEN!
YOU WILL PAY FOR YOUR TRANS-GRESSION.
YOU WILL PAY DEARLY.
THAT IS NOT DEAD WHICH CAN ETERNAL LIE, AND WITH STRANGE EONS EVEN DEATH MAY DIE.
SILENCE!
YOUR TONGUE HAS TASTED OUR SECRETS FOR THE LAST TIME.
NOW IT BELONGS TO ME.
NO!
NOOAAHH--GGRGLL--AGH

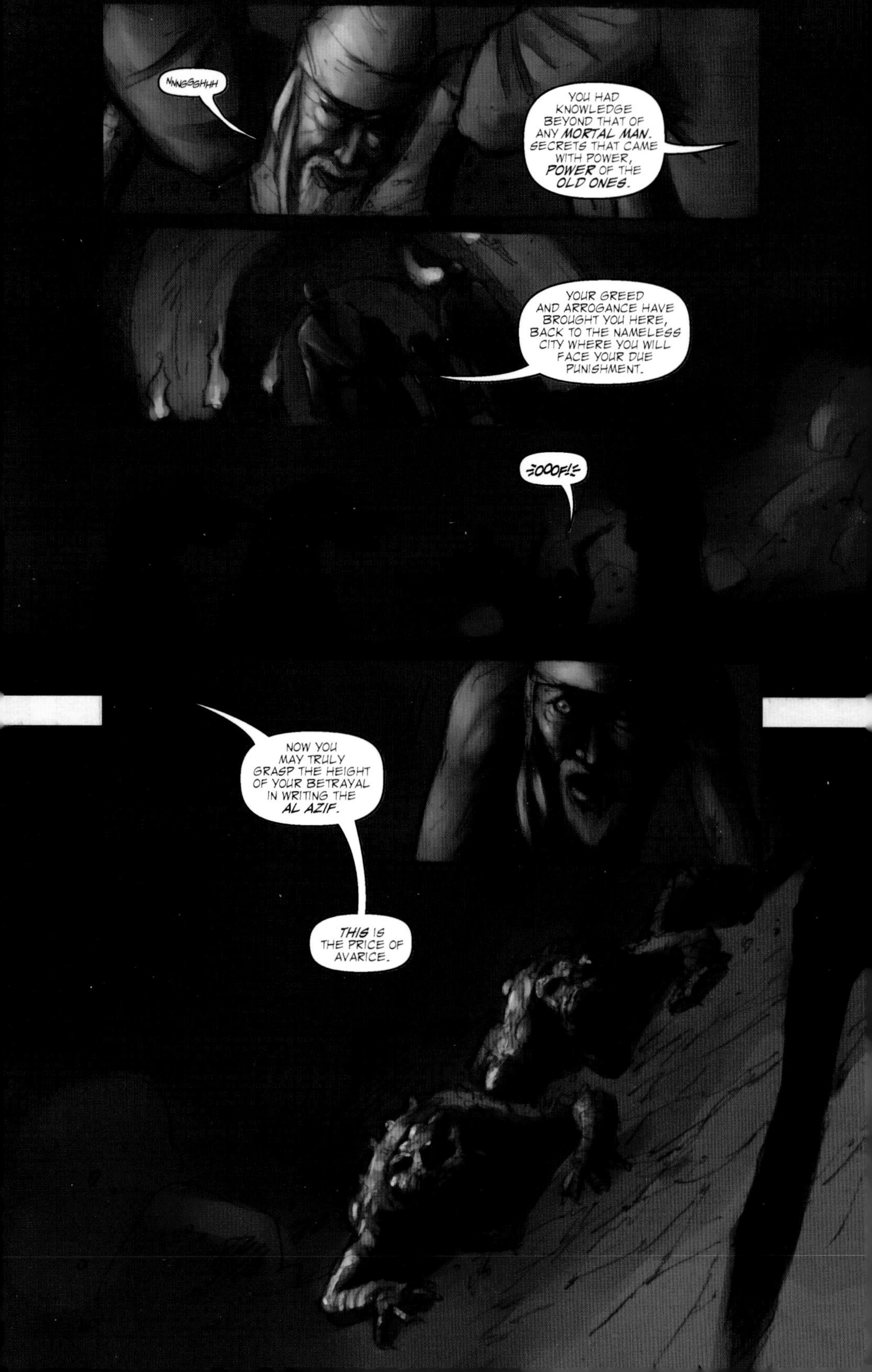
NNNGGSHHH
YOU HAD KNOWLEDGE BEYOND THAT OF ANY MORTAL MAN. SECRETS THAT CAME WITH POWER, POWER OF THE OLD ONES.
YOUR GREED AND ARROGANCE HAVE BROUGHT YOU HERE, BACK TO THE NAMELESS CITY WHERE YOU WILL FACE YOUR DUE PUNISHMENT.
OOOF!
NOW YOU MAY TRULY GRASP THE HEIGHT OF YOUR BETRAYAL IN WRITING THE AL AZIF.
THIS IS THE PRICE OF AVARICE.

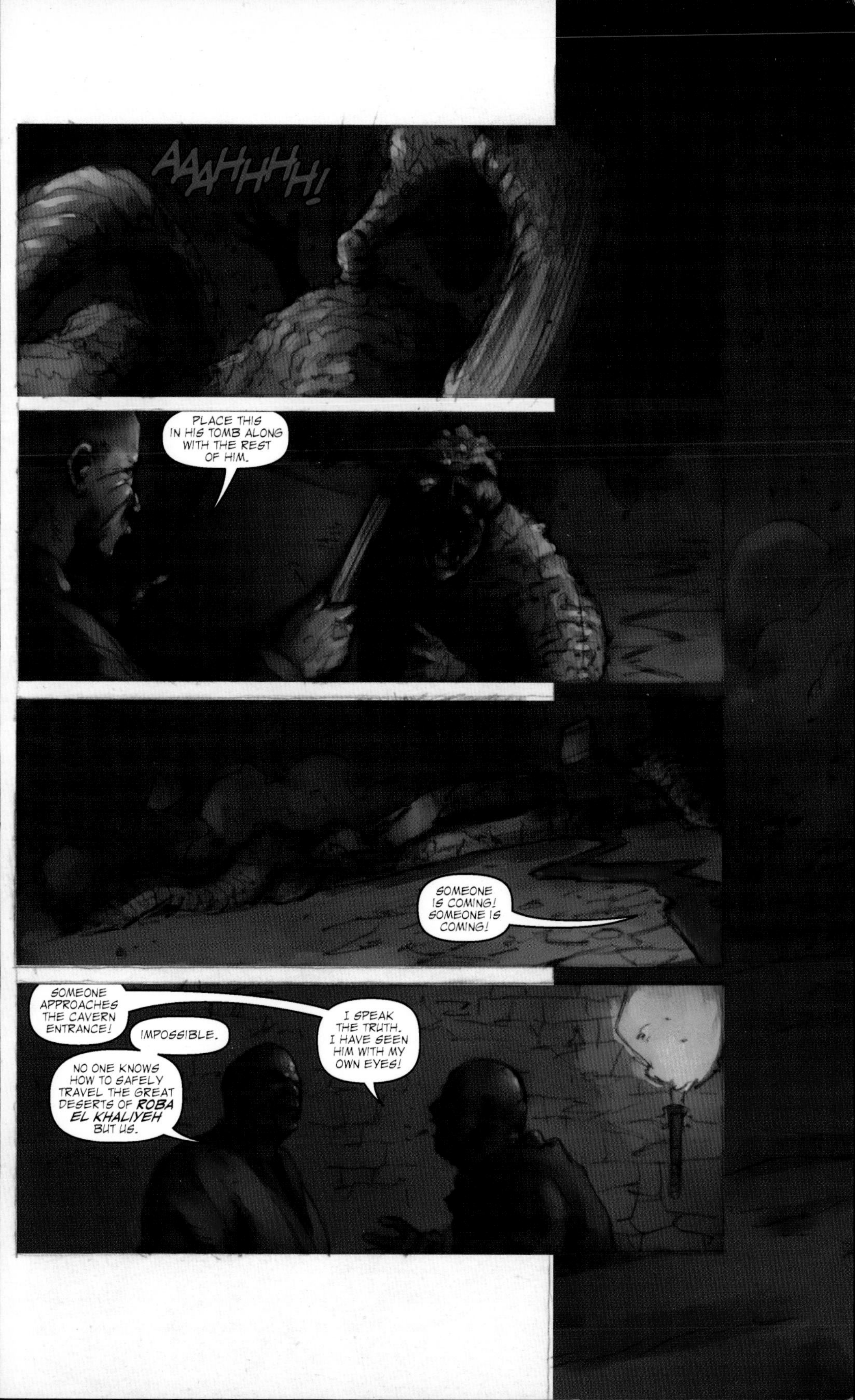
AAAHHHH!
PLACE THIS IN HIS TOMB ALONG WITH THE REST OF HIM.
SOMEONE IS COMING! SOMEONE IS COMING!
SOMEONE APPROACHES THE CAVERN ENTRANCE!
IMPOSSIBLE.
NO ONE KNOWS HOW TO SAFELY TRAVEL THE GREAT DESERTS OF ROBA EL KHALIYEH BUT US.
I SPEAK THE TRUTH. I HAVE SEEN HIM WITH MY OWN EYES!

"HE IS ALMOST UPON US!"

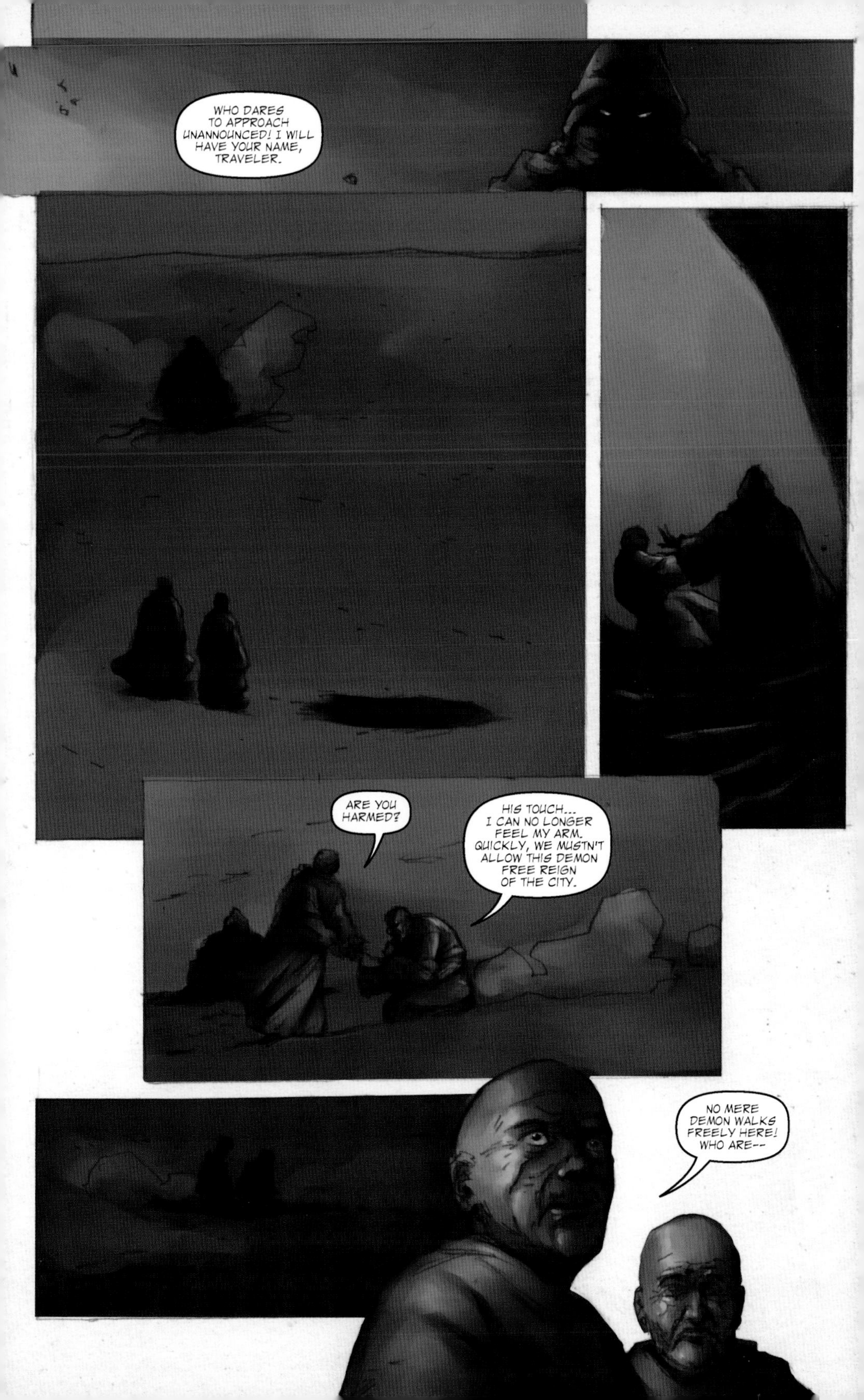
WHO DARES TO APPROACH UNANNOUNCED! I WILL HAVE YOUR NAME, TRAVELER.
ARE YOU HARMED?
HIS TOUCH... I CAN NO LONGER FEEL MY ARM. QUICKLY, WE MUSTN'T ALLOW THIS DEMON FREE REIGN OF THE CITY.
NO MERE DEMON WALKS FREELY HERE! WHO ARE--

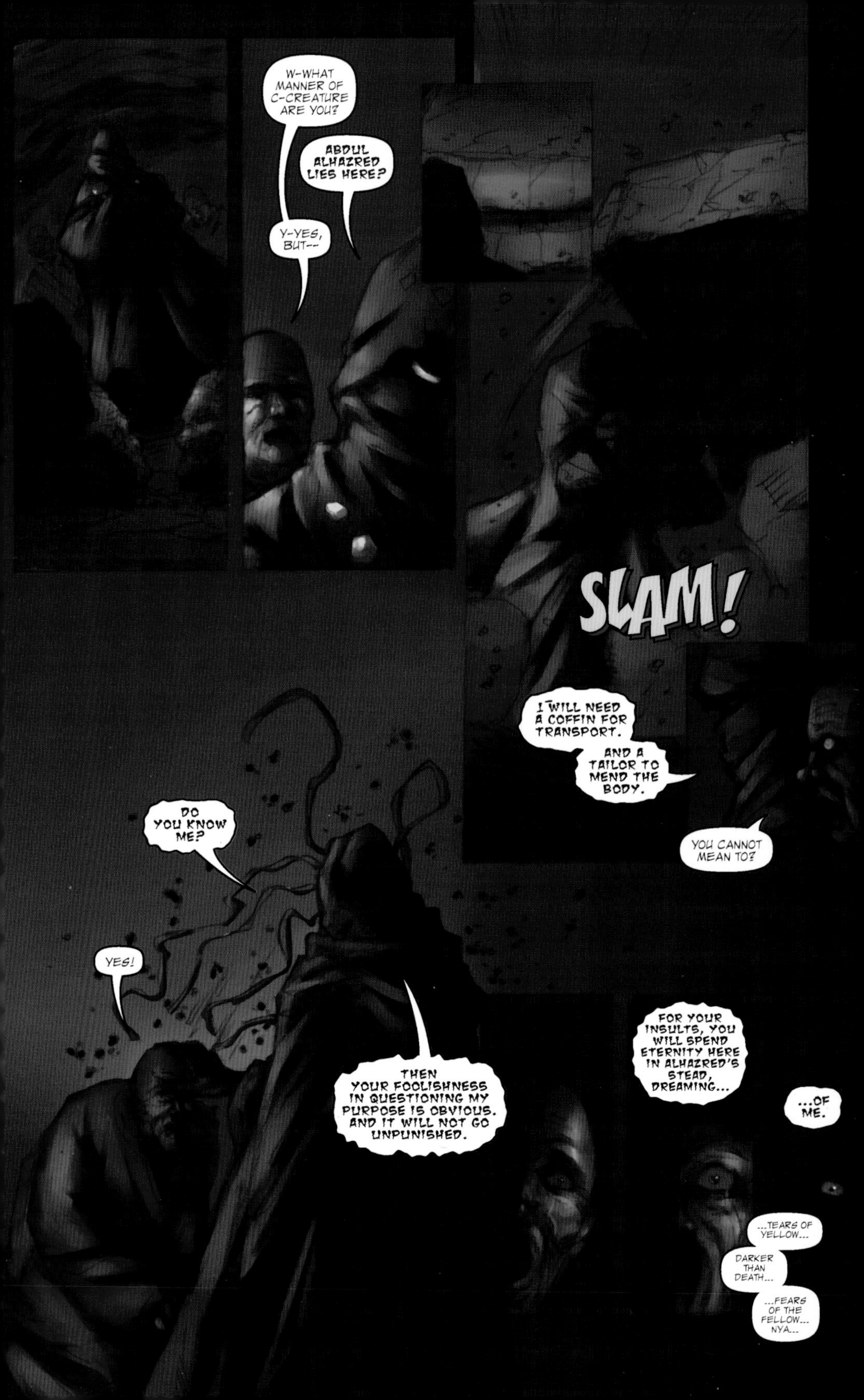
W-WHAT MANNER OF C-CREATURE ARE YOU?
ABDUL ALHAZRED LIES HERE?
Y-YES, BUT--
SLAM!
I WILL NEED A COFFIN FOR TRANSPORT.
AND A TAILOR TO MEND THE BODY.
YOU CANNOT MEAN TO?
DO YOU KNOW ME?
YES!
THEN YOUR FOOLISHNESS IN QUESTIONING MY PURPOSE IS OBVIOUS. AND IT WILL NOT GO UNPUNISHED.
FOR YOUR INSULTS, YOU WILL SPEND ETERNITY HERE IN ALHAZRED'S STEAD, DREAMING...
...OF ME.
...TEARS OF YELLOW...
DARKER THAN DEATH...
...FEARS OF THE FELLOW... NYA...

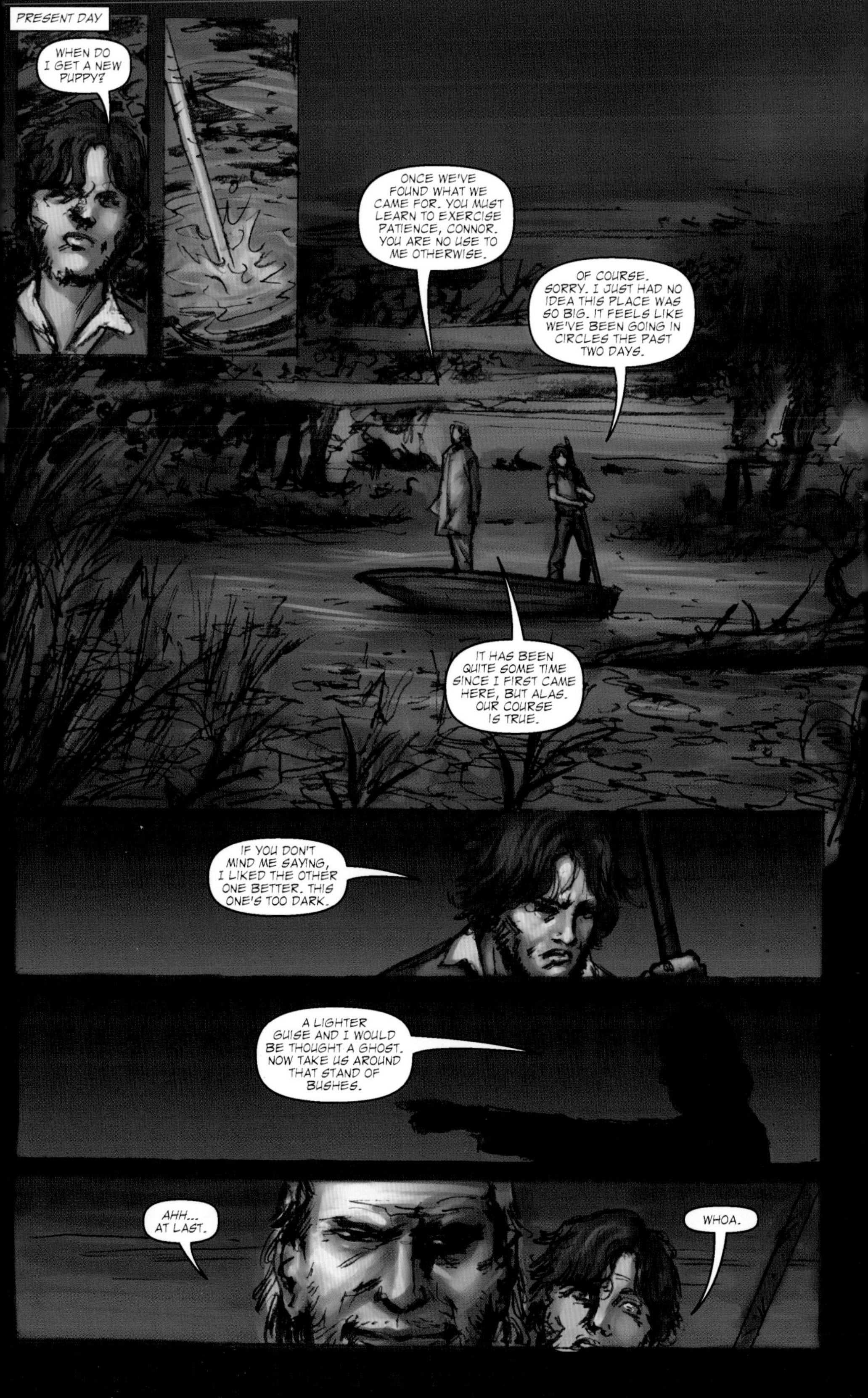
PRESENT DAY
WHEN DO I GET A NEW PUPPY?
ONCE WE'VE FOUND WHAT WE CAME FOR. YOU MUST LEARN TO EXERCISE PATIENCE, CONNOR. YOU ARE NO USE TO ME OTHERWISE.
OF COURSE. SORRY. I JUST HAD NO IDEA THIS PLACE WAS SO BIG. IT FEELS LIKE WE'VE BEEN GOING IN CIRCLES THE PAST TWO DAYS.
IT HAS BEEN QUITE SOME TIME SINCE I FIRST CAME HERE, BUT ALAS. OUR COURSE IS TRUE.
IF YOU DON'T MIND ME SAYING, I LIKED THE OTHER ONE BETTER. THIS ONE'S TOO DARK.
A LIGHTER GUISE AND I WOULD BE THOUGHT A GHOST. NOW TAKE US AROUND THAT STAND OF BUSHES.
AHH... AT LAST.
WHOA.

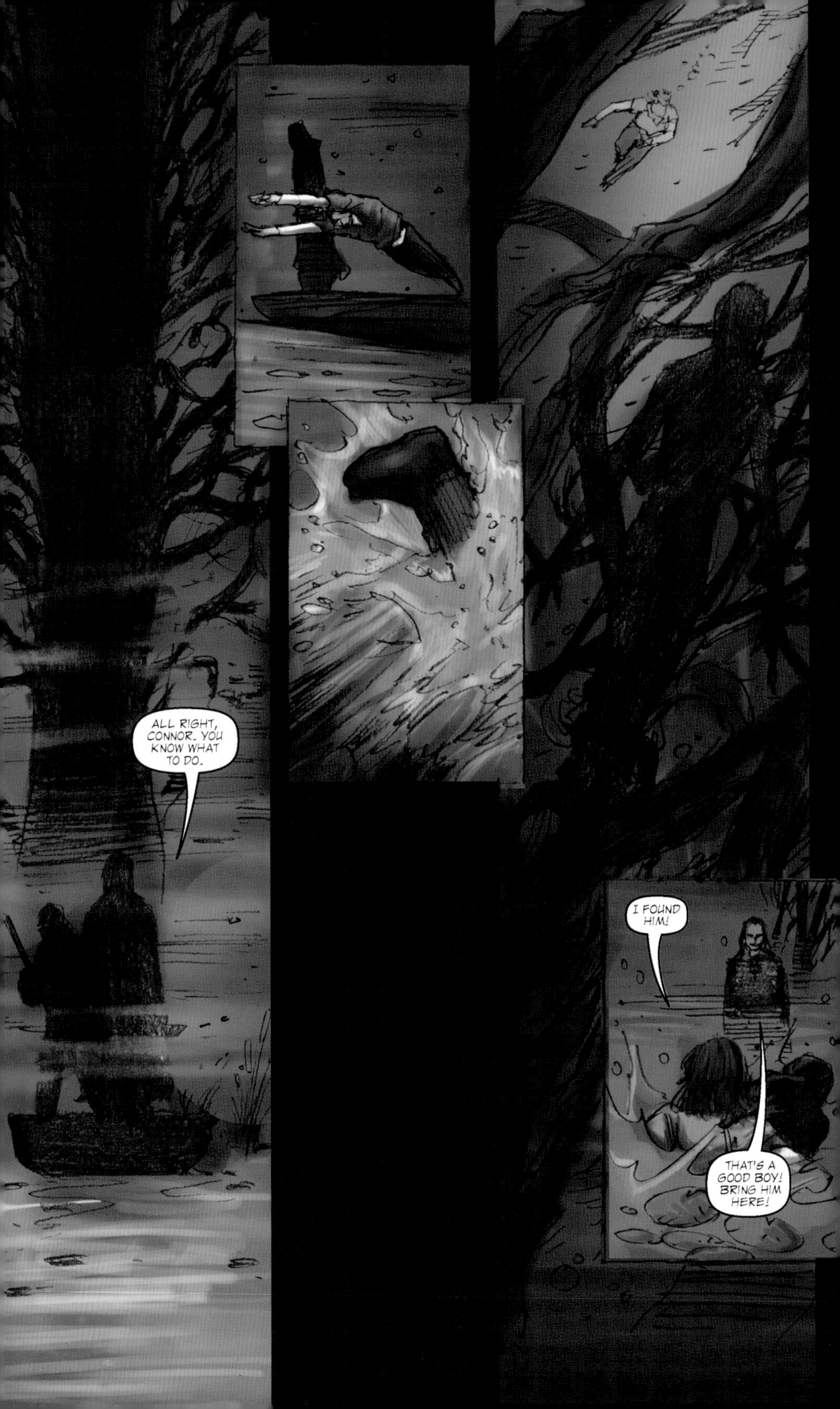
ALL RIGHT, CONNOR. YOU KNOW WHAT TO DO.
I FOUND HIM!
THAT'S A GOOD BOY! BRING HIM HERE!

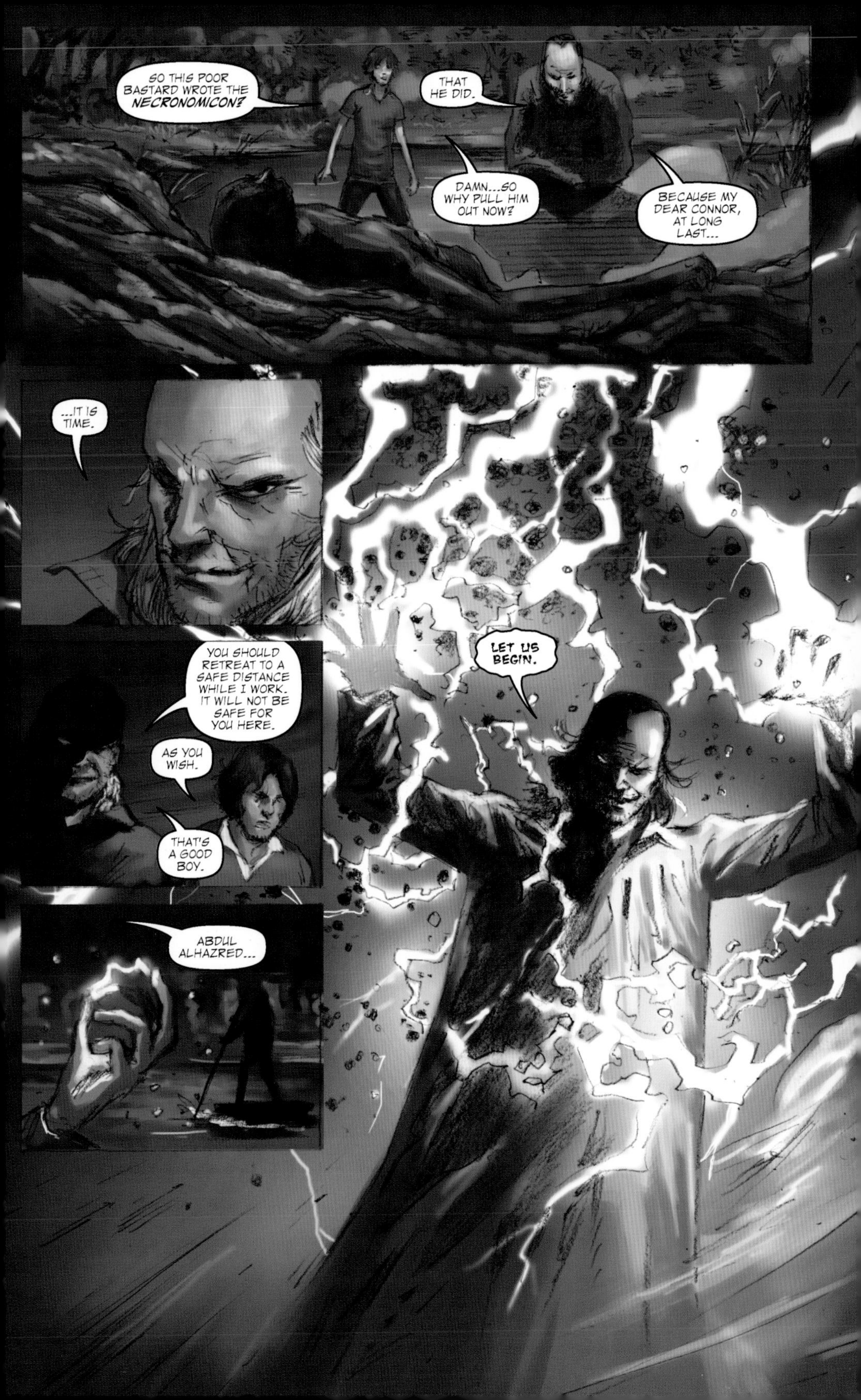
SO THIS POOR BASTARD WROTE THE *NECRONOMICON*?
THAT HE DID.
DAMN...SO WHY PULL HIM OUT NOW?
BECAUSE MY DEAR CONNOR, AT LONG LAST...
...IT IS TIME.
YOU SHOULD RETREAT TO A SAFE DISTANCE WHILE I WORK. IT WILL NOT BE SAFE FOR YOU HERE.
AS YOU WISH.
THAT'S A GOOD BOY.
ABDUL ALHAZRED...
LET US BEGIN.

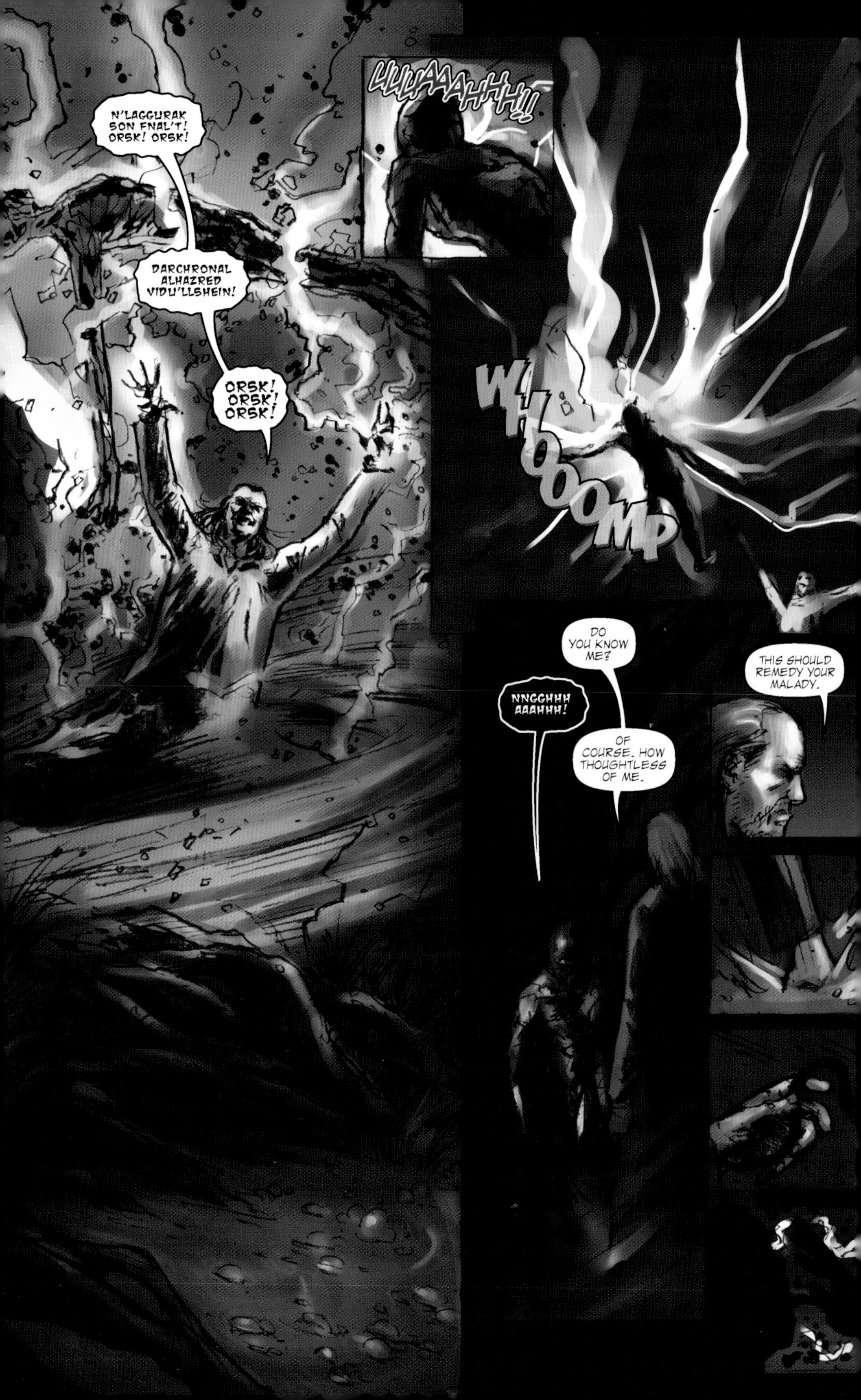
N'LAGGURAK SON FNAL'T! ORSK! ORSK!
DARCHRONAL ALHAZRED VIDU'LLSHEIN!
ORSK! ORSK! ORSK!
UUUAAAHHH!!
WHOOOOMP
DO YOU KNOW ME?
NNGGHHH AAAHHH!
OF COURSE. HOW THOUGHTLESS OF ME.
THIS SHOULD REMEDY YOUR MALADY.

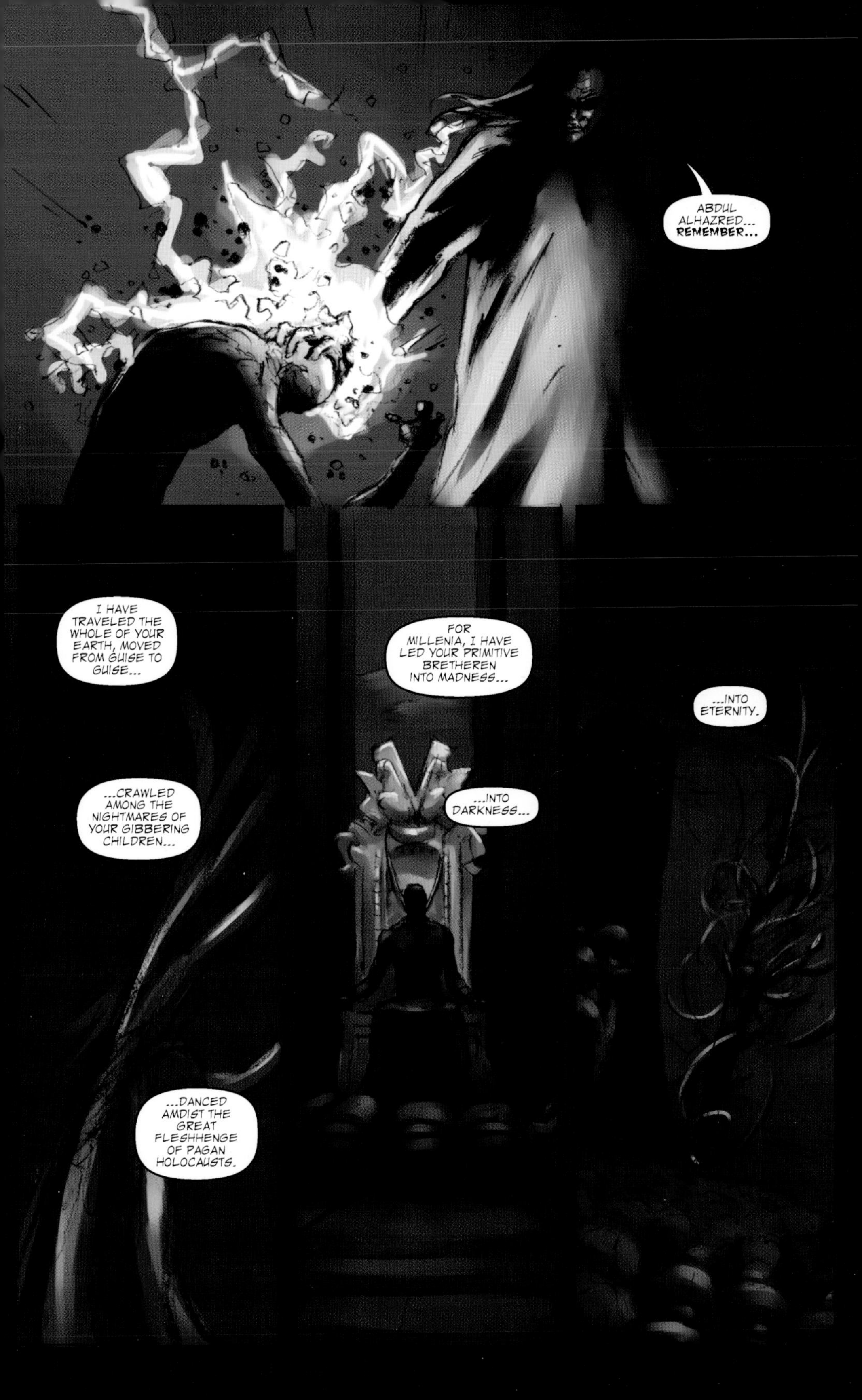
ABDUL ALHAZRED... REMEMBER...
I HAVE TRAVELED THE WHOLE OF YOUR EARTH, MOVED FROM GUISE TO GUISE...
FOR MILLENIA, I HAVE LED YOUR PRIMITIVE BRETHEREN INTO MADNESS...
...INTO ETERNITY.
...CRAWLED AMONG THE NIGHTMARES OF YOUR GIBBERING CHILDREN...
...INTO DARKNESS...
...DANCED AMDIST THE GREAT FLESHHENGE OF PAGAN HOLOCAUSTS.

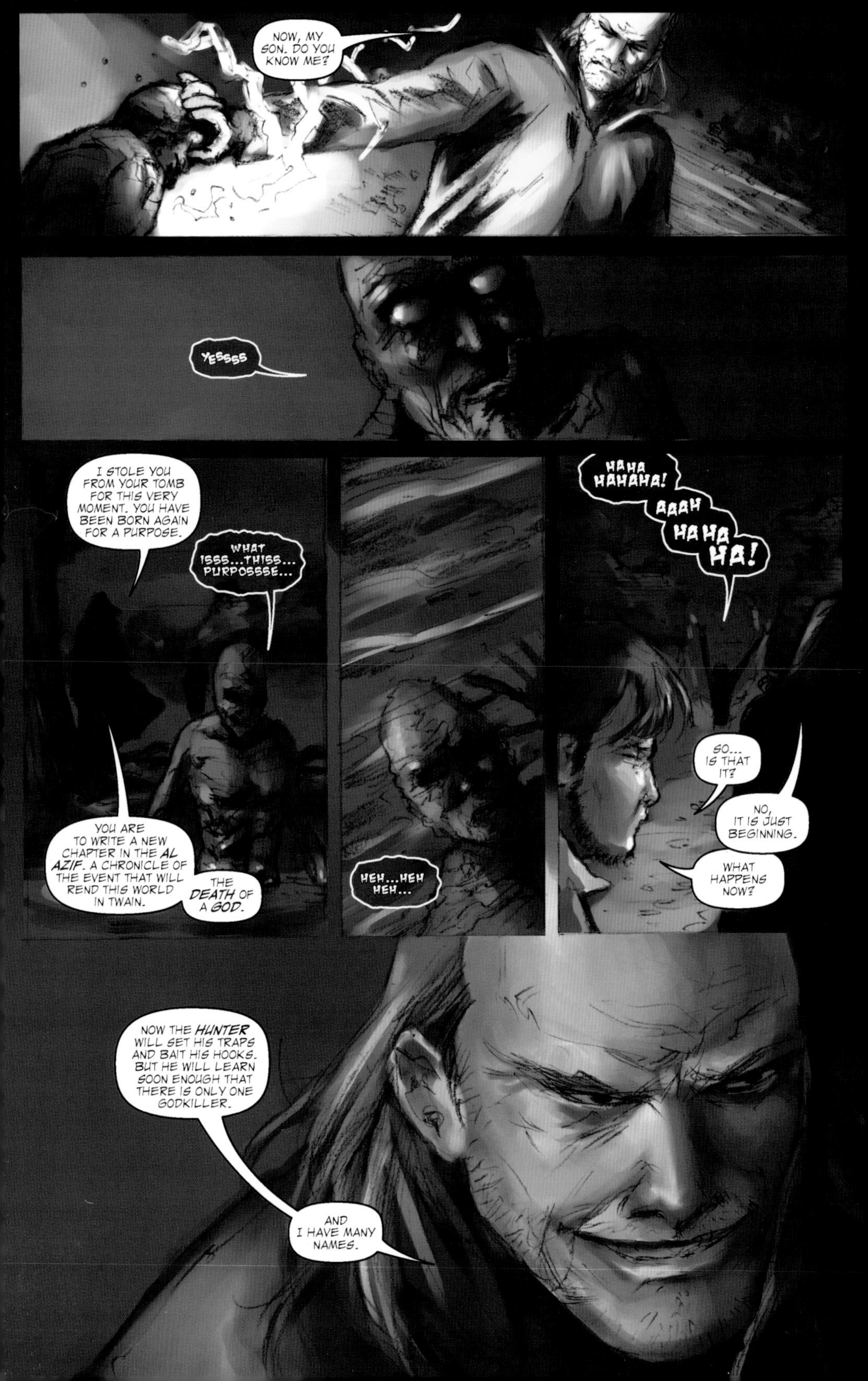
NOW, MY SON. DO YOU KNOW ME?
YESSSS
I STOLE YOU FROM YOUR TOMB FOR THIS VERY MOMENT. YOU HAVE BEEN BORN AGAIN FOR A PURPOSE.
WHAT ISSS...THISS... PURPOSSSE...
YOU ARE TO WRITE A NEW CHAPTER IN THE *AL AZIF*. A CHRONICLE OF THE EVENT THAT WILL REND THIS WORLD IN TWAIN.
THE *DEATH* OF A *GOD*.
HEH...HEH HEH...
HAHA HAHAHA!
AAAH HAHA HA!
SO... IS THAT IT?
NO, IT IS JUST BEGINNING.
WHAT HAPPENS NOW?
NOW THE *HUNTER* WILL SET HIS TRAPS AND BAIT HIS HOOKS. BUT HE WILL LEARN SOON ENOUGH THAT THERE IS ONLY ONE GODKILLER.
AND I HAVE MANY NAMES.

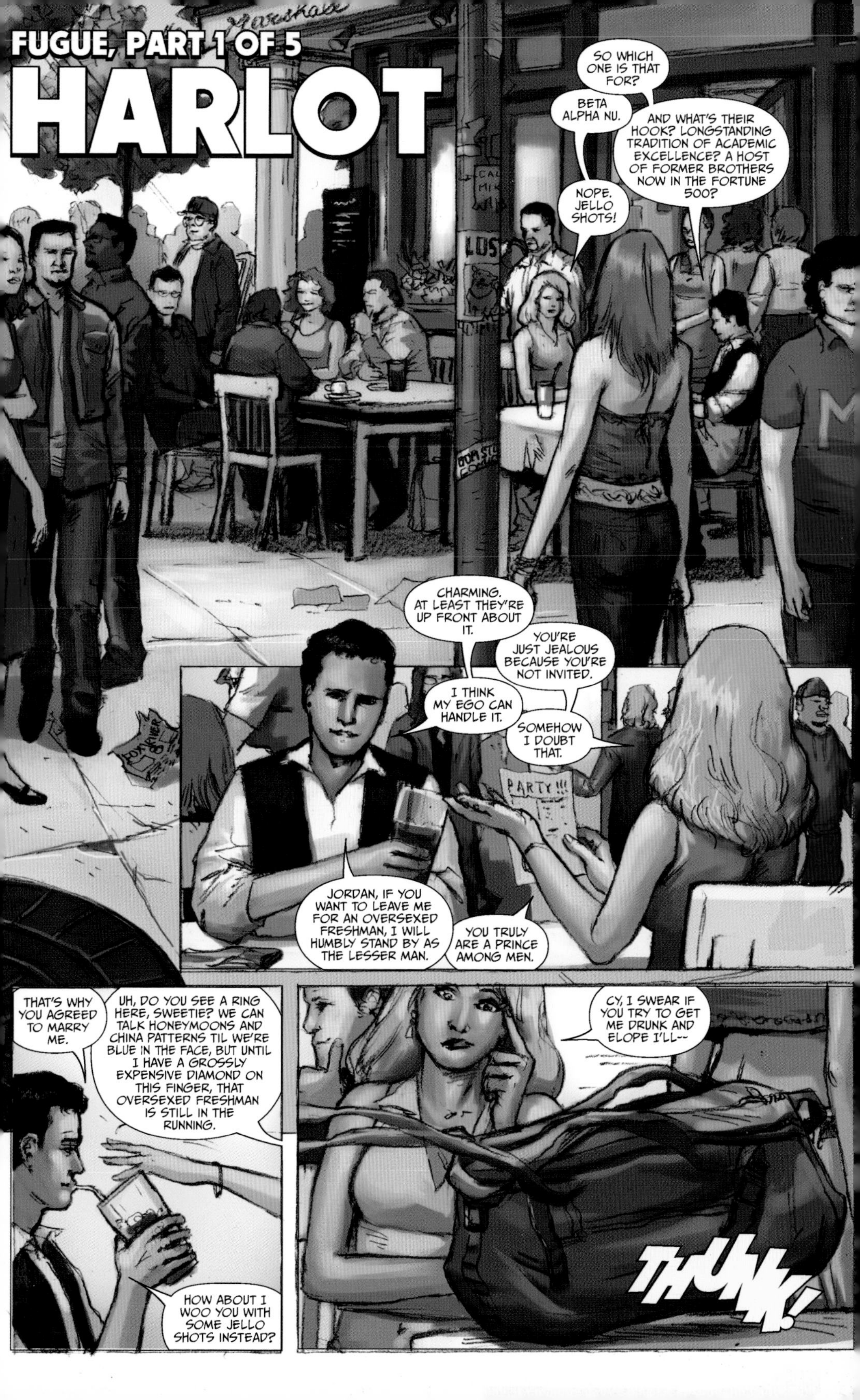
FUGUE, PART 1 OF 5
HARLOT
SO WHICH ONE IS THAT FOR?
BETA ALPHA NU.
AND WHAT'S THEIR HOOK? LONGSTANDING TRADITION OF ACADEMIC EXCELLENCE? A HOST OF FORMER BROTHERS NOW IN THE FORTUNE 500?
NOPE. JELLO SHOTS!
CHARMING. AT LEAST THEY'RE UP FRONT ABOUT IT.
YOU'RE JUST JEALOUS BECAUSE YOU'RE NOT INVITED.
I THINK MY EGO CAN HANDLE IT.
SOMEHOW I DOUBT THAT.
PARTY!!!
JORDAN, IF YOU WANT TO LEAVE ME FOR AN OVERSEXED FRESHMAN, I WILL HUMBLY STAND BY AS THE LESSER MAN.
YOU TRULY ARE A PRINCE AMONG MEN.
THAT'S WHY YOU AGREED TO MARRY ME.
UH, DO YOU SEE A RING HERE, SWEETIE? WE CAN TALK HONEYMOONS AND CHINA PATTERNS TIL WE'RE BLUE IN THE FACE, BUT UNTIL I HAVE A GROSSLY EXPENSIVE DIAMOND ON THIS FINGER, THAT OVERSEXED FRESHMAN IS STILL IN THE RUNNING.
HOW ABOUT I WOO YOU WITH SOME JELLO SHOTS INSTEAD?
CY, I SWEAR IF YOU TRY TO GET ME DRUNK AND ELOPE I'LL--
THUNK!

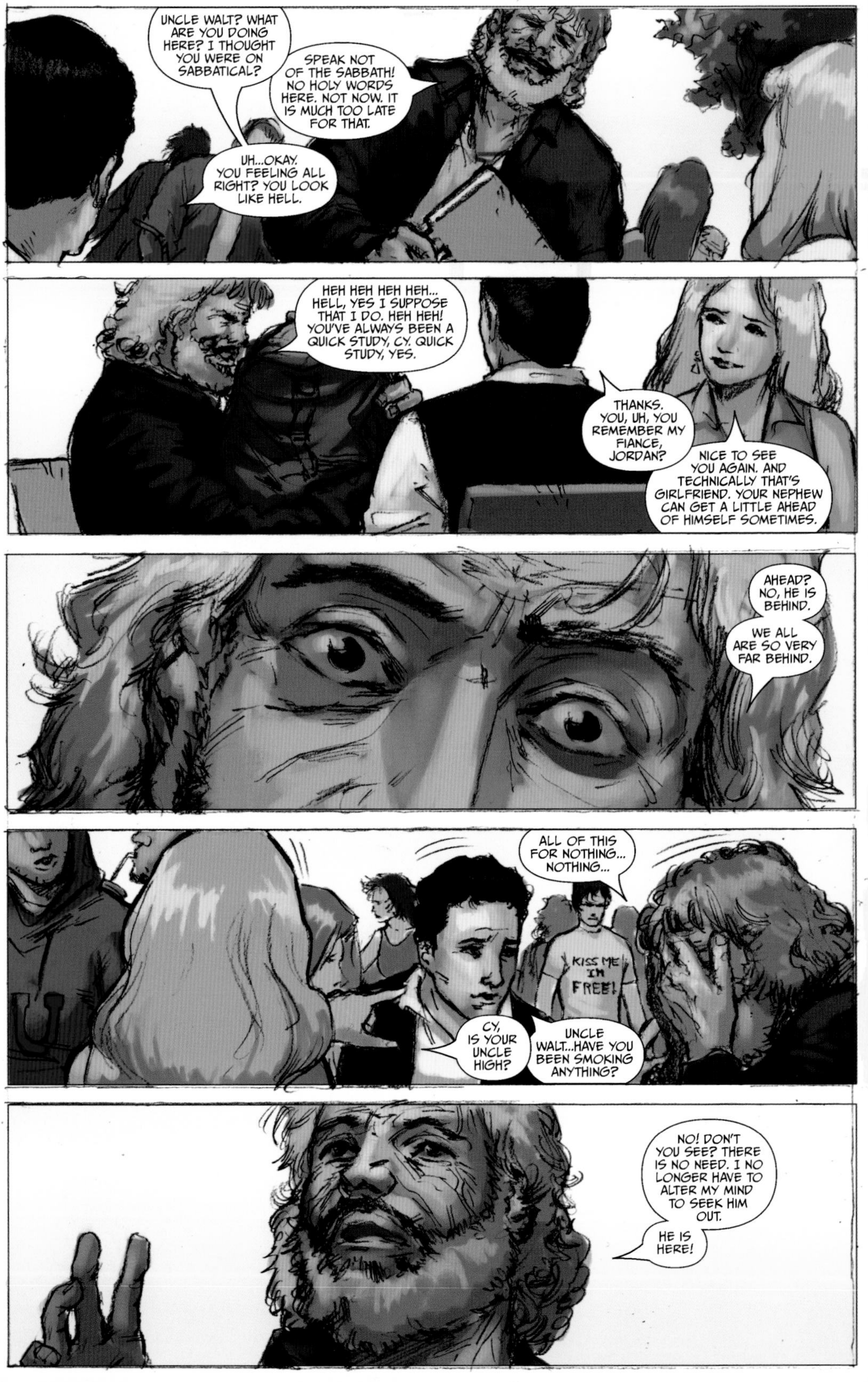
UNCLE WALT? WHAT ARE YOU DOING HERE? I THOUGHT YOU WERE ON SABBATICAL?
SPEAK NOT OF THE SABBATH! NO HOLY WORDS HERE. NOT NOW. IT IS MUCH TOO LATE FOR THAT.
UH...OKAY. YOU FEELING ALL RIGHT? YOU LOOK LIKE HELL.
HEH HEH HEH HEH... HELL, YES I SUPPOSE THAT I DO. HEH HEH! YOU'VE ALWAYS BEEN A QUICK STUDY, CY. QUICK STUDY, YES.
THANKS. YOU, UH, YOU REMEMBER MY FIANCE, JORDAN?
NICE TO SEE YOU AGAIN. AND TECHNICALLY THAT'S GIRLFRIEND. YOUR NEPHEW CAN GET A LITTLE AHEAD OF HIMSELF SOMETIMES.
AHEAD? NO, HE IS BEHIND.
WE ALL ARE SO VERY FAR BEHIND.
ALL OF THIS FOR NOTHING... NOTHING...
KISS ME I'M FREE!
CY, IS YOUR UNCLE HIGH?
UNCLE WALT...HAVE YOU BEEN SMOKING ANYTHING?
NO! DON'T YOU SEE? THERE IS NO NEED. I NO LONGER HAVE TO ALTER MY MIND TO SEEK HIM OUT.
HE IS HERE!

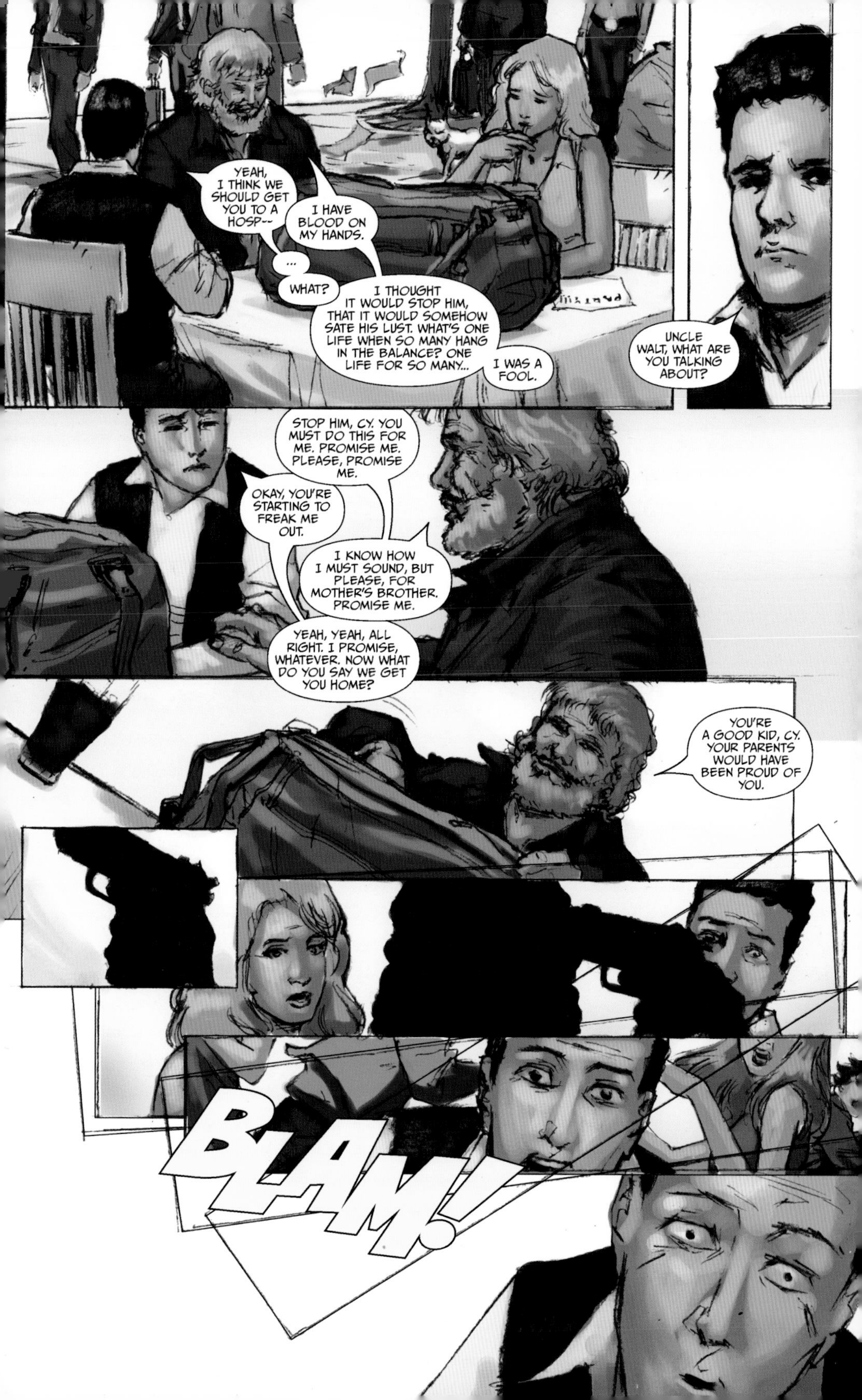
YEAH, I THINK WE SHOULD GET YOU TO A HOSP--
I HAVE BLOOD ON MY HANDS.
...
WHAT?
I THOUGHT IT WOULD STOP HIM, THAT IT WOULD SOMEHOW SATE HIS LUST. WHAT'S ONE LIFE WHEN SO MANY HANG IN THE BALANCE? ONE LIFE FOR SO MANY...
I WAS A FOOL.
UNCLE WALT, WHAT ARE YOU TALKING ABOUT?
STOP HIM, CY. YOU MUST DO THIS FOR ME. PROMISE ME. PLEASE, PROMISE ME.
OKAY, YOU'RE STARTING TO FREAK ME OUT.
I KNOW HOW I MUST SOUND, BUT PLEASE, FOR MOTHER'S BROTHER. PROMISE ME.
YEAH, YEAH, ALL RIGHT. I PROMISE, WHATEVER. NOW WHAT DO YOU SAY WE GET YOU HOME?
YOU'RE A GOOD KID, CY. YOUR PARENTS WOULD HAVE BEEN PROUD OF YOU.
BLAM!

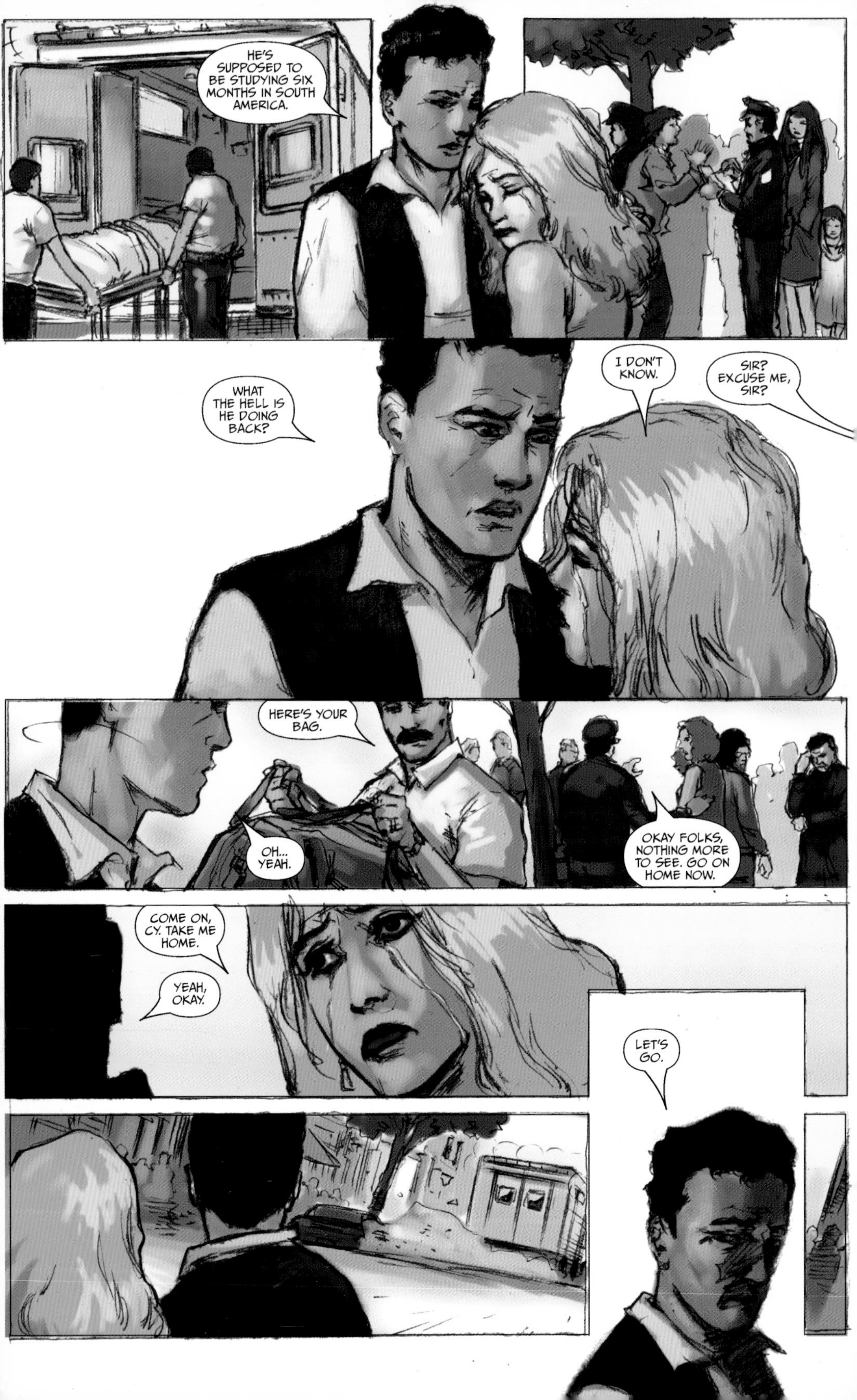
HE'S SUPPOSED TO BE STUDYING SIX MONTHS IN SOUTH AMERICA.
WHAT THE HELL IS HE DOING BACK?
I DON'T KNOW.
SIR? EXCUSE ME, SIR?
HERE'S YOUR BAG.
OH... YEAH.
OKAY FOLKS, NOTHING MORE TO SEE. GO ON HOME NOW.
COME ON, CY. TAKE ME HOME.
YEAH, OKAY.
LET'S GO.

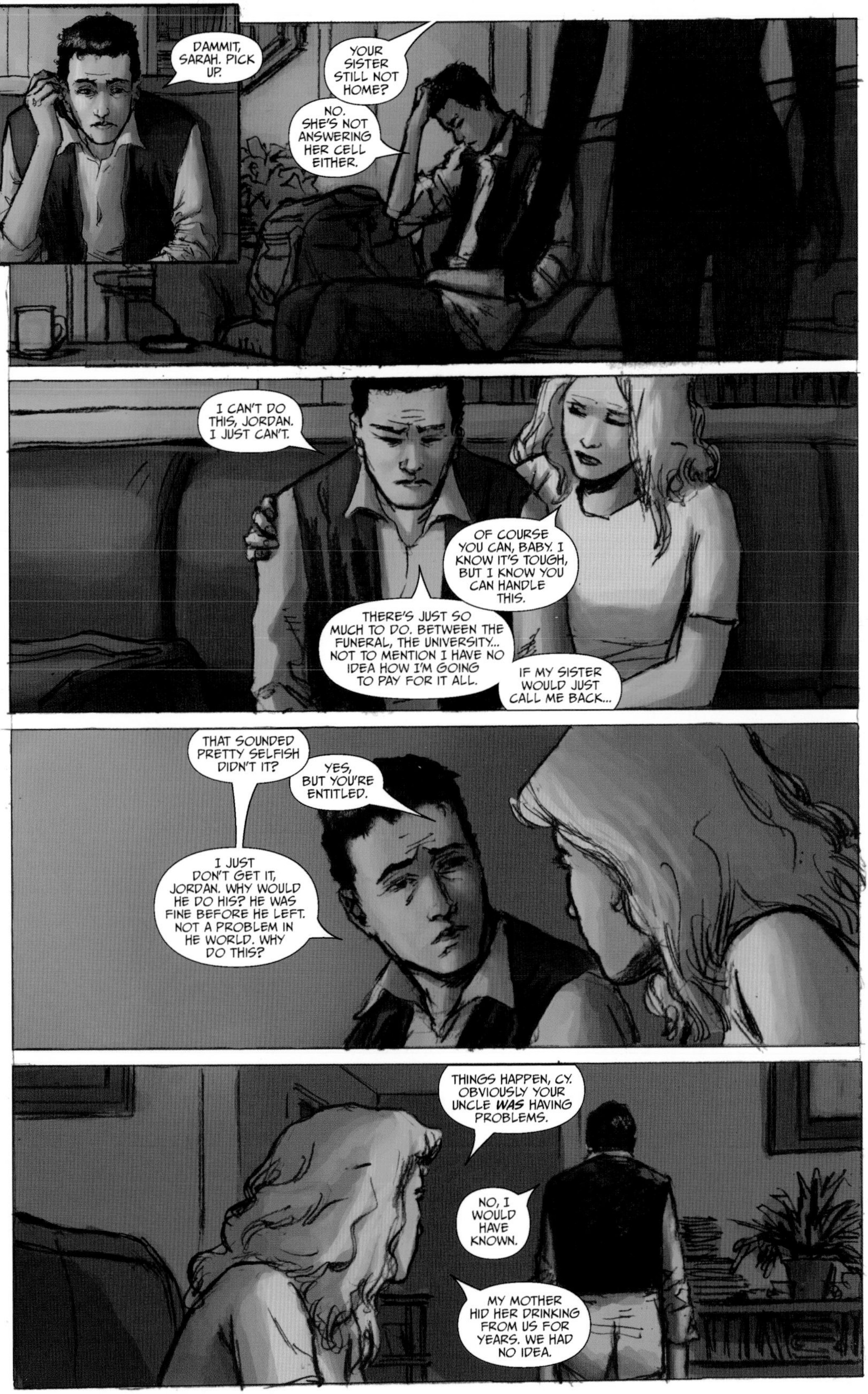
DAMMIT, SARAH. PICK UP.
YOUR SISTER STILL NOT HOME?
NO. SHE'S NOT ANSWERING HER CELL EITHER.
I CAN'T DO THIS, JORDAN. I JUST CAN'T.
OF COURSE YOU CAN, BABY. I KNOW IT'S TOUGH, BUT I KNOW YOU CAN HANDLE THIS.
THERE'S JUST SO MUCH TO DO. BETWEEN THE FUNERAL, THE UNIVERSITY... NOT TO MENTION I HAVE NO IDEA HOW I'M GOING TO PAY FOR IT ALL.
IF MY SISTER WOULD JUST CALL ME BACK...
THAT SOUNDED PRETTY SELFISH DIDN'T IT?
YES, BUT YOU'RE ENTITLED.
I JUST DON'T GET IT, JORDAN. WHY WOULD HE DO HIS? HE WAS FINE BEFORE HE LEFT. NOT A PROBLEM IN HE WORLD. WHY DO THIS?
THINGS HAPPEN, CY. OBVIOUSLY YOUR UNCLE WAS HAVING PROBLEMS.
NO, I WOULD HAVE KNOWN.
MY MOTHER HID HER DRINKING FROM US FOR YEARS. WE HAD NO IDEA.

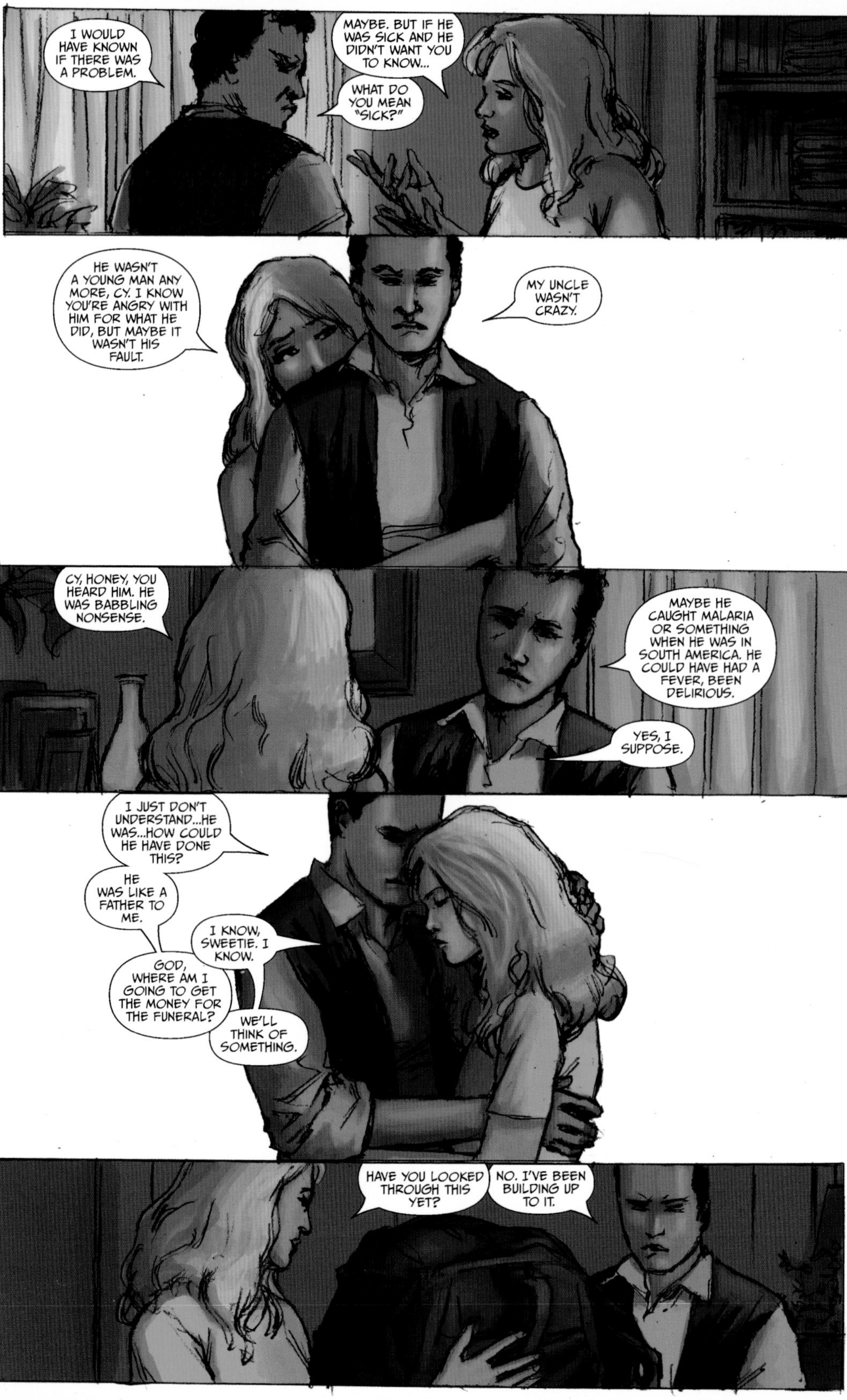
I WOULD HAVE KNOWN IF THERE WAS A PROBLEM.
MAYBE. BUT IF HE WAS SICK AND HE DIDN'T WANT YOU TO KNOW...
WHAT DO YOU MEAN "SICK?"
HE WASN'T A YOUNG MAN ANY MORE, CY. I KNOW YOU'RE ANGRY WITH HIM FOR WHAT HE DID, BUT MAYBE IT WASN'T HIS FAULT.
MY UNCLE WASN'T CRAZY.
CY, HONEY, YOU HEARD HIM. HE WAS BABBLING NONSENSE.
MAYBE HE CAUGHT MALARIA OR SOMETHING WHEN HE WAS IN SOUTH AMERICA. HE COULD HAVE HAD A FEVER, BEEN DELIRIOUS.
YES, I SUPPOSE.
I JUST DON'T UNDERSTAND...HE WAS...HOW COULD HE HAVE DONE THIS?
HE WAS LIKE A FATHER TO ME.
I KNOW, SWEETIE. I KNOW.
GOD, WHERE AM I GOING TO GET THE MONEY FOR THE FUNERAL?
WE'LL THINK OF SOMETHING.
HAVE YOU LOOKED THROUGH THIS YET?
NO. I'VE BEEN BUILDING UP TO IT.

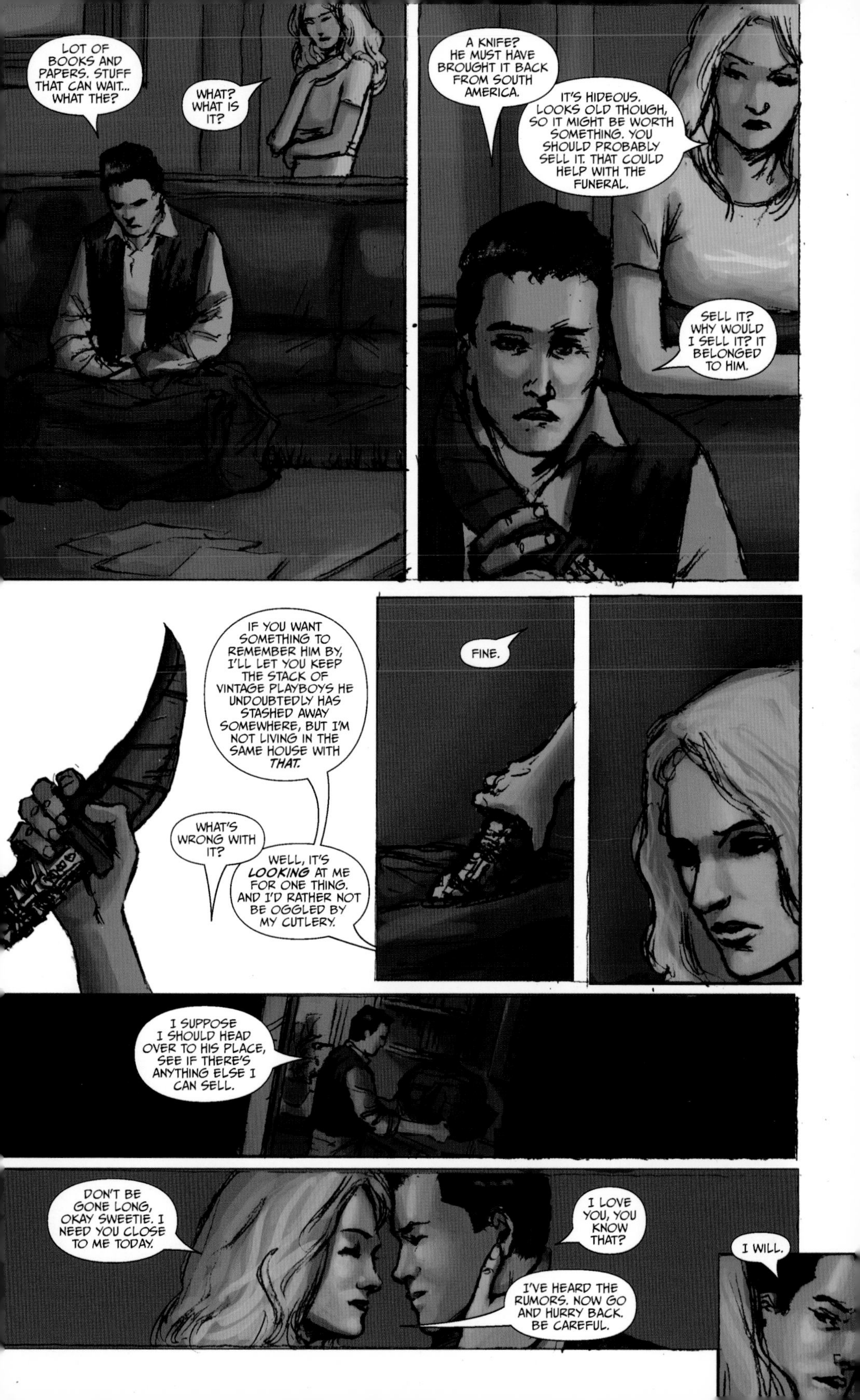
LOT OF BOOKS AND PAPERS. STUFF THAT CAN WAIT... WHAT THE?
WHAT? WHAT IS IT?
A KNIFE? HE MUST HAVE BROUGHT IT BACK FROM SOUTH AMERICA.
IT'S HIDEOUS. LOOKS OLD THOUGH, SO IT MIGHT BE WORTH SOMETHING. YOU SHOULD PROBABLY SELL IT. THAT COULD HELP WITH THE FUNERAL.
SELL IT? WHY WOULD I SELL IT? IT BELONGED TO HIM.
IF YOU WANT SOMETHING TO REMEMBER HIM BY, I'LL LET YOU KEEP THE STACK OF VINTAGE PLAYBOYS HE UNDOUBTEDLY HAS STASHED AWAY SOMEWHERE, BUT I'M NOT LIVING IN THE SAME HOUSE WITH *THAT.*
WHAT'S WRONG WITH IT?
WELL, IT'S *LOOKING* AT ME FOR ONE THING. AND I'D RATHER NOT BE OGGLED BY MY CUTLERY.
FINE.
I SUPPOSE I SHOULD HEAD OVER TO HIS PLACE, SEE IF THERE'S ANYTHING ELSE I CAN SELL.
DON'T BE GONE LONG, OKAY SWEETIE. I NEED YOU CLOSE TO ME TODAY.
I LOVE YOU, YOU KNOW THAT?
I'VE HEARD THE RUMORS. NOW GO AND HURRY BACK. BE CAREFUL.
I WILL.

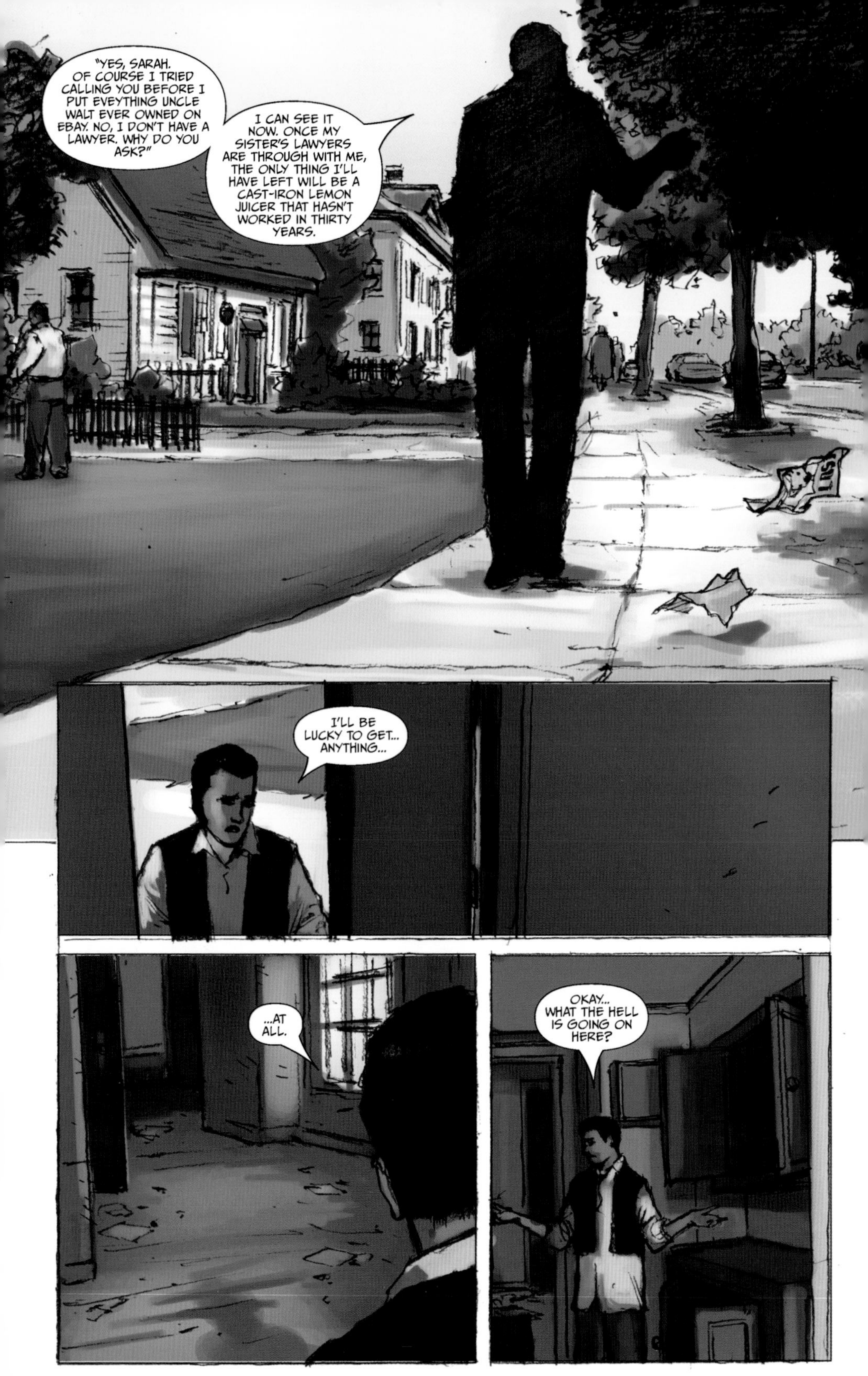
"YES, SARAH. OF COURSE I TRIED CALLING YOU BEFORE I PUT EVEYTHING UNCLE WALT EVER OWNED ON EBAY. NO, I DON'T HAVE A LAWYER. WHY DO YOU ASK?"
I CAN SEE IT NOW. ONCE MY SISTER'S LAWYERS ARE THROUGH WITH ME, THE ONLY THING I'LL HAVE LEFT WILL BE A CAST-IRON LEMON JUICER THAT HASN'T WORKED IN THIRTY YEARS.
I'LL BE LUCKY TO GET... ANYTHING...
...AT ALL.
OKAY... WHAT THE HELL IS GOING ON HERE?

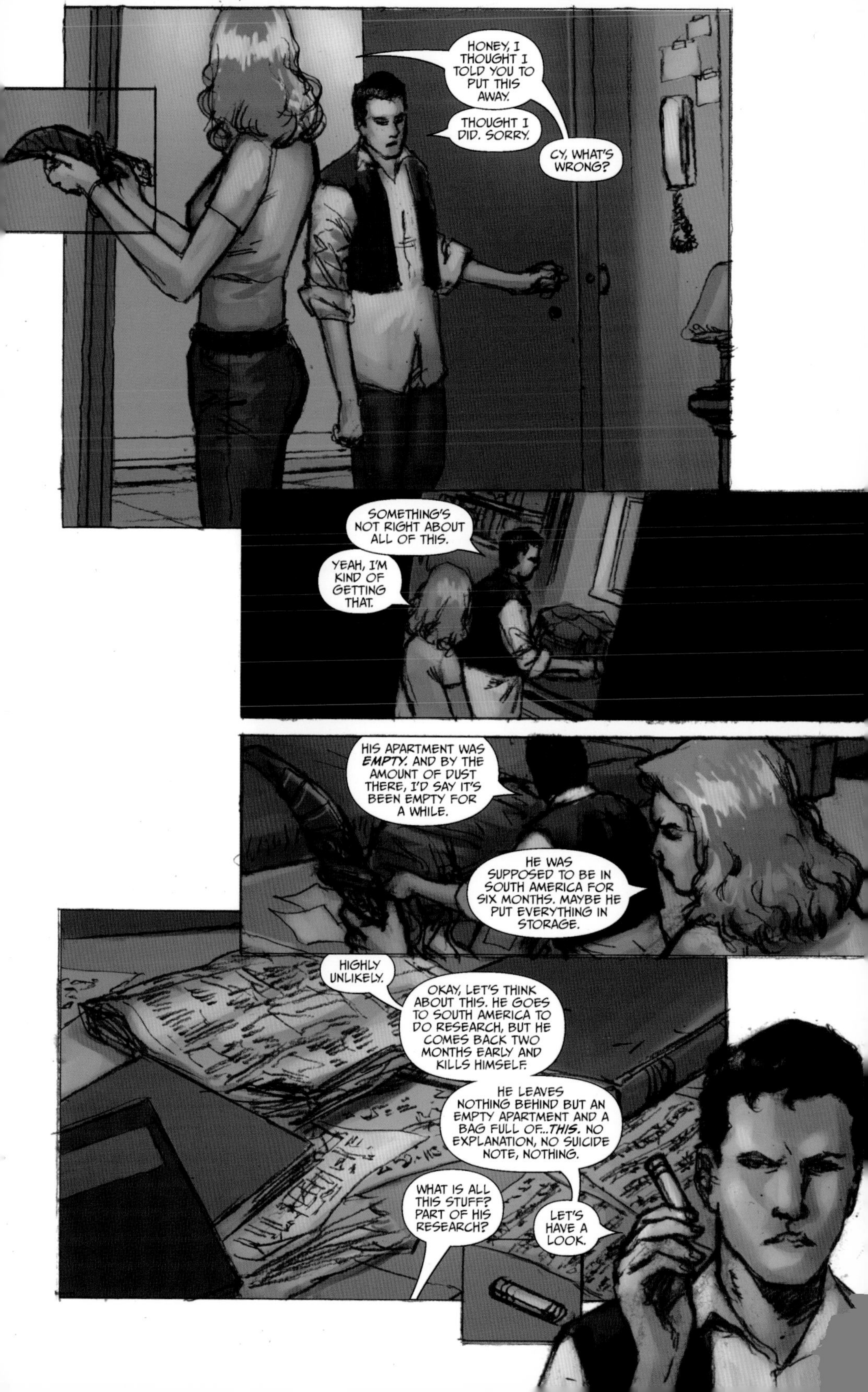
HONEY, I THOUGHT I TOLD YOU TO PUT THIS AWAY.
THOUGHT I DID. SORRY.
CY, WHAT'S WRONG?
SOMETHING'S NOT RIGHT ABOUT ALL OF THIS.
YEAH, I'M KIND OF GETTING THAT.
HIS APARTMENT WAS *EMPTY.* AND BY THE AMOUNT OF DUST THERE, I'D SAY IT'S BEEN EMPTY FOR A WHILE.
HE WAS SUPPOSED TO BE IN SOUTH AMERICA FOR SIX MONTHS. MAYBE HE PUT EVERYTHING IN STORAGE.
HIGHLY UNLIKELY.
OKAY, LET'S THINK ABOUT THIS. HE GOES TO SOUTH AMERICA TO DO RESEARCH, BUT HE COMES BACK TWO MONTHS EARLY AND KILLS HIMSELF.
HE LEAVES NOTHING BEHIND BUT AN EMPTY APARTMENT AND A BAG FULL OF...*THIS.* NO EXPLANATION, NO SUICIDE NOTE, NOTHING.
WHAT IS ALL THIS STUFF? PART OF HIS RESEARCH?
LET'S HAVE A LOOK.

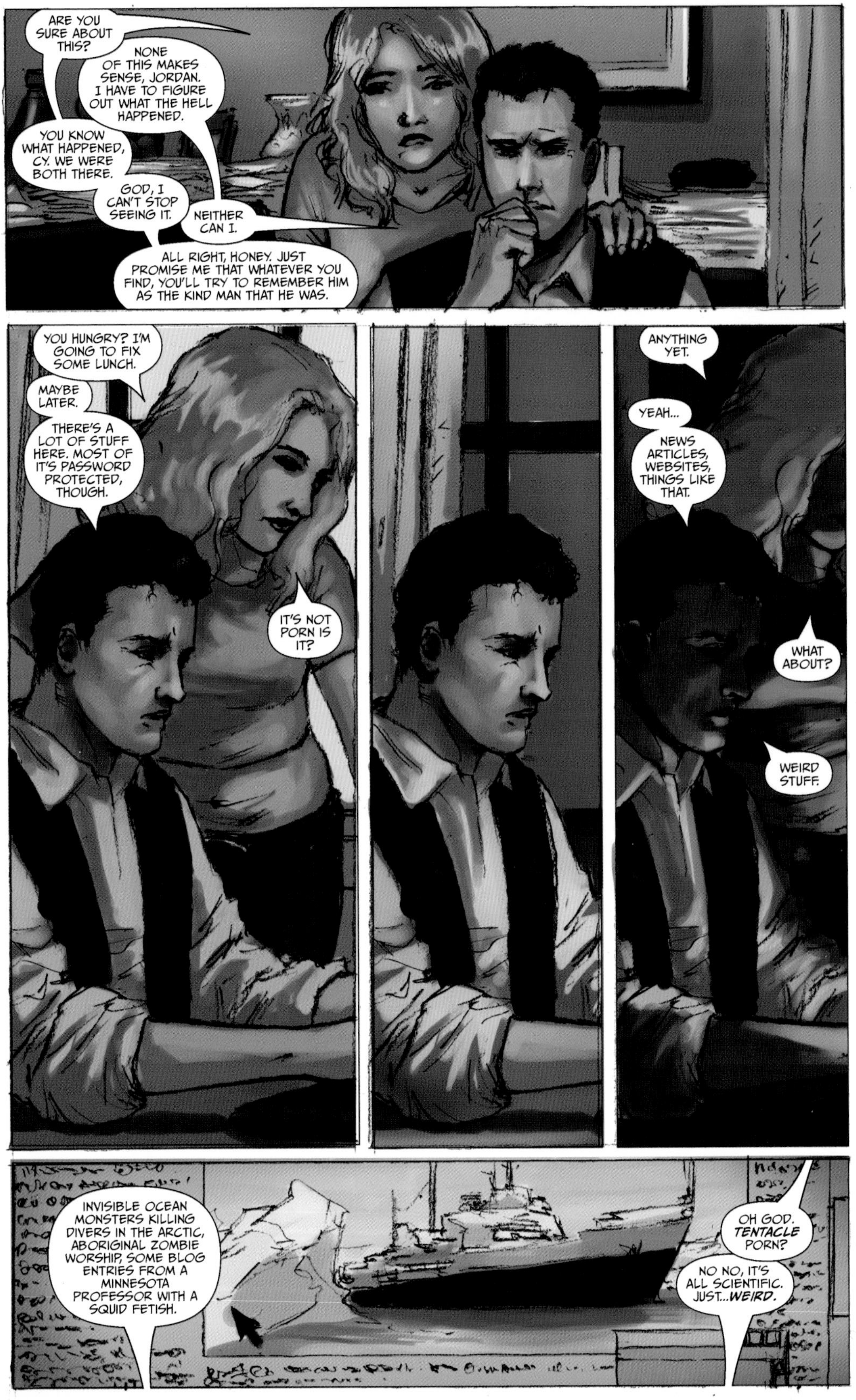
ARE YOU SURE ABOUT THIS?
NONE OF THIS MAKES SENSE, JORDAN. I HAVE TO FIGURE OUT WHAT THE HELL HAPPENED.
YOU KNOW WHAT HAPPENED, CY. WE WERE BOTH THERE.
GOD, I CAN'T STOP SEEING IT.
NEITHER CAN I.
ALL RIGHT, HONEY. JUST PROMISE ME THAT WHATEVER YOU FIND, YOU'LL TRY TO REMEMBER HIM AS THE KIND MAN THAT HE WAS.
YOU HUNGRY? I'M GOING TO FIX SOME LUNCH.
MAYBE LATER.
THERE'S A LOT OF STUFF HERE. MOST OF IT'S PASSWORD PROTECTED, THOUGH.
IT'S NOT PORN IS IT?
ANYTHING YET.
YEAH...
NEWS ARTICLES, WEBSITES, THINGS LIKE THAT.
WHAT ABOUT?
WEIRD STUFF.
INVISIBLE OCEAN MONSTERS KILLING DIVERS IN THE ARCTIC, ABORIGINAL ZOMBIE WORSHIP, SOME BLOG ENTRIES FROM A MINNESOTA PROFESSOR WITH A SQUID FETISH.
OH GOD. TENTACLE PORN?
NO NO, IT'S ALL SCIENTIFIC. JUST...WEIRD.

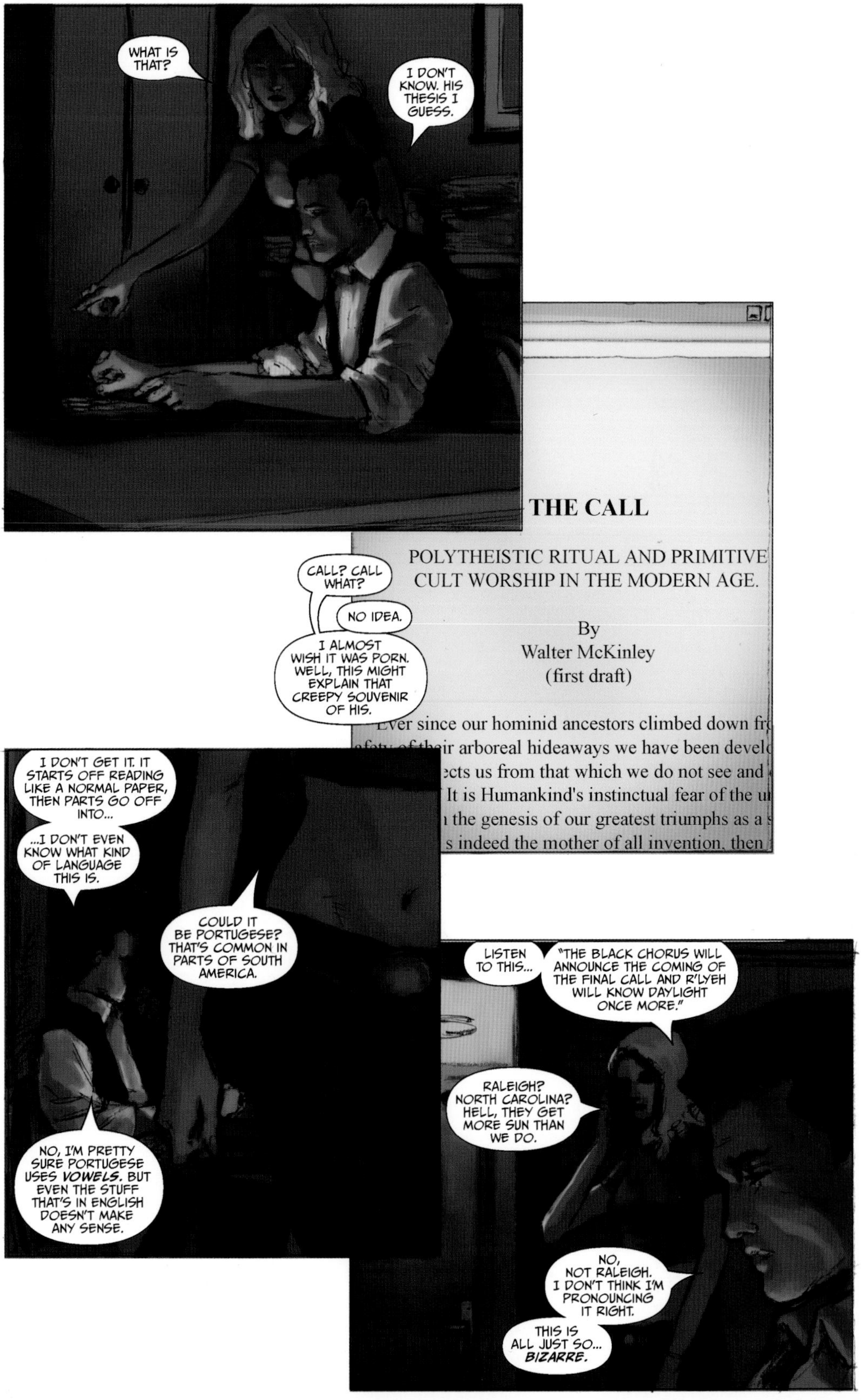
WHAT IS THAT?
I DON'T KNOW. HIS THESIS I GUESS.
THE CALL
POLYTHEISTIC RITUAL AND PRIMITIVE CULT WORSHIP IN THE MODERN AGE.
By
Walter McKinley
(first draft)
Ever since our hominid ancestors climbed down fr
afety of their arboreal hideaways we have been devel
ects us from that which we do not see and
It is Humankind's instinctual fear of the u
the genesis of our greatest triumphs as a
s indeed the mother of all invention, then
CALL? CALL WHAT?
NO IDEA.
I ALMOST WISH IT WAS PORN. WELL, THIS MIGHT EXPLAIN THAT CREEPY SOUVENIR OF HIS.
I DON'T GET IT. IT STARTS OFF READING LIKE A NORMAL PAPER, THEN PARTS GO OFF INTO...
...I DON'T EVEN KNOW WHAT KIND OF LANGUAGE THIS IS.
COULD IT BE PORTUGESE? THAT'S COMMON IN PARTS OF SOUTH AMERICA.
NO, I'M PRETTY SURE PORTUGESE USES ***VOWELS.*** BUT EVEN THE STUFF THAT'S IN ENGLISH DOESN'T MAKE ANY SENSE.
LISTEN TO THIS...
"THE BLACK CHORUS WILL ANNOUNCE THE COMING OF THE FINAL CALL AND R'LYEH WILL KNOW DAYLIGHT ONCE MORE."
RALEIGH? NORTH CAROLINA? HELL, THEY GET MORE SUN THAN WE DO.
NO, NOT RALEIGH. I DON'T THINK I'M PRONOUNCING IT RIGHT.
THIS IS ALL JUST SO... ***BIZARRE.***

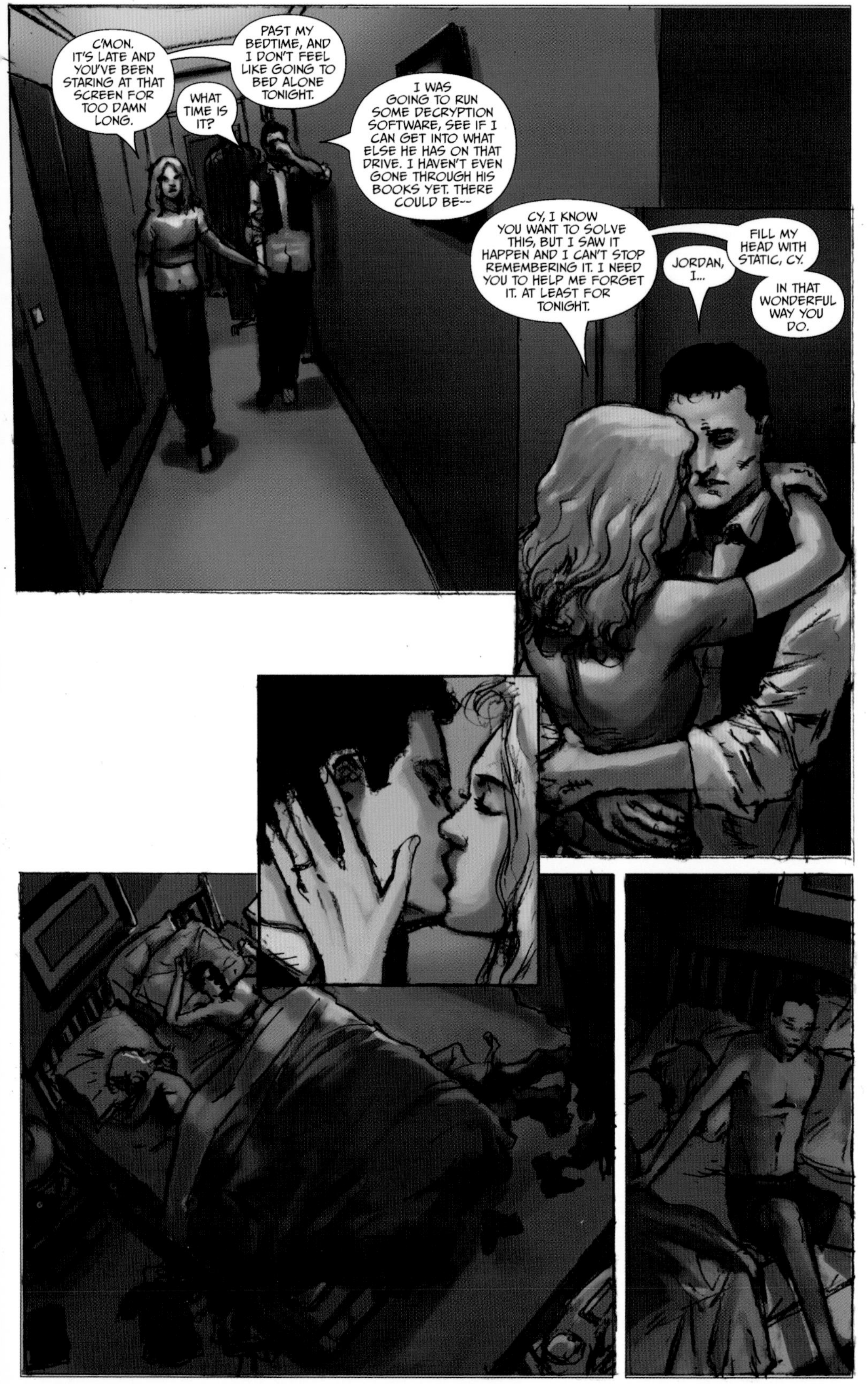
C'MON. IT'S LATE AND YOU'VE BEEN STARING AT THAT SCREEN FOR TOO DAMN LONG.
WHAT TIME IS IT?
PAST MY BEDTIME, AND I DON'T FEEL LIKE GOING TO BED ALONE TONIGHT.
I WAS GOING TO RUN SOME DECRYPTION SOFTWARE, SEE IF I CAN GET INTO WHAT ELSE HE HAS ON THAT DRIVE. I HAVEN'T EVEN GONE THROUGH HIS BOOKS YET. THERE COULD BE--
CY, I KNOW YOU WANT TO SOLVE THIS, BUT I SAW IT HAPPEN AND I CAN'T STOP REMEMBERING IT. I NEED YOU TO HELP ME FORGET IT. AT LEAST FOR TONIGHT.
JORDAN, I...
FILL MY HEAD WITH STATIC, CY.
IN THAT WONDERFUL WAY YOU DO.

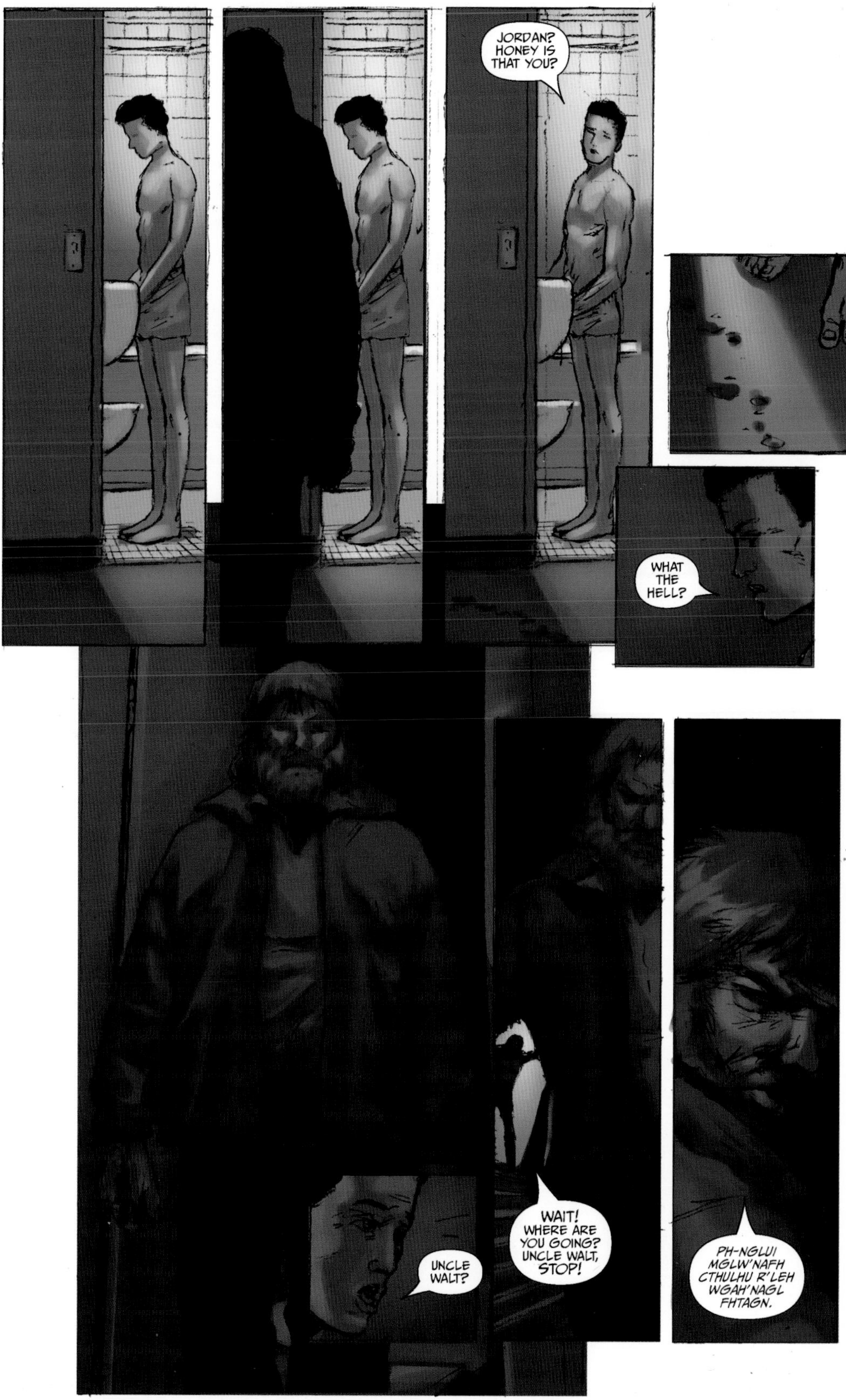
JORDAN? HONEY IS THAT YOU?
WHAT THE HELL?
UNCLE WALT?
WAIT! WHERE ARE YOU GOING? UNCLE WALT, STOP!
PH-NGLUI MGLW'NAFH CTHULHU R'LEH WGAH'NAGL FHTAGN.

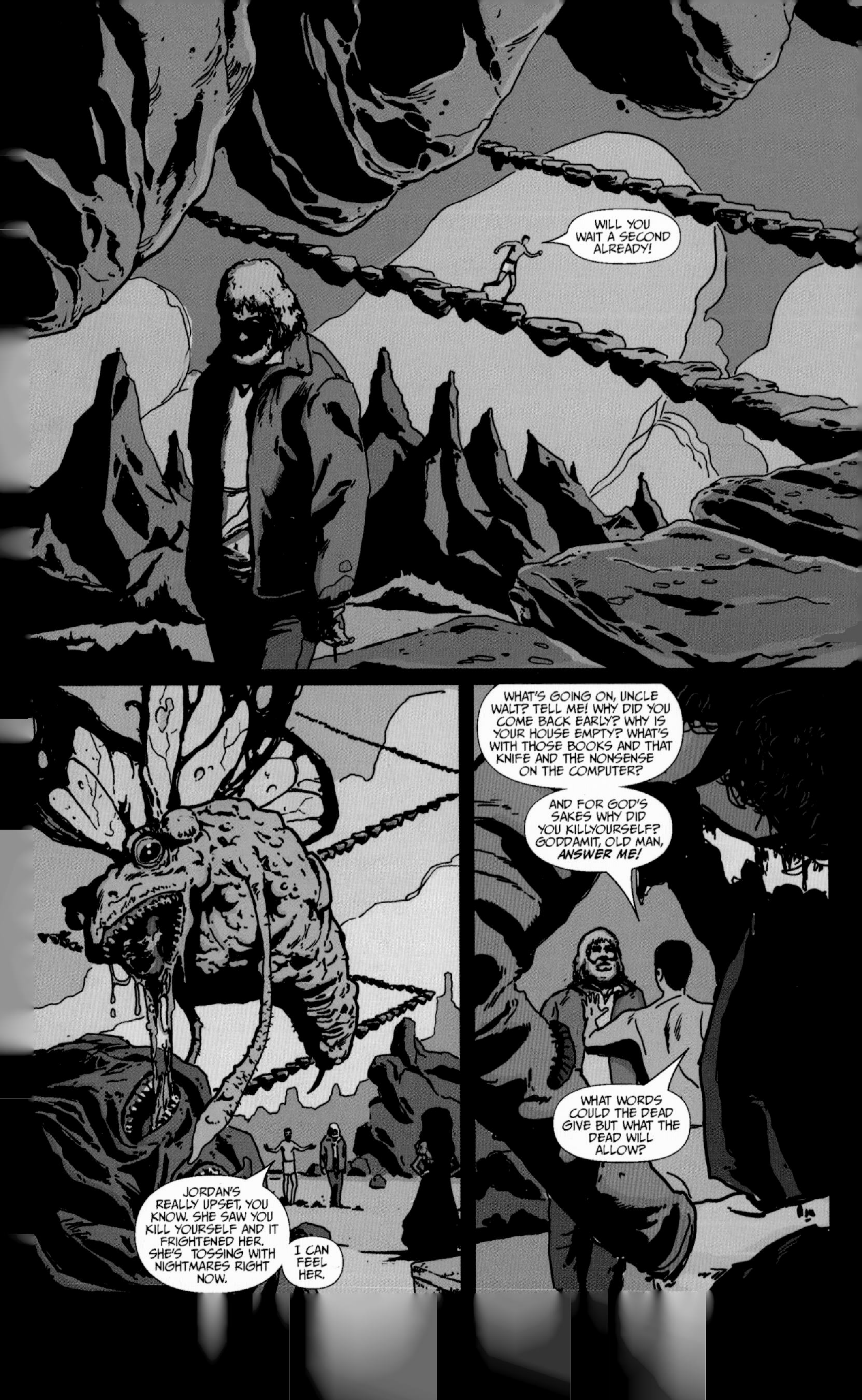

WILL YOU WAIT A SECOND ALREADY!
JORDAN'S REALLY UPSET, YOU KNOW. SHE SAW YOU KILL YOURSELF AND IT FRIGHTENED HER. SHE'S TOSSING WITH NIGHTMARES RIGHT NOW.
I CAN FEEL HER.
WHAT'S GOING ON, UNCLE WALT? TELL ME! WHY DID YOU COME BACK EARLY? WHY IS YOUR HOUSE EMPTY? WHAT'S WITH THOSE BOOKS AND THAT KNIFE AND THE NONSENSE ON THE COMPUTER?
AND FOR GOD'S SAKES WHY DID YOU KILLYOURSELF? GODDAMIT, OLD MAN, ***ANSWER ME!***
WHAT WORDS COULD THE DEAD GIVE BUT WHAT THE DEAD WILL ALLOW?

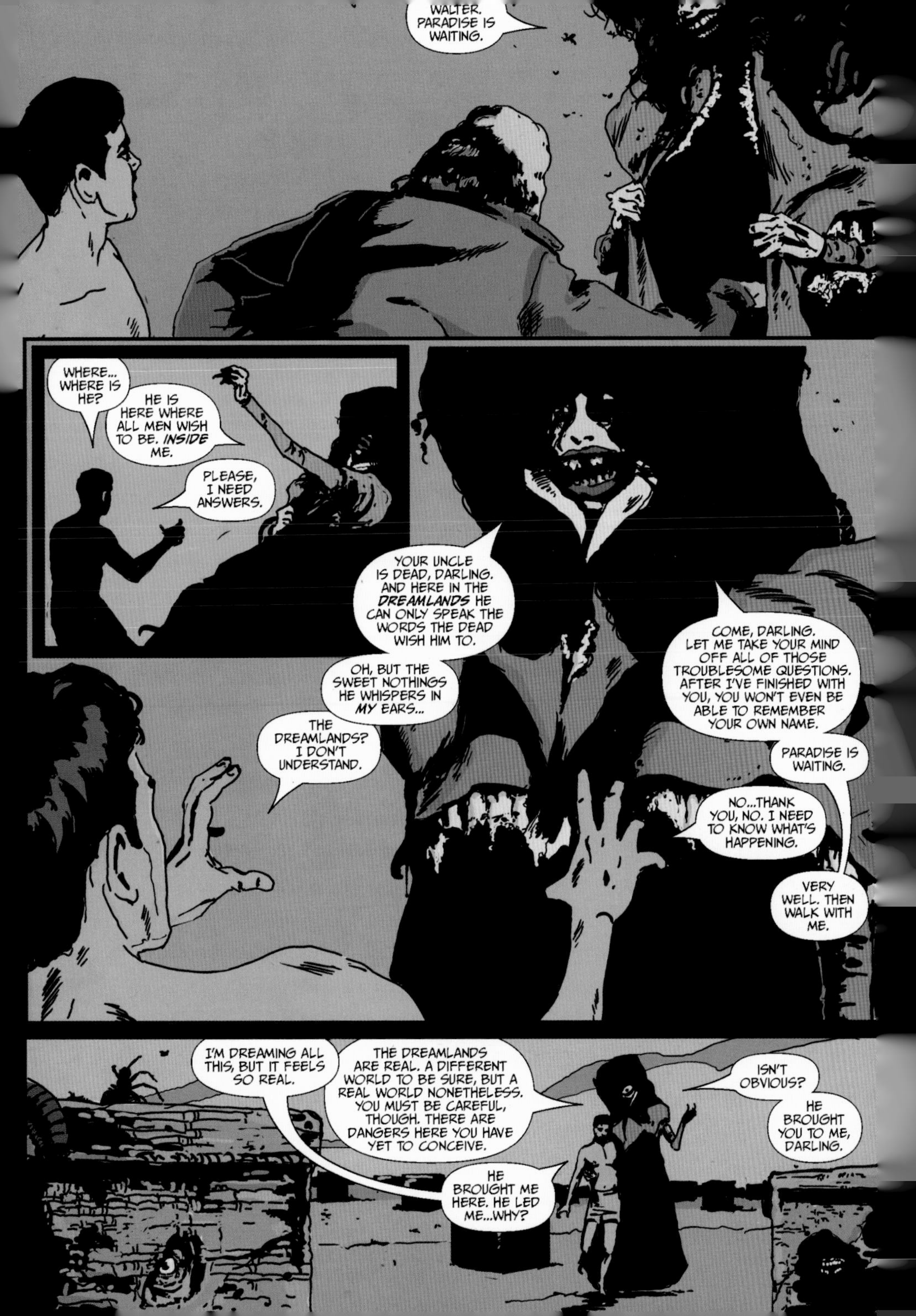
WALTER. PARADISE IS WAITING.
WHERE... WHERE IS HE?
HE IS HERE WHERE ALL MEN WISH TO BE. *INSIDE* ME.
PLEASE, I NEED ANSWERS.
YOUR UNCLE IS DEAD, DARLING. AND HERE IN THE *DREAMLANDS* HE CAN ONLY SPEAK THE WORDS THE DEAD WISH HIM TO.
OH, BUT THE SWEET NOTHINGS HE WHISPERS IN *MY* EARS...
THE DREAMLANDS? I DON'T UNDERSTAND.
COME, DARLING. LET ME TAKE YOUR MIND OFF ALL OF THOSE TROUBLESOME QUESTIONS. AFTER I'VE FINISHED WITH YOU, YOU WON'T EVEN BE ABLE TO REMEMBER YOUR OWN NAME.
PARADISE IS WAITING.
NO...THANK YOU, NO. I NEED TO KNOW WHAT'S HAPPENING.
VERY WELL. THEN WALK WITH ME.
I'M DREAMING ALL THIS, BUT IT FEELS SO REAL.
THE DREAMLANDS ARE REAL. A DIFFERENT WORLD TO BE SURE, BUT A REAL WORLD NONETHELESS. YOU MUST BE CAREFUL, THOUGH. THERE ARE DANGERS HERE YOU HAVE YET TO CONCEIVE.
HE BROUGHT ME HERE. HE LED ME...WHY?
ISN'T OBVIOUS?
HE BROUGHT YOU TO ME, DARLING.

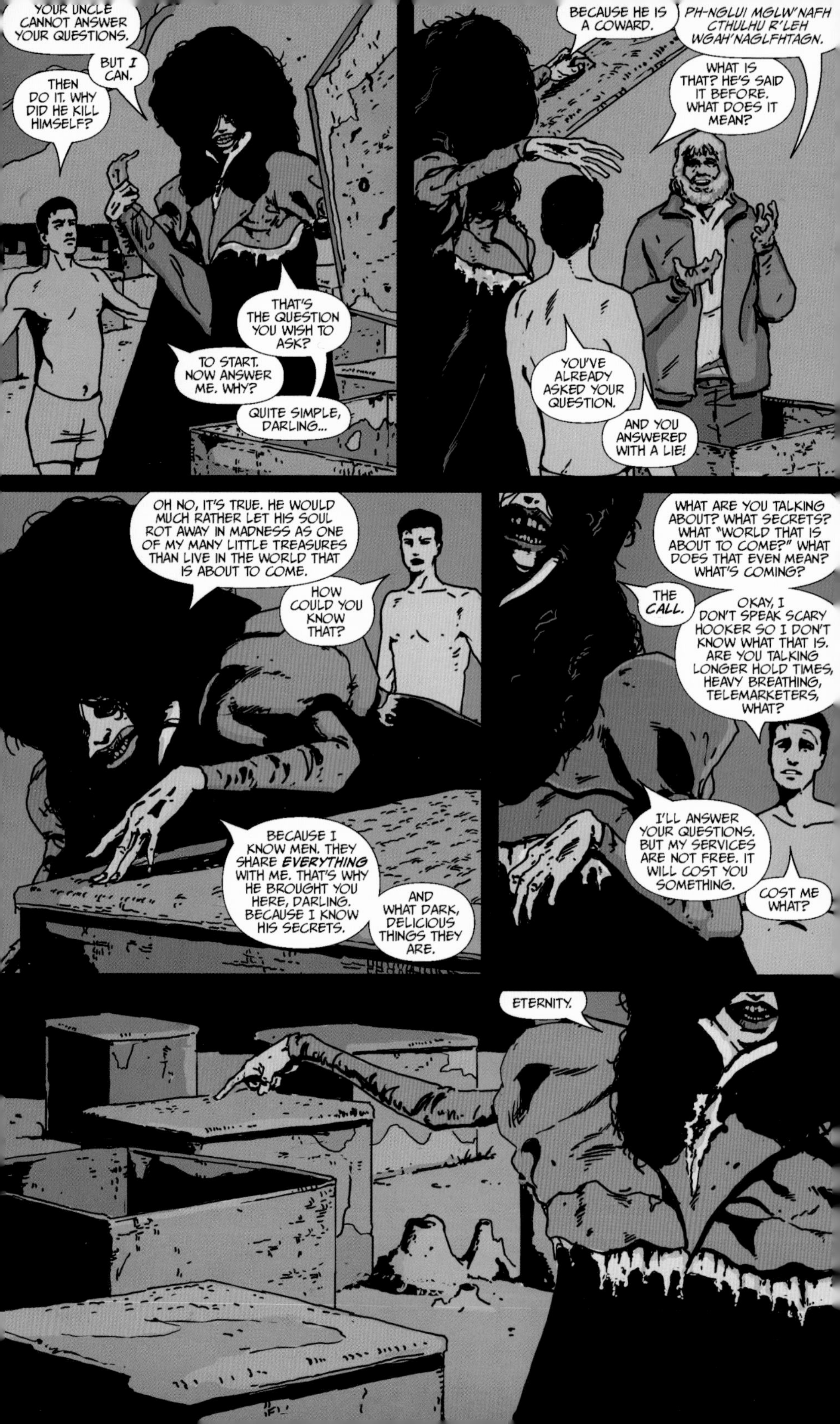
YOUR UNCLE CANNOT ANSWER YOUR QUESTIONS.
BUT I CAN.
THEN DO IT. WHY DID HE KILL HIMSELF?
THAT'S THE QUESTION YOU WISH TO ASK?
TO START. NOW ANSWER ME. WHY?
QUITE SIMPLE, DARLING...
BECAUSE HE IS A COWARD.
PH-NGLUI MGLW'NAFH CTHULHU R'LEH WGAH'NAGLFHTAGN.
WHAT IS THAT? HE'S SAID IT BEFORE. WHAT DOES IT MEAN?
YOU'VE ALREADY ASKED YOUR QUESTION.
AND YOU ANSWERED WITH A LIE!
OH NO, IT'S TRUE. HE WOULD MUCH RATHER LET HIS SOUL ROT AWAY IN MADNESS AS ONE OF MY MANY LITTLE TREASURES THAN LIVE IN THE WORLD THAT IS ABOUT TO COME.
HOW COULD YOU KNOW THAT?
BECAUSE I KNOW MEN. THEY SHARE *EVERYTHING* WITH ME. THAT'S WHY HE BROUGHT YOU HERE, DARLING. BECAUSE I KNOW HIS SECRETS.
AND WHAT DARK, DELICIOUS THINGS THEY ARE.
WHAT ARE YOU TALKING ABOUT? WHAT SECRETS? WHAT "WORLD THAT IS ABOUT TO COME?" WHAT DOES THAT EVEN MEAN? WHAT'S COMING?
THE *CALL*.
OKAY, I DON'T SPEAK SCARY HOOKER SO I DON'T KNOW WHAT THAT IS. ARE YOU TALKING LONGER HOLD TIMES, HEAVY BREATHING, TELEMARKETERS, WHAT?
I'LL ANSWER YOUR QUESTIONS. BUT MY SERVICES ARE NOT FREE. IT WILL COST YOU SOMETHING.
COST ME WHAT?
ETERNITY.

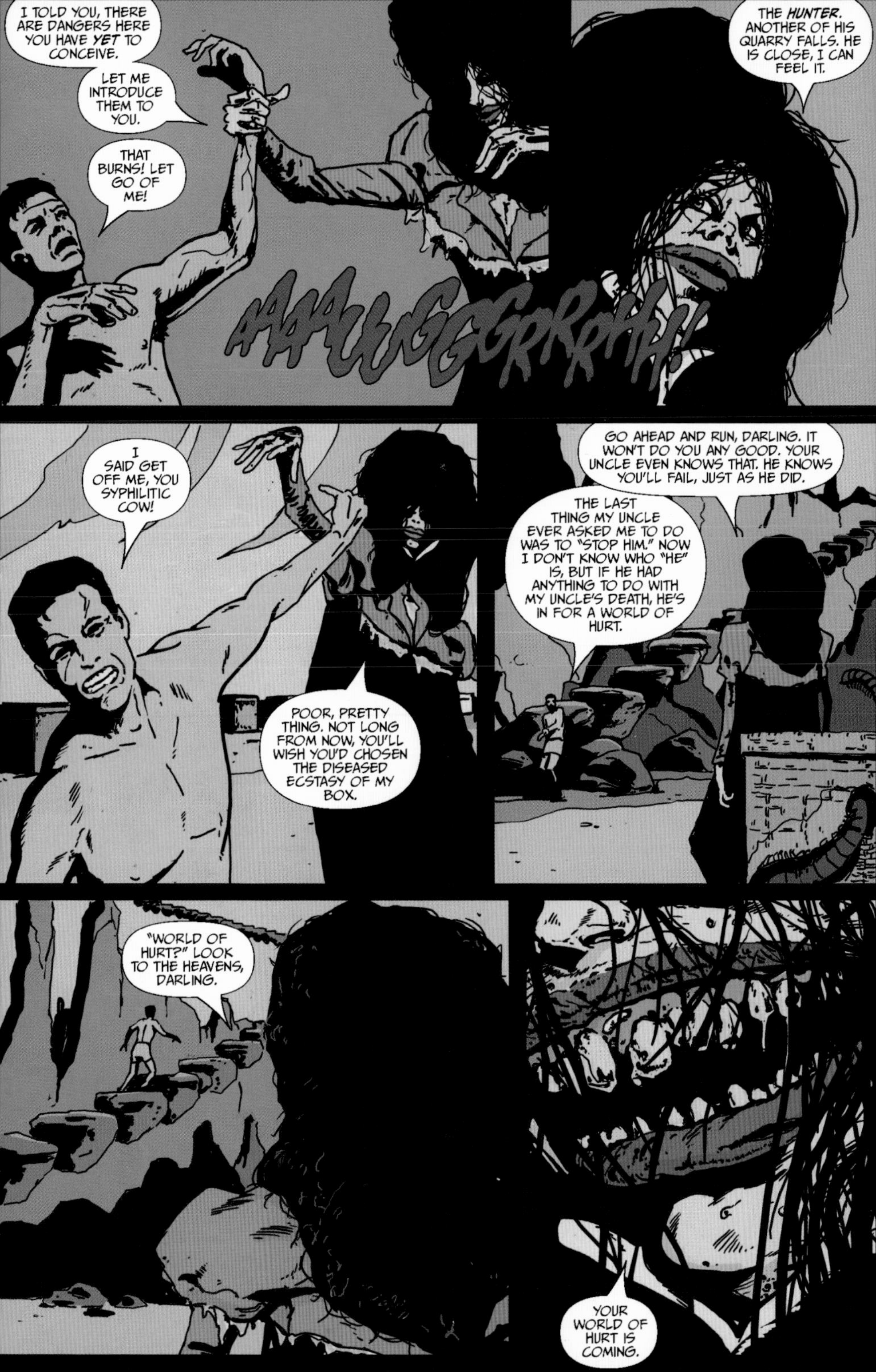

I TOLD YOU, THERE ARE DANGERS HERE YOU HAVE YET TO CONCEIVE.
LET ME INTRODUCE THEM TO YOU.
THAT BURNS! LET GO OF ME!
THE HUNTER. ANOTHER OF HIS QUARRY FALLS. HE IS CLOSE, I CAN FEEL IT.
AAAAUUGGGRRRHH!
I SAID GET OFF ME, YOU SYPHILITIC COW!
POOR, PRETTY THING. NOT LONG FROM NOW, YOU'LL WISH YOU'D CHOSEN THE DISEASED ECSTASY OF MY BOX.
GO AHEAD AND RUN, DARLING. IT WON'T DO YOU ANY GOOD. YOUR UNCLE EVEN KNOWS THAT. HE KNOWS YOU'LL FAIL, JUST AS HE DID.
THE LAST THING MY UNCLE EVER ASKED ME TO DO WAS TO "STOP HIM." NOW I DON'T KNOW WHO "HE" IS, BUT IF HE HAD ANYTHING TO DO WITH MY UNCLE'S DEATH, HE'S IN FOR A WORLD OF HURT.
"WORLD OF HURT?" LOOK TO THE HEAVENS, DARLING.
YOUR WORLD OF HURT IS COMING.

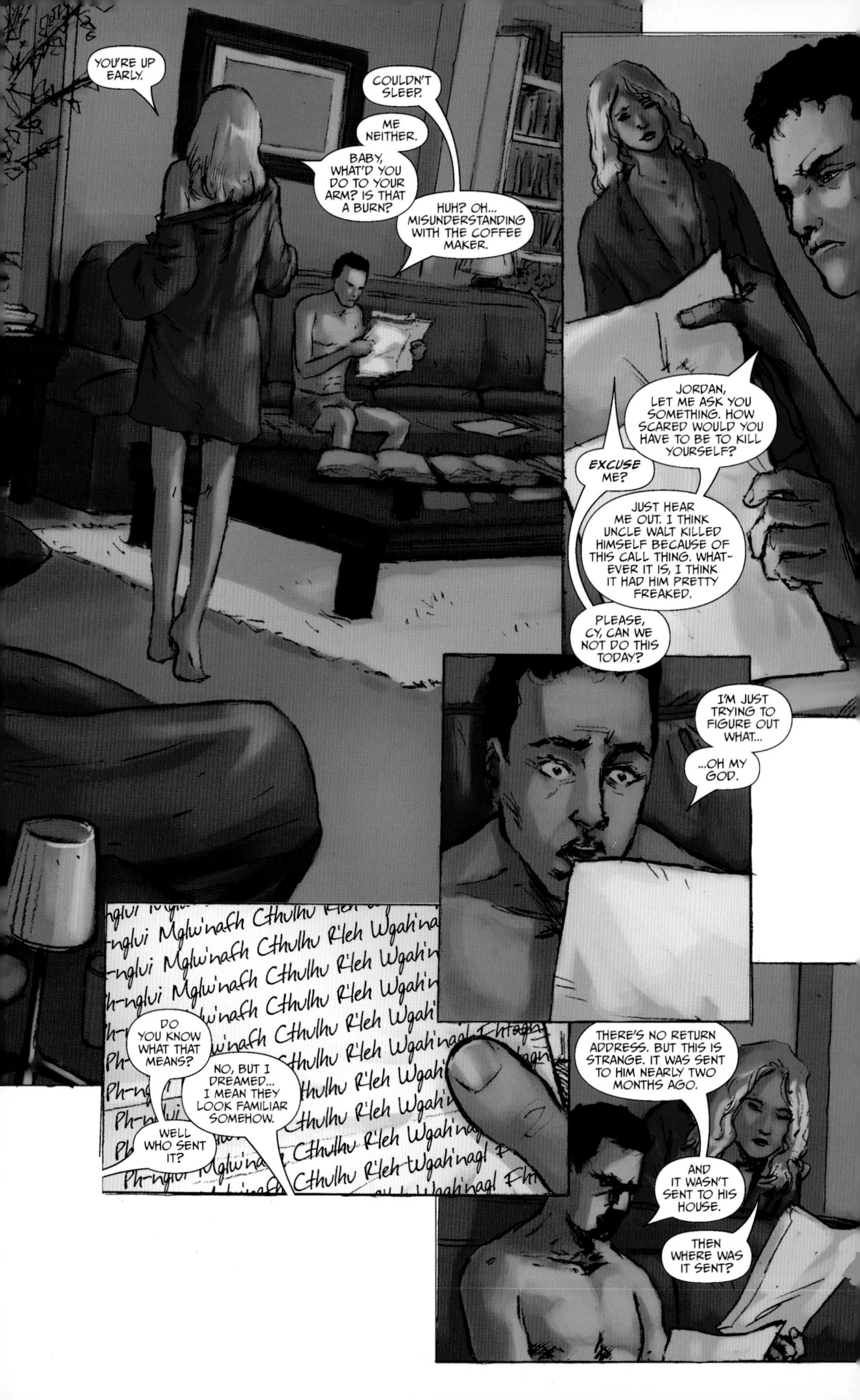
YOU'RE UP EARLY.
COULDN'T SLEEP.
ME NEITHER.
BABY, WHAT'D YOU DO TO YOUR ARM? IS THAT A BURN?
HUH? OH... MISUNDERSTANDING WITH THE COFFEE MAKER.
JORDAN, LET ME ASK YOU SOMETHING. HOW SCARED WOULD YOU HAVE TO BE TO KILL YOURSELF?
EXCUSE ME?
JUST HEAR ME OUT. I THINK UNCLE WALT KILLED HIMSELF BECAUSE OF THIS CALL THING. WHAT-EVER IT IS, I THINK IT HAD HIM PRETTY FREAKED.
PLEASE, CY, CAN WE NOT DO THIS TODAY?
I'M JUST TRYING TO FIGURE OUT WHAT...
...OH MY GOD.
DO YOU KNOW WHAT THAT MEANS?
NO, BUT I DREAMED... I MEAN THEY LOOK FAMILIAR SOMEHOW.
WELL WHO SENT IT?
THERE'S NO RETURN ADDRESS. BUT THIS IS STRANGE. IT WAS SENT TO HIM NEARLY TWO MONTHS AGO.
AND IT WASN'T SENT TO HIS HOUSE.
THEN WHERE WAS IT SENT?

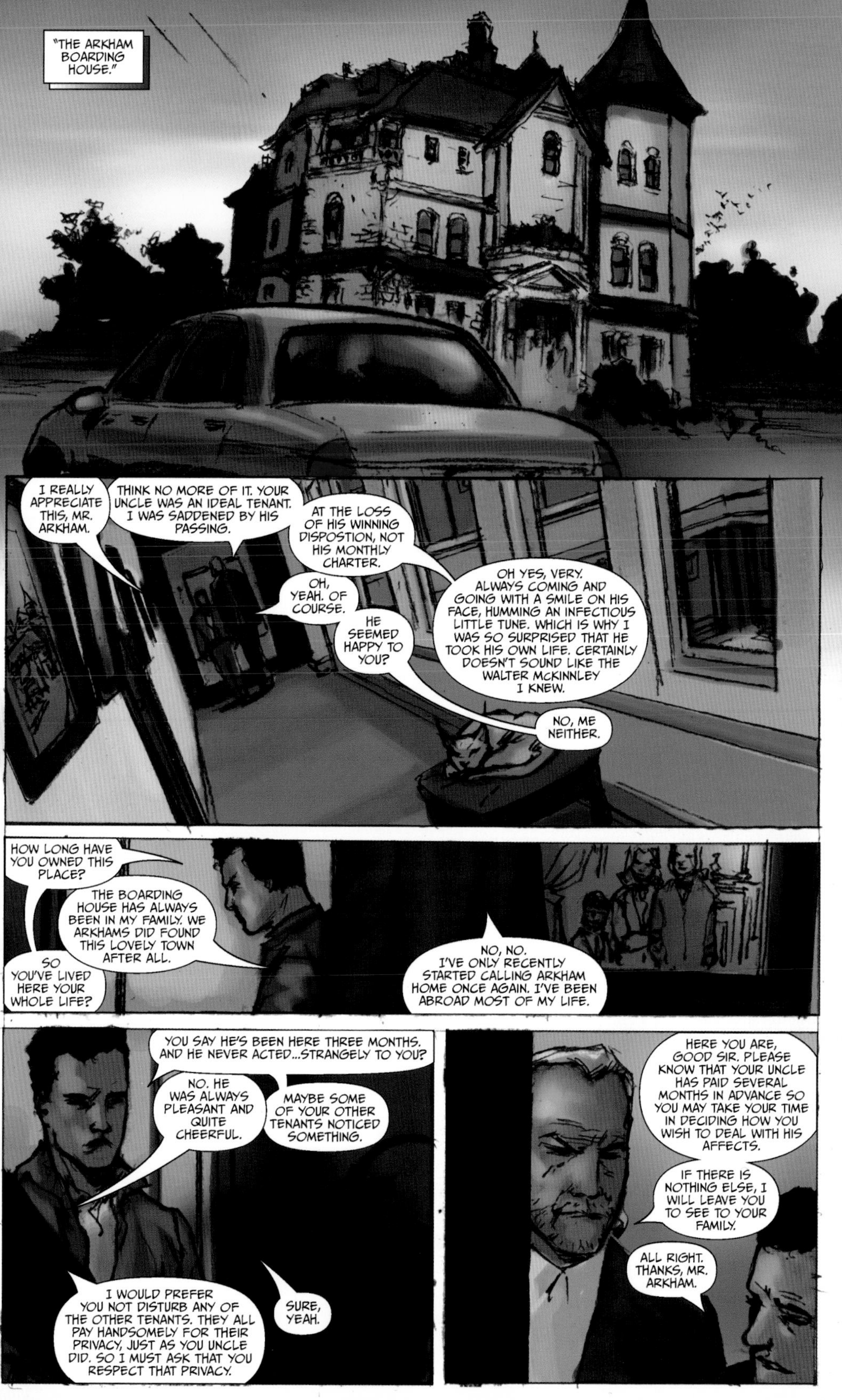
"THE ARKHAM BOARDING HOUSE."
I REALLY APPRECIATE THIS, MR. ARKHAM.
THINK NO MORE OF IT. YOUR UNCLE WAS AN IDEAL TENANT. I WAS SADDENED BY HIS PASSING.
AT THE LOSS OF HIS WINNING DISPOSTION, NOT HIS MONTHLY CHARTER.
OH, YEAH. OF COURSE.
HE SEEMED HAPPY TO YOU?
OH YES, VERY. ALWAYS COMING AND GOING WITH A SMILE ON HIS FACE, HUMMING AN INFECTIOUS LITTLE TUNE. WHICH IS WHY I WAS SO SURPRISED THAT HE TOOK HIS OWN LIFE. CERTAINLY DOESN'T SOUND LIKE THE WALTER MCKINNLEY I KNEW.
NO, ME NEITHER.
HOW LONG HAVE YOU OWNED THIS PLACE?
THE BOARDING HOUSE HAS ALWAYS BEEN IN MY FAMILY. WE ARKHAMS DID FOUND THIS LOVELY TOWN AFTER ALL.
SO YOU'VE LIVED HERE YOUR WHOLE LIFE?
NO, NO. I'VE ONLY RECENTLY STARTED CALLING ARKHAM HOME ONCE AGAIN. I'VE BEEN ABROAD MOST OF MY LIFE.
YOU SAY HE'S BEEN HERE THREE MONTHS. AND HE NEVER ACTED...STRANGELY TO YOU?
NO. HE WAS ALWAYS PLEASANT AND QUITE CHEERFUL.
MAYBE SOME OF YOUR OTHER TENANTS NOTICED SOMETHING.
I WOULD PREFER YOU NOT DISTURB ANY OF THE OTHER TENANTS. THEY ALL PAY HANDSOMELY FOR THEIR PRIVACY, JUST AS YOU UNCLE DID. SO I MUST ASK THAT YOU RESPECT THAT PRIVACY.
SURE, YEAH.
HERE YOU ARE, GOOD SIR. PLEASE KNOW THAT YOUR UNCLE HAS PAID SEVERAL MONTHS IN ADVANCE SO YOU MAY TAKE YOUR TIME IN DECIDING HOW YOU WISH TO DEAL WITH HIS AFFECTS.
IF THERE IS NOTHING ELSE, I WILL LEAVE YOU TO SEE TO YOUR FAMILY.
ALL RIGHT. THANKS, MR. ARKHAM.

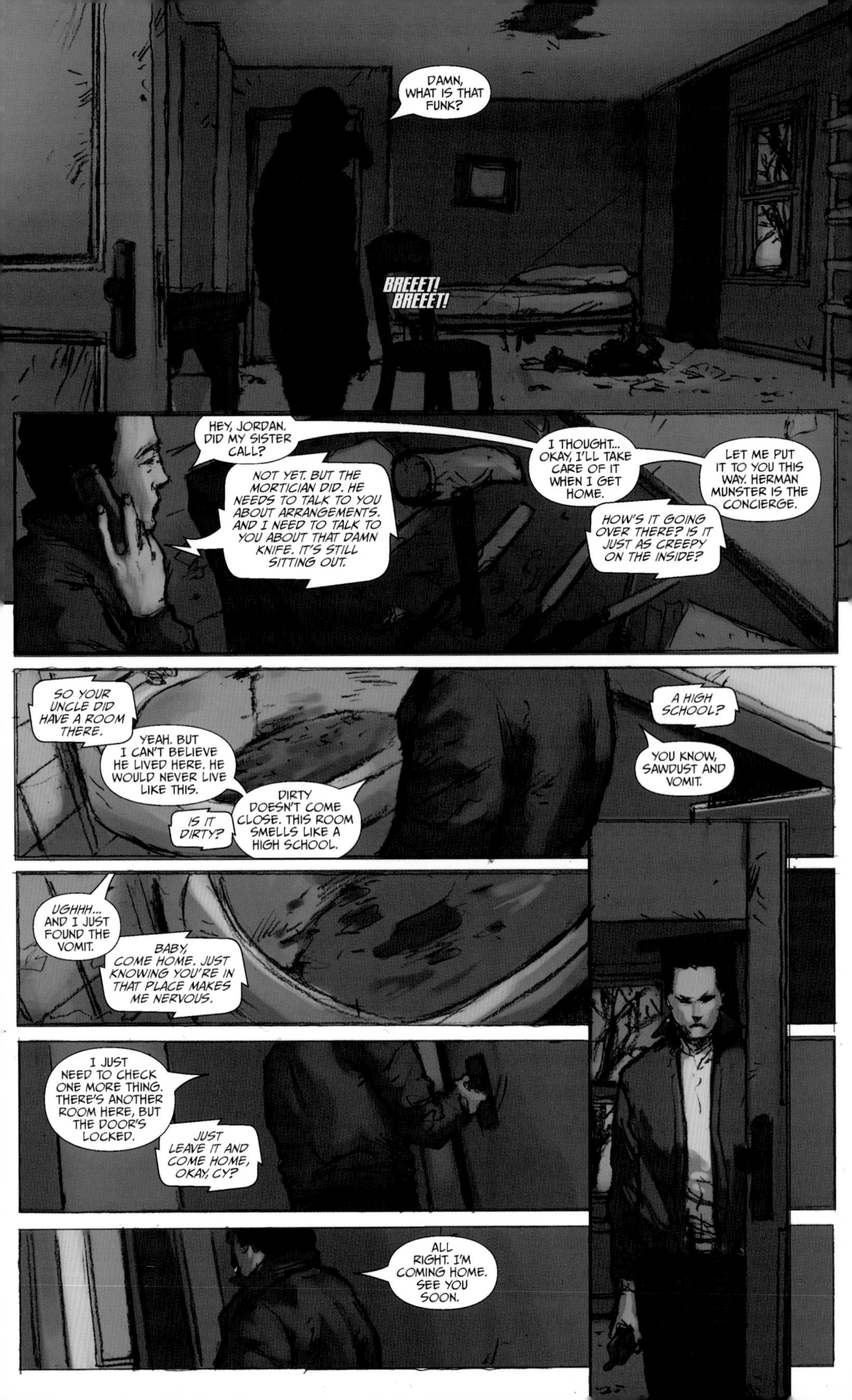
DAMN, WHAT IS THAT FUNK?
BREEET! BREEET!
HEY, JORDAN. DID MY SISTER CALL?
NOT YET. BUT THE MORTICIAN DID. HE NEEDS TO TALK TO YOU ABOUT ARRANGEMENTS. AND I NEED TO TALK TO YOU ABOUT THAT DAMN KNIFE. IT'S STILL SITTING OUT.
I THOUGHT... OKAY, I'LL TAKE CARE OF IT WHEN I GET HOME.
HOW'S IT GOING OVER THERE? IS IT JUST AS CREEPY ON THE INSIDE?
LET ME PUT IT TO YOU THIS WAY. HERMAN MUNSTER IS THE CONCIERGE.
SO YOUR UNCLE DID HAVE A ROOM THERE.
YEAH. BUT I CAN'T BELIEVE HE LIVED HERE. HE WOULD NEVER LIVE LIKE THIS.
IS IT DIRTY?
DIRTY DOESN'T COME CLOSE. THIS ROOM SMELLS LIKE A HIGH SCHOOL.
A HIGH SCHOOL?
YOU KNOW, SAWDUST AND VOMIT.
UGHHH... AND I JUST FOUND THE VOMIT.
BABY, COME HOME. JUST KNOWING YOU'RE IN THAT PLACE MAKES ME NERVOUS.
I JUST NEED TO CHECK ONE MORE THING. THERE'S ANOTHER ROOM HERE, BUT THE DOOR'S LOCKED.
JUST LEAVE IT AND COME HOME, OKAY, CY?
ALL RIGHT. I'M COMING HOME. SEE YOU SOON.

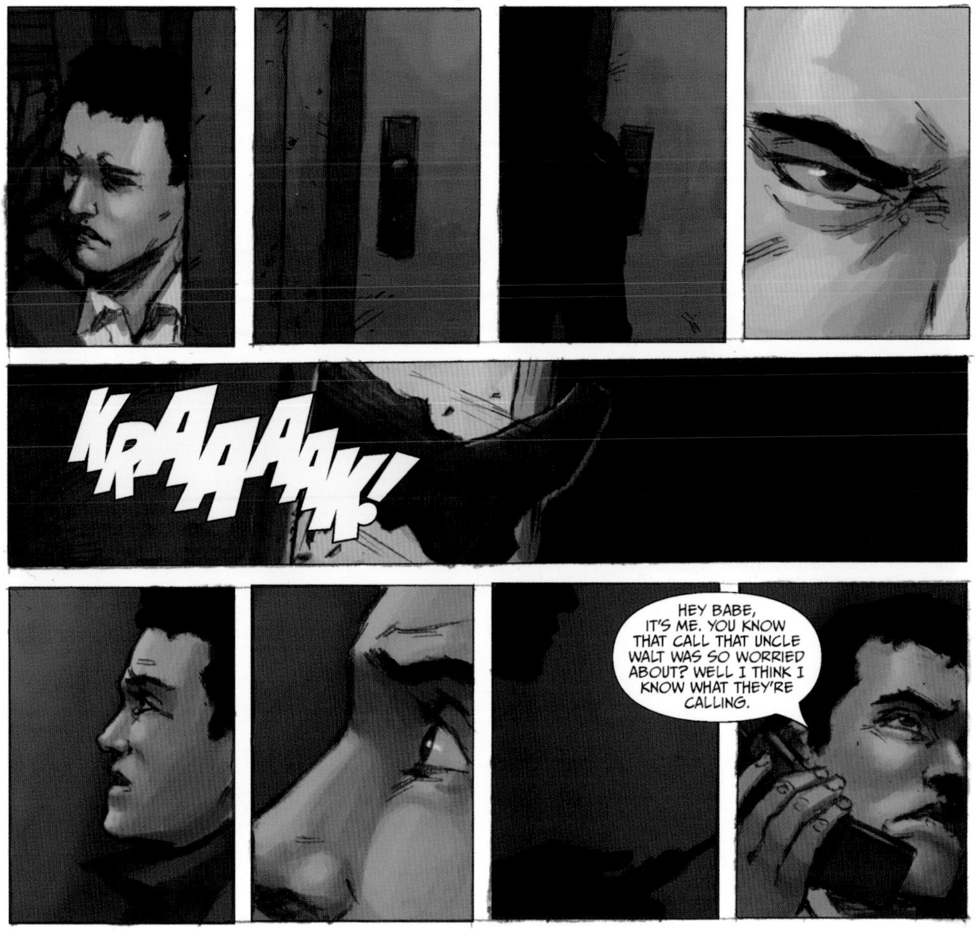
KRAAAAAK!
HEY BABE, IT'S ME. YOU KNOW THAT CALL THAT UNCLE WALT WAS SO WORRIED ABOUT? WELL I THINK I KNOW WHAT THEY'RE CALLING.

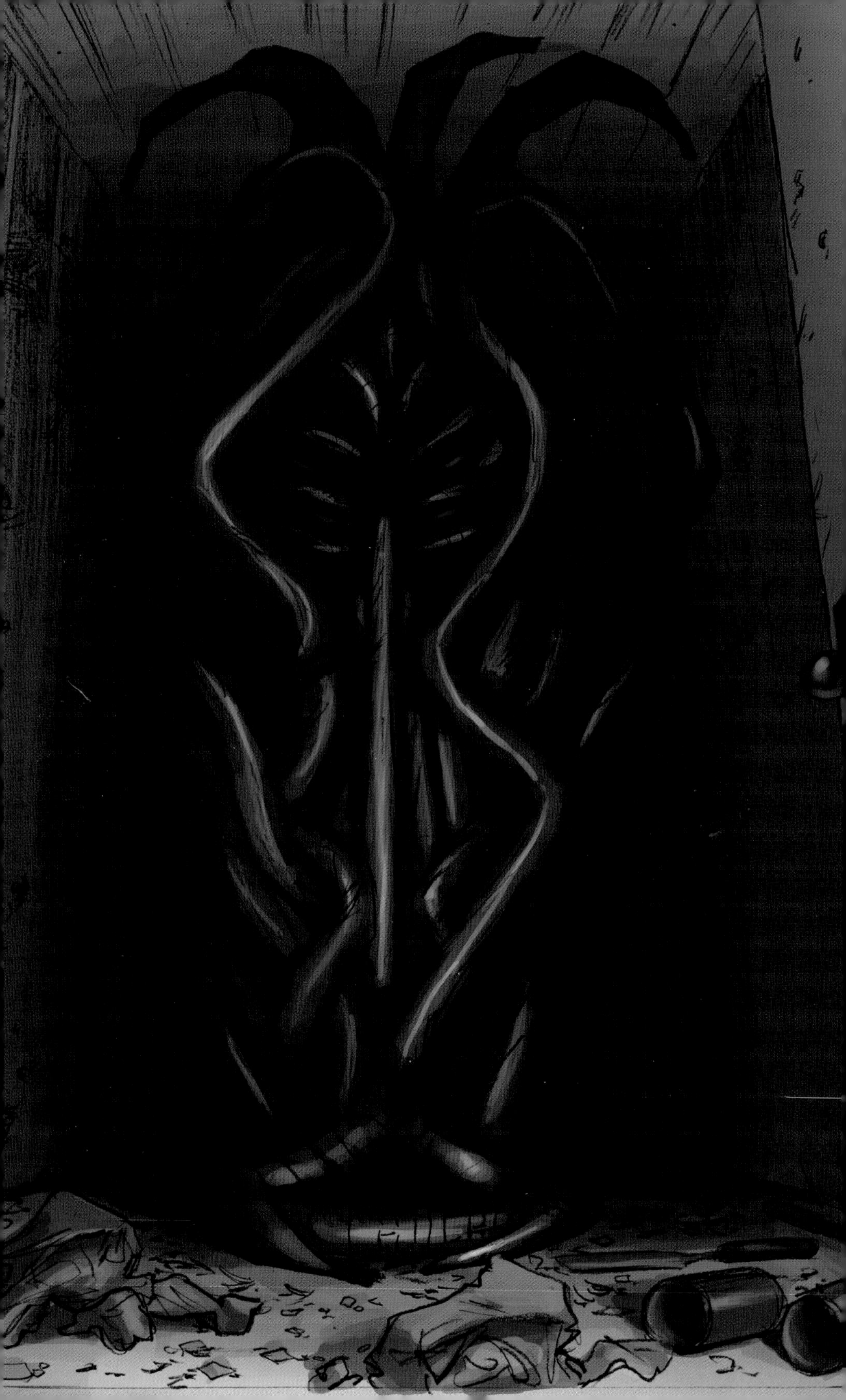

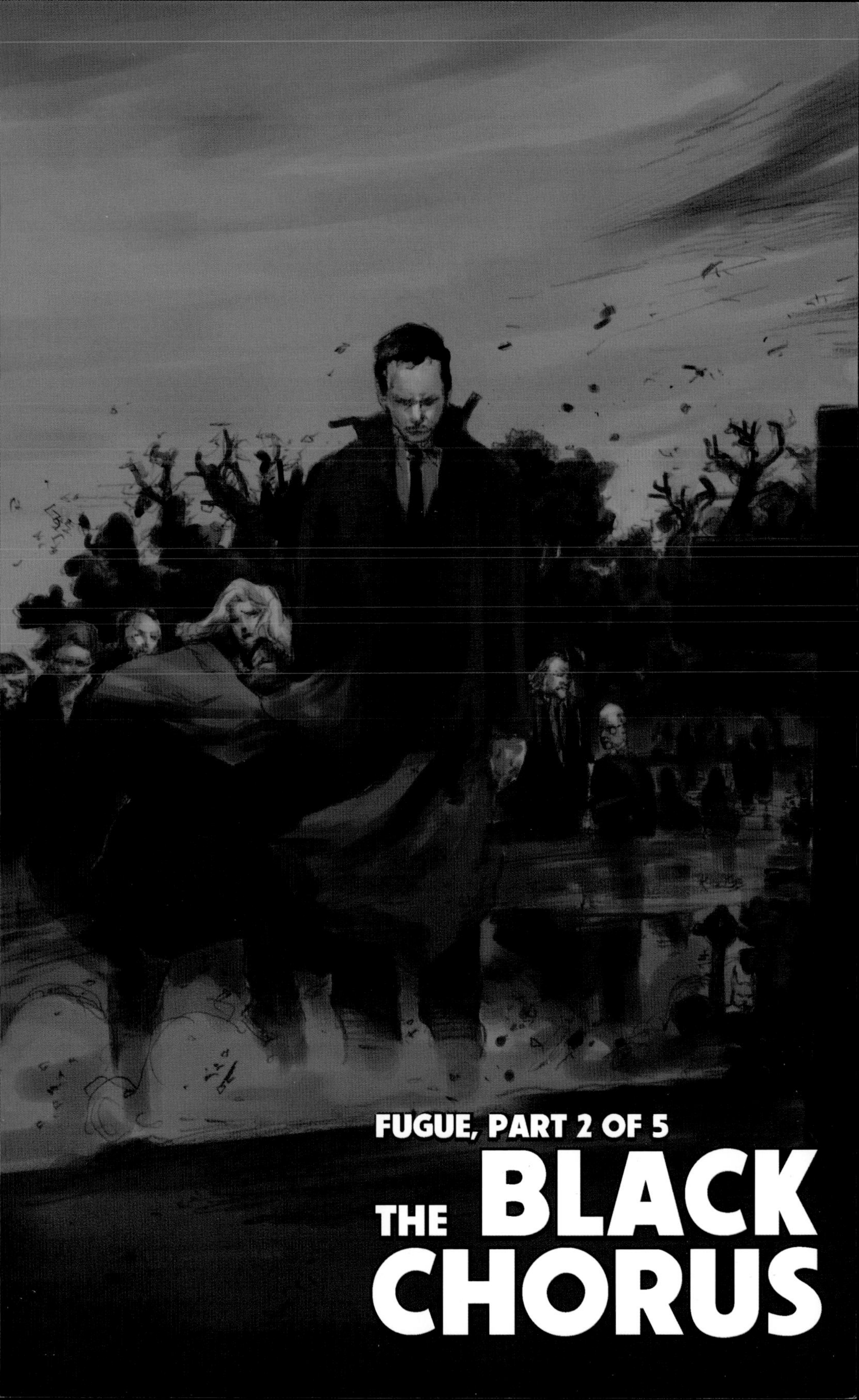
FUGUE, PART 2 OF 5
THE BLACK
CHORUS

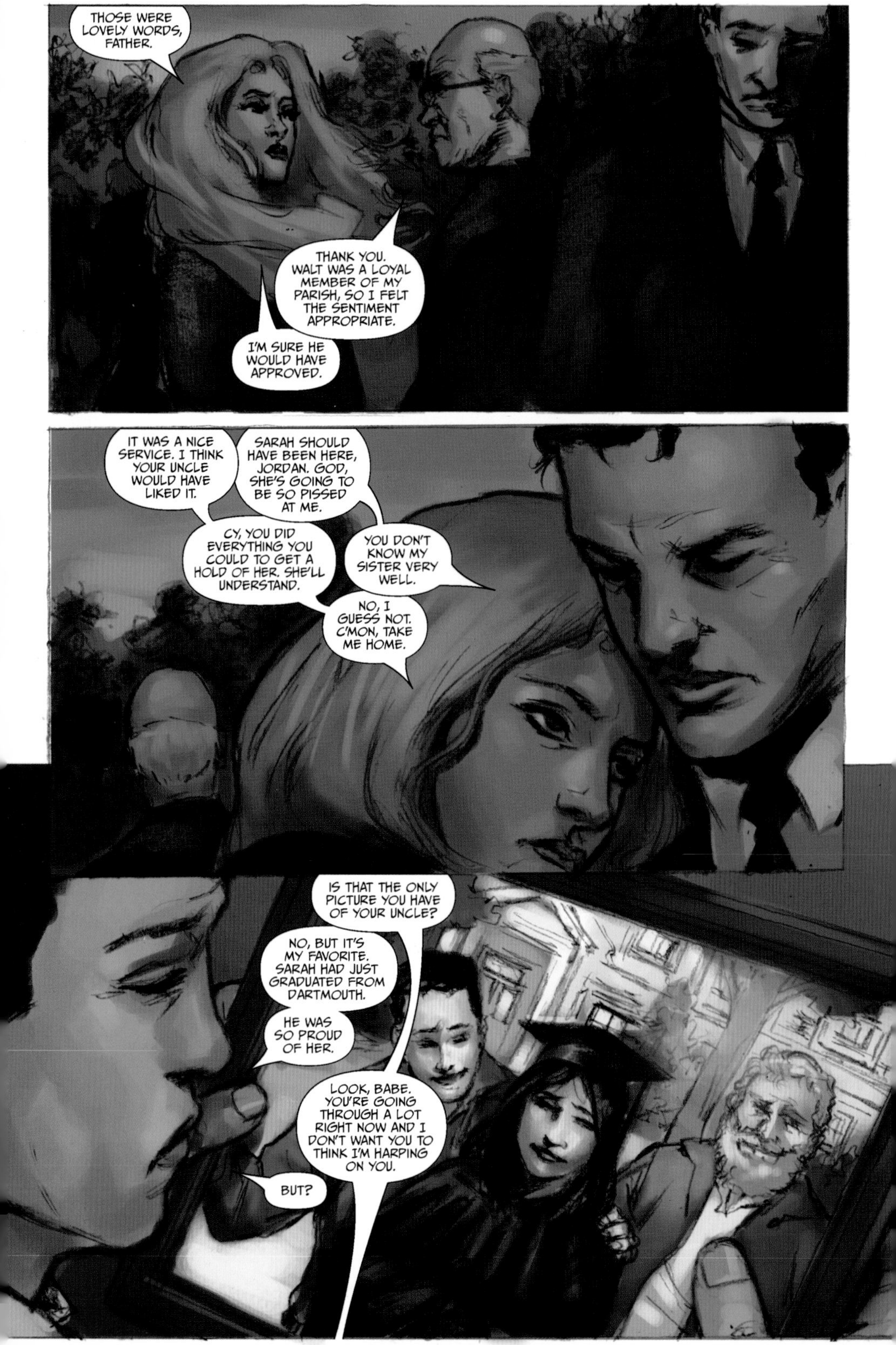
THOSE WERE LOVELY WORDS, FATHER.
THANK YOU. WALT WAS A LOYAL MEMBER OF MY PARISH, SO I FELT THE SENTIMENT APPROPRIATE.
I'M SURE HE WOULD HAVE APPROVED.
IT WAS A NICE SERVICE. I THINK YOUR UNCLE WOULD HAVE LIKED IT.
SARAH SHOULD HAVE BEEN HERE, JORDAN. GOD, SHE'S GOING TO BE SO PISSED AT ME.
CY, YOU DID EVERYTHING YOU COULD TO GET A HOLD OF HER. SHE'LL UNDERSTAND.
YOU DON'T KNOW MY SISTER VERY WELL.
NO, I GUESS NOT. C'MON, TAKE ME HOME.
IS THAT THE ONLY PICTURE YOU HAVE OF YOUR UNCLE?
NO, BUT IT'S MY FAVORITE. SARAH HAD JUST GRADUATED FROM DARTMOUTH.
HE WAS SO PROUD OF HER.
LOOK, BABE. YOU'RE GOING THROUGH A LOT RIGHT NOW AND I DON'T WANT YOU TO THINK I'M HARPING ON YOU.
BUT?

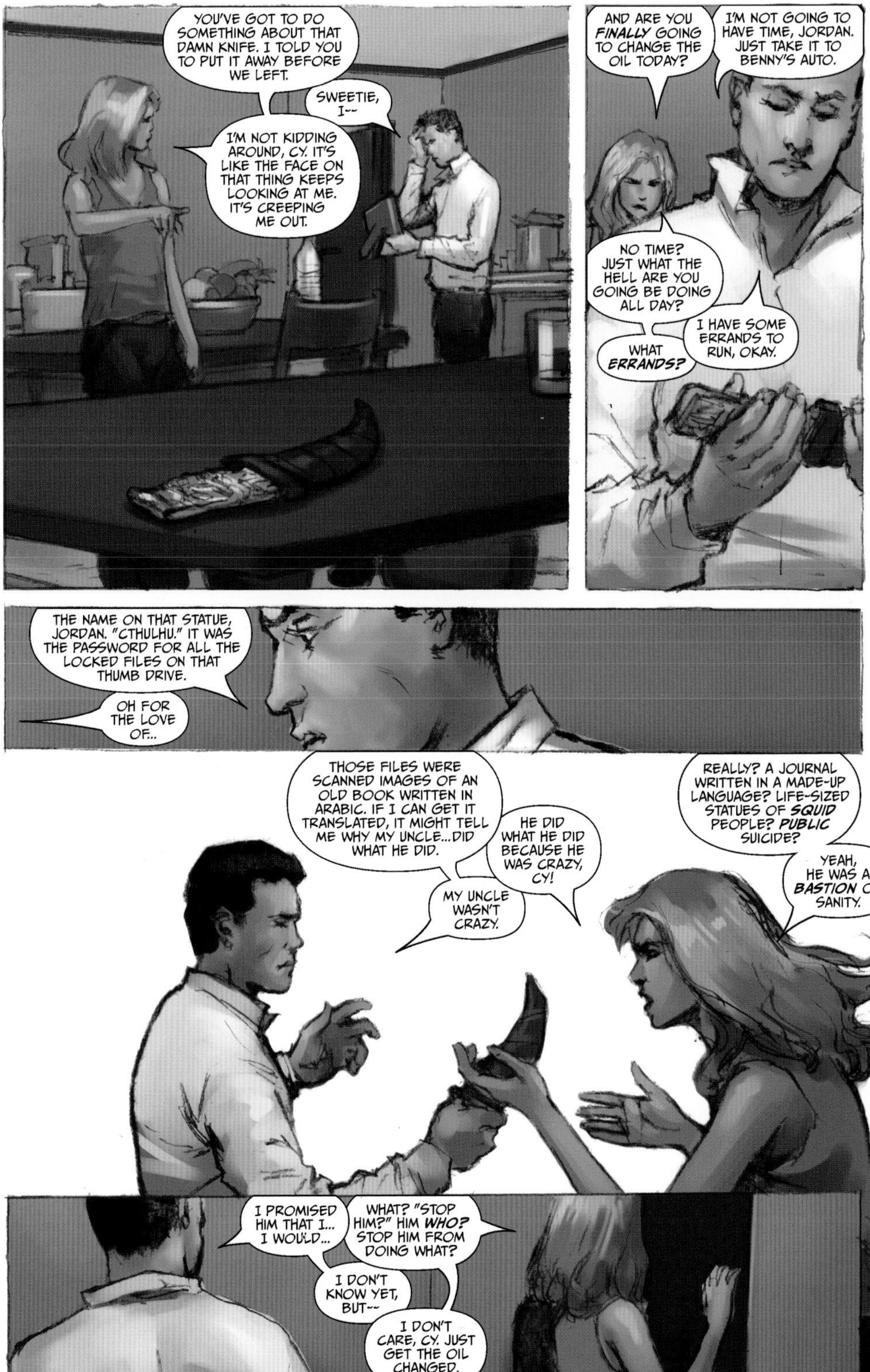
YOU'VE GOT TO DO SOMETHING ABOUT THAT DAMN KNIFE. I TOLD YOU TO PUT IT AWAY BEFORE WE LEFT.
SWEETIE, I--
I'M NOT KIDDING AROUND, CY. IT'S LIKE THE FACE ON THAT THING KEEPS LOOKING AT ME. IT'S CREEPING ME OUT.
AND ARE YOU *FINALLY* GOING TO CHANGE THE OIL TODAY?
I'M NOT GOING TO HAVE TIME, JORDAN. JUST TAKE IT TO BENNY'S AUTO.
NO TIME? JUST WHAT THE HELL ARE YOU GOING BE DOING ALL DAY?
I HAVE SOME ERRANDS TO RUN, OKAY.
WHAT *ERRANDS?*
THE NAME ON THAT STATUE, JORDAN. "CTHULHU." IT WAS THE PASSWORD FOR ALL THE LOCKED FILES ON THAT THUMB DRIVE.
OH FOR THE LOVE OF...
THOSE FILES WERE SCANNED IMAGES OF AN OLD BOOK WRITTEN IN ARABIC. IF I CAN GET IT TRANSLATED, IT MIGHT TELL ME WHY MY UNCLE...DID WHAT HE DID.
HE DID WHAT HE DID BECAUSE HE WAS CRAZY, CY!
MY UNCLE WASN'T CRAZY.
REALLY? A JOURNAL WRITTEN IN A MADE-UP LANGUAGE? LIFE-SIZED STATUES OF *SQUID* PEOPLE? *PUBLIC* SUICIDE?
YEAH, HE WAS A *BASTION* OF SANITY.
I PROMISED HIM THAT I... I WOULD...
WHAT? "STOP HIM?" HIM *WHO?* STOP HIM FROM DOING WHAT?
I DON'T KNOW YET, BUT--
I DON'T CARE, CY. JUST GET THE OIL CHANGED.

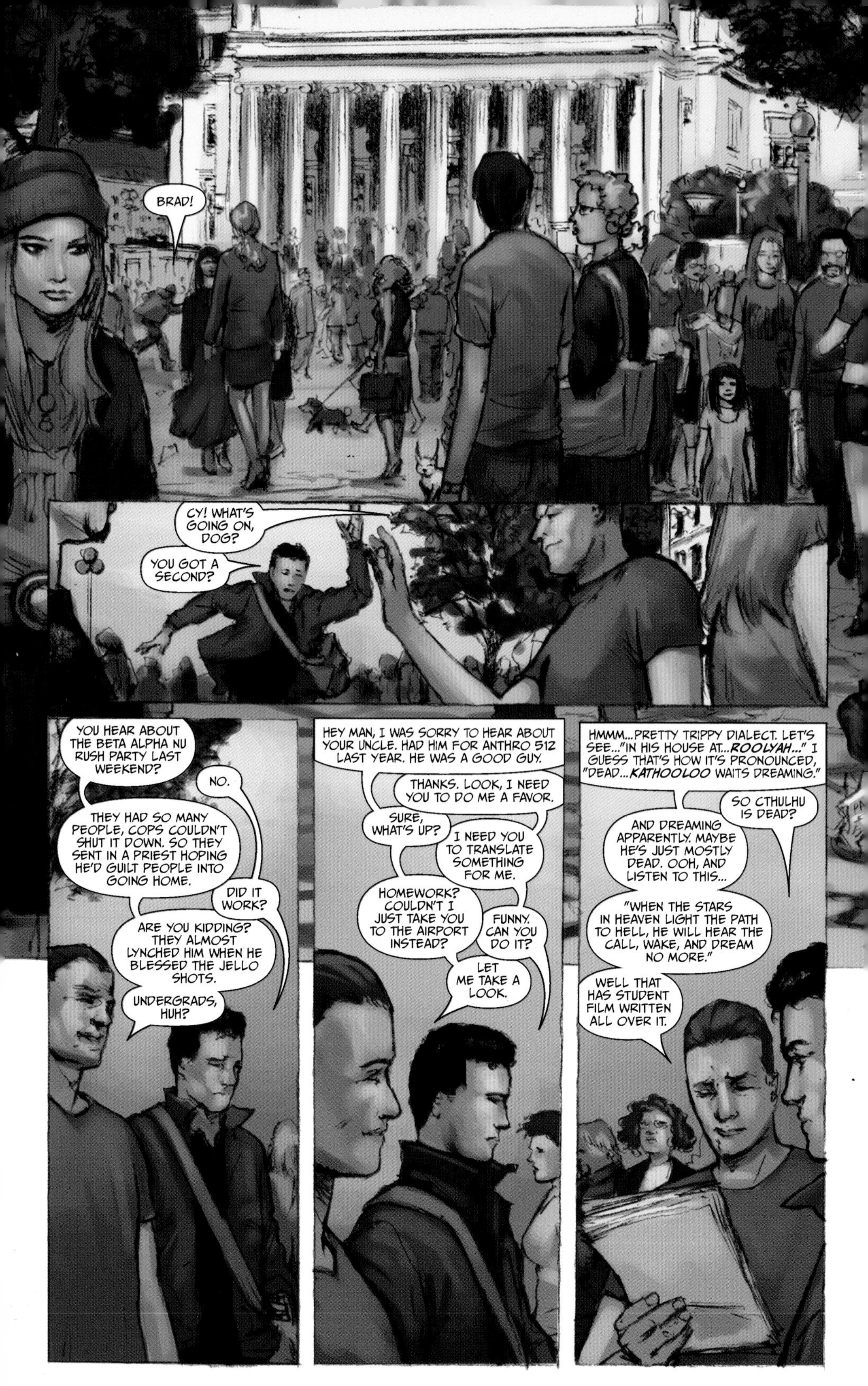
BRAD!
CY! WHAT'S GOING ON, DOG?
YOU GOT A SECOND?
YOU HEAR ABOUT THE BETA ALPHA NU RUSH PARTY LAST WEEKEND?
NO.
THEY HAD SO MANY PEOPLE, COPS COULDN'T SHUT IT DOWN. SO THEY SENT IN A PRIEST HOPING HE'D GUILT PEOPLE INTO GOING HOME.
DID IT WORK?
ARE YOU KIDDING? THEY ALMOST LYNCHED HIM WHEN HE BLESSED THE JELLO SHOTS.
UNDERGRADS, HUH?
HEY MAN, I WAS SORRY TO HEAR ABOUT YOUR UNCLE. HAD HIM FOR ANTHRO 512 LAST YEAR. HE WAS A GOOD GUY.
THANKS. LOOK, I NEED YOU TO DO ME A FAVOR.
SURE, WHAT'S UP?
I NEED YOU TO TRANSLATE SOMETHING FOR ME.
HOMEWORK? COULDN'T I JUST TAKE YOU TO THE AIRPORT INSTEAD?
FUNNY. CAN YOU DO IT?
LET ME TAKE A LOOK.
HMMM...PRETTY TRIPPY DIALECT. LET'S SEE..."IN HIS HOUSE AT...*ROOLYAH...*" I GUESS THAT'S HOW IT'S PRONOUNCED, "DEAD...*KATHOOLOO* WAITS DREAMING."
SO CTHULHU IS DEAD?
AND DREAMING APPARENTLY. MAYBE HE'S JUST MOSTLY DEAD. OOH, AND LISTEN TO THIS...
"WHEN THE STARS IN HEAVEN LIGHT THE PATH TO HELL, HE WILL HEAR THE CALL, WAKE, AND DREAM NO MORE."
WELL THAT HAS STUDENT FILM WRITTEN ALL OVER IT.

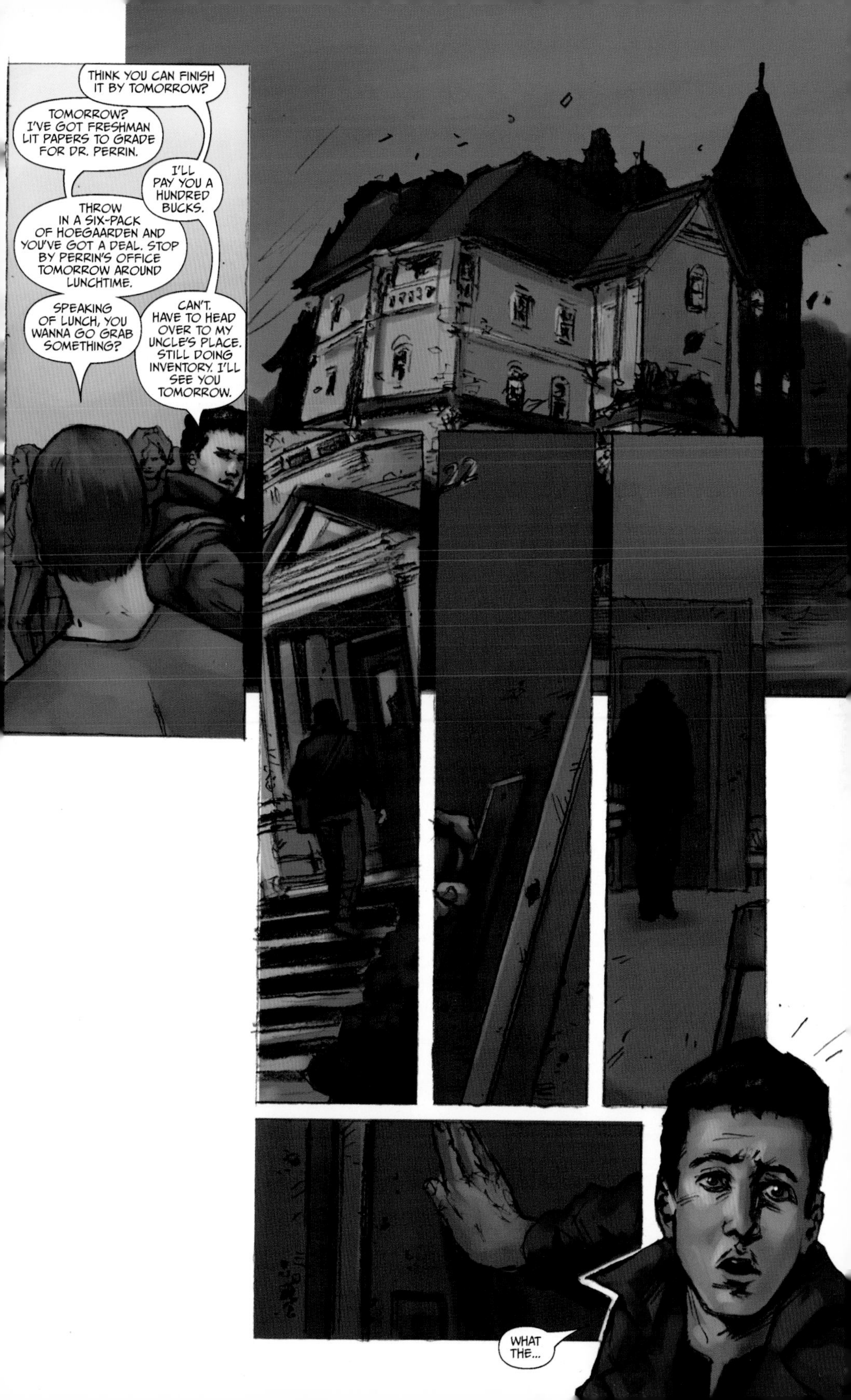
THINK YOU CAN FINISH IT BY TOMORROW?
TOMORROW? I'VE GOT FRESHMAN LIT PAPERS TO GRADE FOR DR. PERRIN.
I'LL PAY YOU A HUNDRED BUCKS.
THROW IN A SIX-PACK OF HOEGAARDEN AND YOU'VE GOT A DEAL. STOP BY PERRIN'S OFFICE TOMORROW AROUND LUNCHTIME.
SPEAKING OF LUNCH, YOU WANNA GO GRAB SOMETHING?
CAN'T. HAVE TO HEAD OVER TO MY UNCLE'S PLACE. STILL DOING INVENTORY. I'LL SEE YOU TOMORROW.
WHAT THE...

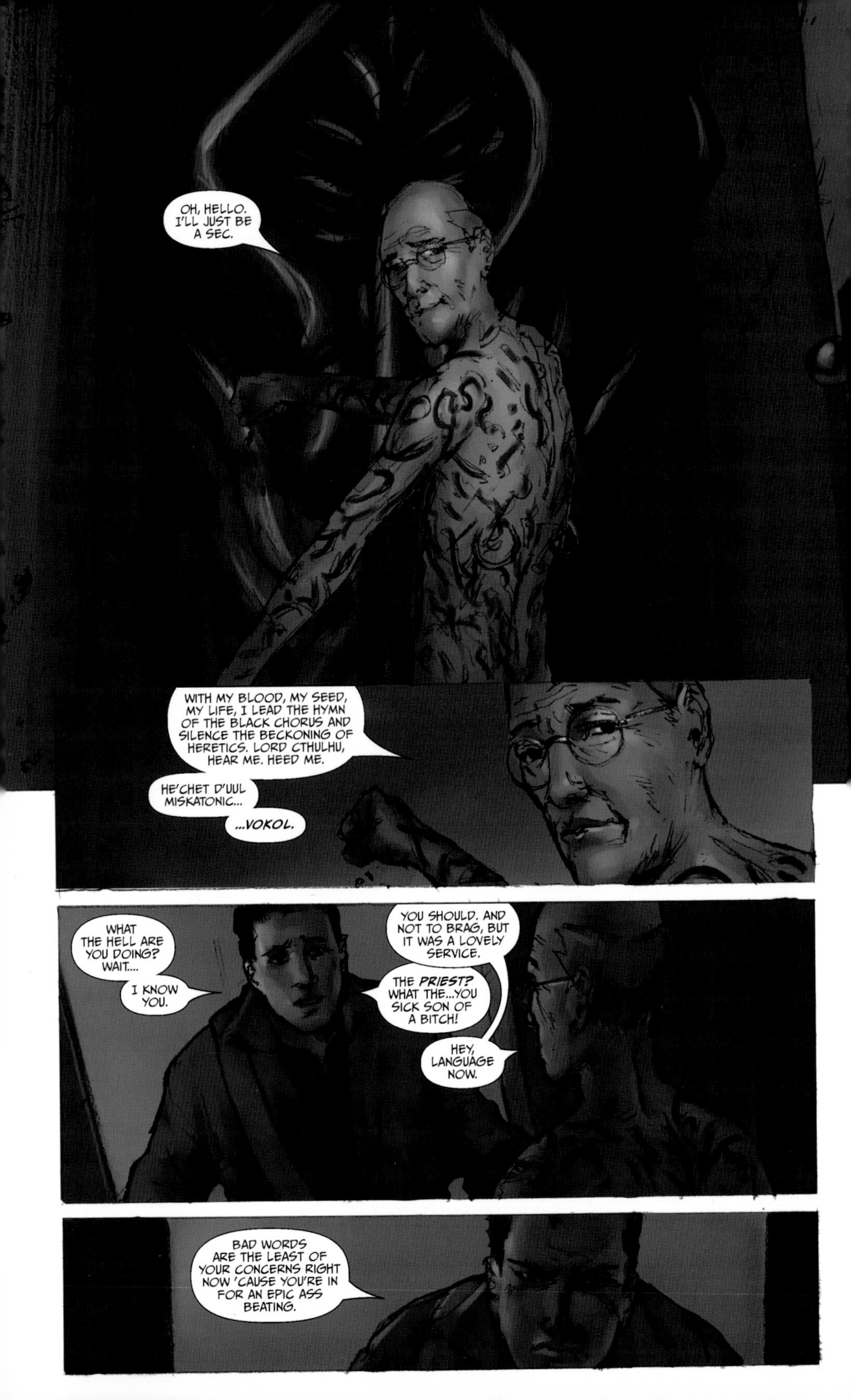
OH, HELLO. I'LL JUST BE A SEC.
WITH MY BLOOD, MY SEED, MY LIFE, I LEAD THE HYMN OF THE BLACK CHORUS AND SILENCE THE BECKONING OF HERETICS. LORD CTHULHU, HEAR ME. HEED ME.
HE'CHET D'UUL MISKATONIC...
...VOKOL.
WHAT THE HELL ARE YOU DOING? WAIT....
I KNOW YOU.
YOU SHOULD. AND NOT TO BRAG, BUT IT WAS A LOVELY SERVICE.
THE PRIEST? WHAT THE...YOU SICK SON OF A BITCH!
HEY, LANGUAGE NOW.
BAD WORDS ARE THE LEAST OF YOUR CONCERNS RIGHT NOW 'CAUSE YOU'RE IN FOR AN EPIC ASS BEATING.

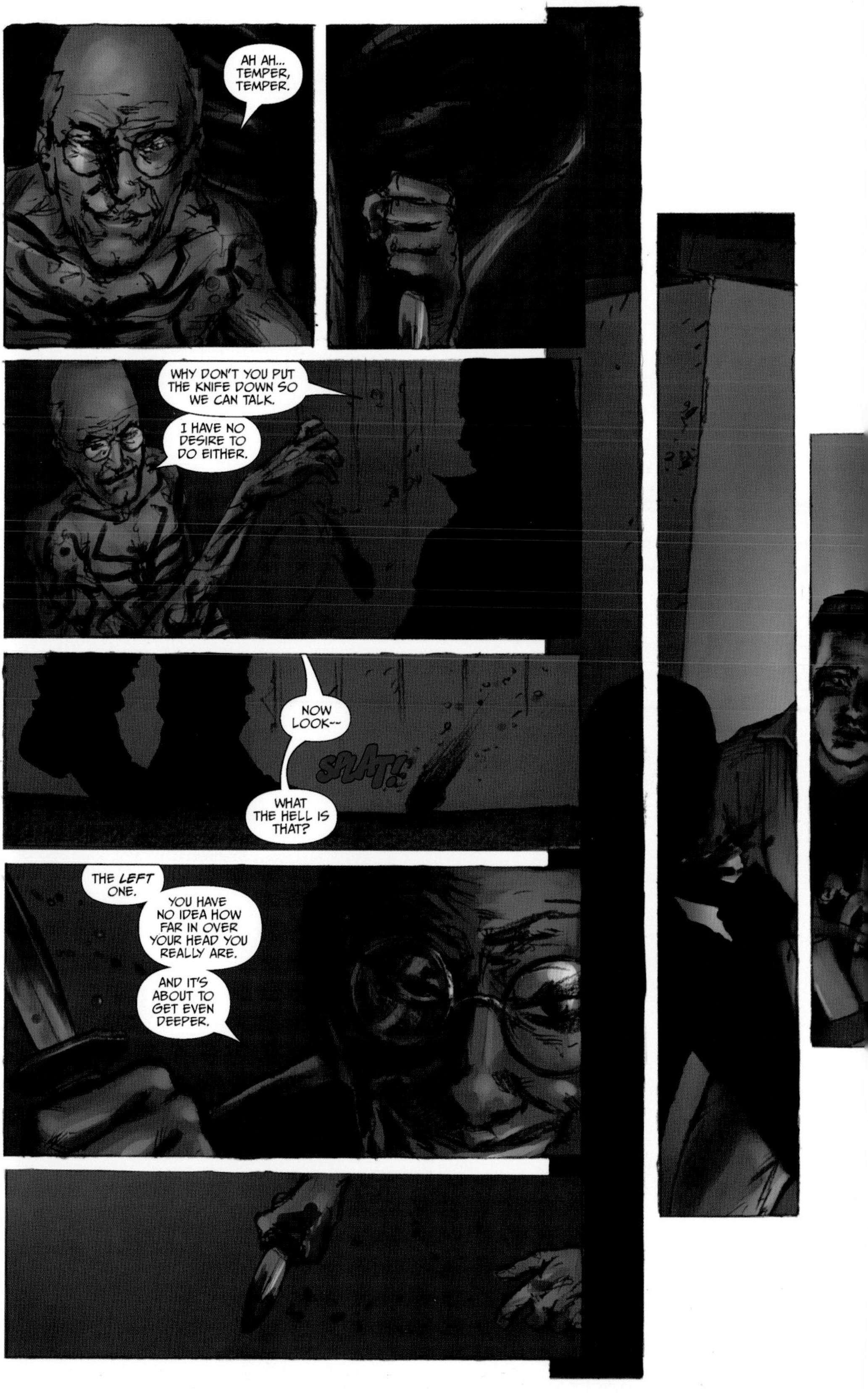
AH AH... TEMPER, TEMPER.
WHY DON'T YOU PUT THE KNIFE DOWN SO WE CAN TALK.
I HAVE NO DESIRE TO DO EITHER.
NOW LOOK--
SPLAT!
WHAT THE HELL IS THAT?
THE *LEFT* ONE.
YOU HAVE NO IDEA HOW FAR IN OVER YOUR HEAD YOU REALLY ARE.
AND IT'S ABOUT TO GET EVEN DEEPER.

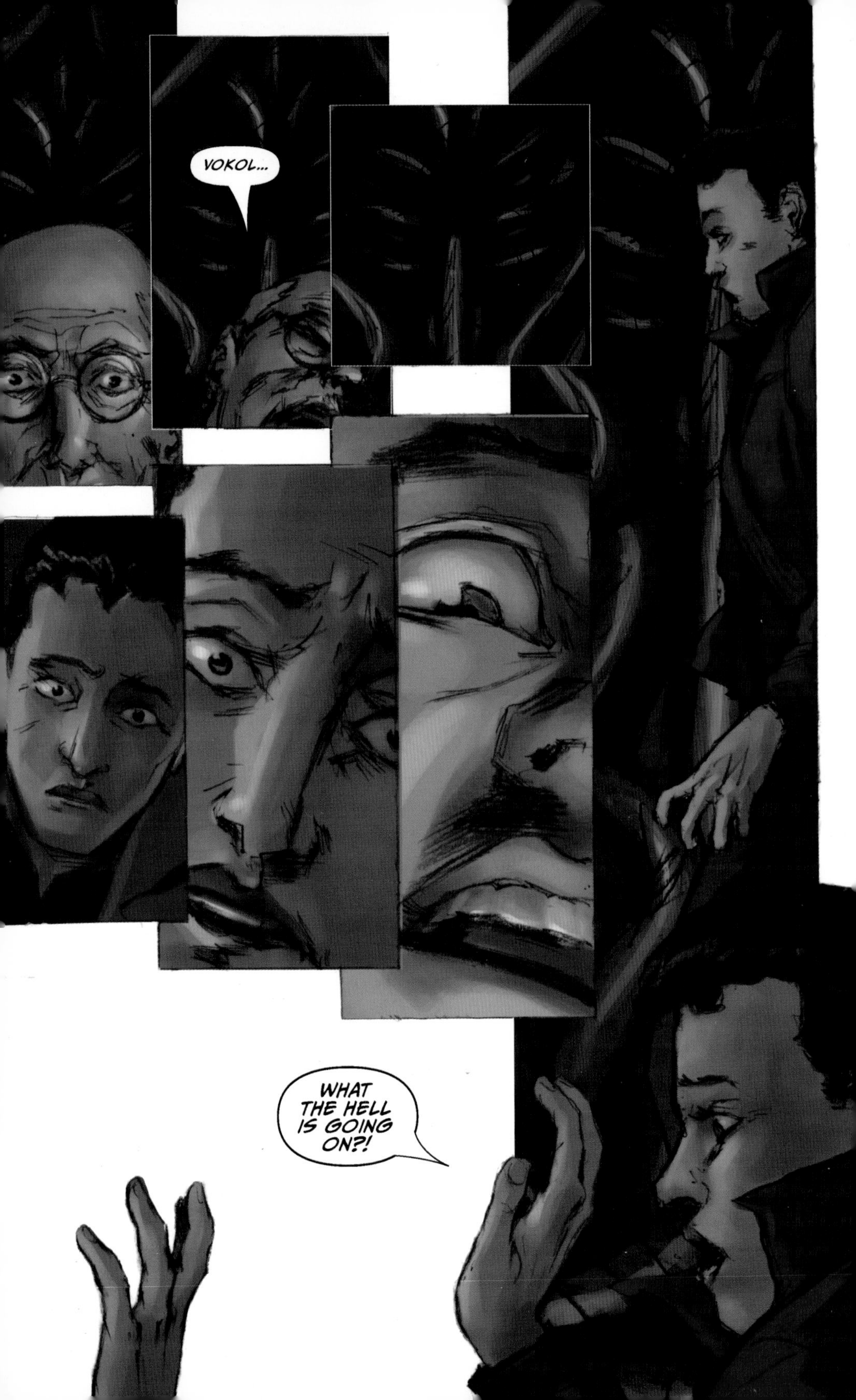
VOKOL...
WHAT THE HELL IS GOING ON?!

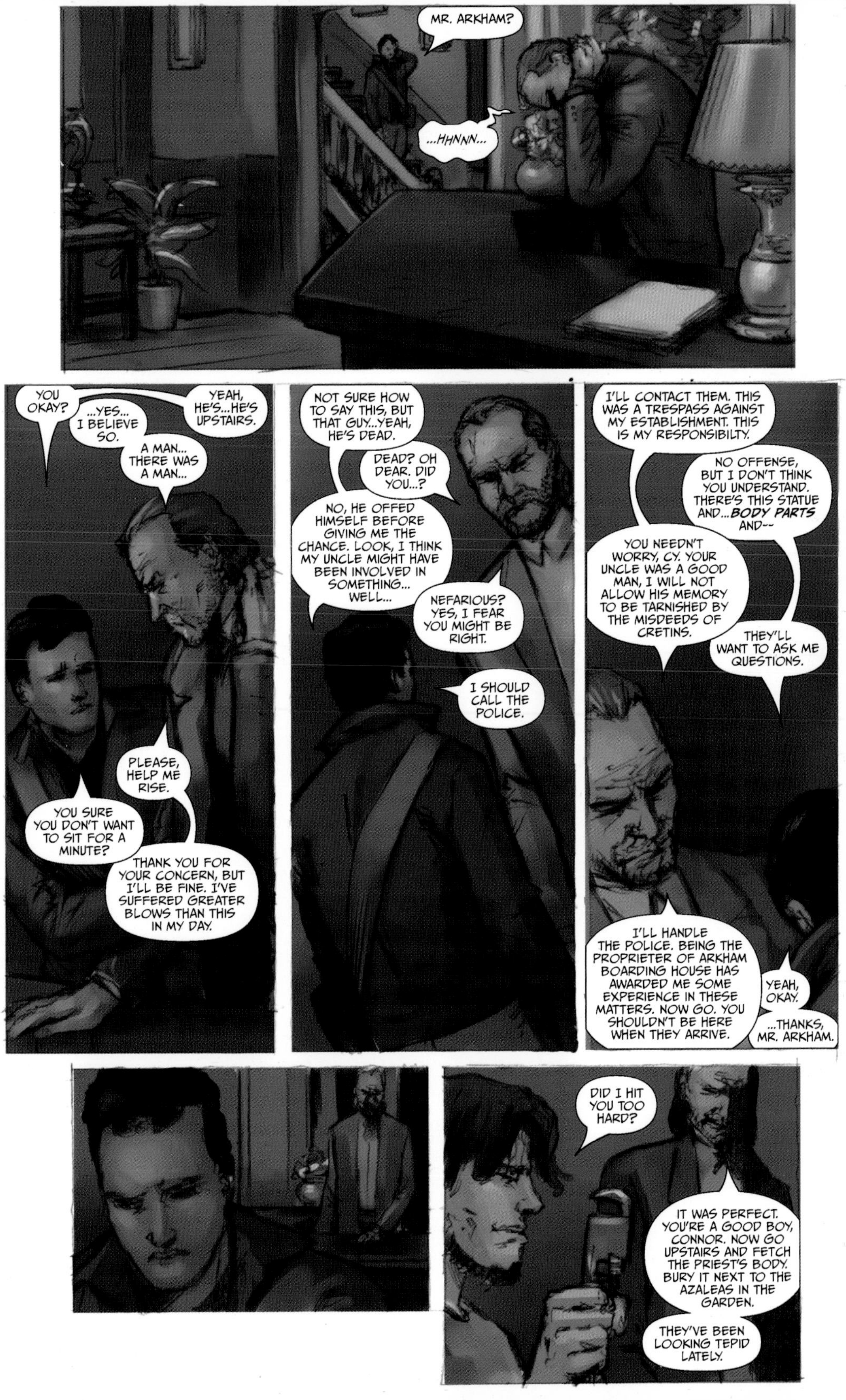
MR. ARKHAM?
...HHNNN...
YOU OKAY?
...YES... I BELIEVE SO.
YEAH, HE'S...HE'S UPSTAIRS.
A MAN... THERE WAS A MAN...
PLEASE, HELP ME RISE.
YOU SURE YOU DON'T WANT TO SIT FOR A MINUTE?
THANK YOU FOR YOUR CONCERN, BUT I'LL BE FINE. I'VE SUFFERED GREATER BLOWS THAN THIS IN MY DAY.
NOT SURE HOW TO SAY THIS, BUT THAT GUY...YEAH, HE'S DEAD.
DEAD? OH DEAR. DID YOU...?
NO, HE OFFED HIMSELF BEFORE GIVING ME THE CHANCE. LOOK, I THINK MY UNCLE MIGHT HAVE BEEN INVOLVED IN SOMETHING... WELL...
NEFARIOUS? YES, I FEAR YOU MIGHT BE RIGHT.
I SHOULD CALL THE POLICE.
I'LL CONTACT THEM. THIS WAS A TRESPASS AGAINST MY ESTABLISHMENT. THIS IS MY RESPONSIBILTY.
NO OFFENSE, BUT I DON'T THINK YOU UNDERSTAND. THERE'S THIS STATUE AND...BODY PARTS AND~~
YOU NEEDN'T WORRY, CY. YOUR UNCLE WAS A GOOD MAN, I WILL NOT ALLOW HIS MEMORY TO BE TARNISHED BY THE MISDEEDS OF CRETINS.
THEY'LL WANT TO ASK ME QUESTIONS.
I'LL HANDLE THE POLICE. BEING THE PROPRIETER OF ARKHAM BOARDING HOUSE HAS AWARDED ME SOME EXPERIENCE IN THESE MATTERS. NOW GO. YOU SHOULDN'T BE HERE WHEN THEY ARRIVE.
YEAH, OKAY.
...THANKS, MR. ARKHAM.
DID I HIT YOU TOO HARD?
IT WAS PERFECT. YOU'RE A GOOD BOY, CONNOR. NOW GO UPSTAIRS AND FETCH THE PRIEST'S BODY. BURY IT NEXT TO THE AZALEAS IN THE GARDEN.
THEY'VE BEEN LOOKING TEPID LATELY.

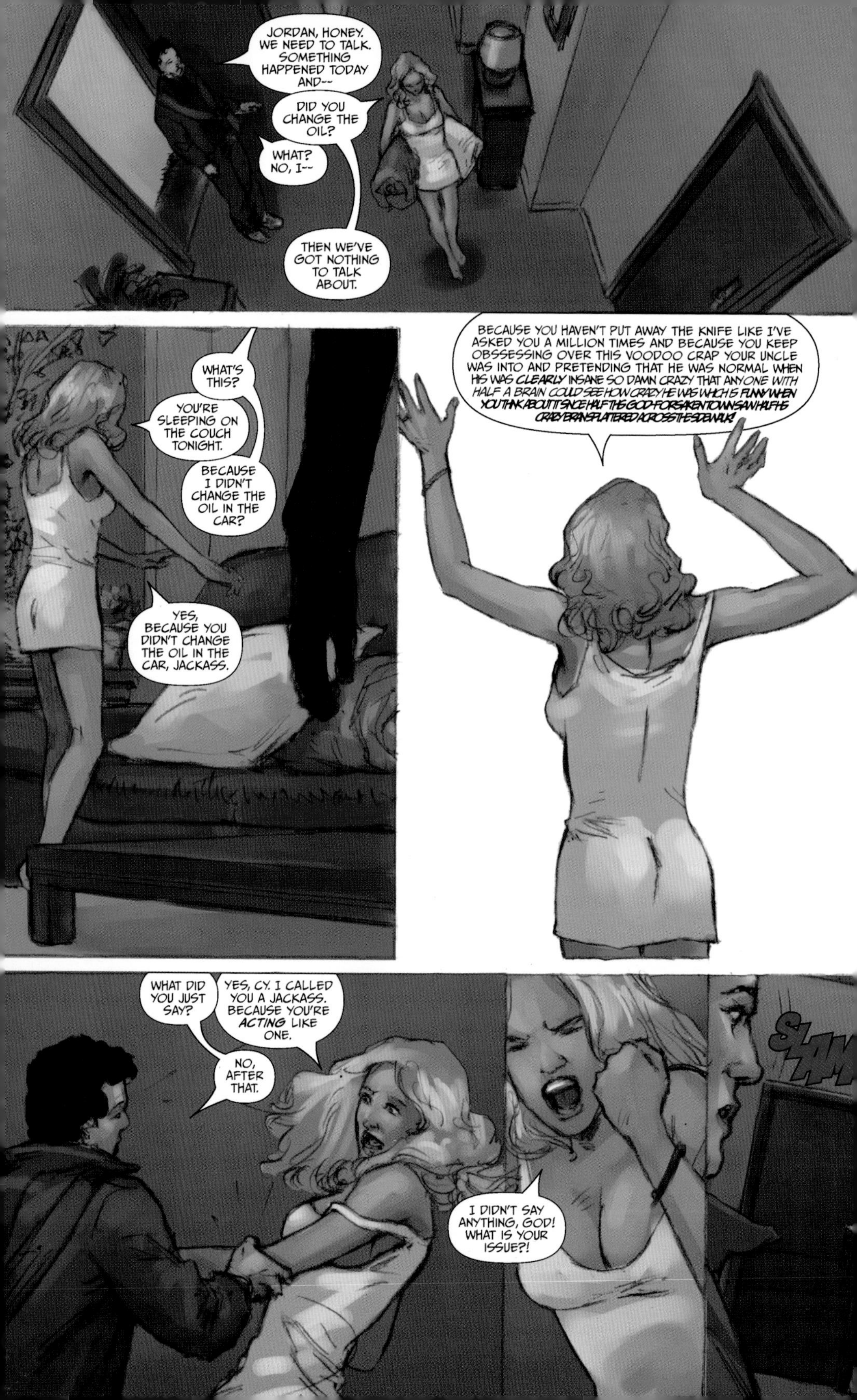
JORDAN, HONEY. WE NEED TO TALK. SOMETHING HAPPENED TODAY AND--
DID YOU CHANGE THE OIL?
WHAT? NO, I--
THEN WE'VE GOT NOTHING TO TALK ABOUT.
WHAT'S THIS?
YOU'RE SLEEPING ON THE COUCH TONIGHT.
BECAUSE I DIDN'T CHANGE THE OIL IN THE CAR?
YES, BECAUSE YOU DIDN'T CHANGE THE OIL IN THE CAR, JACKASS.
BECAUSE YOU HAVEN'T PUT AWAY THE KNIFE LIKE I'VE ASKED YOU A MILLION TIMES AND BECAUSE YOU KEEP OBSSESSING OVER THIS VOODOO CRAP YOUR UNCLE WAS INTO AND PRETENDING THAT HE WAS NORMAL WHEN HIS WAS CLEARLY INSANE SO DAMN CRAZY THAT ANYONE WITH HALF A BRAIN COULD SEE HOW CRAZY HE WAS WHICH IS FUNNY WHEN YOU THINK ABOUT IT SINCE HALF THIS GOD-FORSAKEN TOWN SAN HALF HIS CRAZY BRAIN SPLATTERED ACROSS THE SIDEWALK!
WHAT DID YOU JUST SAY?
YES, CY. I CALLED YOU A JACKASS. BECAUSE YOU'RE ACTING LIKE ONE.
NO, AFTER THAT.
I DIDN'T SAY ANYTHING, GOD! WHAT IS YOUR ISSUE?!
SLAM

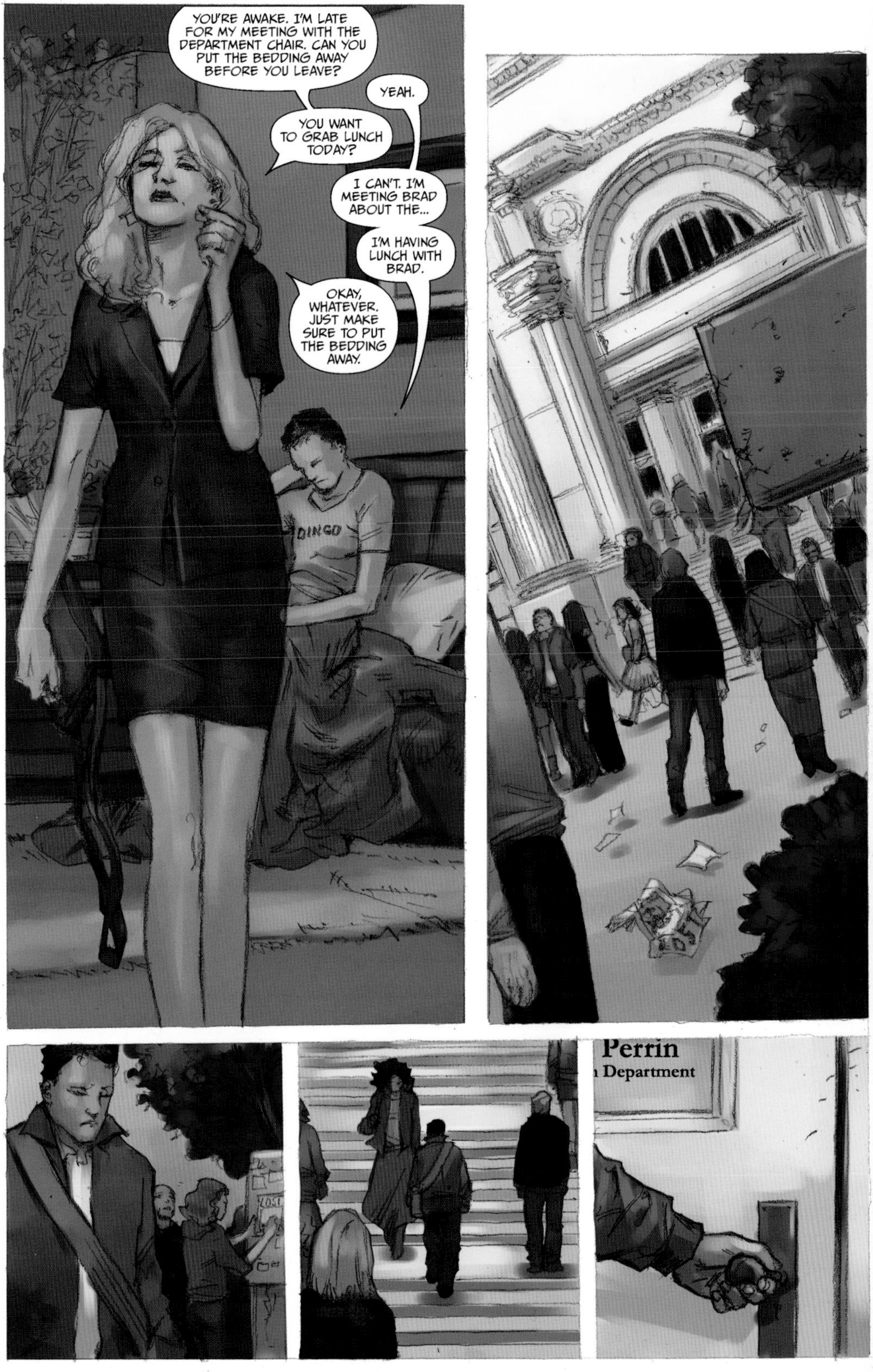
YOU'RE AWAKE. I'M LATE FOR MY MEETING WITH THE DEPARTMENT CHAIR. CAN YOU PUT THE BEDDING AWAY BEFORE YOU LEAVE?
YEAH.
YOU WANT TO GRAB LUNCH TODAY?
I CAN'T. I'M MEETING BRAD ABOUT THE...
I'M HAVING LUNCH WITH BRAD.
OKAY, WHATEVER. JUST MAKE SURE TO PUT THE BEDDING AWAY.
DINGO
Pertin
n Department

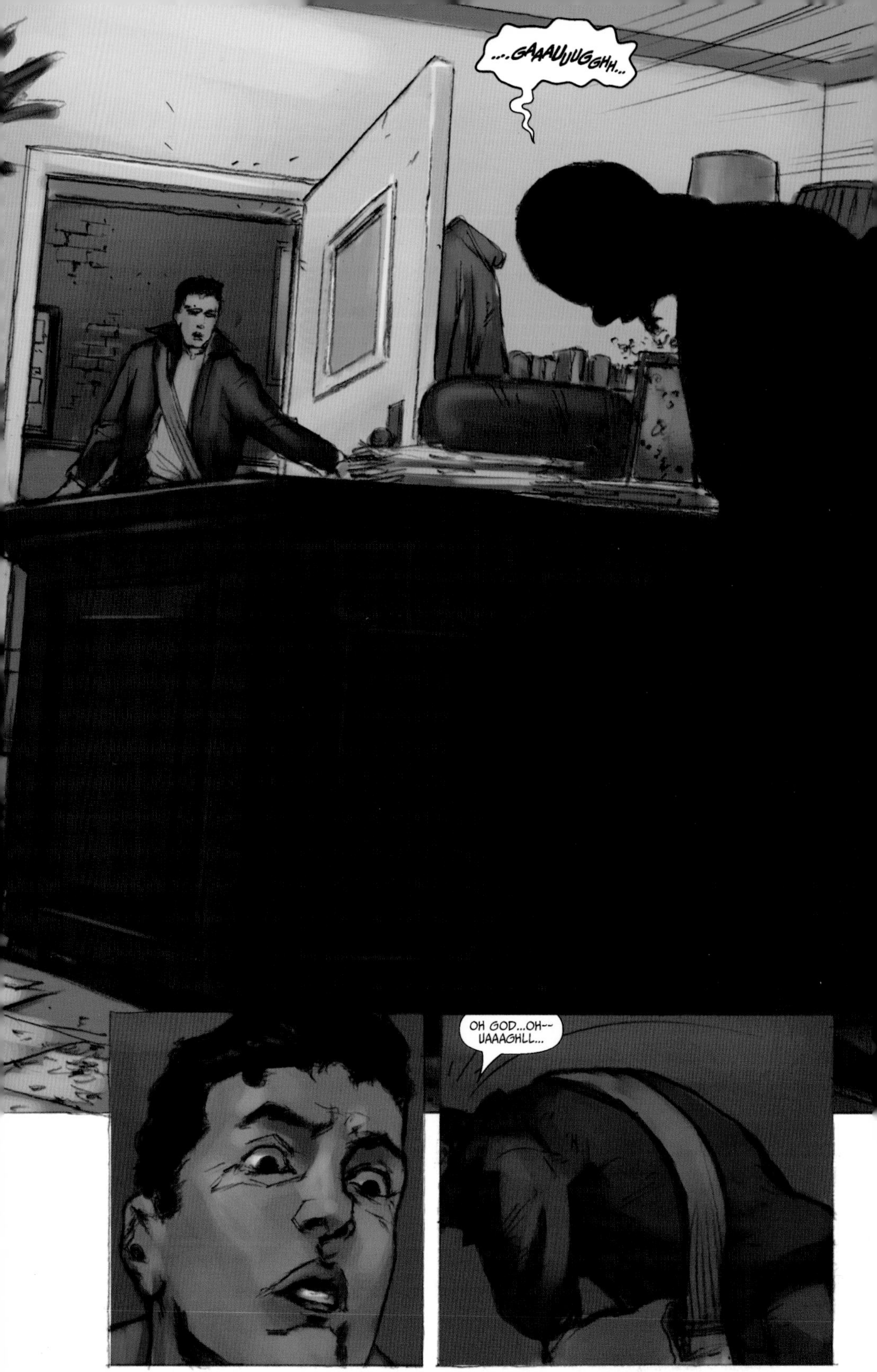
...GAAAUUUGGHH...
OH GOD...OH--
UAAAGHLL...

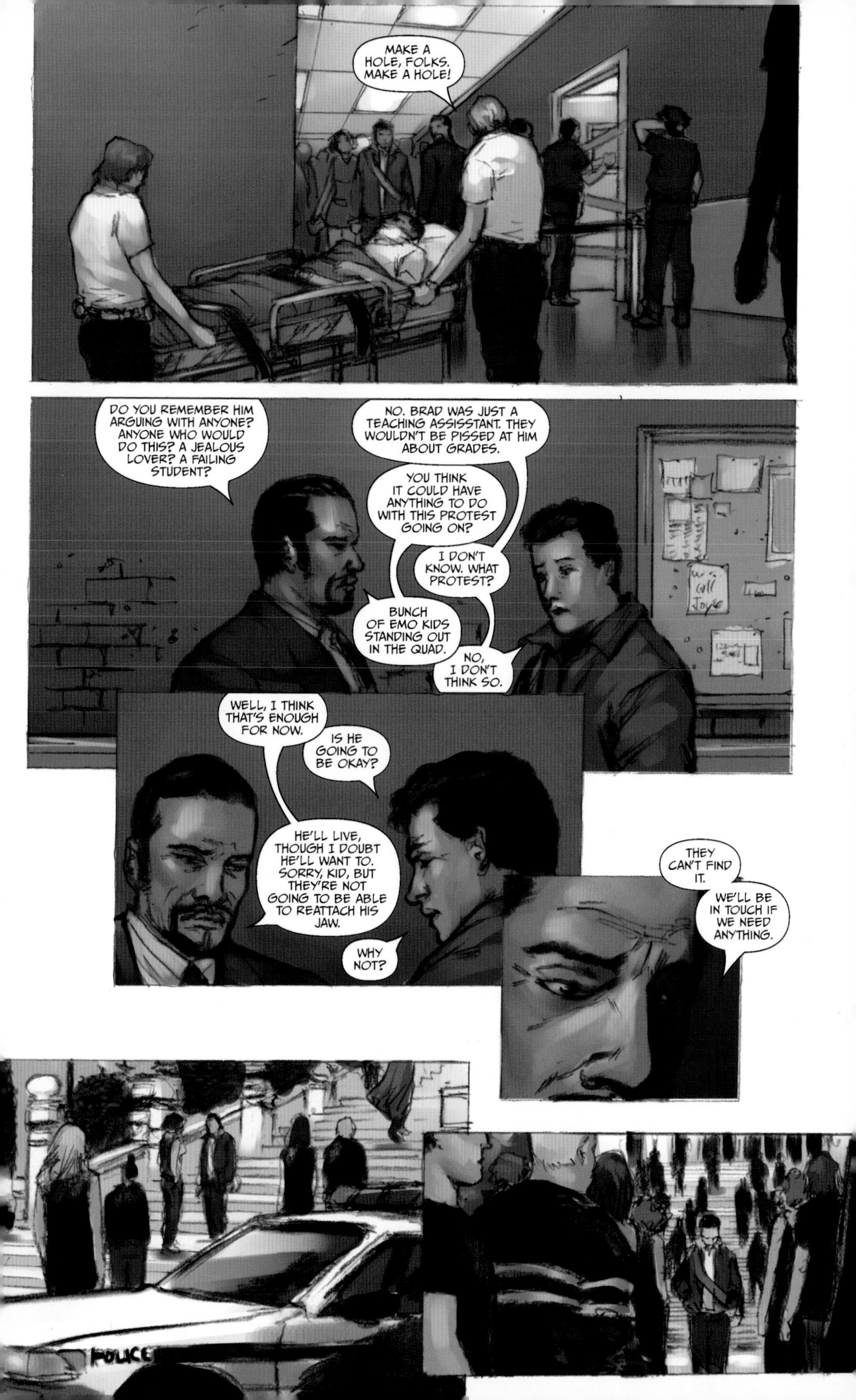
MAKE A HOLE, FOLKS. MAKE A HOLE!
DO YOU REMEMBER HIM ARGUING WITH ANYONE? ANYONE WHO WOULD DO THIS? A JEALOUS LOVER? A FAILING STUDENT?
NO. BRAD WAS JUST A TEACHING ASSISSTANT. THEY WOULDN'T BE PISSED AT HIM ABOUT GRADES.
YOU THINK IT COULD HAVE ANYTHING TO DO WITH THIS PROTEST GOING ON?
I DON'T KNOW. WHAT PROTEST?
BUNCH OF EMO KIDS STANDING OUT IN THE QUAD.
NO, I DON'T THINK SO.
WELL, I THINK THAT'S ENOUGH FOR NOW.
IS HE GOING TO BE OKAY?
HE'LL LIVE, THOUGH I DOUBT HE'LL WANT TO. SORRY, KID, BUT THEY'RE NOT GOING TO BE ABLE TO REATTACH HIS JAW.
WHY NOT?
THEY CAN'T FIND IT.
WE'LL BE IN TOUCH IF WE NEED ANYTHING.
POLICE

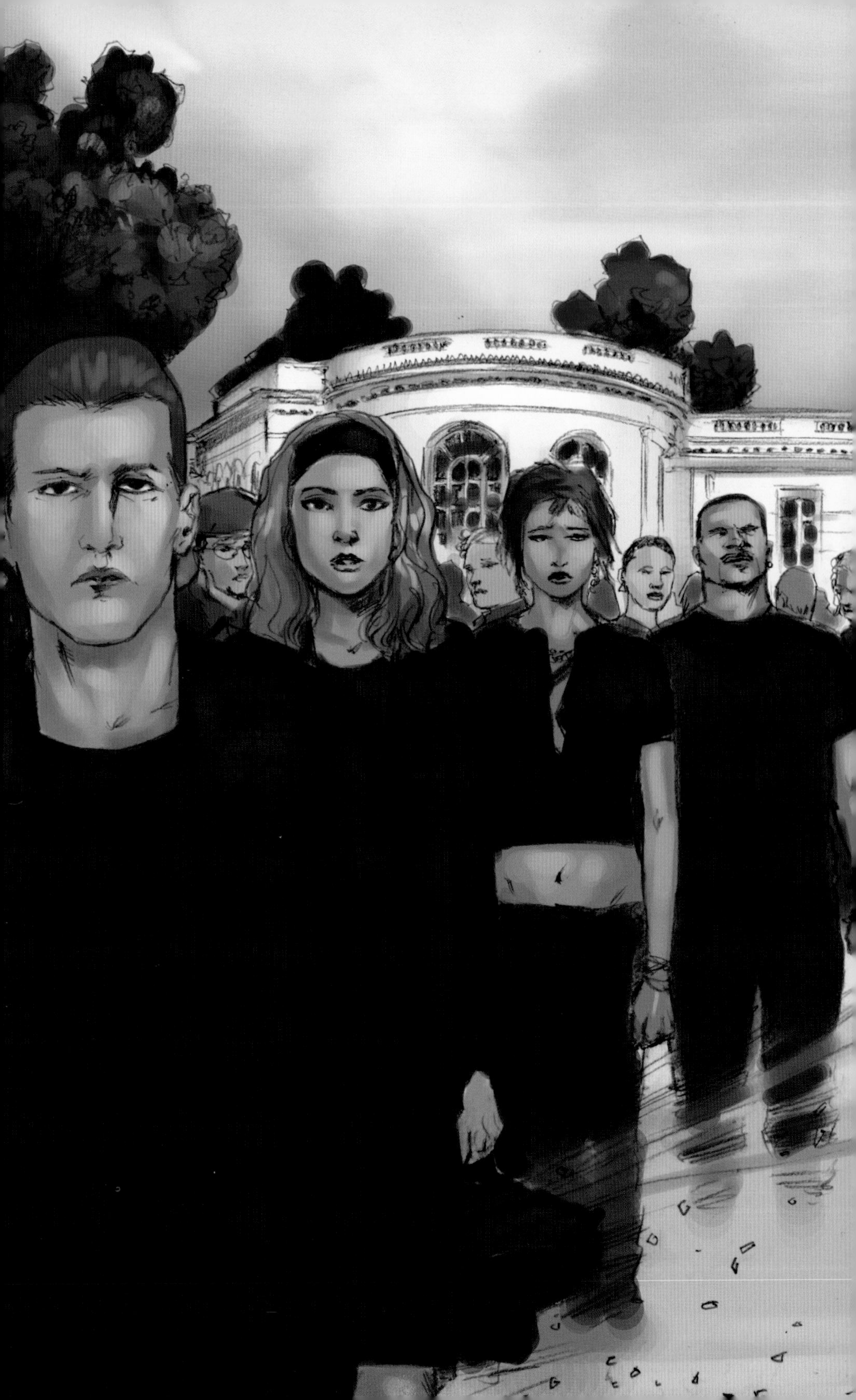

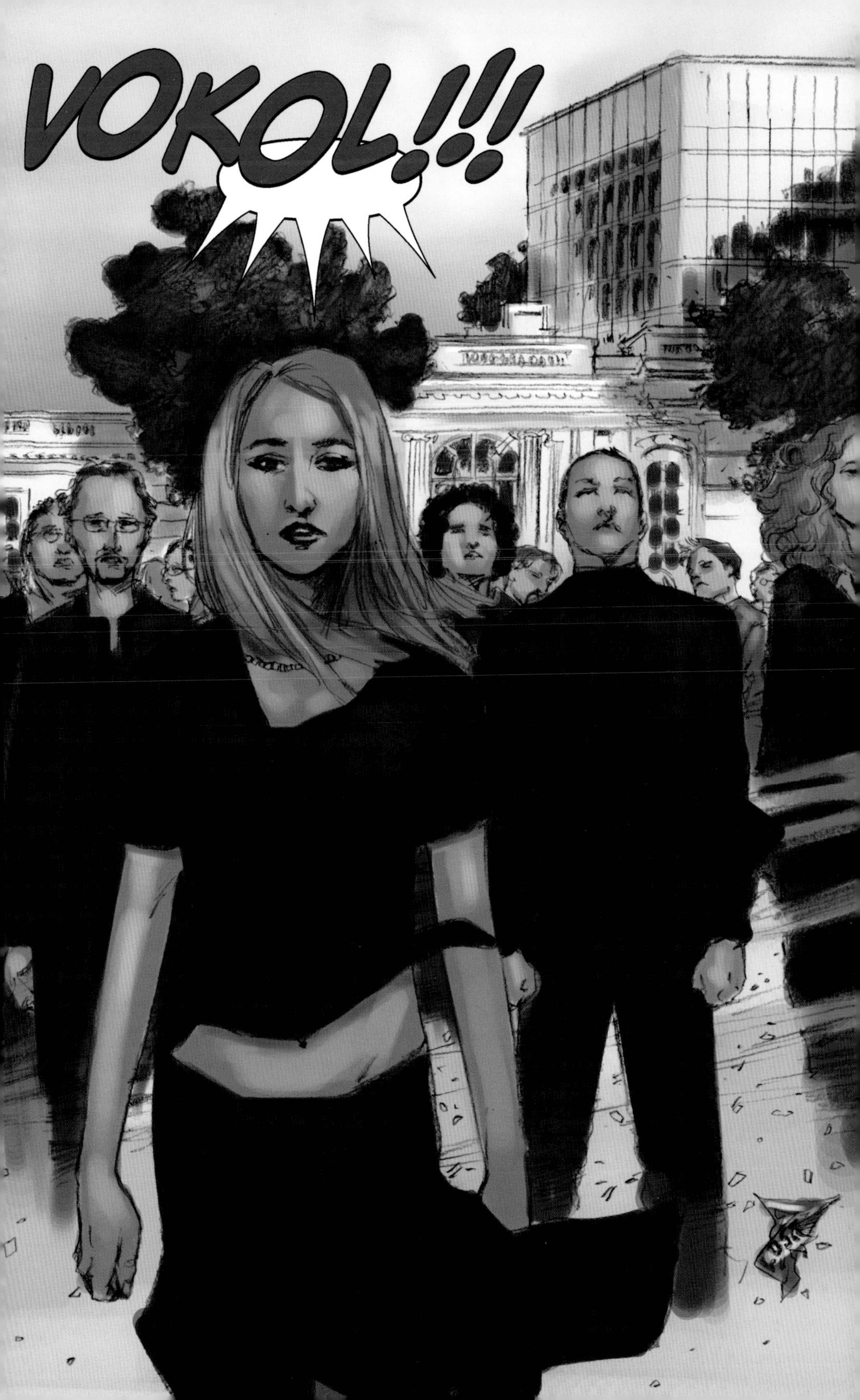
VOKOL!!!

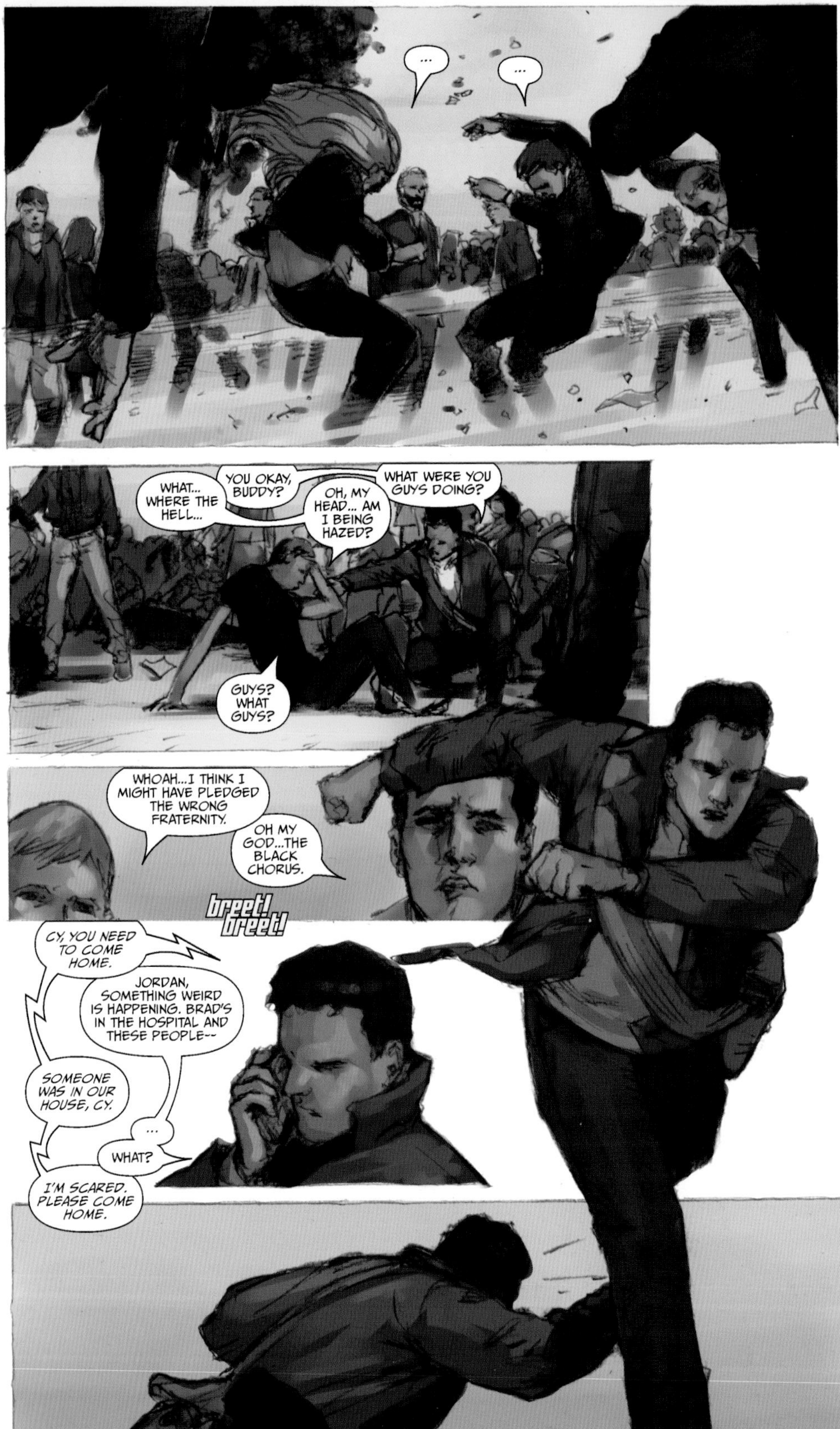
...
...
WHAT... WHERE THE HELL...
YOU OKAY, BUDDY?
OH, MY HEAD... AM I BEING HAZED?
WHAT WERE YOU GUYS DOING?
GUYS? WHAT GUYS?
WHOAH...I THINK I MIGHT HAVE PLEDGED THE WRONG FRATERNITY.
OH MY GOD...THE BLACK CHORUS.
breet! breet!
CY, YOU NEED TO COME HOME.
JORDAN, SOMETHING WEIRD IS HAPPENING. BRAD'S IN THE HOSPITAL AND THESE PEOPLE--
SOMEONE WAS IN OUR HOUSE, CY.
...
WHAT?
I'M SCARED. PLEASE COME HOME.

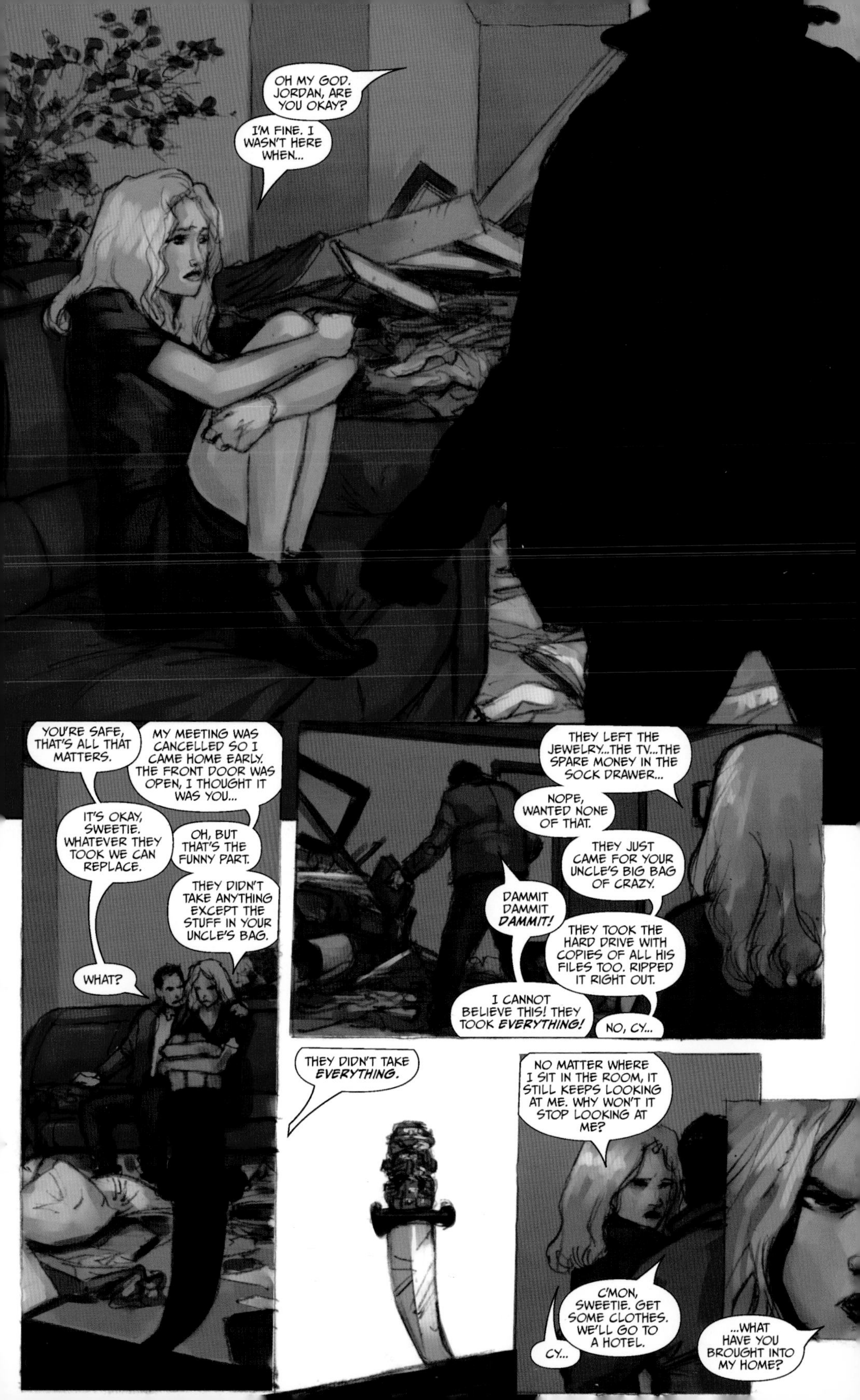
OH MY GOD. JORDAN, ARE YOU OKAY?
I'M FINE. I WASN'T HERE WHEN...
YOU'RE SAFE, THAT'S ALL THAT MATTERS.
MY MEETING WAS CANCELLED SO I CAME HOME EARLY. THE FRONT DOOR WAS OPEN, I THOUGHT IT WAS YOU...
IT'S OKAY, SWEETIE. WHATEVER THEY TOOK WE CAN REPLACE.
OH, BUT THAT'S THE FUNNY PART.
THEY DIDN'T TAKE ANYTHING EXCEPT THE STUFF IN YOUR UNCLE'S BAG.
WHAT?
THEY LEFT THE JEWELRY...THE TV...THE SPARE MONEY IN THE SOCK DRAWER...
NOPE, WANTED NONE OF THAT.
THEY JUST CAME FOR YOUR UNCLE'S BIG BAG OF CRAZY.
DAMMIT DAMMIT *DAMMIT!*
THEY TOOK THE HARD DRIVE WITH COPIES OF ALL HIS FILES TOO. RIPPED IT RIGHT OUT.
I CANNOT BELIEVE THIS! THEY TOOK *EVERYTHING!*
NO, CY...
THEY DIDN'T TAKE *EVERYTHING.*
NO MATTER WHERE I SIT IN THE ROOM, IT STILL KEEPS LOOKING AT ME. WHY WON'T IT STOP LOOKING AT ME?
C'MON, SWEETIE. GET SOME CLOTHES. WE'LL GO TO A HOTEL.
CY...
...WHAT HAVE YOU BROUGHT INTO MY HOME?

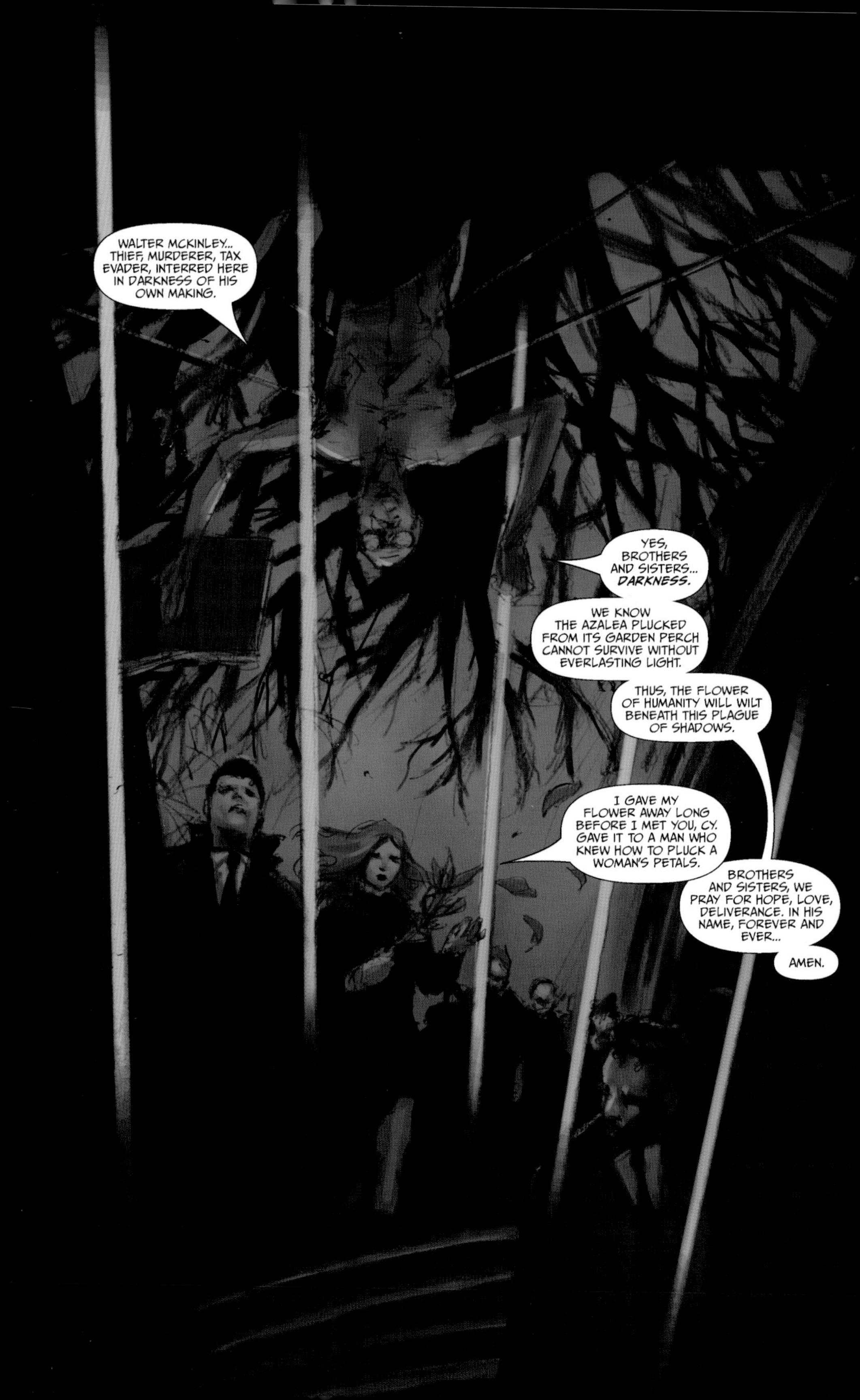
WALTER MCKINLEY... THIEF, MURDERER, TAX EVADER, INTERRED HERE IN DARKNESS OF HIS OWN MAKING.
YES, BROTHERS AND SISTERS... *DARKNESS.*
WE KNOW THE AZALEA PLUCKED FROM ITS GARDEN PERCH CANNOT SURVIVE WITHOUT EVERLASTING LIGHT.
THUS, THE FLOWER OF HUMANITY WILL WILT BENEATH THIS PLAGUE OF SHADOWS.
I GAVE MY FLOWER AWAY LONG BEFORE I MET YOU, CY. GAVE IT TO A MAN WHO KNEW HOW TO PLUCK A WOMAN'S PETALS.
BROTHERS AND SISTERS, WE PRAY FOR HOPE, LOVE, DELIVERANCE. IN HIS NAME, FOREVER AND EVER...
AMEN.

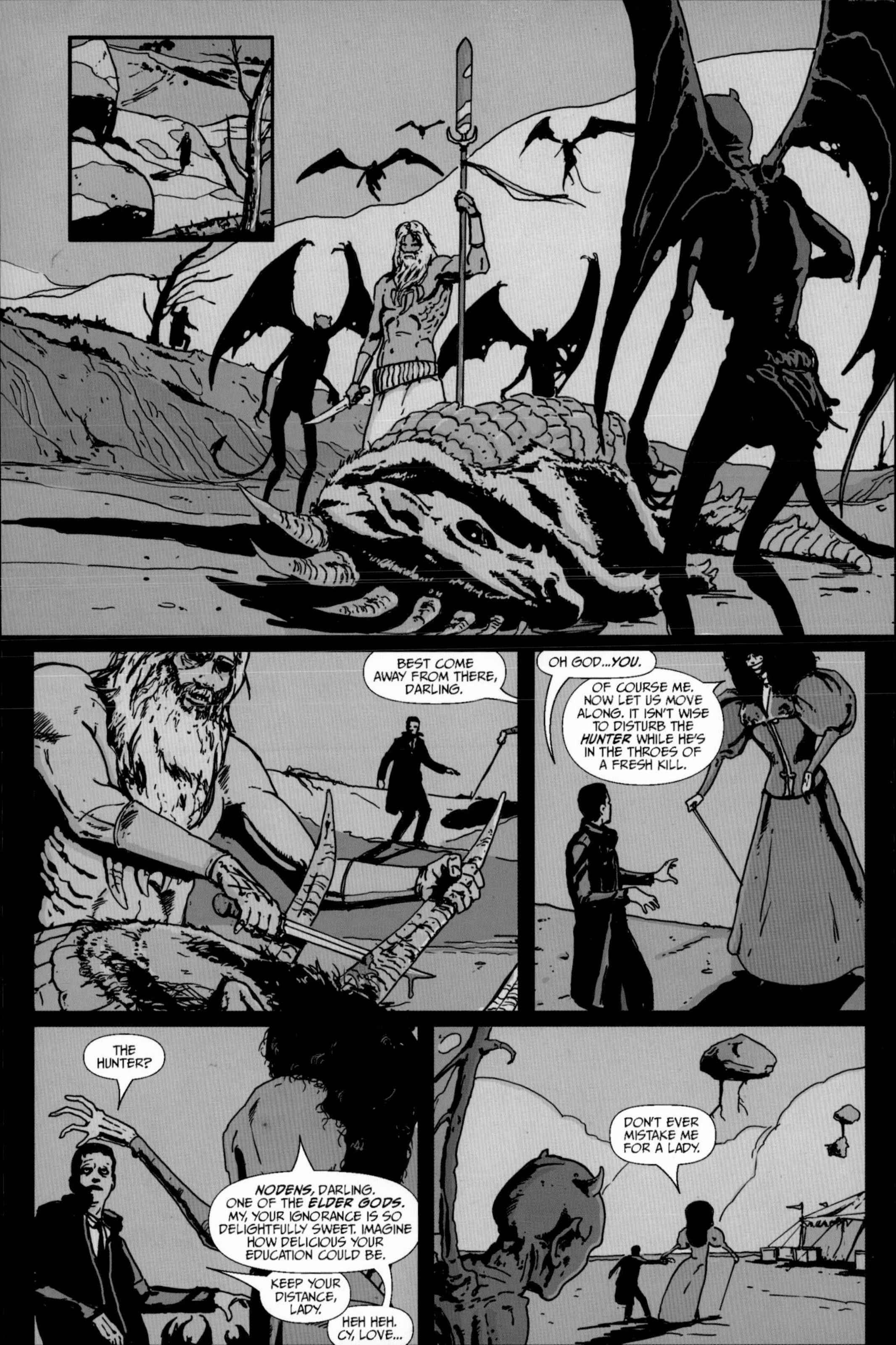
BEST COME AWAY FROM THERE, DARLING.
OH GOD...YOU.
OF COURSE ME. NOW LET US MOVE ALONG. IT ISN'T WISE TO DISTURB THE HUNTER WHILE HE'S IN THE THROES OF A FRESH KILL.
THE HUNTER?
NODENS, DARLING. ONE OF THE ELDER GODS. MY, YOUR IGNORANCE IS SO DELIGHTFULLY SWEET. IMAGINE HOW DELICIOUS YOUR EDUCATION COULD BE.
KEEP YOUR DISTANCE, LADY.
HEH HEH. CY, LOVE...
DON'T EVER MISTAKE ME FOR A LADY.

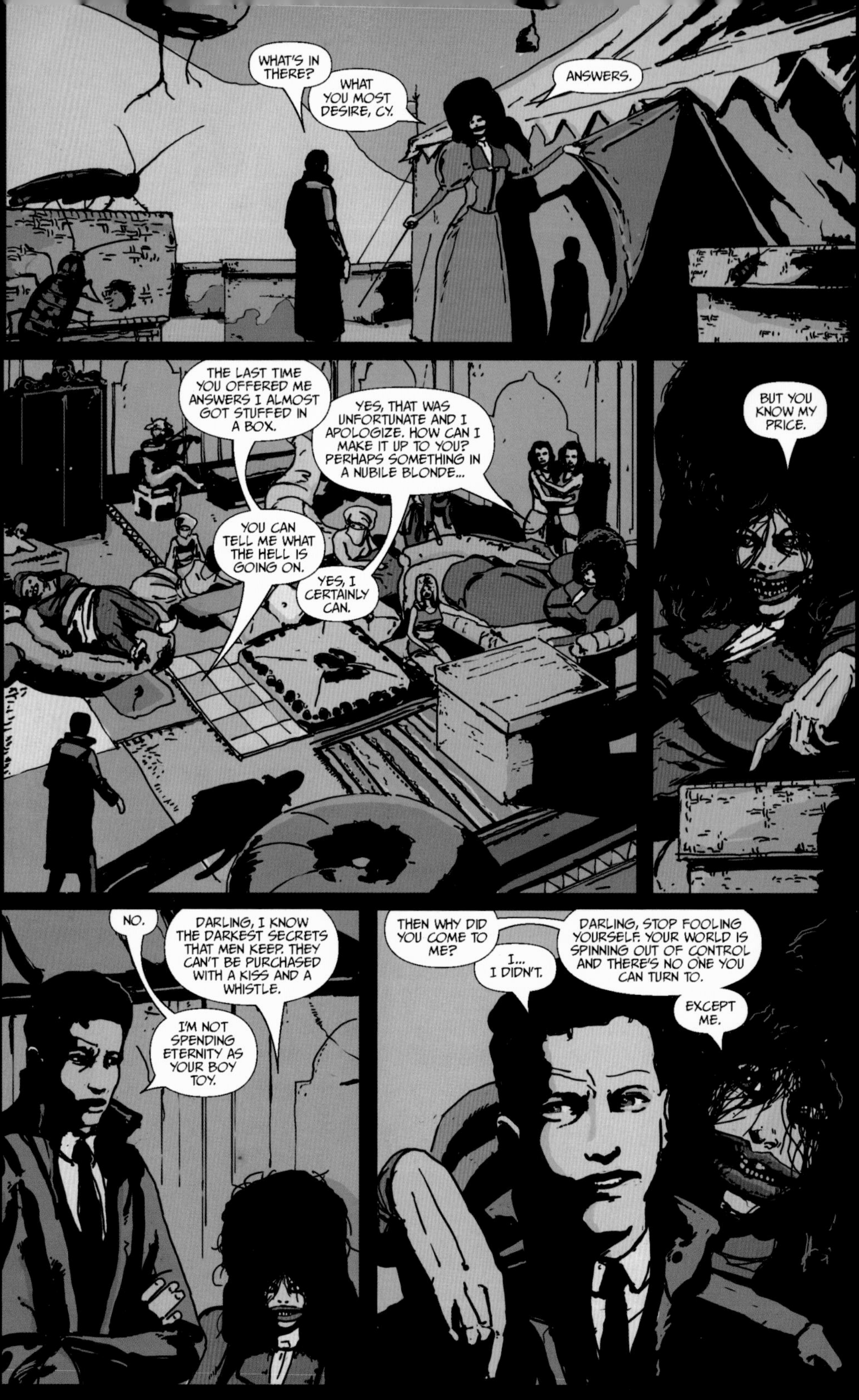

WHAT'S IN THERE?
WHAT YOU MOST DESIRE, CY.
ANSWERS.
THE LAST TIME YOU OFFERED ME ANSWERS I ALMOST GOT STUFFED IN A BOX.
YES, THAT WAS UNFORTUNATE AND I APOLOGIZE. HOW CAN I MAKE IT UP TO YOU? PERHAPS SOMETHING IN A NUBILE BLONDE...
YOU CAN TELL ME WHAT THE HELL IS GOING ON.
YES, I CERTAINLY CAN.
BUT YOU KNOW MY PRICE.
NO.
DARLING, I KNOW THE DARKEST SECRETS THAT MEN KEEP. THEY CAN'T BE PURCHASED WITH A KISS AND A WHISTLE.
I'M NOT SPENDING ETERNITY AS YOUR BOY TOY.
THEN WHY DID YOU COME TO ME?
I... I DIDN'T.
DARLING, STOP FOOLING YOURSELF. YOUR WORLD IS SPINNING OUT OF CONTROL AND THERE'S NO ONE YOU CAN TURN TO.
EXCEPT ME.

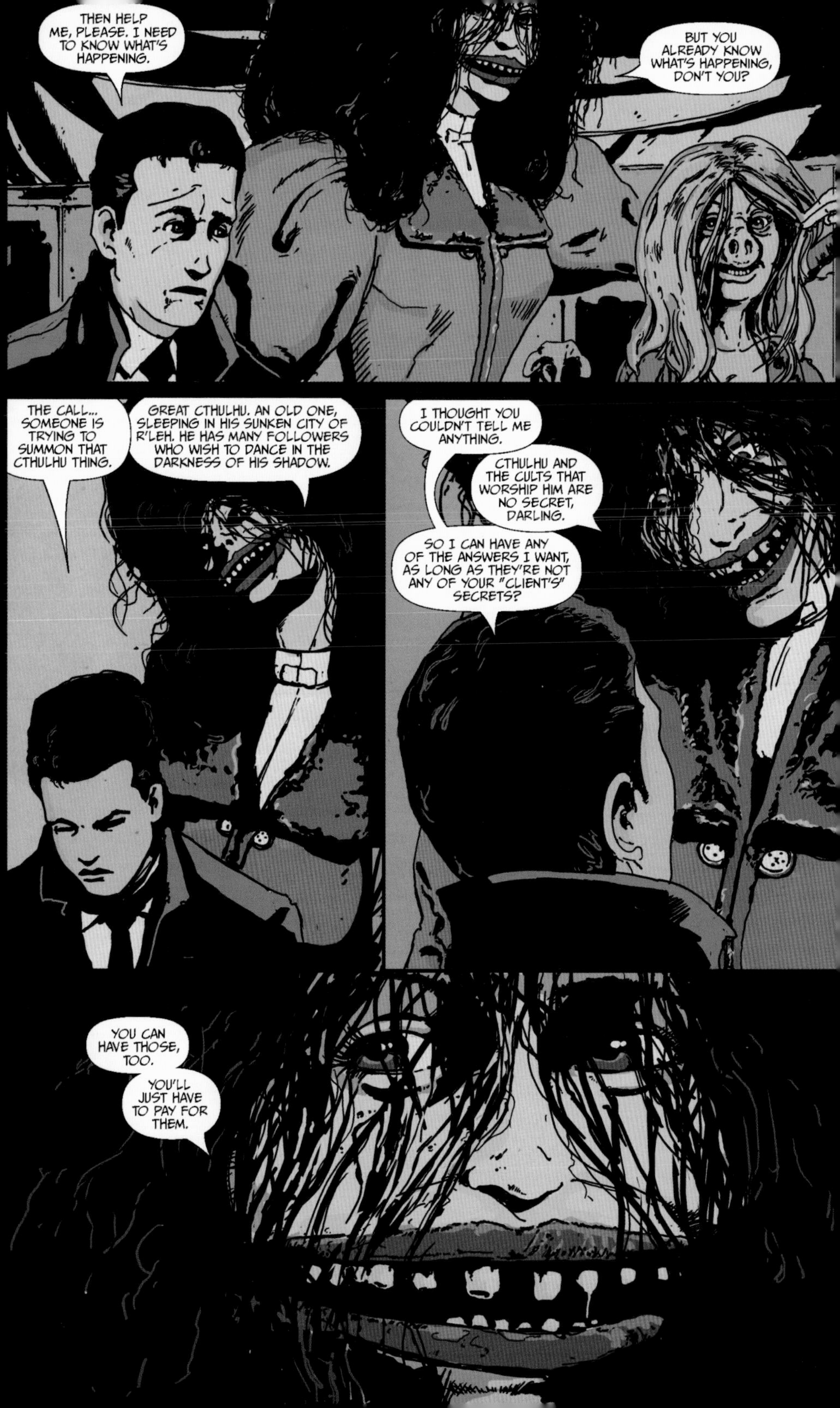

THEN HELP ME, PLEASE. I NEED TO KNOW WHAT'S HAPPENING.
BUT YOU ALREADY KNOW WHAT'S HAPPENING, DON'T YOU?
THE CALL... SOMEONE IS TRYING TO SUMMON THAT CTHULHU THING.
GREAT CTHULHU. AN OLD ONE, SLEEPING IN HIS SUNKEN CITY OF R'LEH. HE HAS MANY FOLLOWERS WHO WISH TO DANCE IN THE DARKNESS OF HIS SHADOW.
I THOUGHT YOU COULDN'T TELL ME ANYTHING.
CTHULHU AND THE CULTS THAT WORSHIP HIM ARE NO SECRET, DARLING.
SO I CAN HAVE ANY OF THE ANSWERS I WANT, AS LONG AS THEY'RE NOT ANY OF YOUR "CLIENT'S" SECRETS?
YOU CAN HAVE THOSE, TOO.
YOU'LL JUST HAVE TO PAY FOR THEM.

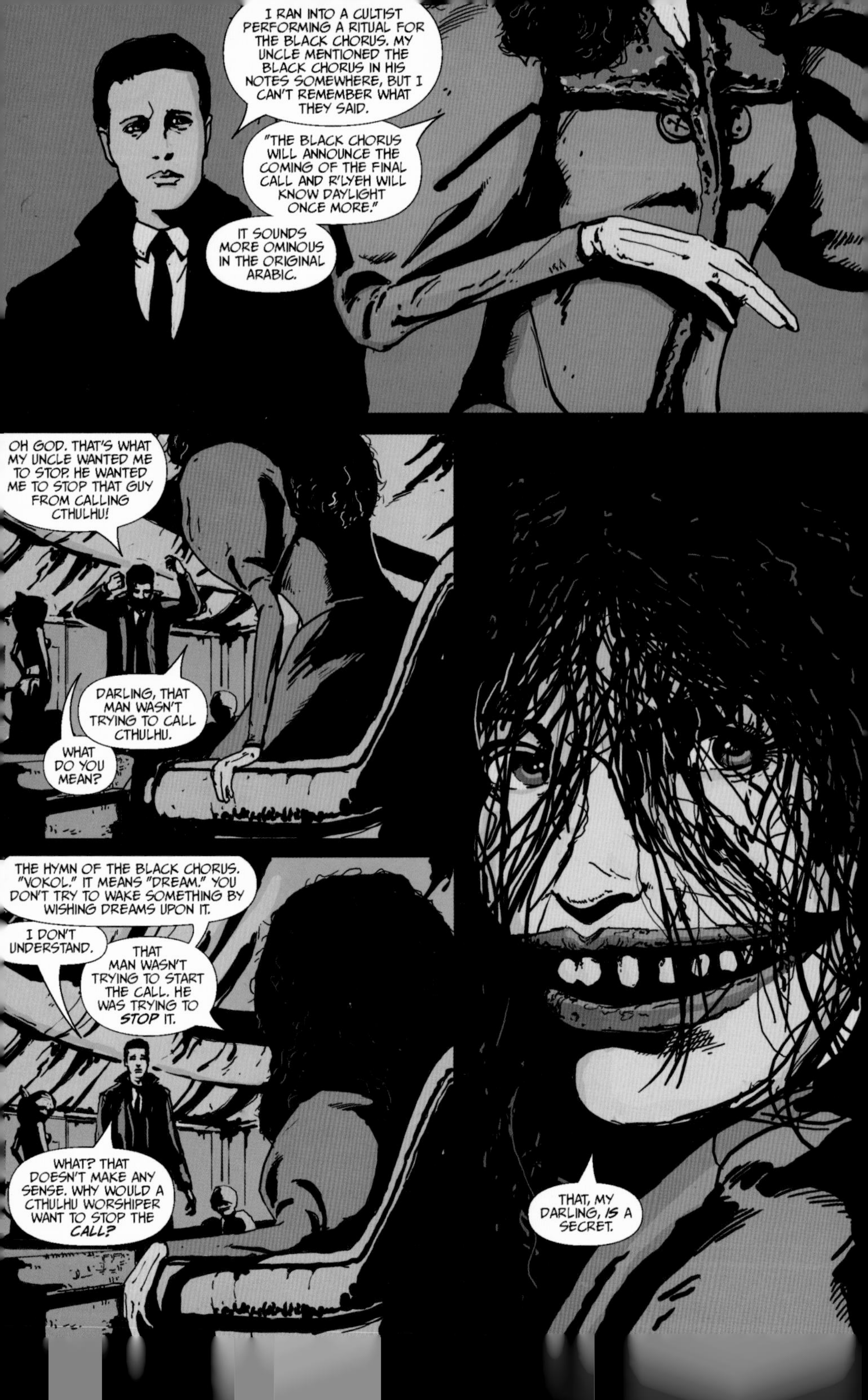
I RAN INTO A CULTIST PERFORMING A RITUAL FOR THE BLACK CHORUS. MY UNCLE MENTIONED THE BLACK CHORUS IN HIS NOTES SOMEWHERE, BUT I CAN'T REMEMBER WHAT THEY SAID.
"THE BLACK CHORUS WILL ANNOUNCE THE COMING OF THE FINAL CALL AND R'LYEH WILL KNOW DAYLIGHT ONCE MORE."
IT SOUNDS MORE OMINOUS IN THE ORIGINAL ARABIC.
OH GOD. THAT'S WHAT MY UNCLE WANTED ME TO STOP. HE WANTED ME TO STOP THAT GUY FROM CALLING CTHULHU!
DARLING, THAT MAN WASN'T TRYING TO CALL CTHULHU.
WHAT DO YOU MEAN?
THE HYMN OF THE BLACK CHORUS. "VOKOL." IT MEANS "DREAM." YOU DON'T TRY TO WAKE SOMETHING BY WISHING DREAMS UPON IT.
I DON'T UNDERSTAND.
THAT MAN WASN'T TRYING TO START THE CALL. HE WAS TRYING TO *STOP* IT.
WHAT? THAT DOESN'T MAKE ANY SENSE. WHY WOULD A CTHULHU WORSHIPER WANT TO STOP THE *CALL?*
THAT, MY DARLING, *IS* A SECRET.

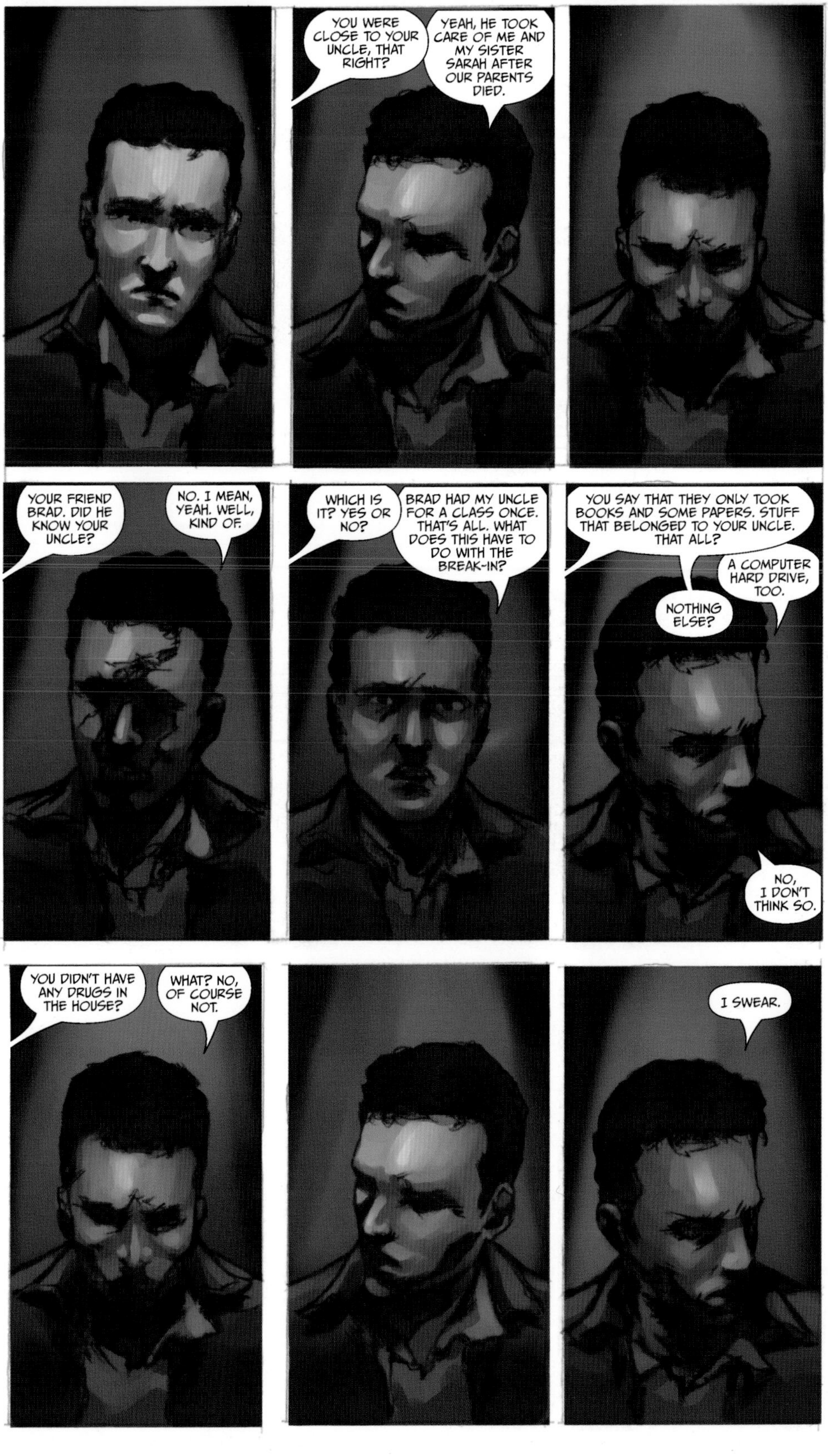
YOU WERE CLOSE TO YOUR UNCLE, THAT RIGHT?
YEAH, HE TOOK CARE OF ME AND MY SISTER SARAH AFTER OUR PARENTS DIED.
YOUR FRIEND BRAD. DID HE KNOW YOUR UNCLE?
NO. I MEAN, YEAH. WELL, KIND OF.
WHICH IS IT? YES OR NO?
BRAD HAD MY UNCLE FOR A CLASS ONCE. THAT'S ALL. WHAT DOES THIS HAVE TO DO WITH THE BREAK-IN?
YOU SAY THAT THEY ONLY TOOK BOOKS AND SOME PAPERS. STUFF THAT BELONGED TO YOUR UNCLE. THAT ALL?
A COMPUTER HARD DRIVE, TOO.
NOTHING ELSE?
NO, I DON'T THINK SO.
YOU DIDN'T HAVE ANY DRUGS IN THE HOUSE?
WHAT? NO, OF COURSE NOT.
I SWEAR.

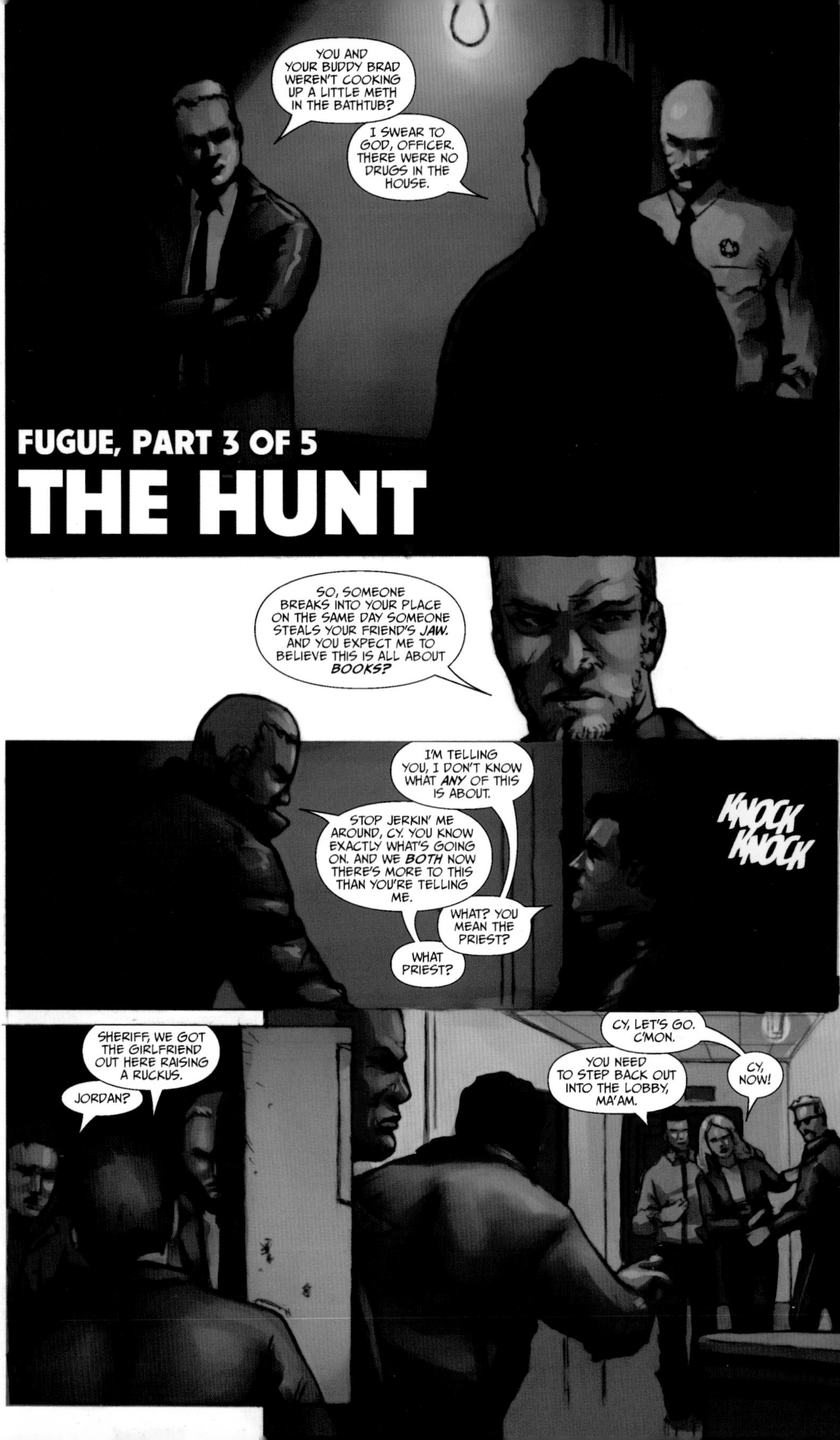
YOU AND YOUR BUDDY BRAD WEREN'T COOKING UP A LITTLE METH IN THE BATHTUB?
I SWEAR TO GOD, OFFICER. THERE WERE NO DRUGS IN THE HOUSE.
FUGUE, PART 3 OF 5
THE HUNT
SO, SOMEONE BREAKS INTO YOUR PLACE ON THE SAME DAY SOMEONE STEALS YOUR FRIEND'S JAW. AND YOU EXPECT ME TO BELIEVE THIS IS ALL ABOUT BOOKS?
I'M TELLING YOU, I DON'T KNOW WHAT ANY OF THIS IS ABOUT.
STOP JERKIN' ME AROUND, CY. YOU KNOW EXACTLY WHAT'S GOING ON. AND WE BOTH NOW THERE'S MORE TO THIS THAN YOU'RE TELLING ME.
WHAT? YOU MEAN THE PRIEST?
WHAT PRIEST?
KNOCK KNOCK
SHERIFF, WE GOT THE GIRLFRIEND OUT HERE RAISING A RUCKUS.
JORDAN?
CY, LET'S GO. C'MON.
YOU NEED TO STEP BACK OUT INTO THE LOBBY, MA'AM.
CY, NOW!

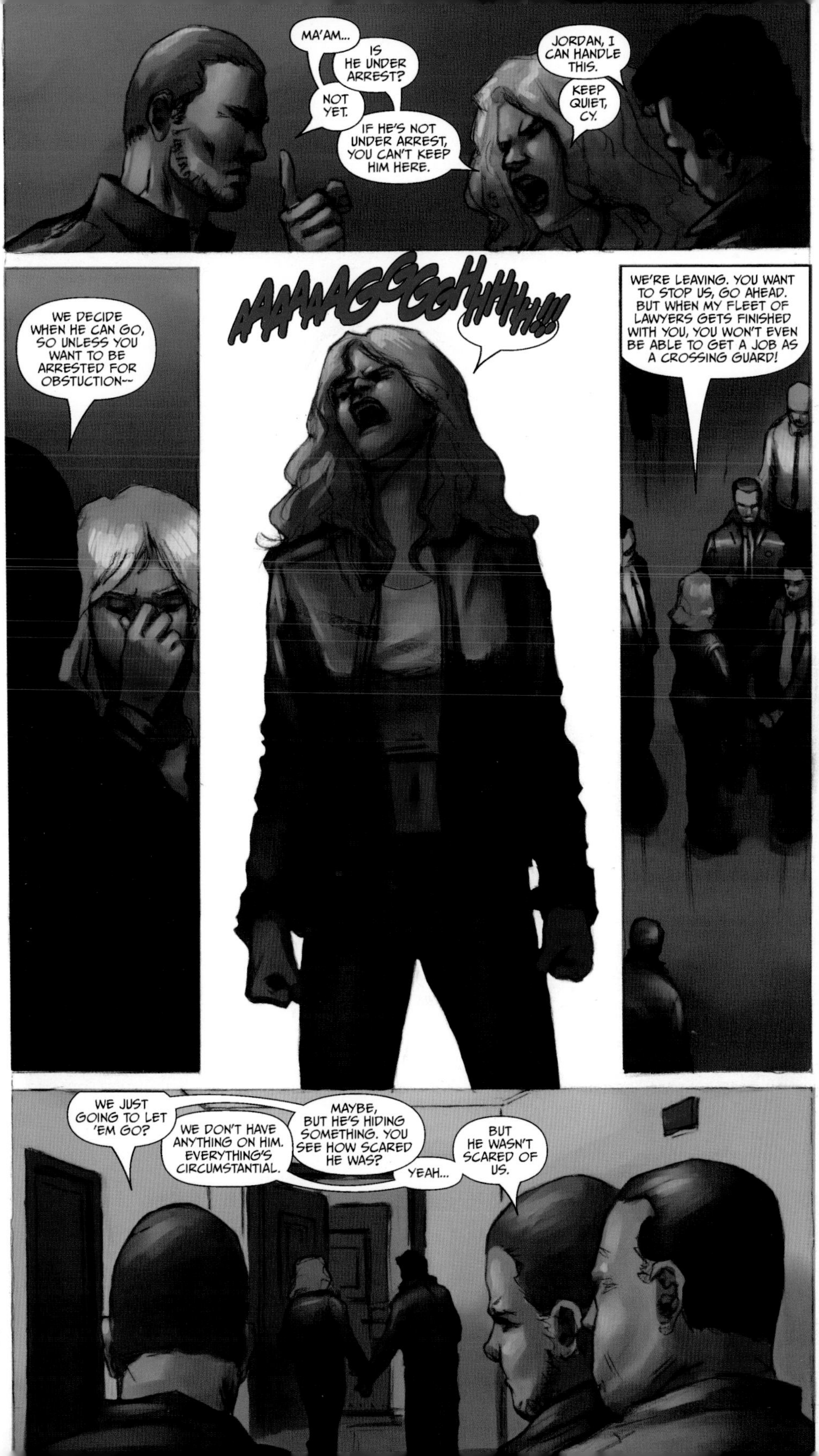
MA'AM...
IS HE UNDER ARREST?
NOT YET.
IF HE'S NOT UNDER ARREST, YOU CAN'T KEEP HIM HERE.
JORDAN, I CAN HANDLE THIS.
KEEP QUIET, CY.
WE DECIDE WHEN HE CAN GO, SO UNLESS YOU WANT TO BE ARRESTED FOR OBSTUCTION--
AAAAAAGGGGHHHHH!!!
WE'RE LEAVING. YOU WANT TO STOP US, GO AHEAD. BUT WHEN MY FLEET OF LAWYERS GETS FINISHED WITH YOU, YOU WON'T EVEN BE ABLE TO GET A JOB AS A CROSSING GUARD!
WE JUST GOING TO LET 'EM GO?
WE DON'T HAVE ANYTHING ON HIM. EVERYTHING'S CIRCUMSTANTIAL.
MAYBE, BUT HE'S HIDING SOMETHING. YOU SEE HOW SCARED HE WAS?
YEAH...
BUT HE WASN'T SCARED OF US.

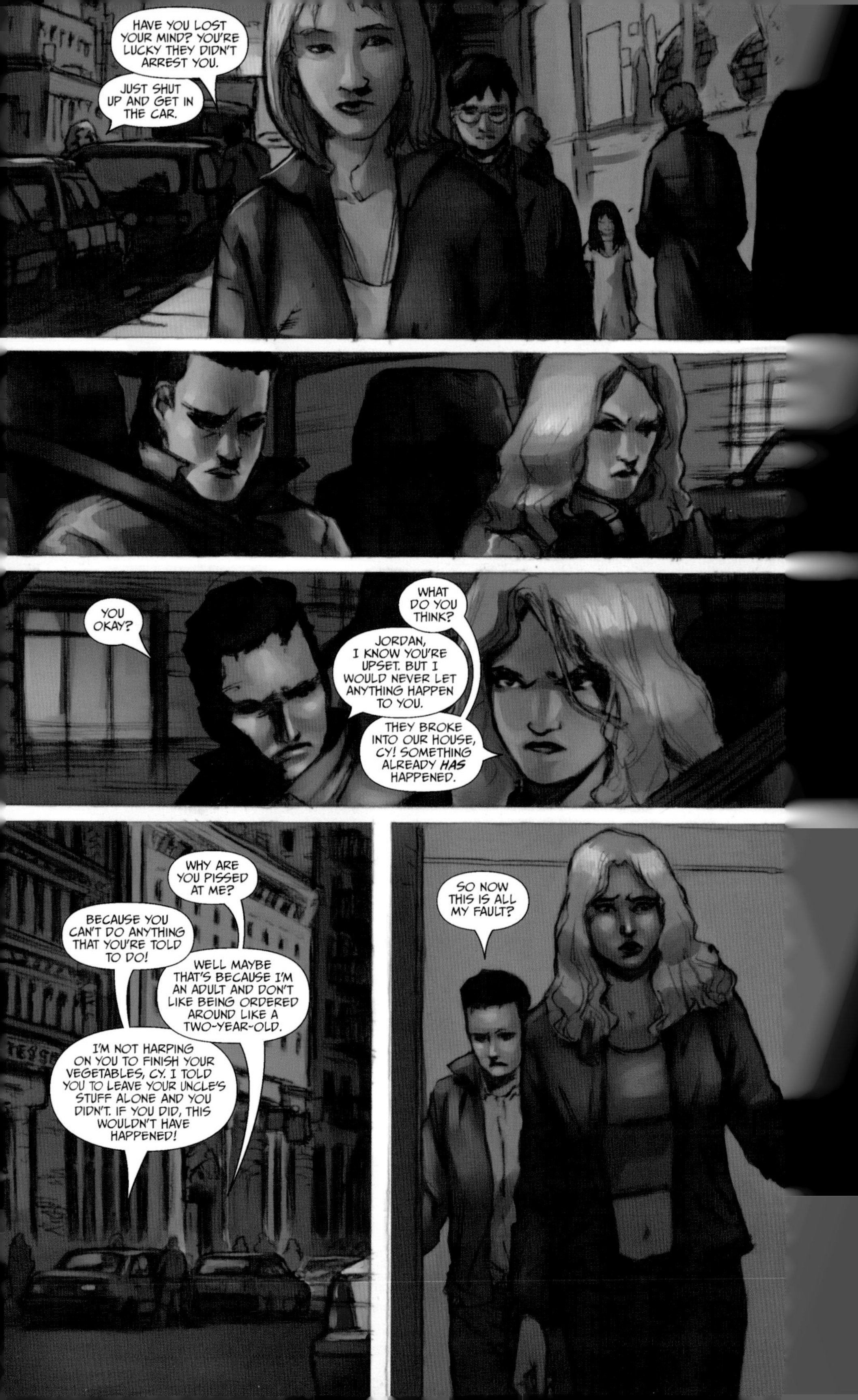
HAVE YOU LOST YOUR MIND? YOU'RE LUCKY THEY DIDN'T ARREST YOU.
JUST SHUT UP AND GET IN THE CAR.
YOU OKAY?
WHAT DO YOU THINK?
JORDAN, I KNOW YOU'RE UPSET. BUT I WOULD NEVER LET ANYTHING HAPPEN TO YOU.
THEY BROKE INTO OUR HOUSE, CY! SOMETHING ALREADY *HAS* HAPPENED.
WHY ARE YOU PISSED AT ME?
BECAUSE YOU CAN'T DO ANYTHING THAT YOU'RE TOLD TO DO!
WELL MAYBE THAT'S BECAUSE I'M AN ADULT AND DON'T LIKE BEING ORDERED AROUND LIKE A TWO-YEAR-OLD.
I'M NOT HARPING ON YOU TO FINISH YOUR VEGETABLES, CY. I TOLD YOU TO LEAVE YOUR UNCLE'S STUFF ALONE AND YOU DIDN'T. IF YOU DID, THIS WOULDN'T HAVE HAPPENED!
SO NOW THIS IS ALL MY FAULT?

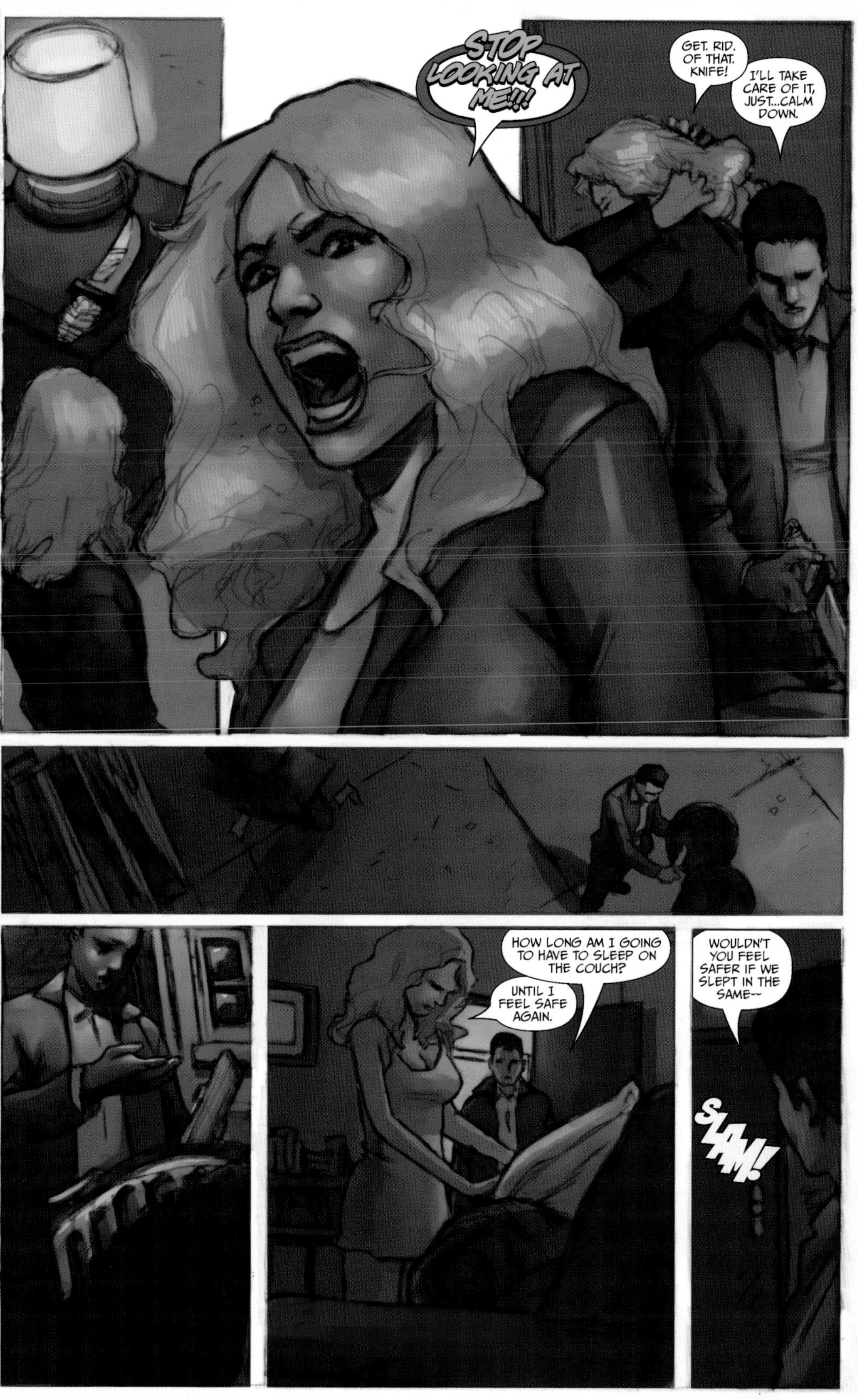
STOP LOOKING AT ME!!!
GET. RID. OF THAT. KNIFE!
I'LL TAKE CARE OF IT, JUST...CALM DOWN.
HOW LONG AM I GOING TO HAVE TO SLEEP ON THE COUCH?
UNTIL I FEEL SAFE AGAIN.
WOULDN'T YOU FEEL SAFER IF WE SLEPT IN THE SAME--
SLAM!

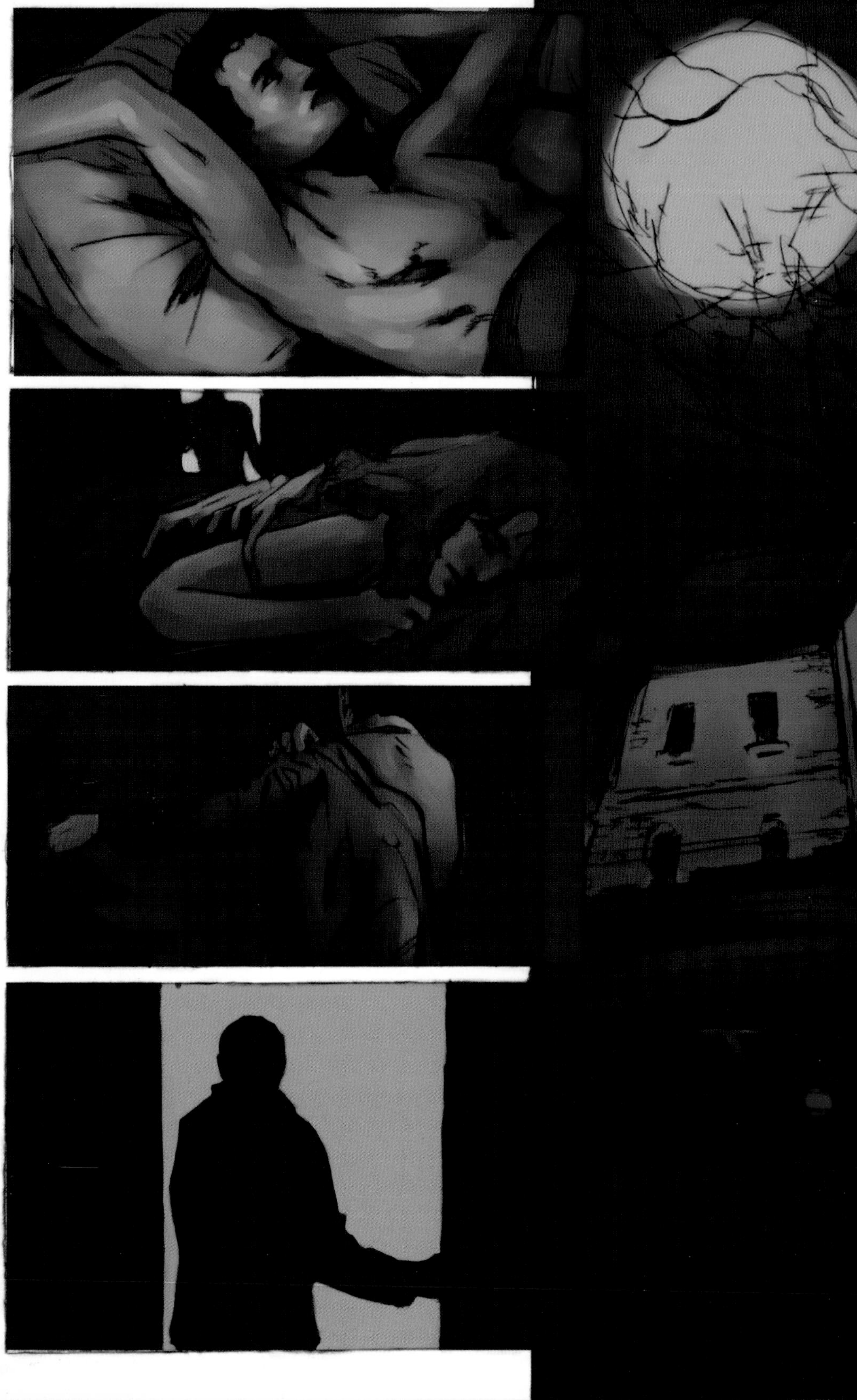

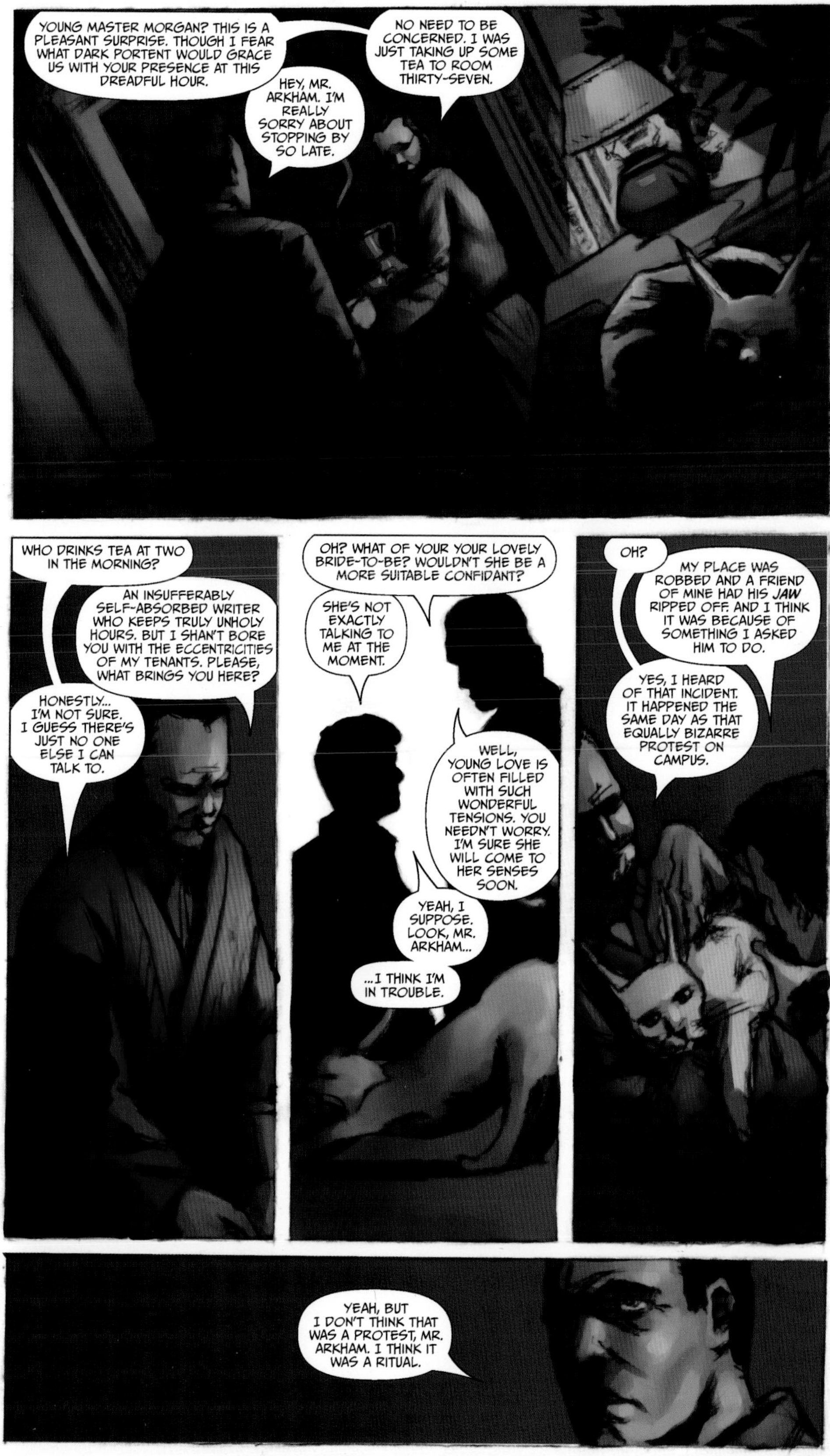
YOUNG MASTER MORGAN? THIS IS A PLEASANT SURPRISE. THOUGH I FEAR WHAT DARK PORTENT WOULD GRACE US WITH YOUR PRESENCE AT THIS DREADFUL HOUR.
NO NEED TO BE CONCERNED. I WAS JUST TAKING UP SOME TEA TO ROOM THIRTY-SEVEN.
HEY, MR. ARKHAM. I'M REALLY SORRY ABOUT STOPPING BY SO LATE.
WHO DRINKS TEA AT TWO IN THE MORNING?
AN INSUFFERABLY SELF-ABSORBED WRITER WHO KEEPS TRULY UNHOLY HOURS. BUT I SHAN'T BORE YOU WITH THE ECCENTRICITIES OF MY TENANTS. PLEASE, WHAT BRINGS YOU HERE?
HONESTLY... I'M NOT SURE. I GUESS THERE'S JUST NO ONE ELSE I CAN TALK TO.
OH? WHAT OF YOUR YOUR LOVELY BRIDE-TO-BE? WOULDN'T SHE BE A MORE SUITABLE CONFIDANT?
SHE'S NOT EXACTLY TALKING TO ME AT THE MOMENT.
WELL, YOUNG LOVE IS OFTEN FILLED WITH SUCH WONDERFUL TENSIONS. YOU NEEDN'T WORRY. I'M SURE SHE WILL COME TO HER SENSES SOON.
YEAH, I SUPPOSE. LOOK, MR. ARKHAM...
...I THINK I'M IN TROUBLE.
OH?
MY PLACE WAS ROBBED AND A FRIEND OF MINE HAD HIS JAW RIPPED OFF. AND I THINK IT WAS BECAUSE OF SOMETHING I ASKED HIM TO DO.
YES, I HEARD OF THAT INCIDENT. IT HAPPENED THE SAME DAY AS THAT EQUALLY BIZARRE PROTEST ON CAMPUS.
YEAH, BUT I DON'T THINK THAT WAS A PROTEST, MR. ARKHAM. I THINK IT WAS A RITUAL.

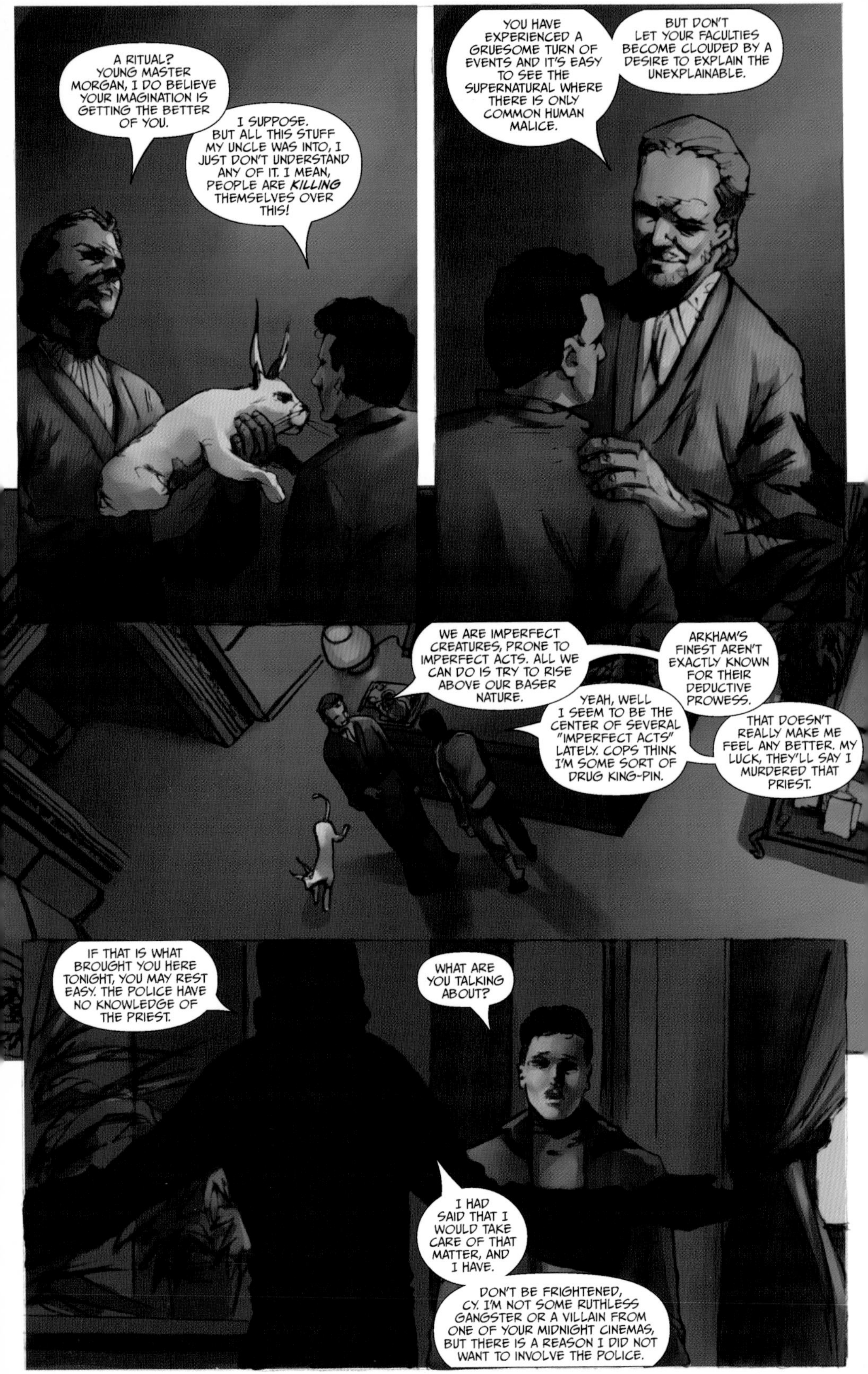
A RITUAL? YOUNG MASTER MORGAN, I DO BELIEVE YOUR IMAGINATION IS GETTING THE BETTER OF YOU.
I SUPPOSE. BUT ALL THIS STUFF MY UNCLE WAS INTO, I JUST DON'T UNDERSTAND ANY OF IT. I MEAN, PEOPLE ARE KILLING THEMSELVES OVER THIS!
YOU HAVE EXPERIENCED A GRUESOME TURN OF EVENTS AND IT'S EASY TO SEE THE SUPERNATURAL WHERE THERE IS ONLY COMMON HUMAN MALICE.
BUT DON'T LET YOUR FACULTIES BECOME CLOUDED BY A DESIRE TO EXPLAIN THE UNEXPLAINABLE.
WE ARE IMPERFECT CREATURES, PRONE TO IMPERFECT ACTS. ALL WE CAN DO IS TRY TO RISE ABOVE OUR BASER NATURE.
YEAH, WELL I SEEM TO BE THE CENTER OF SEVERAL "IMPERFECT ACTS" LATELY. COPS THINK I'M SOME SORT OF DRUG KING-PIN.
ARKHAM'S FINEST AREN'T EXACTLY KNOWN FOR THEIR DEDUCTIVE PROWESS.
THAT DOESN'T REALLY MAKE ME FEEL ANY BETTER. MY LUCK, THEY'LL SAY I MURDERED THAT PRIEST.
IF THAT IS WHAT BROUGHT YOU HERE TONIGHT, YOU MAY REST EASY. THE POLICE HAVE NO KNOWLEDGE OF THE PRIEST.
WHAT ARE YOU TALKING ABOUT?
I HAD SAID THAT I WOULD TAKE CARE OF THAT MATTER, AND I HAVE.
DON'T BE FRIGHTENED, CY. I'M NOT SOME RUTHLESS GANGSTER OR A VILLAIN FROM ONE OF YOUR MIDNIGHT CINEMAS, BUT THERE IS A REASON I DID NOT WANT TO INVOLVE THE POLICE.

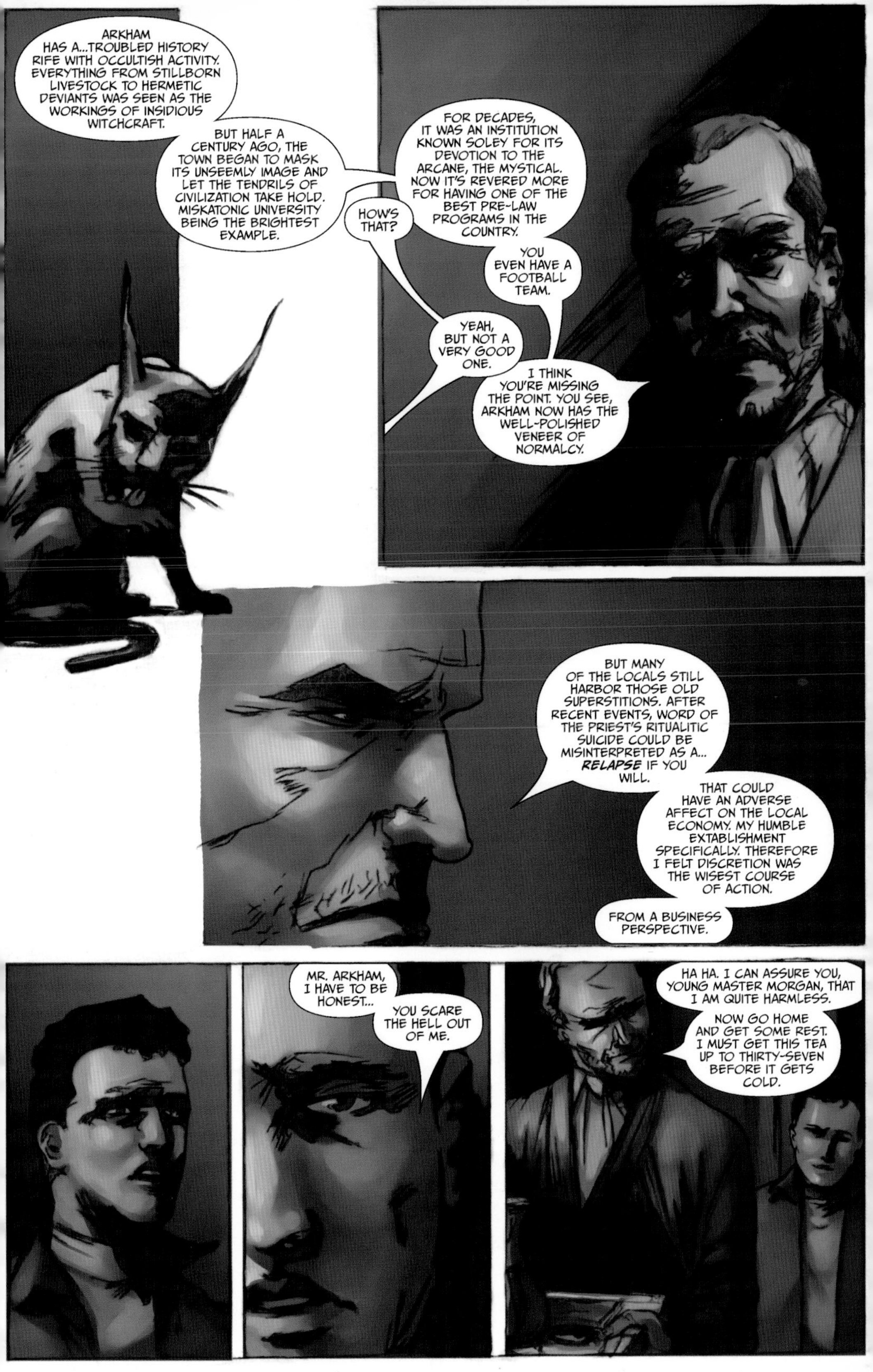
ARKHAM HAS A...TROUBLED HISTORY RIFE WITH OCCULTISH ACTIVITY. EVERYTHING FROM STILLBORN LIVESTOCK TO HERMETIC DEVIANTS WAS SEEN AS THE WORKINGS OF INSIDIOUS WITCHCRAFT.
BUT HALF A CENTURY AGO, THE TOWN BEGAN TO MASK ITS UNSEEMLY IMAGE AND LET THE TENDRILS OF CIVILIZATION TAKE HOLD. MISKATONIC UNIVERSITY BEING THE BRIGHTEST EXAMPLE.
FOR DECADES, IT WAS AN INSTITUTION KNOWN SOLEY FOR ITS DEVOTION TO THE ARCANE, THE MYSTICAL. NOW IT'S REVERED MORE FOR HAVING ONE OF THE BEST PRE-LAW PROGRAMS IN THE COUNTRY.
HOW'S THAT?
YOU EVEN HAVE A FOOTBALL TEAM.
YEAH, BUT NOT A VERY GOOD ONE.
I THINK YOU'RE MISSING THE POINT. YOU SEE, ARKHAM NOW HAS THE WELL-POLISHED VENEER OF NORMALCY.
BUT MANY OF THE LOCALS STILL HARBOR THOSE OLD SUPERSTITIONS. AFTER RECENT EVENTS, WORD OF THE PRIEST'S RITUALITIC SUICIDE COULD BE MISINTERPRETED AS A... ***RELAPSE*** IF YOU WILL.
THAT COULD HAVE AN ADVERSE AFFECT ON THE LOCAL ECONOMY. MY HUMBLE EXTABLISHMENT SPECIFICALLY. THEREFORE I FELT DISCRETION WAS THE WISEST COURSE OF ACTION.
FROM A BUSINESS PERSPECTIVE.
MR. ARKHAM, I HAVE TO BE HONEST...
YOU SCARE THE HELL OUT OF ME.
HA HA. I CAN ASSURE YOU, YOUNG MASTER MORGAN, THAT I AM QUITE HARMLESS.
NOW GO HOME AND GET SOME REST. I MUST GET THIS TEA UP TO THIRTY-SEVEN BEFORE IT GETS COLD.

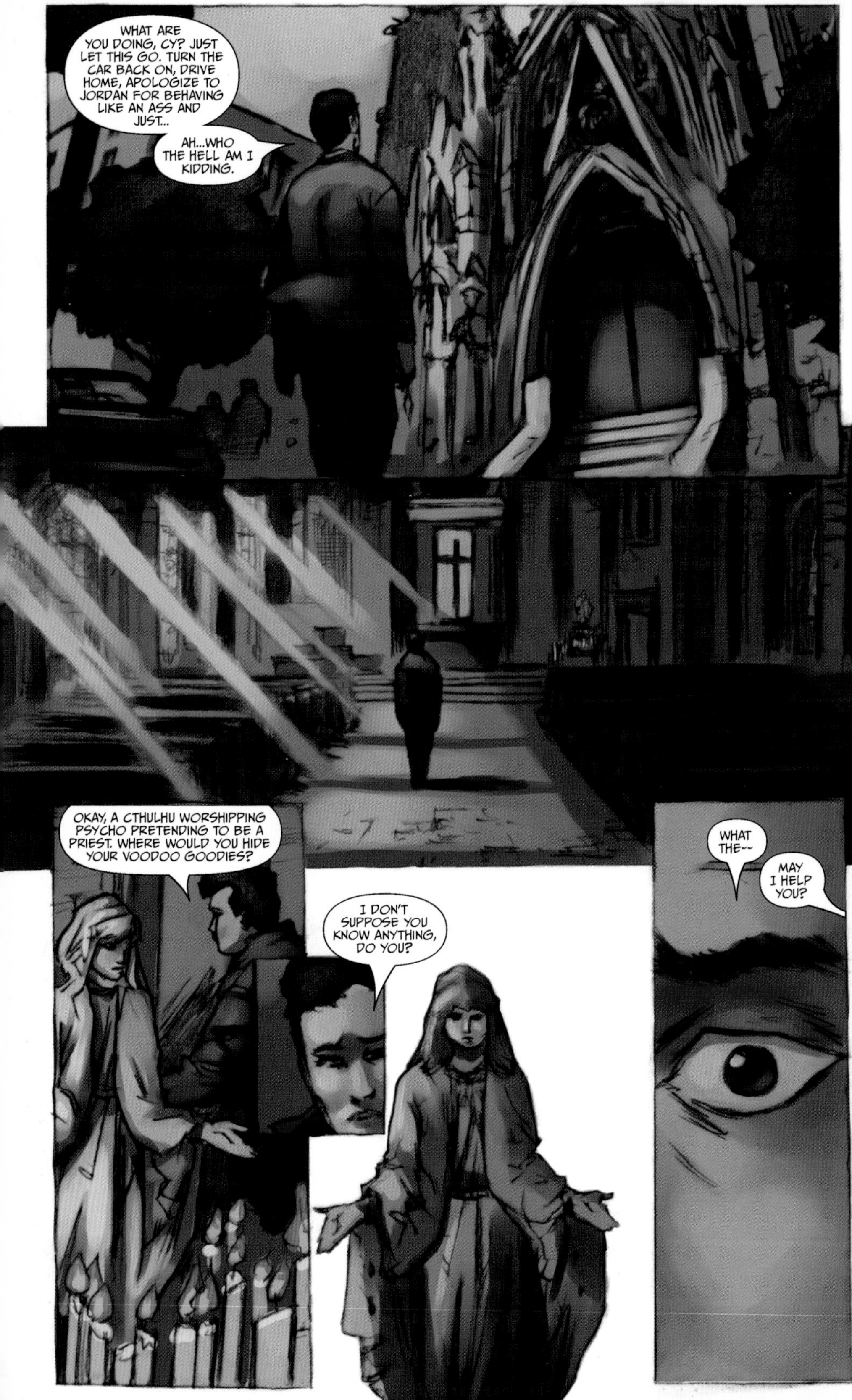
WHAT ARE YOU DOING, CY? JUST LET THIS GO. TURN THE CAR BACK ON, DRIVE HOME, APOLOGIZE TO JORDAN FOR BEHAVING LIKE AN ASS AND JUST...
AH...WHO THE HELL AM I KIDDING.
OKAY, A CTHULHU WORSHIPPING PSYCHO PRETENDING TO BE A PRIEST. WHERE WOULD YOU HIDE YOUR VOODOO GOODIES?
I DON'T SUPPOSE YOU KNOW ANYTHING, DO YOU?
WHAT THE--
MAY I HELP YOU?

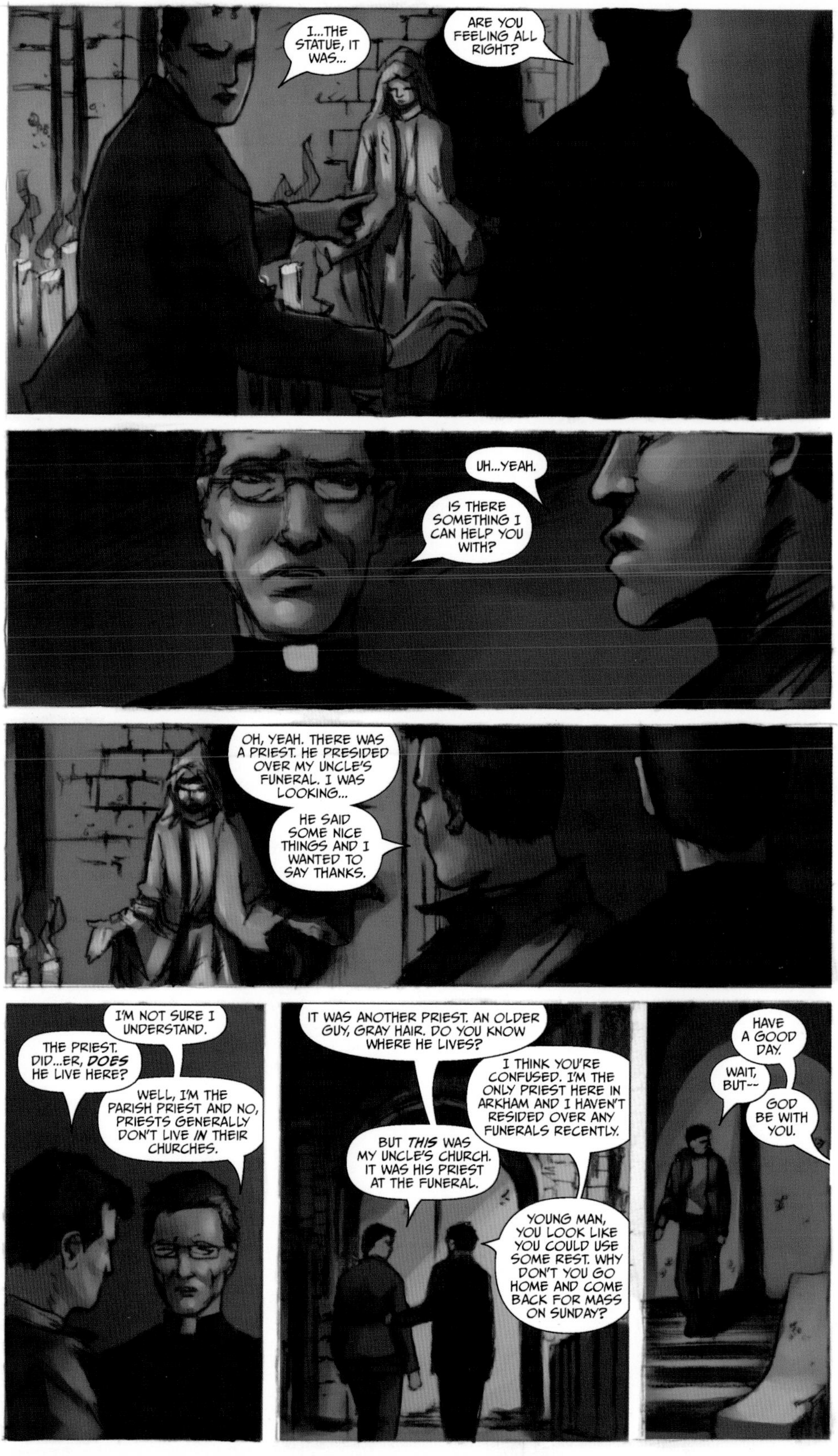
I...THE STATUE, IT WAS...
ARE YOU FEELING ALL RIGHT?
UH...YEAH.
IS THERE SOMETHING I CAN HELP YOU WITH?
OH, YEAH. THERE WAS A PRIEST. HE PRESIDED OVER MY UNCLE'S FUNERAL. I WAS LOOKING...
HE SAID SOME NICE THINGS AND I WANTED TO SAY THANKS.
I'M NOT SURE I UNDERSTAND.
THE PRIEST. DID...ER, *DOES* HE LIVE HERE?
WELL, I'M THE PARISH PRIEST AND NO, PRIESTS GENERALLY DON'T LIVE *IN* THEIR CHURCHES.
IT WAS ANOTHER PRIEST. AN OLDER GUY, GRAY HAIR. DO YOU KNOW WHERE HE LIVES?
I THINK YOU'RE CONFUSED. I'M THE ONLY PRIEST HERE IN ARKHAM AND I HAVEN'T RESIDED OVER ANY FUNERALS RECENTLY.
BUT *THIS* WAS MY UNCLE'S CHURCH. IT WAS HIS PRIEST AT THE FUNERAL.
YOUNG MAN, YOU LOOK LIKE YOU COULD USE SOME REST. WHY DON'T YOU GO HOME AND COME BACK FOR MASS ON SUNDAY?
HAVE A GOOD DAY.
WAIT, BUT--
GOD BE WITH YOU.

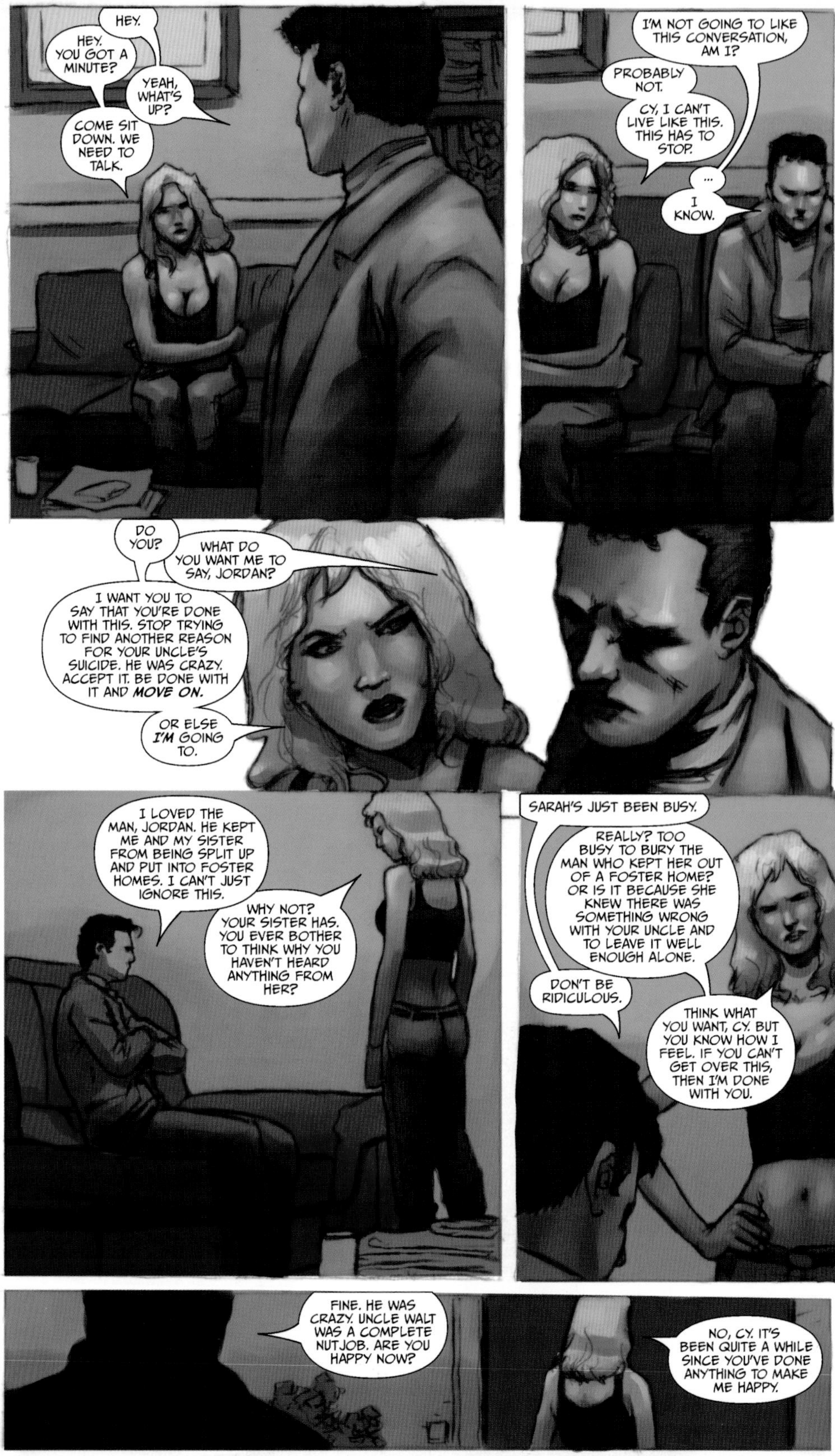
HEY.
HEY. YOU GOT A MINUTE?
YEAH, WHAT'S UP?
COME SIT DOWN. WE NEED TO TALK.
I'M NOT GOING TO LIKE THIS CONVERSATION, AM I?
PROBABLY NOT.
CY, I CAN'T LIVE LIKE THIS. THIS HAS TO STOP.
...
I KNOW.
DO YOU?
WHAT DO YOU WANT ME TO SAY, JORDAN?
I WANT YOU TO SAY THAT YOU'RE DONE WITH THIS. STOP TRYING TO FIND ANOTHER REASON FOR YOUR UNCLE'S SUICIDE. HE WAS CRAZY. ACCEPT IT. BE DONE WITH IT AND *MOVE ON.*
OR ELSE *I'M* GOING TO.
I LOVED THE MAN, JORDAN. HE KEPT ME AND MY SISTER FROM BEING SPLIT UP AND PUT INTO FOSTER HOMES. I CAN'T JUST IGNORE THIS.
WHY NOT? YOUR SISTER HAS. YOU EVER BOTHER TO THINK WHY YOU HAVEN'T HEARD ANYTHING FROM HER?
SARAH'S JUST BEEN BUSY.
REALLY? TOO BUSY TO BURY THE MAN WHO KEPT HER OUT OF A FOSTER HOME? OR IS IT BECAUSE SHE KNEW THERE WAS SOMETHING WRONG WITH YOUR UNCLE AND TO LEAVE IT WELL ENOUGH ALONE.
DON'T BE RIDICULOUS.
THINK WHAT YOU WANT, CY. BUT YOU KNOW HOW I FEEL. IF YOU CAN'T GET OVER THIS, THEN I'M DONE WITH YOU.
FINE. HE WAS CRAZY. UNCLE WALT WAS A COMPLETE NUTJOB. ARE YOU HAPPY NOW?
NO, CY. IT'S BEEN QUITE A WHILE SINCE YOU'VE DONE ANYTHING TO MAKE ME HAPPY.

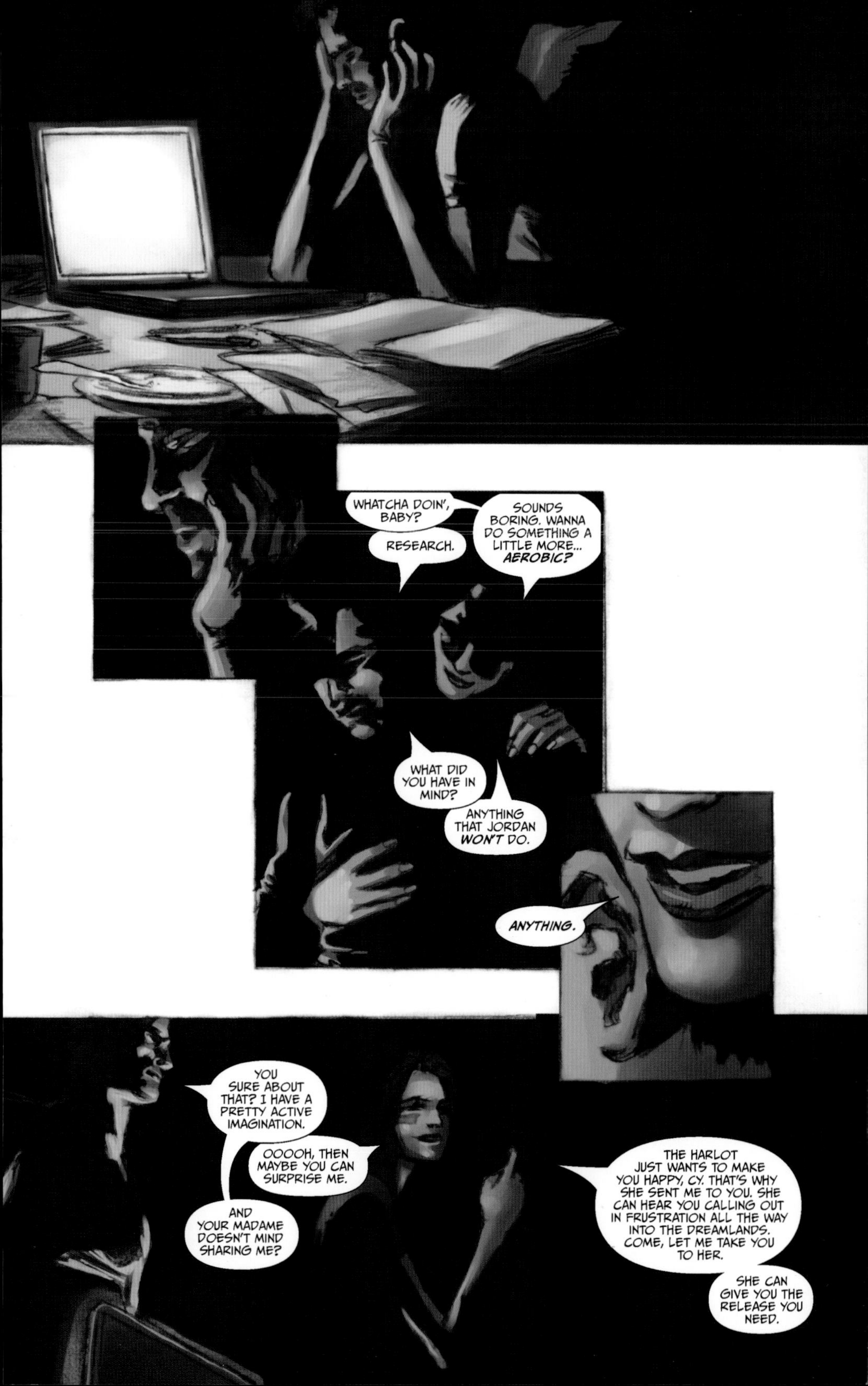
WHATCHA DOIN', BABY?
RESEARCH.
SOUNDS BORING. WANNA DO SOMETHING A LITTLE MORE... AEROBIC?
WHAT DID YOU HAVE IN MIND?
ANYTHING THAT JORDAN WON'T DO.
ANYTHING.
YOU SURE ABOUT THAT? I HAVE A PRETTY ACTIVE IMAGINATION.
OOOOH, THEN MAYBE YOU CAN SURPRISE ME.
AND YOUR MADAME DOESN'T MIND SHARING ME?
THE HARLOT JUST WANTS TO MAKE YOU HAPPY, CY. THAT'S WHY SHE SENT ME TO YOU. SHE CAN HEAR YOU CALLING OUT IN FRUSTRATION ALL THE WAY INTO THE DREAMLANDS. COME, LET ME TAKE YOU TO HER.
SHE CAN GIVE YOU THE RELEASE YOU NEED.

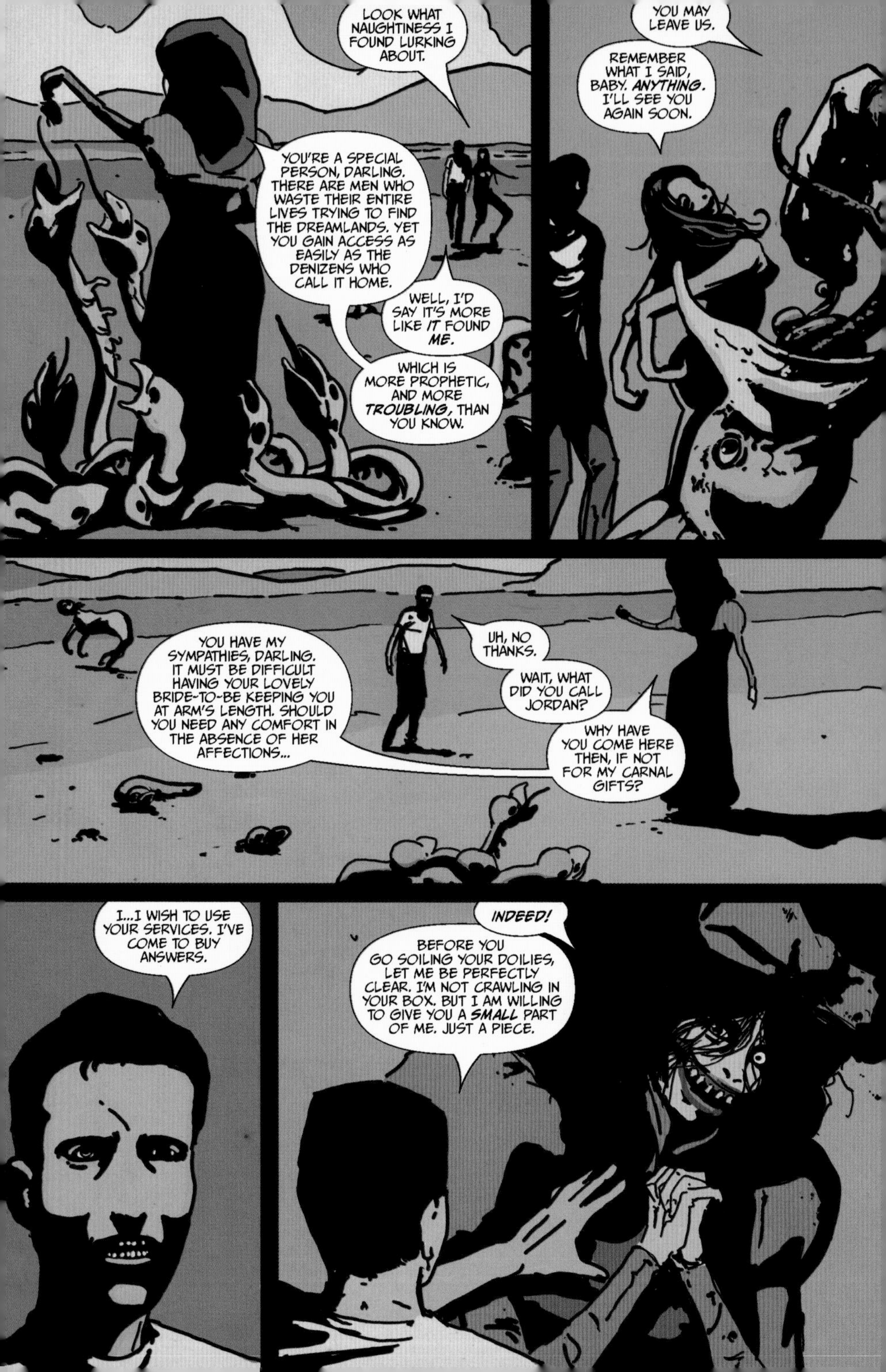
LOOK WHAT NAUGHTINESS I FOUND LURKING ABOUT.
YOU'RE A SPECIAL PERSON, DARLING. THERE ARE MEN WHO WASTE THEIR ENTIRE LIVES TRYING TO FIND THE DREAMLANDS. YET YOU GAIN ACCESS AS EASILY AS THE DENIZENS WHO CALL IT HOME.
WELL, I'D SAY IT'S MORE LIKE *IT* FOUND ***ME.***
WHICH IS MORE PROPHETIC, AND MORE ***TROUBLING,*** THAN YOU KNOW.
YOU MAY LEAVE US.
REMEMBER WHAT I SAID, BABY. ***ANYTHING.*** I'LL SEE YOU AGAIN SOON.
YOU HAVE MY SYMPATHIES, DARLING. IT MUST BE DIFFICULT HAVING YOUR LOVELY BRIDE-TO-BE KEEPING YOU AT ARM'S LENGTH. SHOULD YOU NEED ANY COMFORT IN THE ABSENCE OF HER AFFECTIONS...
UH, NO THANKS.
WAIT, WHAT DID YOU CALL JORDAN?
WHY HAVE YOU COME HERE THEN, IF NOT FOR MY CARNAL GIFTS?
I...I WISH TO USE YOUR SERVICES. I'VE COME TO BUY ANSWERS.
INDEED!
BEFORE YOU GO SOILING YOUR DOILIES, LET ME BE PERFECTLY CLEAR. I'M NOT CRAWLING IN YOUR BOX. BUT I AM WILLING TO GIVE YOU A ***SMALL*** PART OF ME. JUST A PIECE.

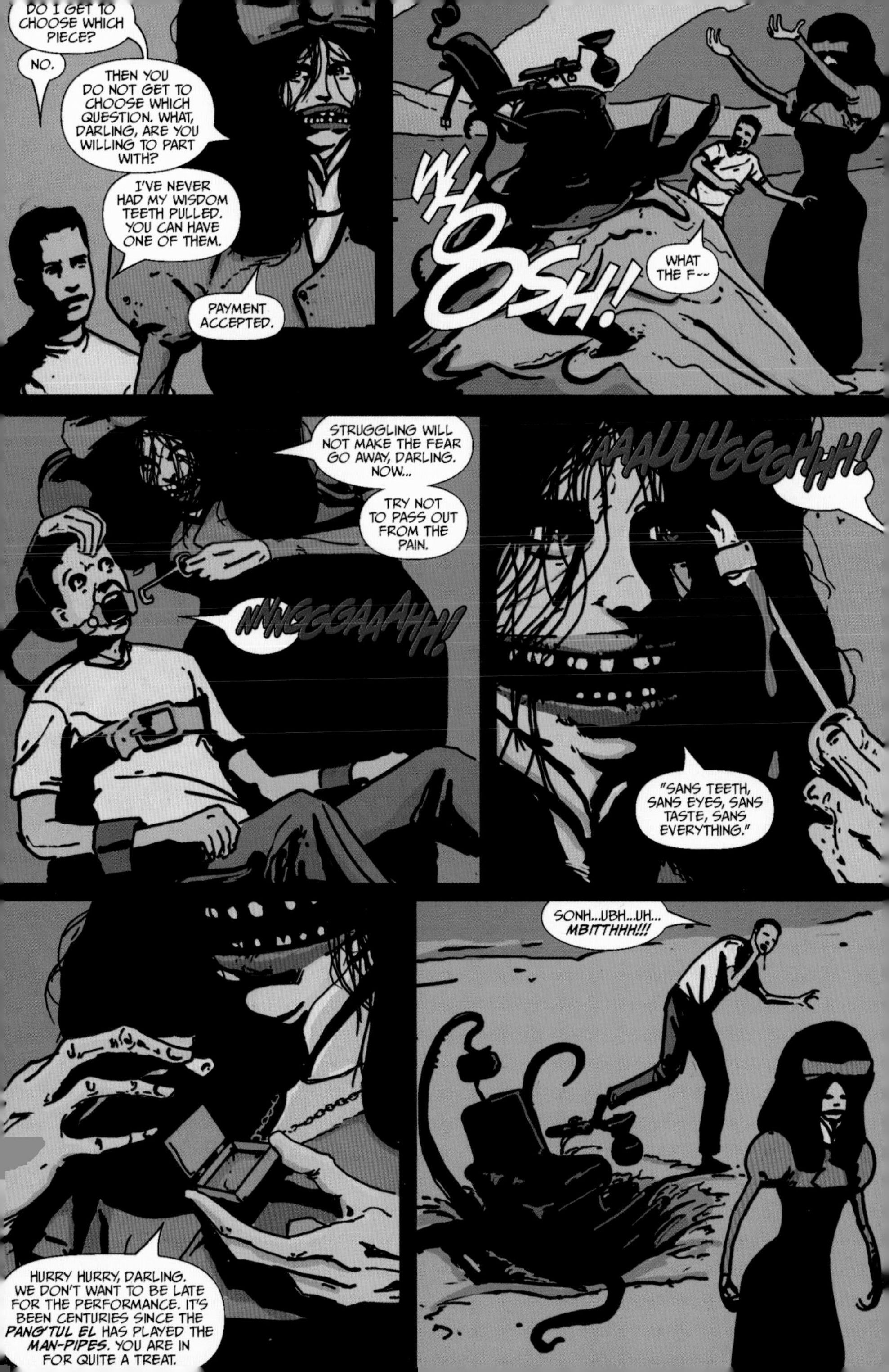
DO I GET TO CHOOSE WHICH PIECE?
NO.
THEN YOU DO NOT GET TO CHOOSE WHICH QUESTION. WHAT, DARLING, ARE YOU WILLING TO PART WITH?
I'VE NEVER HAD MY WISDOM TEETH PULLED. YOU CAN HAVE ONE OF THEM.
PAYMENT ACCEPTED.
WHOOSH!
WHAT THE F--
STRUGGLING WILL NOT MAKE THE FEAR GO AWAY, DARLING. NOW...
TRY NOT TO PASS OUT FROM THE PAIN.
NNNGGGAAAAHH!
AAAUUUGGGHHH!
"SANS TEETH, SANS EYES, SANS TASTE, SANS EVERYTHING."
HURRY HURRY, DARLING. WE DON'T WANT TO BE LATE FOR THE PERFORMANCE. IT'S BEEN CENTURIES SINCE THE ***PANG'TUL EL*** HAS PLAYED THE ***MAN-PIPES***. YOU ARE IN FOR QUITE A TREAT.
SONH...UBH...UH... ***MBITTHHH!!!***

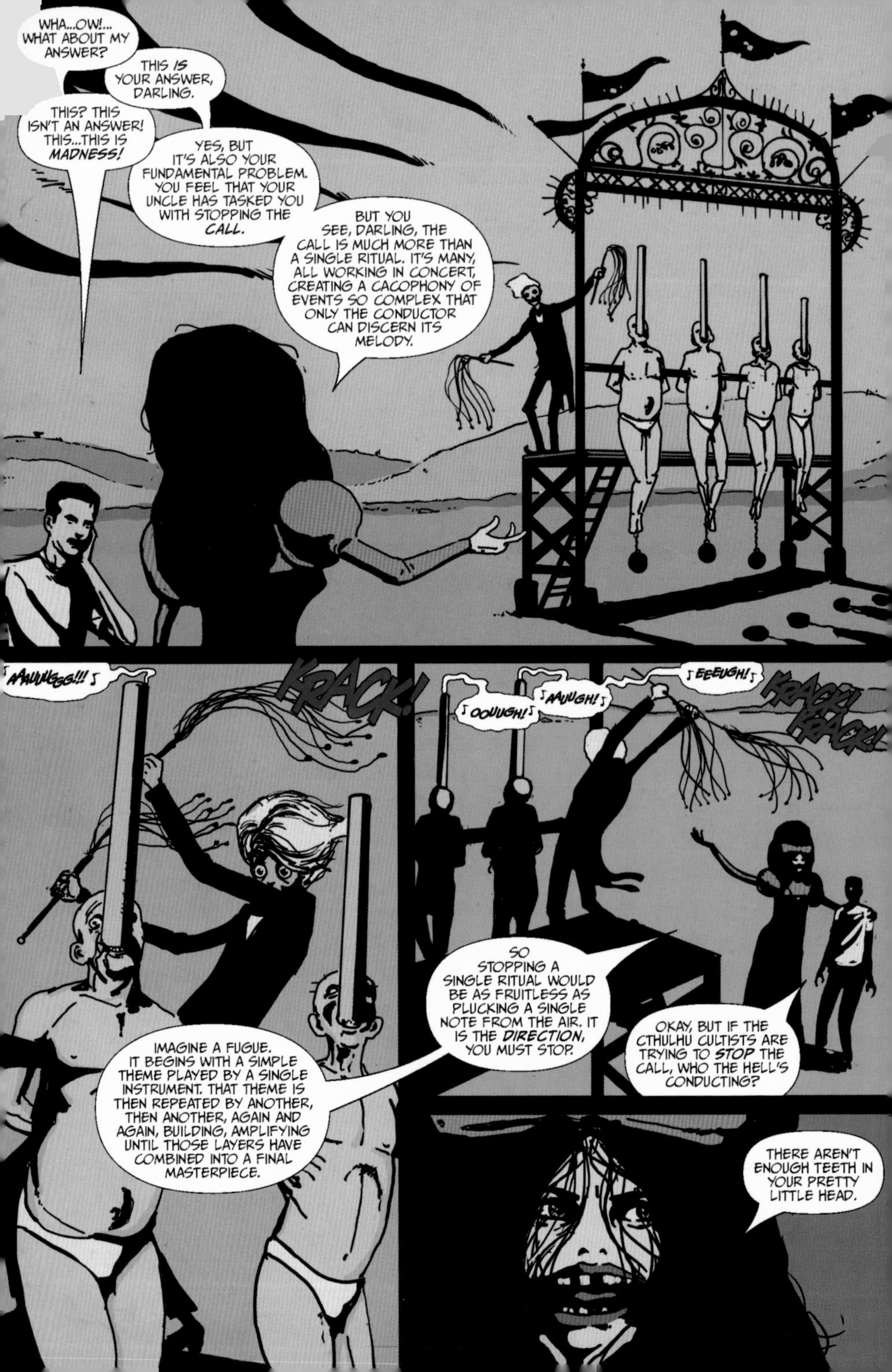
WHA...OW!... WHAT ABOUT MY ANSWER?
THIS *IS* YOUR ANSWER, DARLING.
THIS? THIS ISN'T AN ANSWER! THIS...THIS IS ***MADNESS!***
YES, BUT IT'S ALSO YOUR FUNDAMENTAL PROBLEM. YOU FEEL THAT YOUR UNCLE HAS TASKED YOU WITH STOPPING THE ***CALL.***
BUT YOU SEE, DARLING, THE CALL IS MUCH MORE THAN A SINGLE RITUAL. IT'S MANY, ALL WORKING IN CONCERT, CREATING A CACOPHONY OF EVENTS SO COMPLEX THAT ONLY THE CONDUCTOR CAN DISCERN ITS MELODY.
AAUUUGGG!!!
KRACK!
IMAGINE A FUGUE. IT BEGINS WITH A SIMPLE THEME PLAYED BY A SINGLE INSTRUMENT. THAT THEME IS THEN REPEATED BY ANOTHER, THEN ANOTHER, AGAIN AND AGAIN, BUILDING, AMPLIFYING UNTIL THOSE LAYERS HAVE COMBINED INTO A FINAL MASTERPIECE.
OOUUGH!
AAUUGH!
EEEUGH!
KRACK! KRACK!
SO STOPPING A SINGLE RITUAL WOULD BE AS FRUITLESS AS PLUCKING A SINGLE NOTE FROM THE AIR. IT IS THE ***DIRECTION,*** YOU MUST STOP.
OKAY, BUT IF THE CTHULHU CULTISTS ARE TRYING TO ***STOP*** THE CALL, WHO THE HELL'S CONDUCTING?
THERE AREN'T ENOUGH TEETH IN YOUR PRETTY LITTLE HEAD.

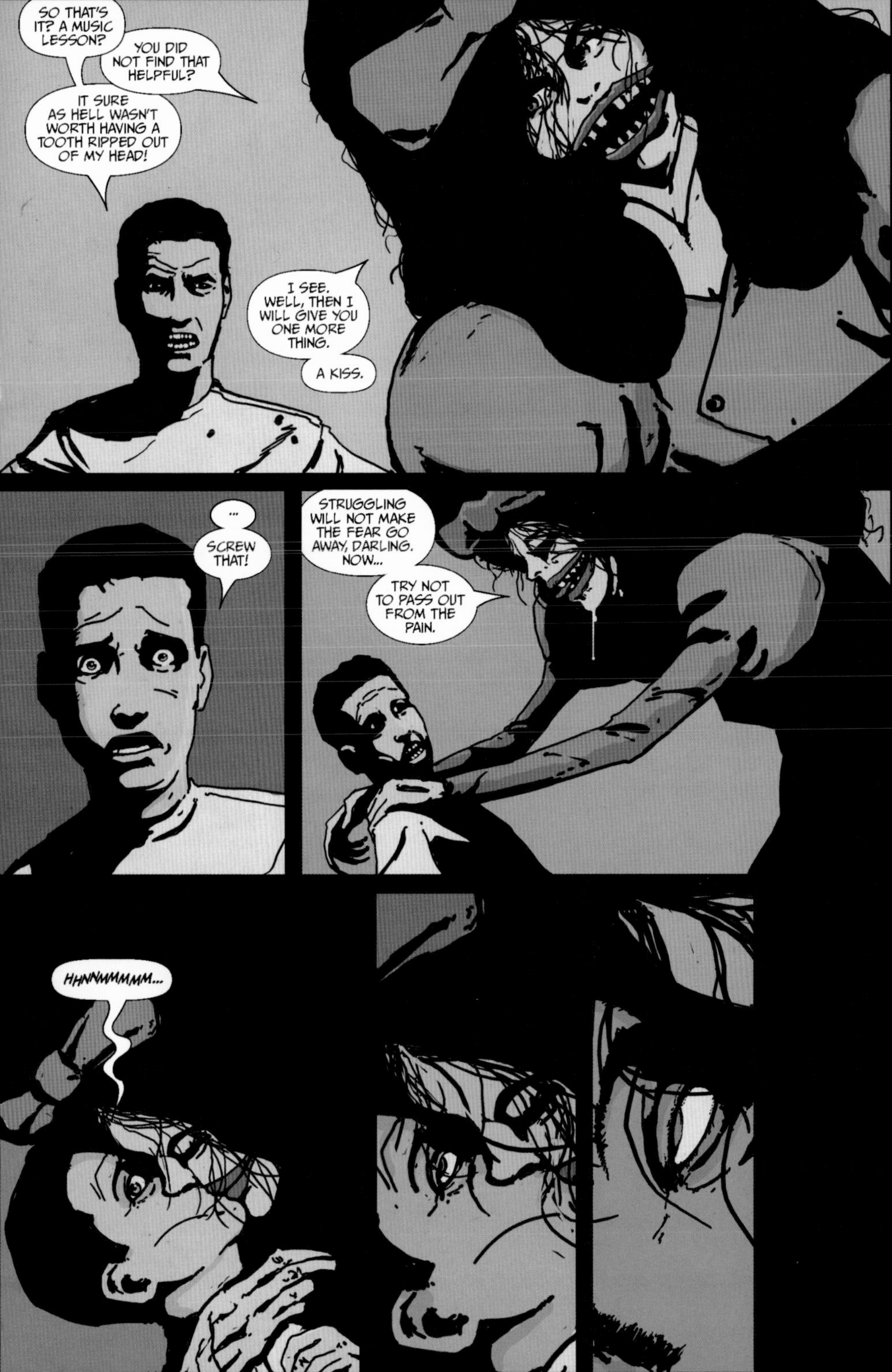
SO THAT'S IT? A MUSIC LESSON?
YOU DID NOT FIND THAT HELPFUL?
IT SURE AS HELL WASN'T WORTH HAVING A TOOTH RIPPED OUT OF MY HEAD!
I SEE. WELL, THEN I WILL GIVE YOU ONE MORE THING.
A KISS.
...
SCREW THAT!
STRUGGLING WILL NOT MAKE THE FEAR GO AWAY, DARLING. NOW...
TRY NOT TO PASS OUT FROM THE PAIN.
HHNNMMMMM...

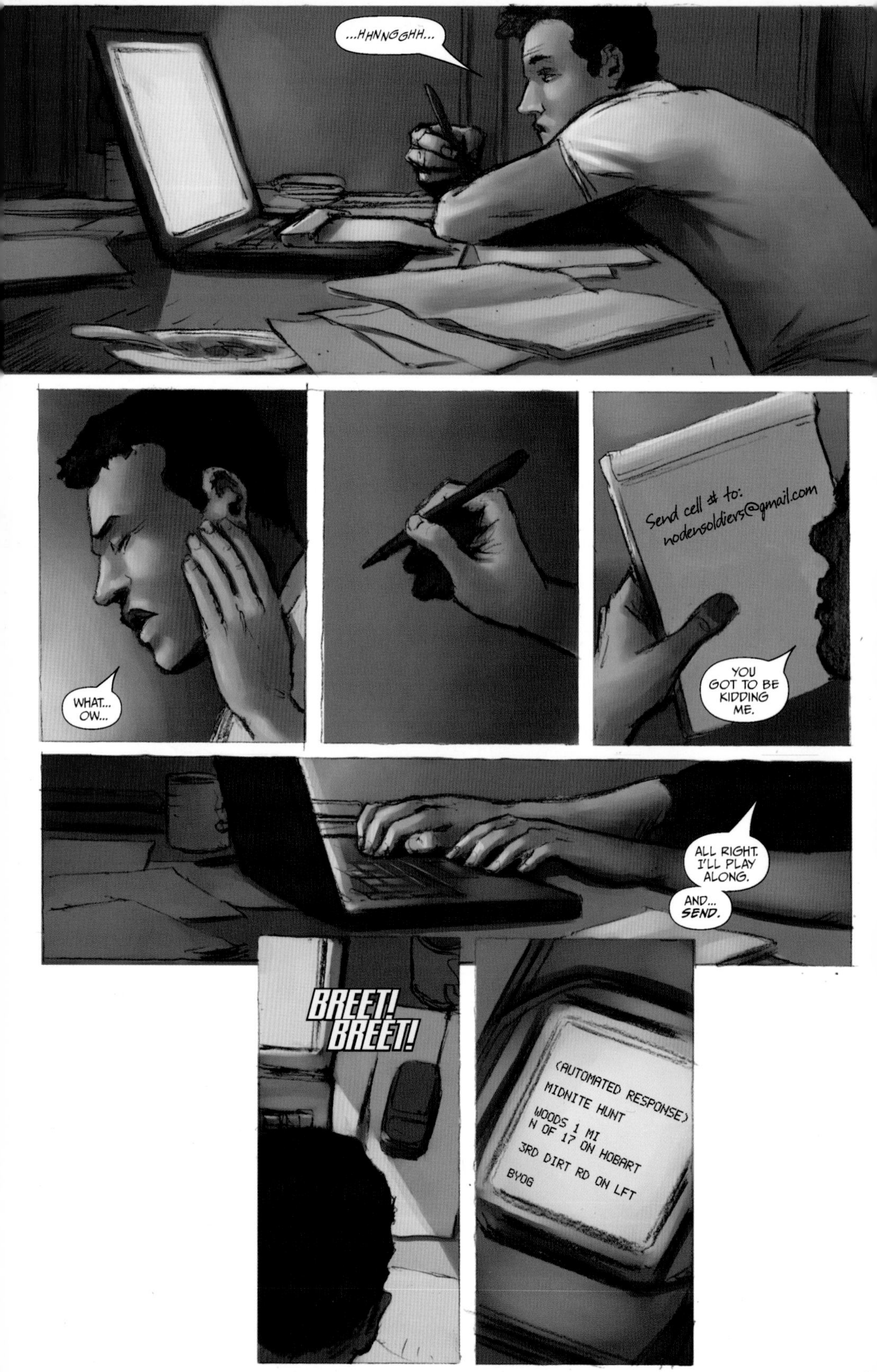
...HHNNGGHH...
WHAT... OW...
Send cell # to: nodensoldiers@gmail.com
YOU GOT TO BE KIDDING ME.
ALL RIGHT. I'LL PLAY ALONG.
AND... SEND.
BREET! BREET!
(AUTOMATED RESPONSE)
MIDNITE HUNT
WOODS 1 MI N OF 17 ON HOBART
3RD DIRT RD ON LFT
BYOG

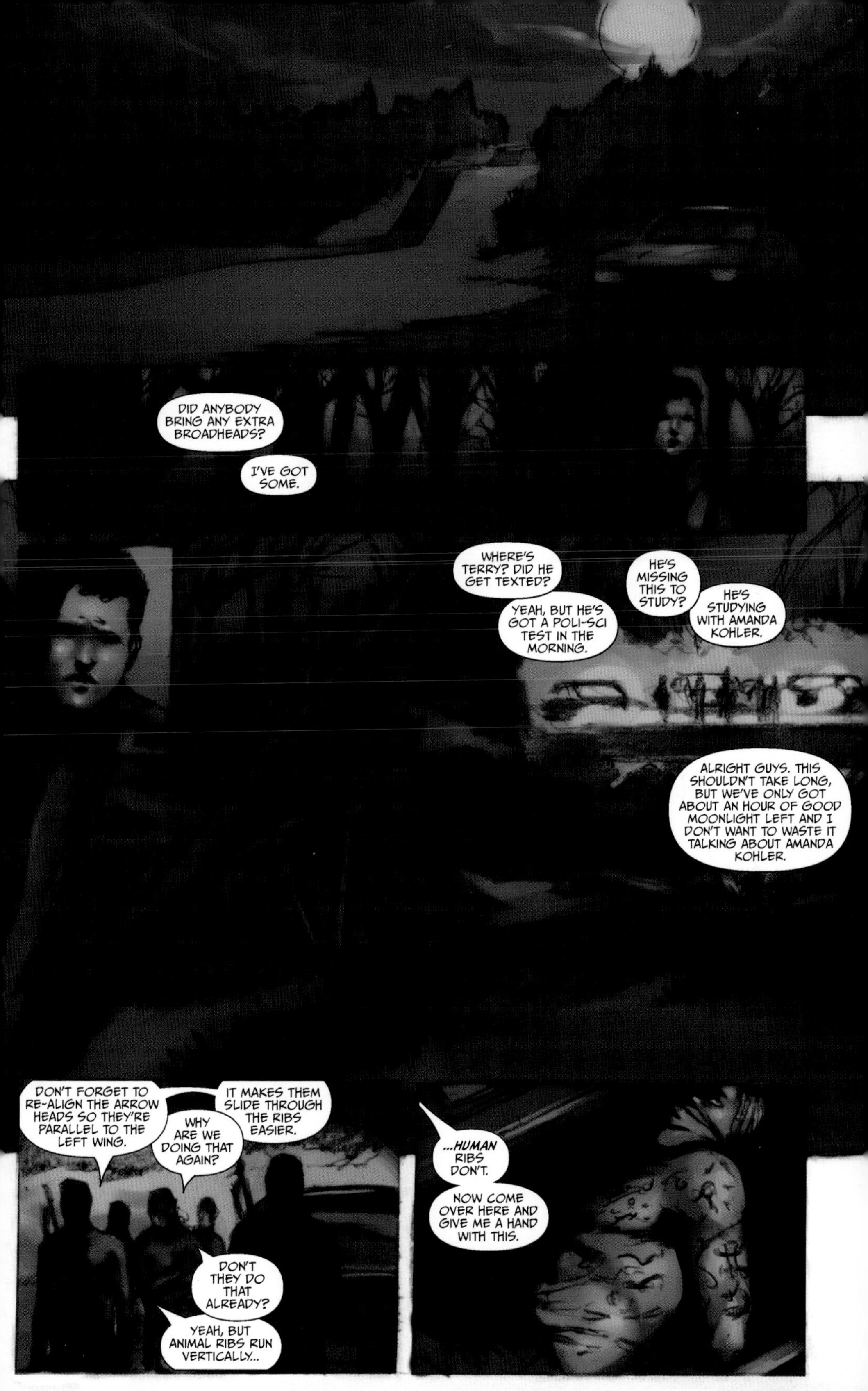
DID ANYBODY BRING ANY EXTRA BROADHEADS?
I'VE GOT SOME.
WHERE'S TERRY? DID HE GET TEXTED?
YEAH, BUT HE'S GOT A POLI-SCI TEST IN THE MORNING.
HE'S MISSING THIS TO STUDY?
HE'S STUDYING WITH AMANDA KOHLER.
ALRIGHT GUYS. THIS SHOULDN'T TAKE LONG, BUT WE'VE ONLY GOT ABOUT AN HOUR OF GOOD MOONLIGHT LEFT AND I DON'T WANT TO WASTE IT TALKING ABOUT AMANDA KOHLER.
DON'T FORGET TO RE-ALIGN THE ARROW HEADS SO THEY'RE PARALLEL TO THE LEFT WING.
WHY ARE WE DOING THAT AGAIN?
IT MAKES THEM SLIDE THROUGH THE RIBS EASIER.
DON'T THEY DO THAT ALREADY?
YEAH, BUT ANIMAL RIBS RUN VERTICALLY...
...*HUMAN* RIBS DON'T.
NOW COME OVER HERE AND GIVE ME A HAND WITH THIS.

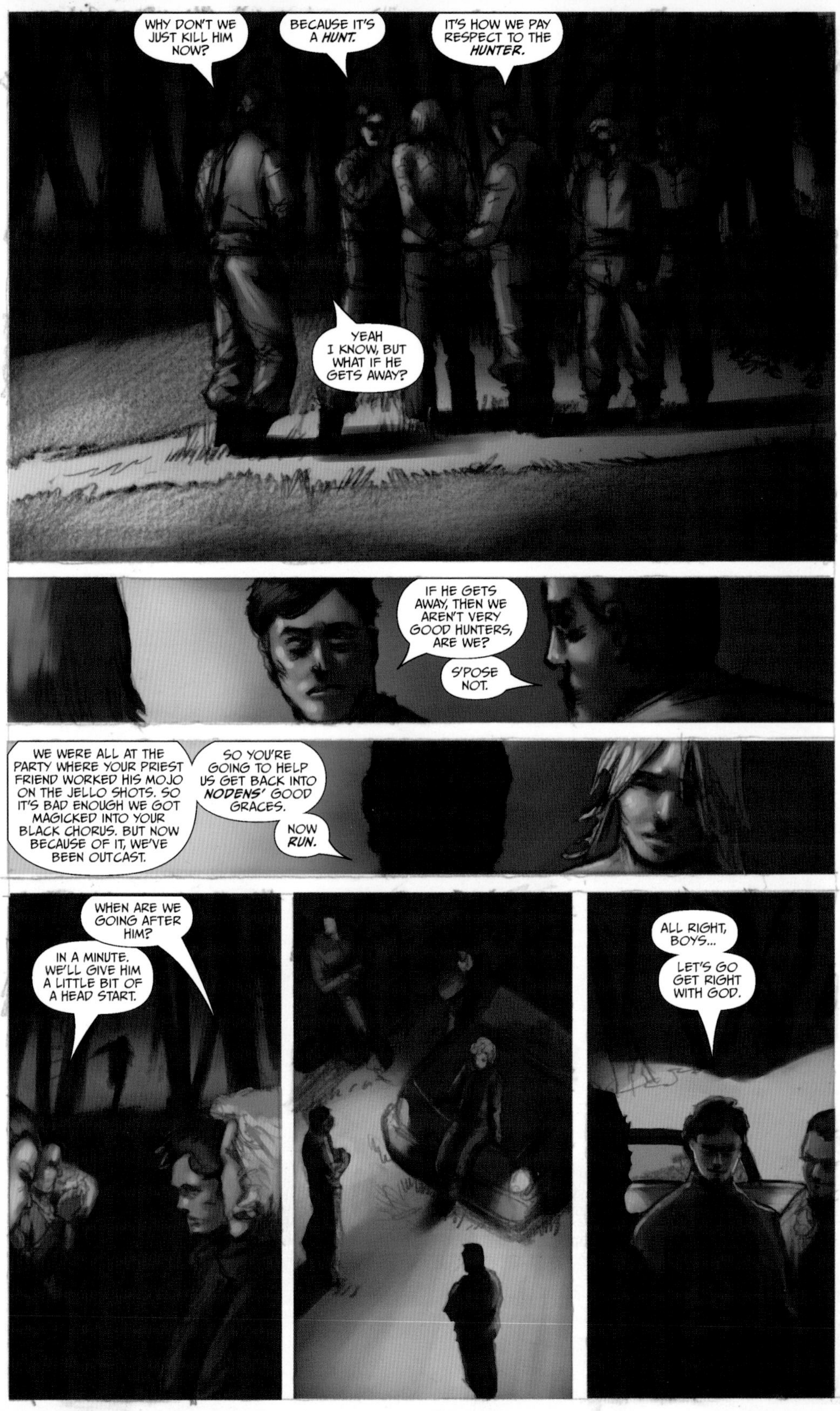
WHY DON'T WE JUST KILL HIM NOW?
BECAUSE IT'S A *HUNT.*
IT'S HOW WE PAY RESPECT TO THE ***HUNTER.***
YEAH I KNOW, BUT WHAT IF HE GETS AWAY?
IF HE GETS AWAY, THEN WE AREN'T VERY GOOD HUNTERS, ARE WE?
S'POSE NOT.
WE WERE ALL AT THE PARTY WHERE YOUR PRIEST FRIEND WORKED HIS MOJO ON THE JELLO SHOTS. SO IT'S BAD ENOUGH WE GOT MAGICKED INTO YOUR BLACK CHORUS. BUT NOW BECAUSE OF IT, WE'VE BEEN OUTCAST.
SO YOU'RE GOING TO HELP US GET BACK INTO ***NODENS'*** GOOD GRACES.
NOW *RUN.*
WHEN ARE WE GOING AFTER HIM?
IN A MINUTE. WE'LL GIVE HIM A LITTLE BIT OF A HEAD START.
ALL RIGHT, BOYS...
LET'S GO GET RIGHT WITH GOD.

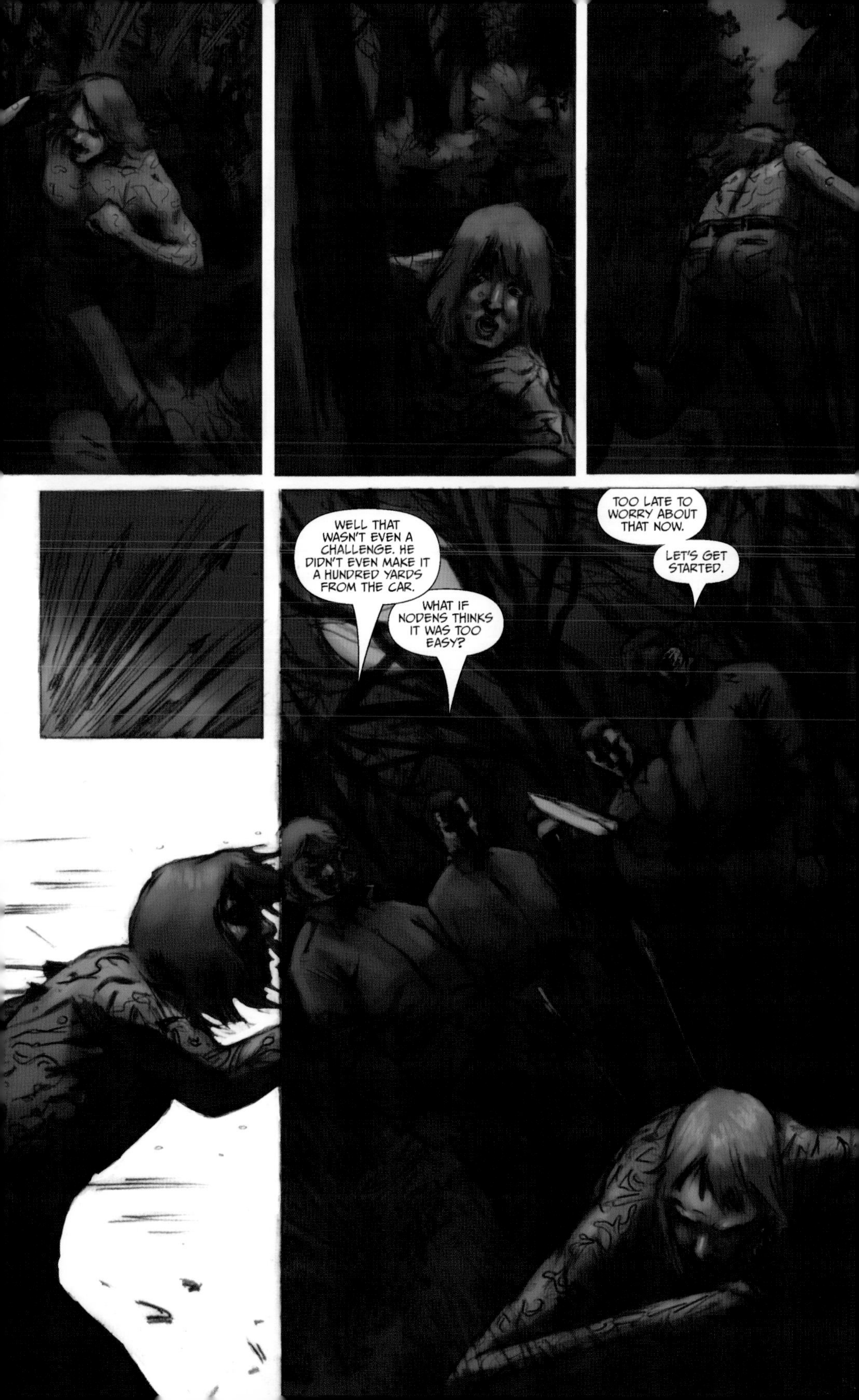
WELL THAT WASN'T EVEN A CHALLENGE. HE DIDN'T EVEN MAKE IT A HUNDRED YARDS FROM THE CAR.
WHAT IF NODENS THINKS IT WAS TOO EASY?
TOO LATE TO WORRY ABOUT THAT NOW.
LET'S GET STARTED.

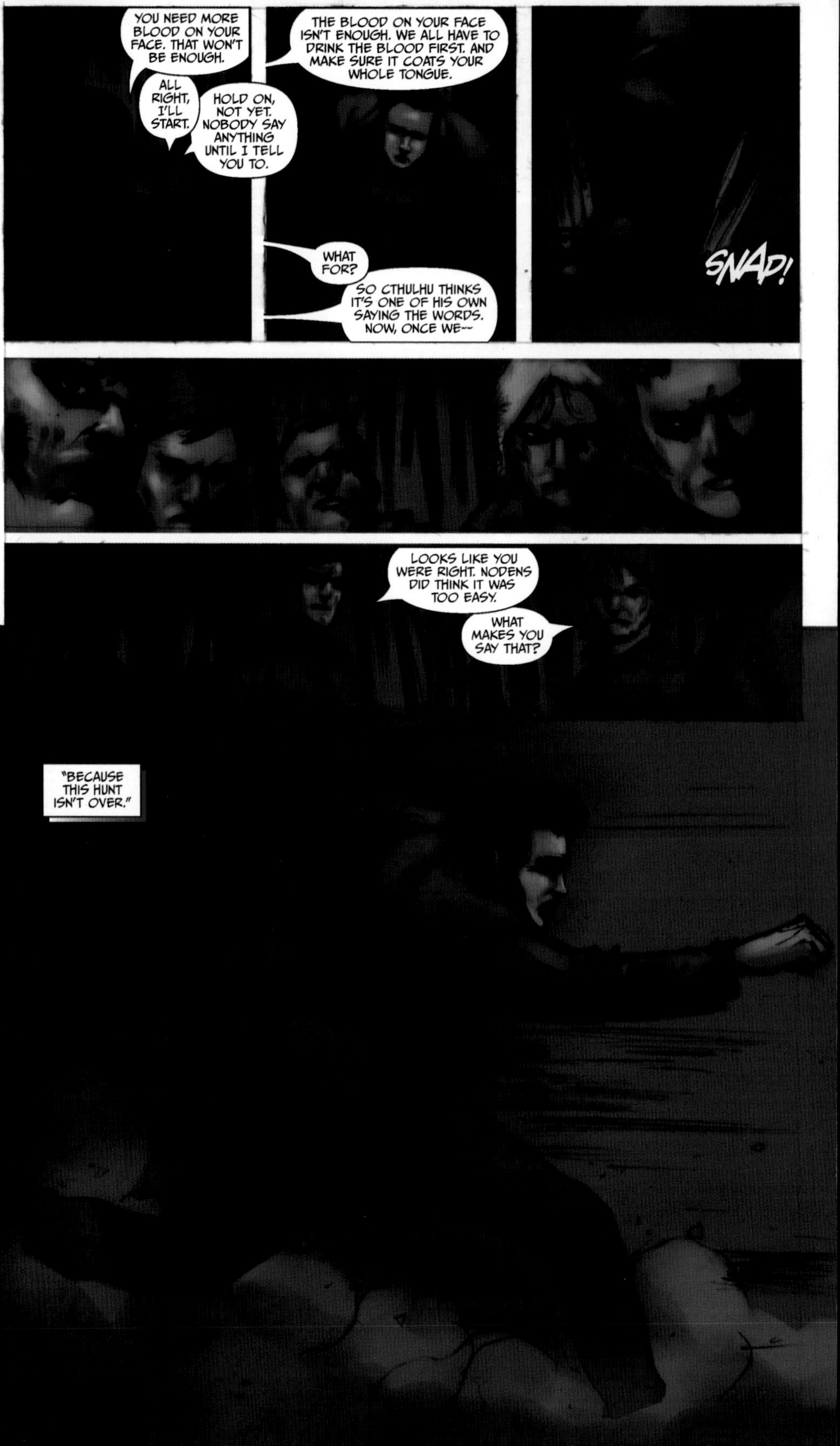
YOU NEED MORE BLOOD ON YOUR FACE. THAT WON'T BE ENOUGH.
ALL RIGHT, I'LL START.
HOLD ON, NOT YET. NOBODY SAY ANYTHING UNTIL I TELL YOU TO.
THE BLOOD ON YOUR FACE ISN'T ENOUGH. WE ALL HAVE TO DRINK THE BLOOD FIRST. AND MAKE SURE IT COATS YOUR WHOLE TONGUE.
WHAT FOR?
SO CTHULHU THINKS IT'S ONE OF HIS OWN SAYING THE WORDS. NOW, ONCE WE--
SNAP!
LOOKS LIKE YOU WERE RIGHT. NODENS DID THINK IT WAS TOO EASY.
WHAT MAKES YOU SAY THAT?
"BECAUSE THIS HUNT ISN'T OVER."

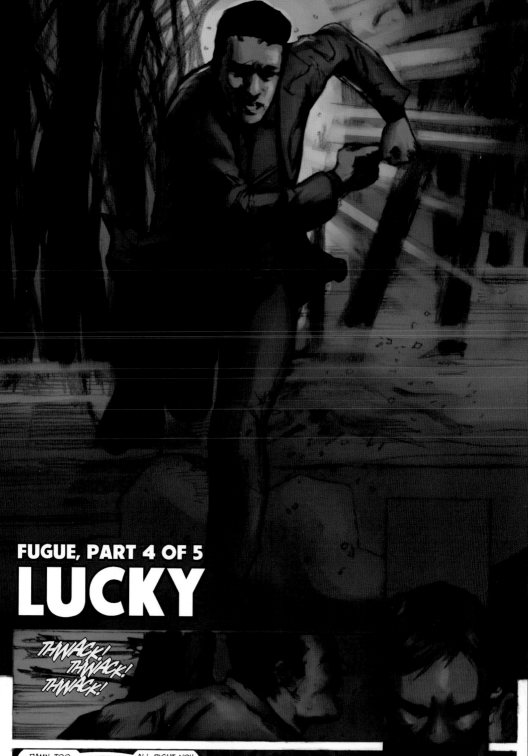

LUCKY

THWACK!
THWACK!
THWACK!

DAMN. TOO MANY TREES TO GET A CLEAR SHOT.

WE'RE LOSING MOONLIGHT HERE GUYS.

ALL RIGHT. YOU ALL GO BACK AND START THE RITUAL THEN.

BUT WHAT ABOUT THIS GUY?

I THINK IT'S TIME WE BROUGHT SOME HOUNDS TO THIS HUNT.

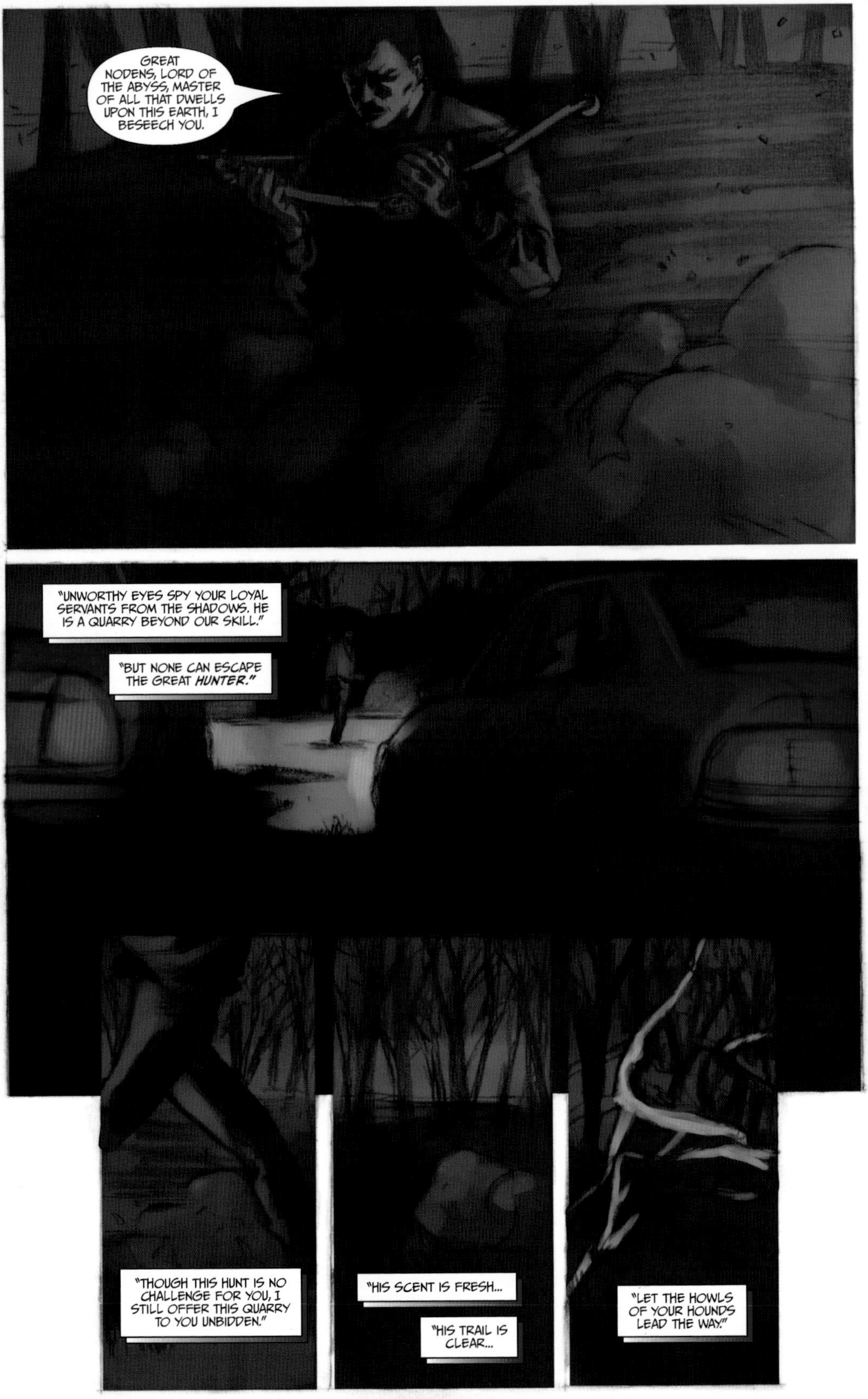
GREAT NODENS, LORD OF THE ABYSS, MASTER OF ALL THAT DWELLS UPON THIS EARTH, I BESEECH YOU.
"UNWORTHY EYES SPY YOUR LOYAL SERVANTS FROM THE SHADOWS. HE IS A QUARRY BEYOND OUR SKILL."
"BUT NONE CAN ESCAPE THE GREAT HUNTER."
"THOUGH THIS HUNT IS NO CHALLENGE FOR YOU, I STILL OFFER THIS QUARRY TO YOU UNBIDDEN."
"HIS SCENT IS FRESH...
"HIS TRAIL IS CLEAR...
"LET THE HOWLS OF YOUR HOUNDS LEAD THE WAY."

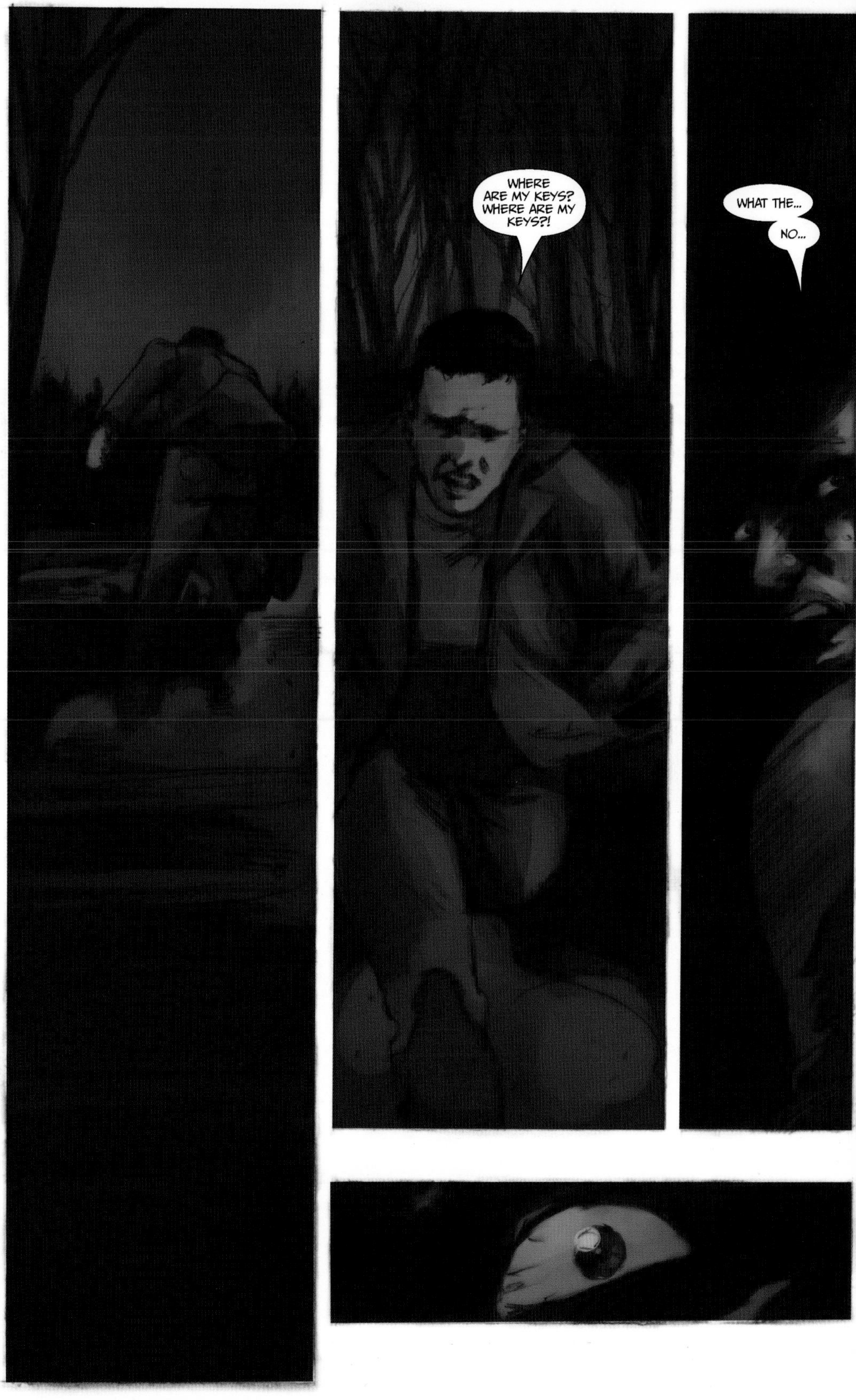
WHERE ARE MY KEYS? WHERE ARE MY KEYS?!
WHAT THE...
NO...

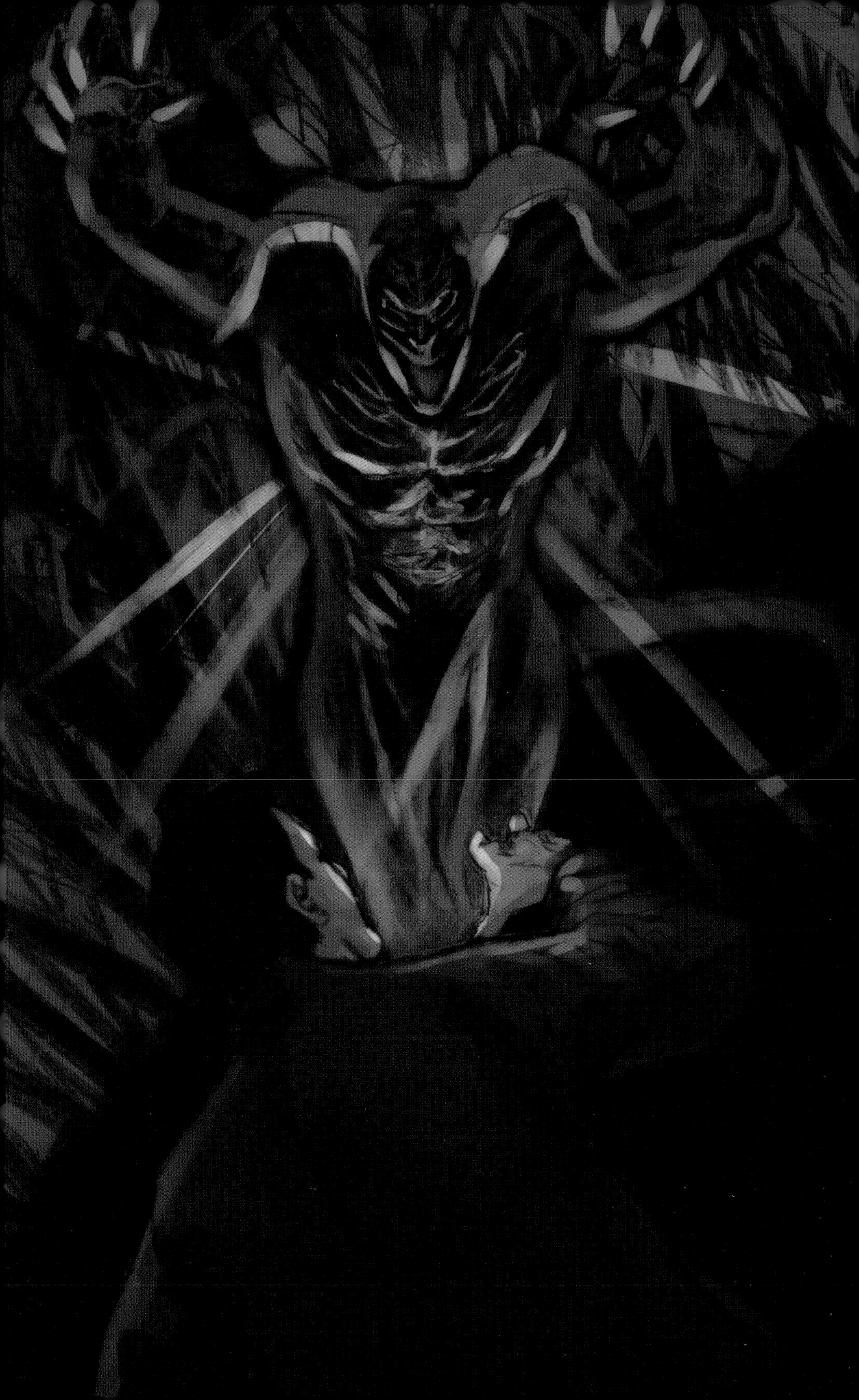

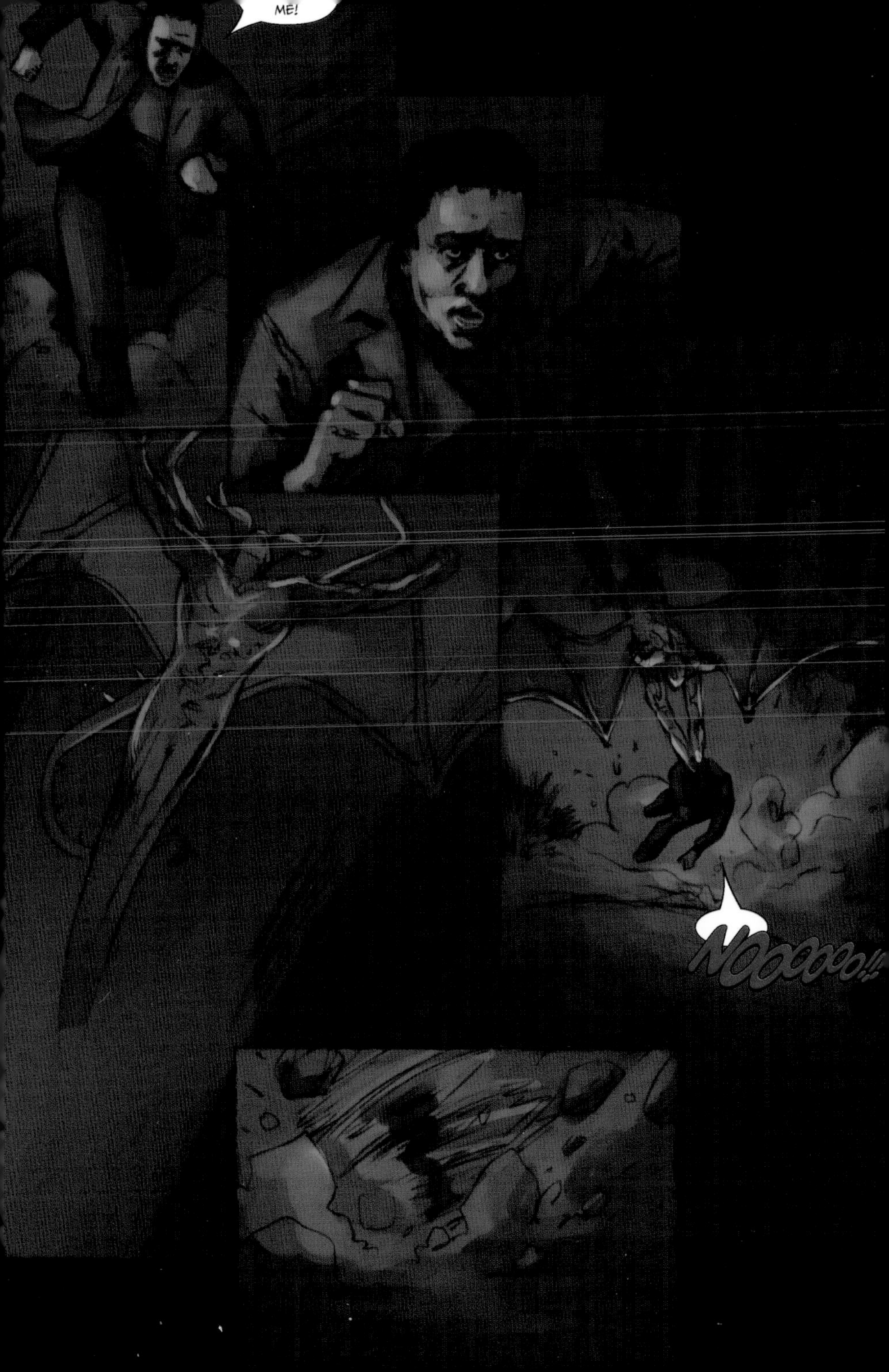
ME!
NOOOOOOO!!

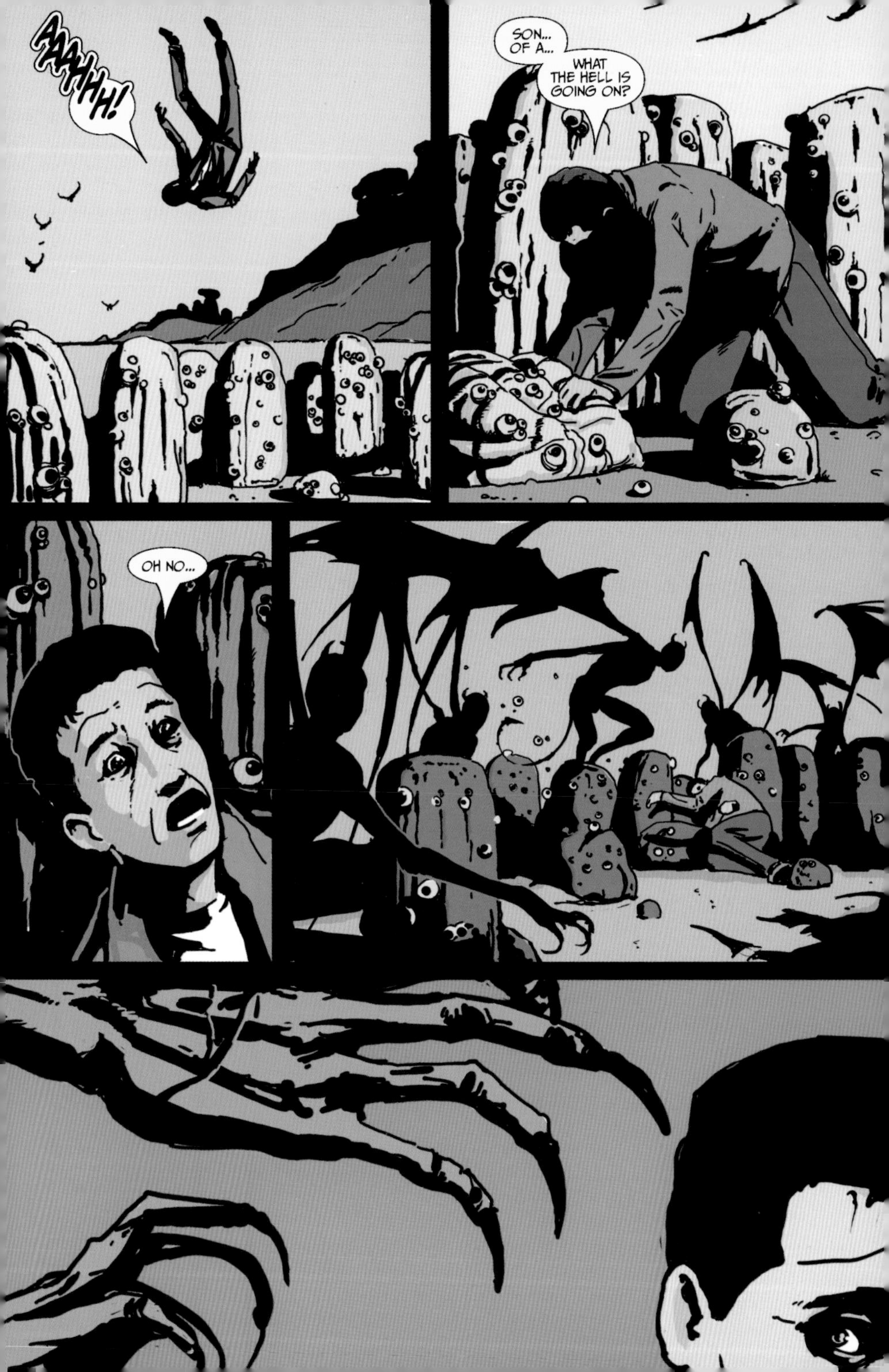
AAAHHH!
SON... OF A...
WHAT THE HELL IS GOING ON?
OH NO...

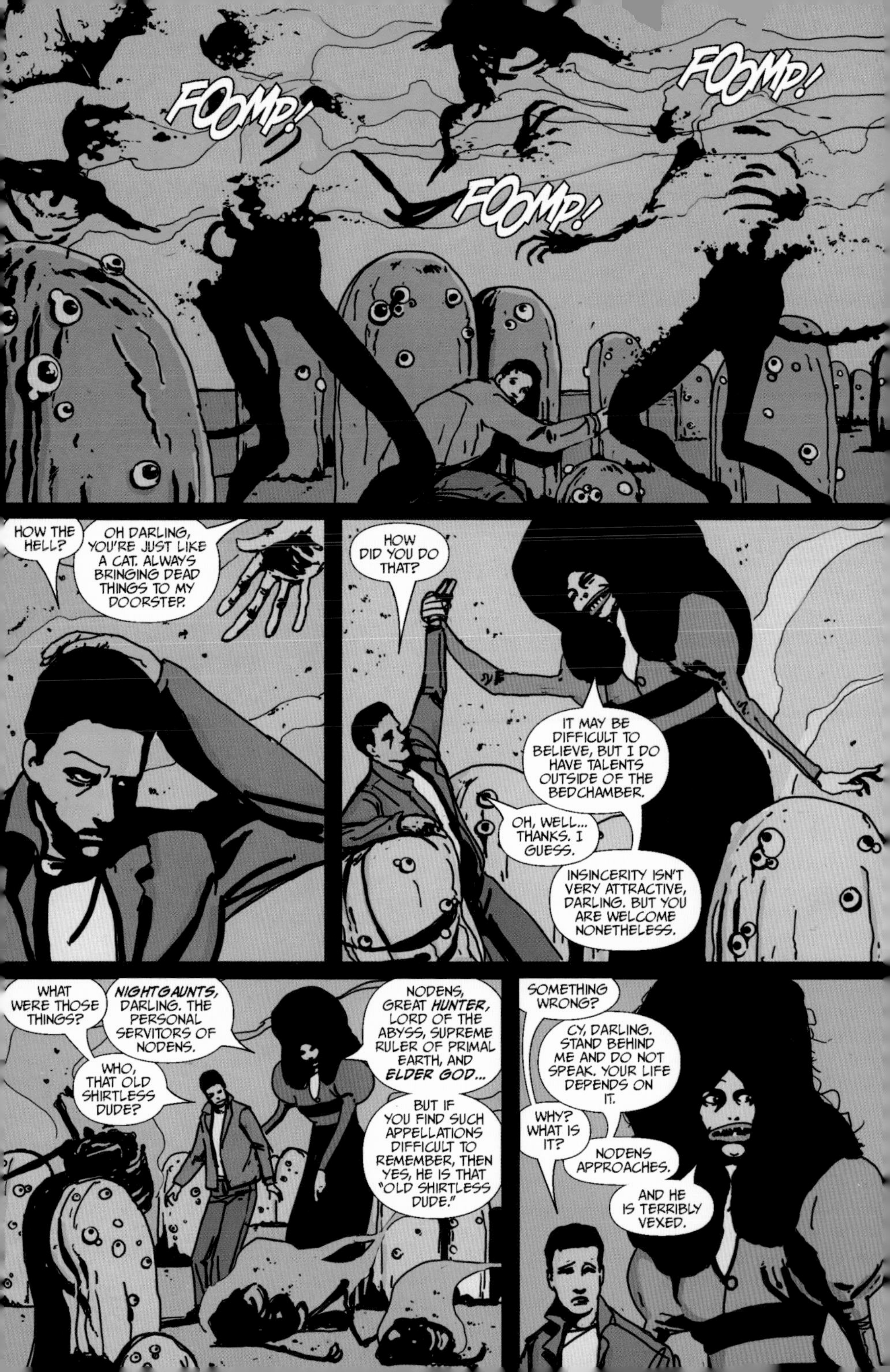
FOOMP!
FOOMP!
FOOMP!
HOW THE HELL?
OH DARLING, YOU'RE JUST LIKE A CAT. ALWAYS BRINGING DEAD THINGS TO MY DOORSTEP.
HOW DID YOU DO THAT?
IT MAY BE DIFFICULT TO BELIEVE, BUT I DO HAVE TALENTS OUTSIDE OF THE BEDCHAMBER.
OH, WELL... THANKS. I GUESS.
INSINCERITY ISN'T VERY ATTRACTIVE, DARLING. BUT YOU ARE WELCOME NONETHELESS.
WHAT WERE THOSE THINGS?
NIGHTGAUNTS, DARLING. THE PERSONAL SERVITORS OF NODENS.
WHO, THAT OLD SHIRTLESS DUDE?
NODENS, GREAT HUNTER, LORD OF THE ABYSS, SUPREME RULER OF PRIMAL EARTH, AND ELDER GOD...
BUT IF YOU FIND SUCH APPELLATIONS DIFFICULT TO REMEMBER, THEN YES, HE IS THAT "OLD SHIRTLESS DUDE."
SOMETHING WRONG?
CY, DARLING. STAND BEHIND ME AND DO NOT SPEAK. YOUR LIFE DEPENDS ON IT.
WHY? WHAT IS IT?
NODENS APPROACHES.
AND HE IS TERRIBLY VEXED.

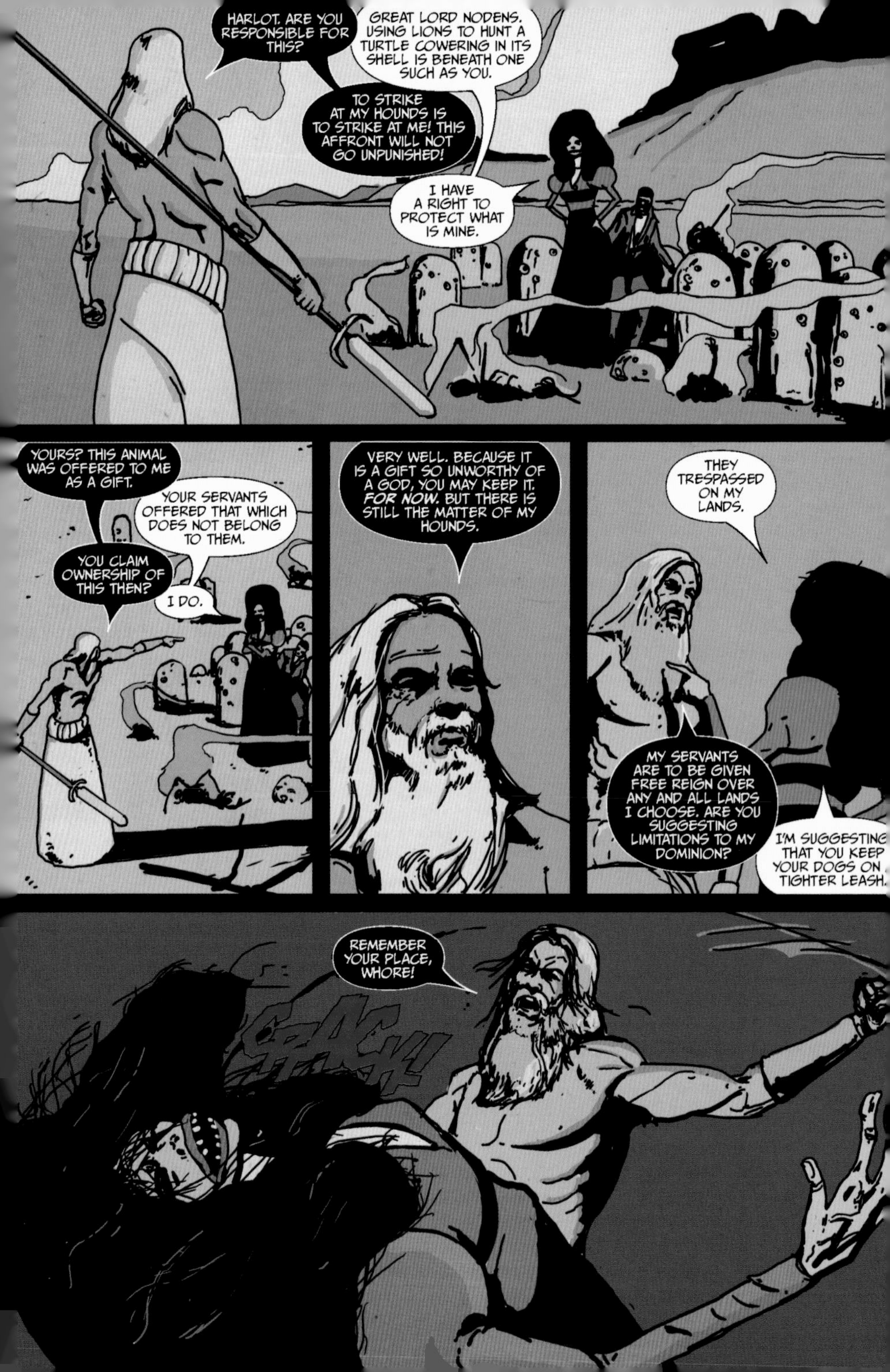
HARLOT. ARE YOU RESPONSIBLE FOR THIS?
GREAT LORD NODENS. USING LIONS TO HUNT A TURTLE COWERING IN ITS SHELL IS BENEATH ONE SUCH AS YOU.
TO STRIKE AT MY HOUNDS IS TO STRIKE AT ME! THIS AFFRONT WILL NOT GO UNPUNISHED!
I HAVE A RIGHT TO PROTECT WHAT IS MINE.
YOURS? THIS ANIMAL WAS OFFERED TO ME AS A GIFT.
YOUR SERVANTS OFFERED THAT WHICH DOES NOT BELONG TO THEM.
YOU CLAIM OWNERSHIP OF THIS THEN?
I DO.
VERY WELL. BECAUSE IT IS A GIFT SO UNWORTHY OF A GOD, YOU MAY KEEP IT. *FOR NOW.* BUT THERE IS STILL THE MATTER OF MY HOUNDS.
THEY TRESPASSED ON MY LANDS.
MY SERVANTS ARE TO BE GIVEN FREE REIGN OVER ANY AND ALL LANDS I CHOOSE. ARE YOU SUGGESTING LIMITATIONS TO MY DOMINION?
I'M SUGGESTING THAT YOU KEEP YOUR DOGS ON TIGHTER LEASH.
REMEMBER YOUR PLACE, WHORE!
SPACK!

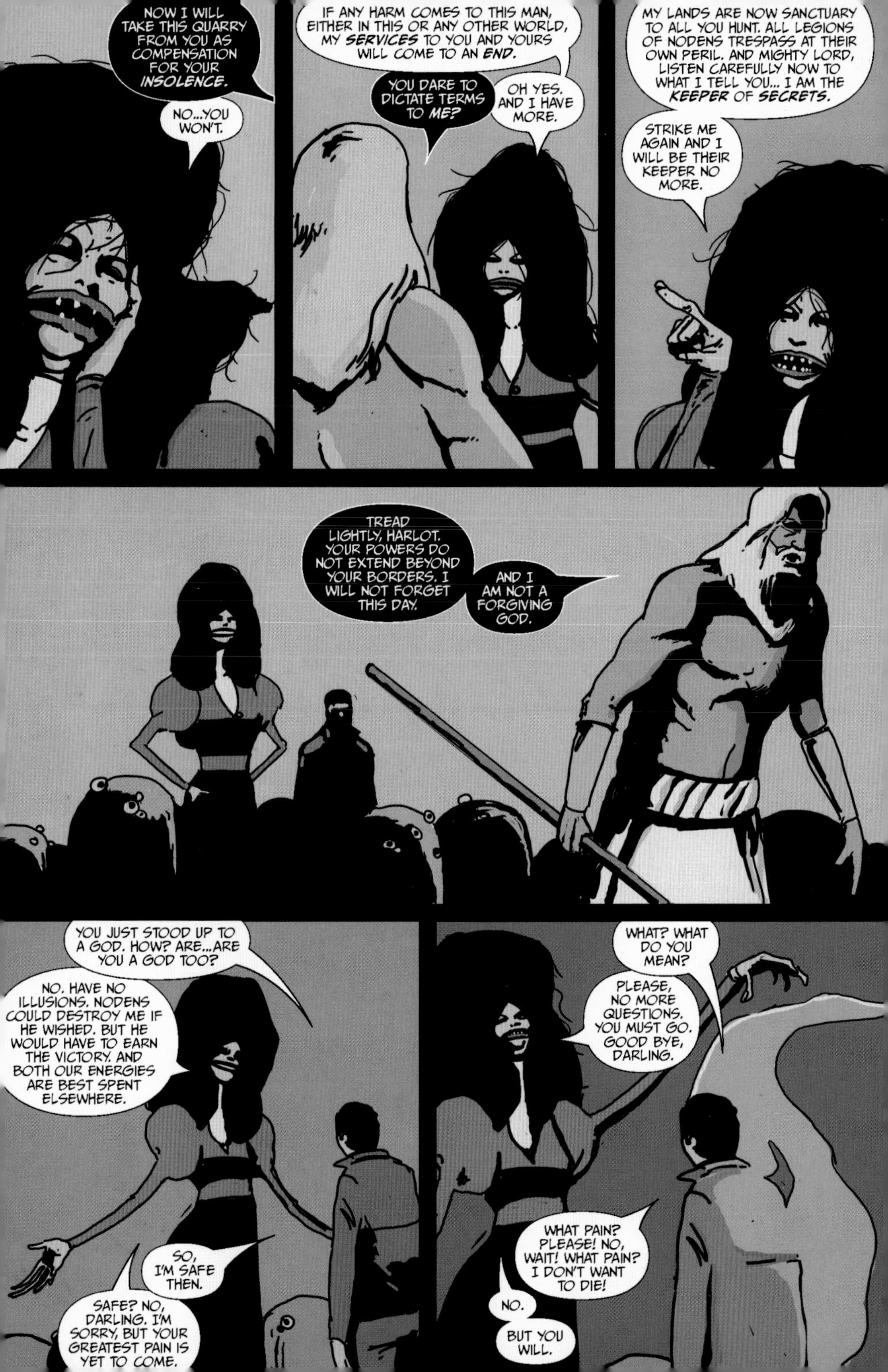
NOW I WILL TAKE THIS QUARRY FROM YOU AS COMPENSATION FOR YOUR INSOLENCE.
NO...YOU WON'T.
IF ANY HARM COMES TO THIS MAN, EITHER IN THIS OR ANY OTHER WORLD, MY SERVICES TO YOU AND YOURS WILL COME TO AN END.
YOU DARE TO DICTATE TERMS TO ME?
OH YES. AND I HAVE MORE.
MY LANDS ARE NOW SANCTUARY TO ALL YOU HUNT. ALL LEGIONS OF NODENS TRESPASS AT THEIR OWN PERIL. AND MIGHTY LORD, LISTEN CAREFULLY NOW TO WHAT I TELL YOU... I AM THE KEEPER OF SECRETS.
STRIKE ME AGAIN AND I WILL BE THEIR KEEPER NO MORE.
TREAD LIGHTLY, HARLOT. YOUR POWERS DO NOT EXTEND BEYOND YOUR BORDERS. I WILL NOT FORGET THIS DAY.
AND I AM NOT A FORGIVING GOD.
YOU JUST STOOD UP TO A GOD. HOW? ARE...ARE YOU A GOD TOO?
NO. HAVE NO ILLUSIONS. NODENS COULD DESTROY ME IF HE WISHED. BUT HE WOULD HAVE TO EARN THE VICTORY. AND BOTH OUR ENERGIES ARE BEST SPENT ELSEWHERE.
SO, I'M SAFE THEN.
SAFE? NO, DARLING. I'M SORRY, BUT YOUR GREATEST PAIN IS YET TO COME.
WHAT? WHAT DO YOU MEAN?
PLEASE, NO MORE QUESTIONS. YOU MUST GO. GOOD BYE, DARLING.
WHAT PAIN? PLEASE! NO, WAIT! WHAT PAIN? I DON'T WANT TO DIE!
NO.
BUT YOU WILL.

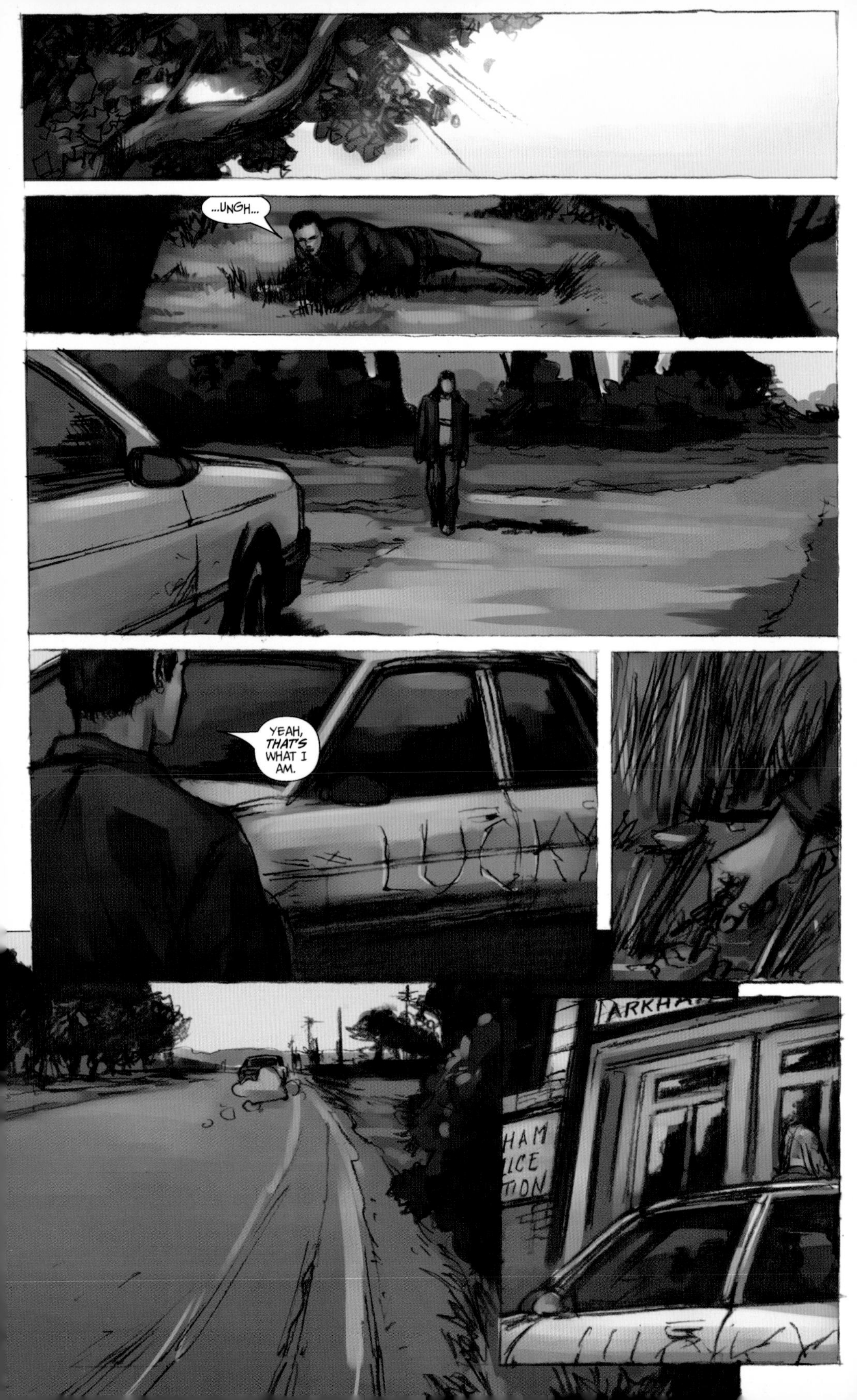

...UNGH...
YEAH, *THAT'S* WHAT I AM.

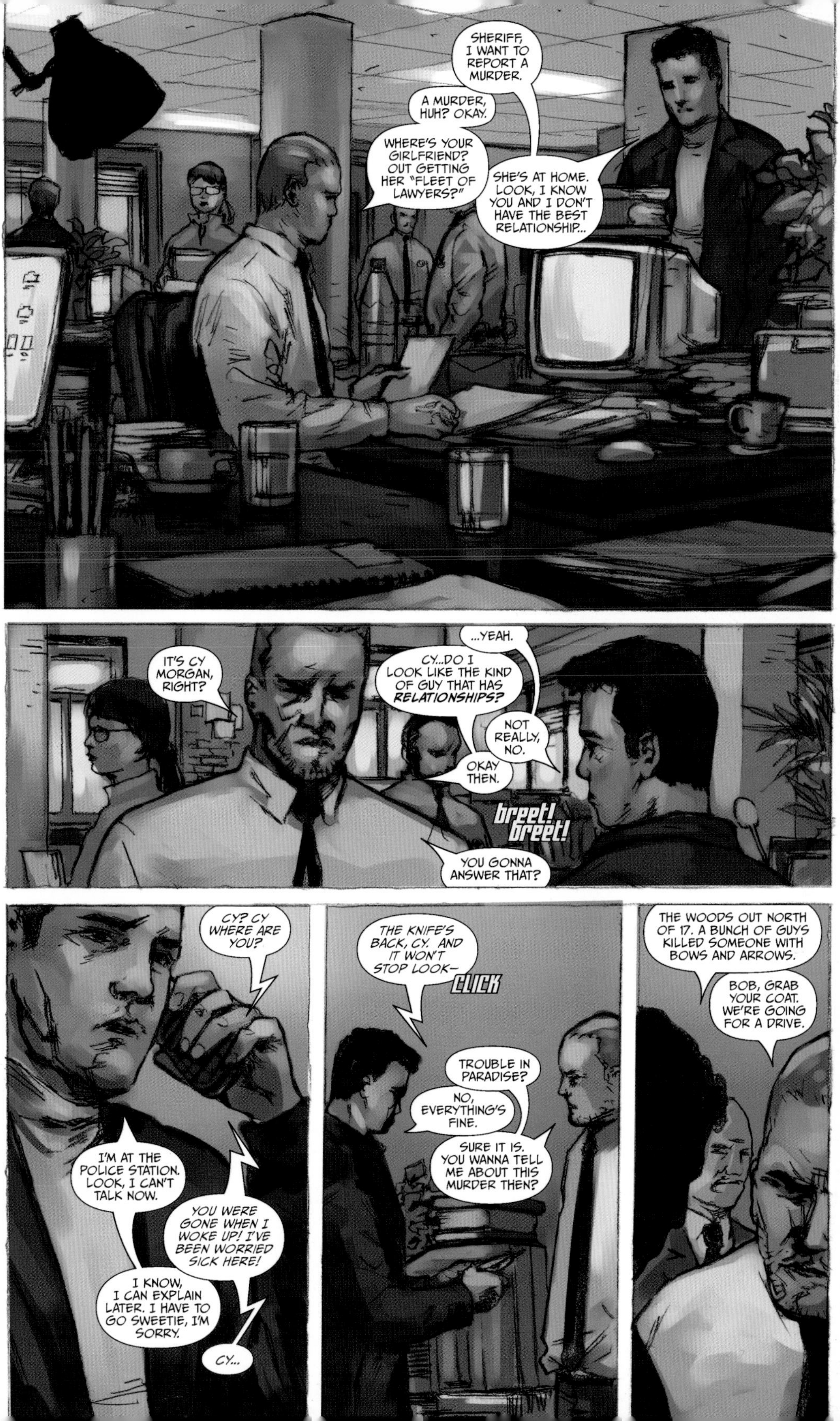
SHERIFF, I WANT TO REPORT A MURDER.
A MURDER, HUH? OKAY.
WHERE'S YOUR GIRLFRIEND? OUT GETTING HER "FLEET OF LAWYERS?"
SHE'S AT HOME. LOOK, I KNOW YOU AND I DON'T HAVE THE BEST RELATIONSHIP...
IT'S CY MORGAN, RIGHT?
...YEAH.
CY...DO I LOOK LIKE THE KIND OF GUY THAT HAS RELATIONSHIPS?
NOT REALLY, NO.
OKAY THEN.
breet! breet!
YOU GONNA ANSWER THAT?
CY? CY WHERE ARE YOU?
I'M AT THE POLICE STATION. LOOK, I CAN'T TALK NOW.
YOU WERE GONE WHEN I WOKE UP! I'VE BEEN WORRIED SICK HERE!
I KNOW, I CAN EXPLAIN LATER. I HAVE TO GO SWEETIE, I'M SORRY.
CY...
THE KNIFE'S BACK, CY. AND IT WON'T STOP LOOK—
CLICK
TROUBLE IN PARADISE?
NO, EVERYTHING'S FINE.
SURE IT IS. YOU WANNA TELL ME ABOUT THIS MURDER THEN?
THE WOODS OUT NORTH OF 17. A BUNCH OF GUYS KILLED SOMEONE WITH BOWS AND ARROWS.
BOB, GRAB YOUR COAT. WE'RE GOING FOR A DRIVE.

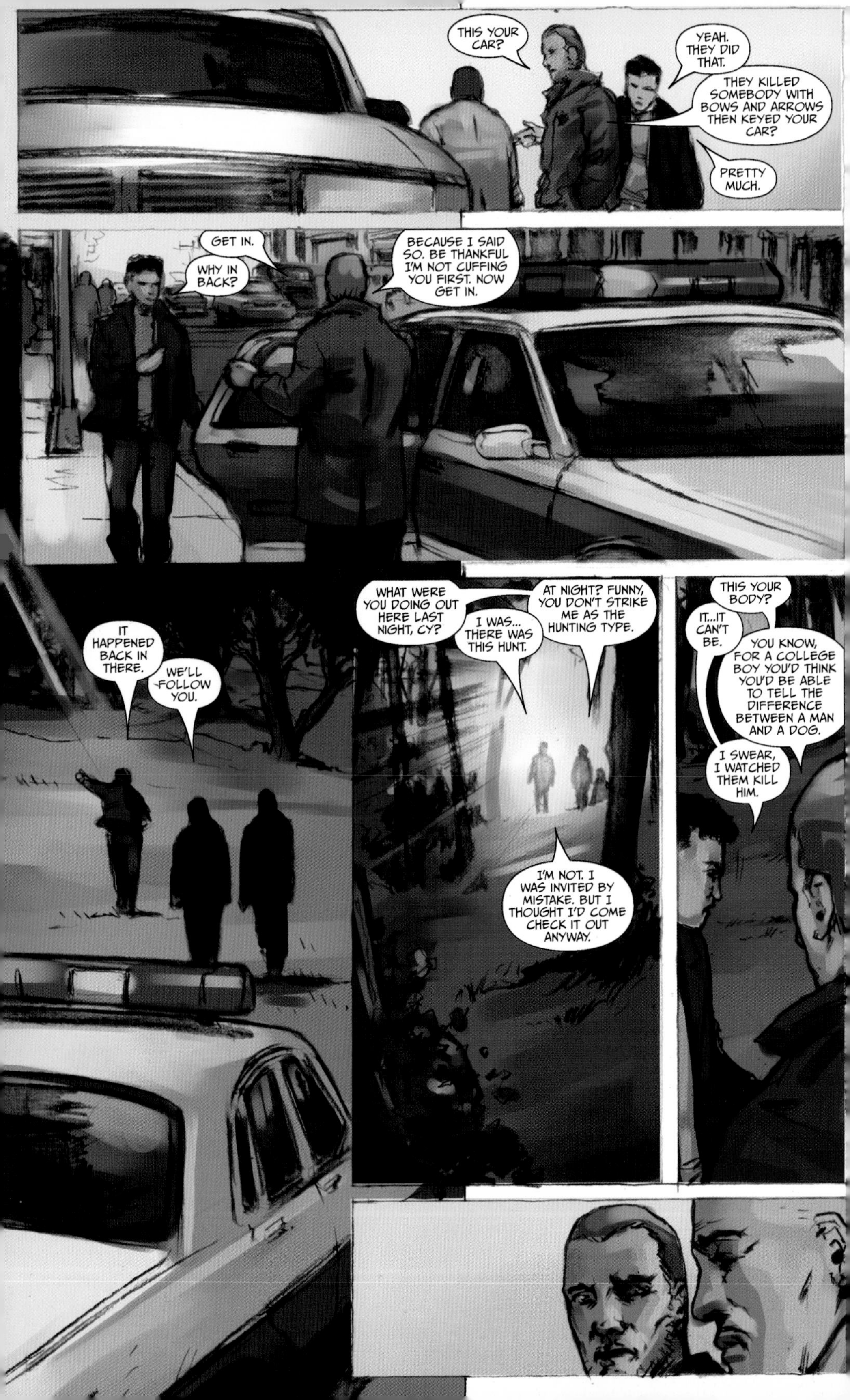
THIS YOUR CAR?
YEAH. THEY DID THAT.
THEY KILLED SOMEBODY WITH BOWS AND ARROWS THEN KEYED YOUR CAR?
PRETTY MUCH.
GET IN.
WHY IN BACK?
BECAUSE I SAID SO. BE THANKFUL I'M NOT CUFFING YOU FIRST. NOW GET IN.
IT HAPPENED BACK IN THERE.
WE'LL FOLLOW YOU.
WHAT WERE YOU DOING OUT HERE LAST NIGHT, CY?
I WAS... THERE WAS THIS HUNT.
AT NIGHT? FUNNY, YOU DON'T STRIKE ME AS THE HUNTING TYPE.
I'M NOT. I WAS INVITED BY MISTAKE. BUT I THOUGHT I'D COME CHECK IT OUT ANYWAY.
THIS YOUR BODY?
IT...IT CAN'T BE.
YOU KNOW, FOR A COLLEGE BOY YOU'D THINK YOU'D BE ABLE TO TELL THE DIFFERENCE BETWEEN A MAN AND A DOG.
I SWEAR, I WATCHED THEM KILL HIM.

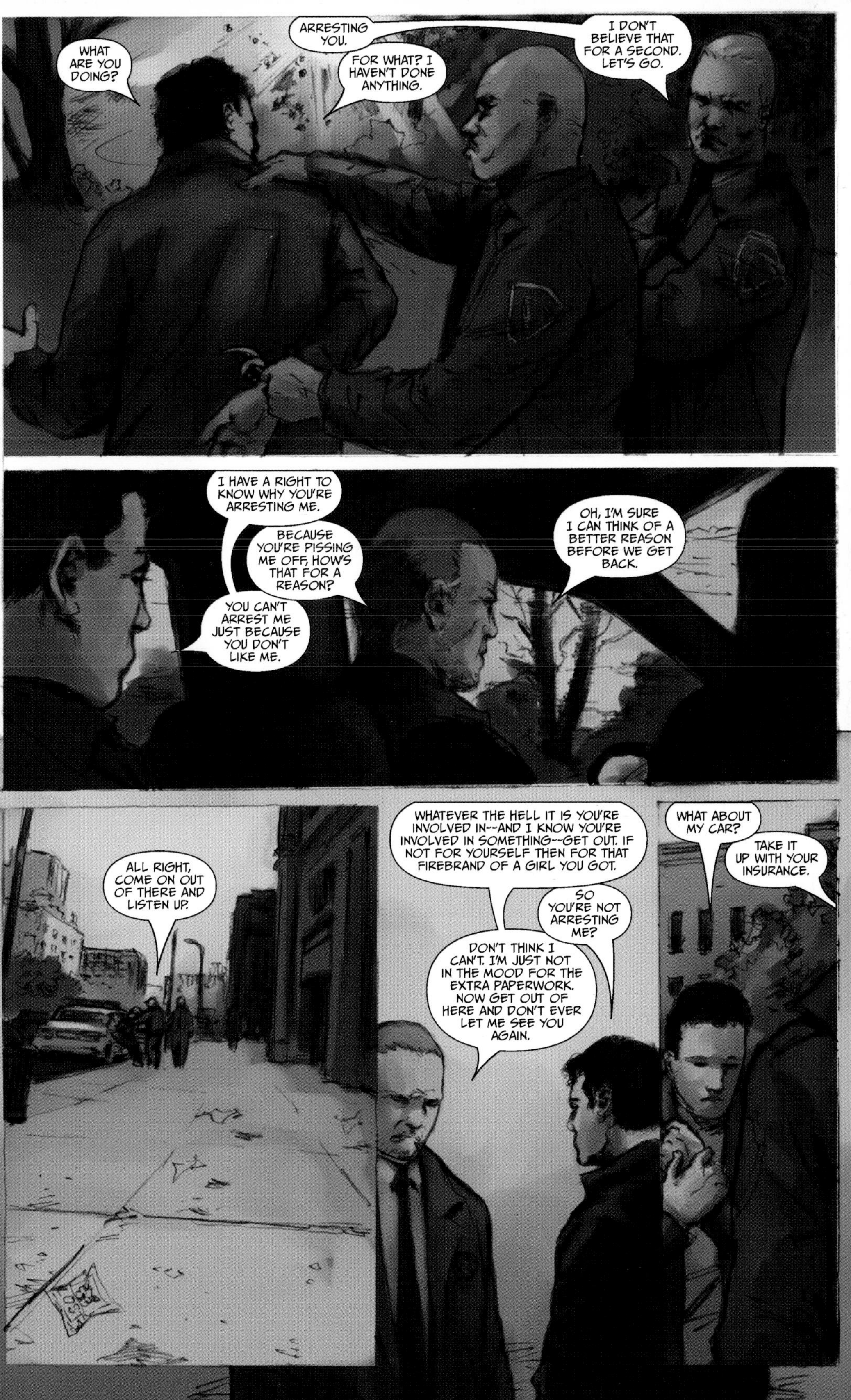
WHAT ARE YOU DOING?
ARRESTING YOU.
FOR WHAT? I HAVEN'T DONE ANYTHING.
I DON'T BELIEVE THAT FOR A SECOND. LET'S GO.
I HAVE A RIGHT TO KNOW WHY YOU'RE ARRESTING ME.
BECAUSE YOU'RE PISSING ME OFF, HOW'S THAT FOR A REASON?
YOU CAN'T ARREST ME JUST BECAUSE YOU DON'T LIKE ME.
OH, I'M SURE I CAN THINK OF A BETTER REASON BEFORE WE GET BACK.
ALL RIGHT, COME ON OUT OF THERE AND LISTEN UP.
WHATEVER THE HELL IT IS YOU'RE INVOLVED IN--AND I KNOW YOU'RE INVOLVED IN SOMETHING--GET OUT. IF NOT FOR YOURSELF THEN FOR THAT FIREBRAND OF A GIRL YOU GOT.
SO YOU'RE NOT ARRESTING ME?
DON'T THINK I CAN'T. I'M JUST NOT IN THE MOOD FOR THE EXTRA PAPERWORK. NOW GET OUT OF HERE AND DON'T EVER LET ME SEE YOU AGAIN.
WHAT ABOUT MY CAR?
TAKE IT UP WITH YOUR INSURANCE.

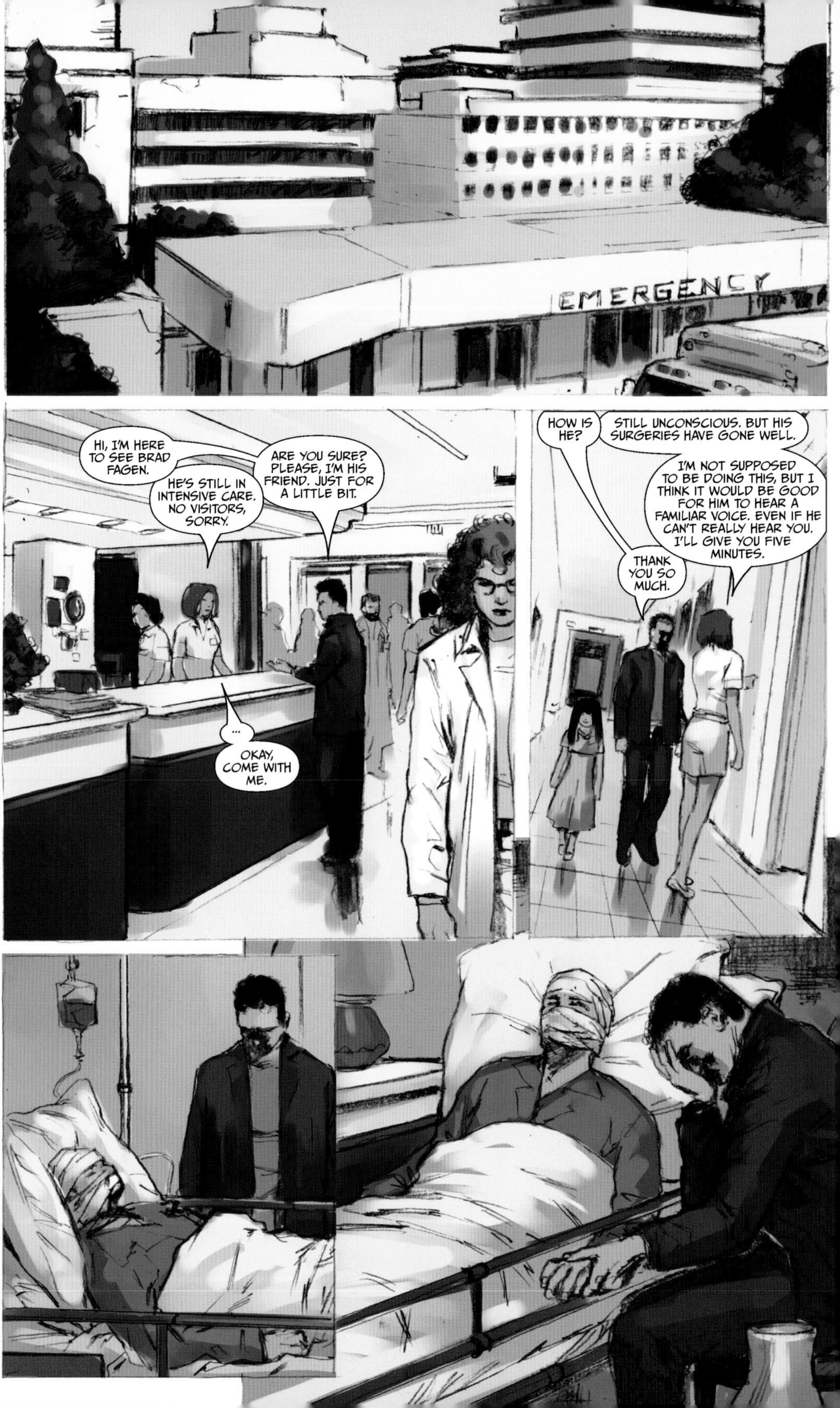
EMERGENCY
HI, I'M HERE TO SEE BRAD FAGEN.
HE'S STILL IN INTENSIVE CARE. NO VISITORS, SORRY.
ARE YOU SURE? PLEASE, I'M HIS FRIEND. JUST FOR A LITTLE BIT.
...
OKAY, COME WITH ME.
HOW IS HE?
STILL UNCONSCIOUS. BUT HIS SURGERIES HAVE GONE WELL.
I'M NOT SUPPOSED TO BE DOING THIS, BUT I THINK IT WOULD BE GOOD FOR HIM TO HEAR A FAMILIAR VOICE. EVEN IF HE CAN'T REALLY HEAR YOU. I'LL GIVE YOU FIVE MINUTES.
THANK YOU SO MUCH.

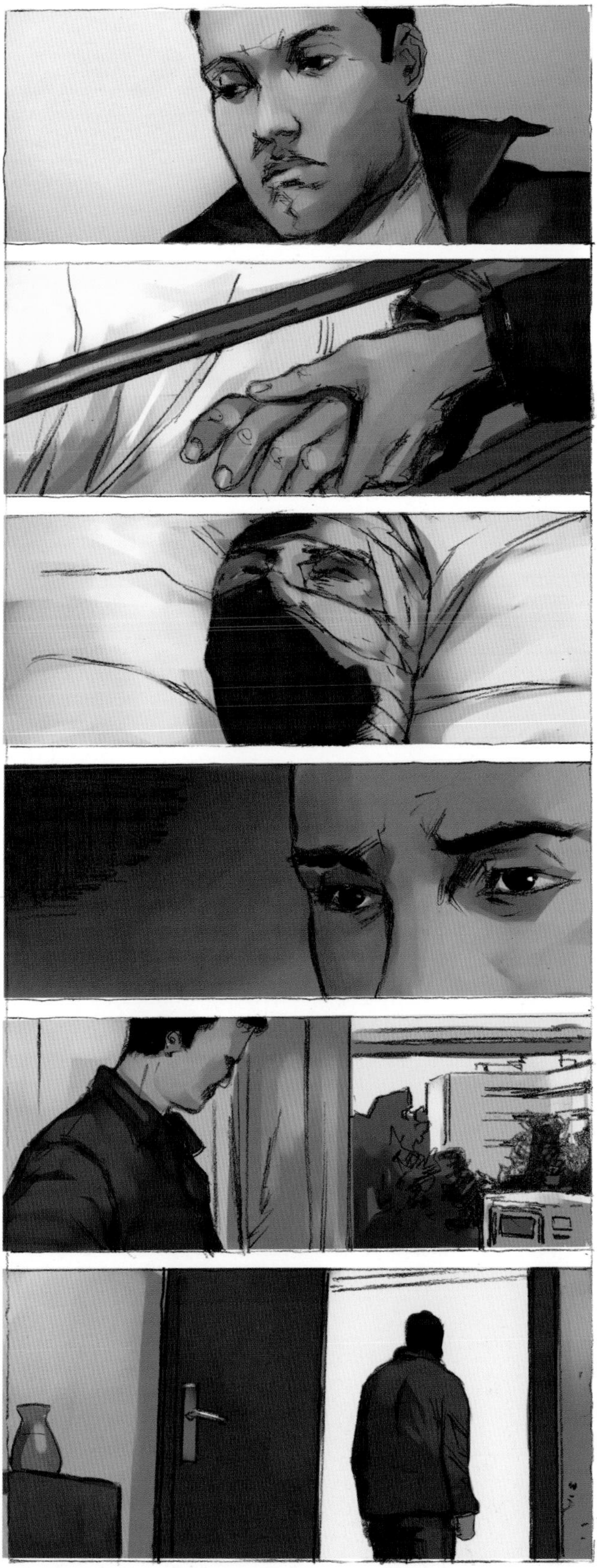

SO, I WENT AND DID SOMETHING REALLY STUPID THE OTHER DAY. I BOUGHT A GUN. I KNOW, ME AND GUNS GO TOGETHER ABOUT AS WELL AS ONIONS AND CHOCOLATE.

TOLD YOU IT WAS STUPID.

SOMEONE BROKE INTO OUR HOUSE THE SAME DAY AS...WELL, ANYWAY I GOT SCARED. I JUST WANTED TO KEEP JORDAN SAFE, YOU KNOW?

THE GUN DOESN'T DO ANY GOOD THOUGH, JUST SITS IN A SHOEBOX UNDER THE COUCH. I'M TOO SCARED TO TOUCH THE DAMN THING.

SUPPOSE THAT'S PROBABLY FOR THE BEST.

I CAN'T STOP IMAGINING JORDAN IN THAT BED INSTEAD OF YOU. GOD, IT MAKES ME SICK INSIDE. I CAN'T TAKE A CHANCE LIKE THAT WITH HER. NOT WITH HER.

SO I WANTED TO LET YOU KNOW THAT I'M DONE WITH ALL OF UNCLE WALT'S BIG BAG OF CRAZY. I KNOW, FAT BIT OF GOOD IT DOES YOU NOW, HUH?

FOR WHAT IT'S WORTH, I'M SORRY. I WON'T ASK FOR FORGIVENESS THAT I DON'T DESERVE. JUST...

JUST GET BETTER, OKAY.

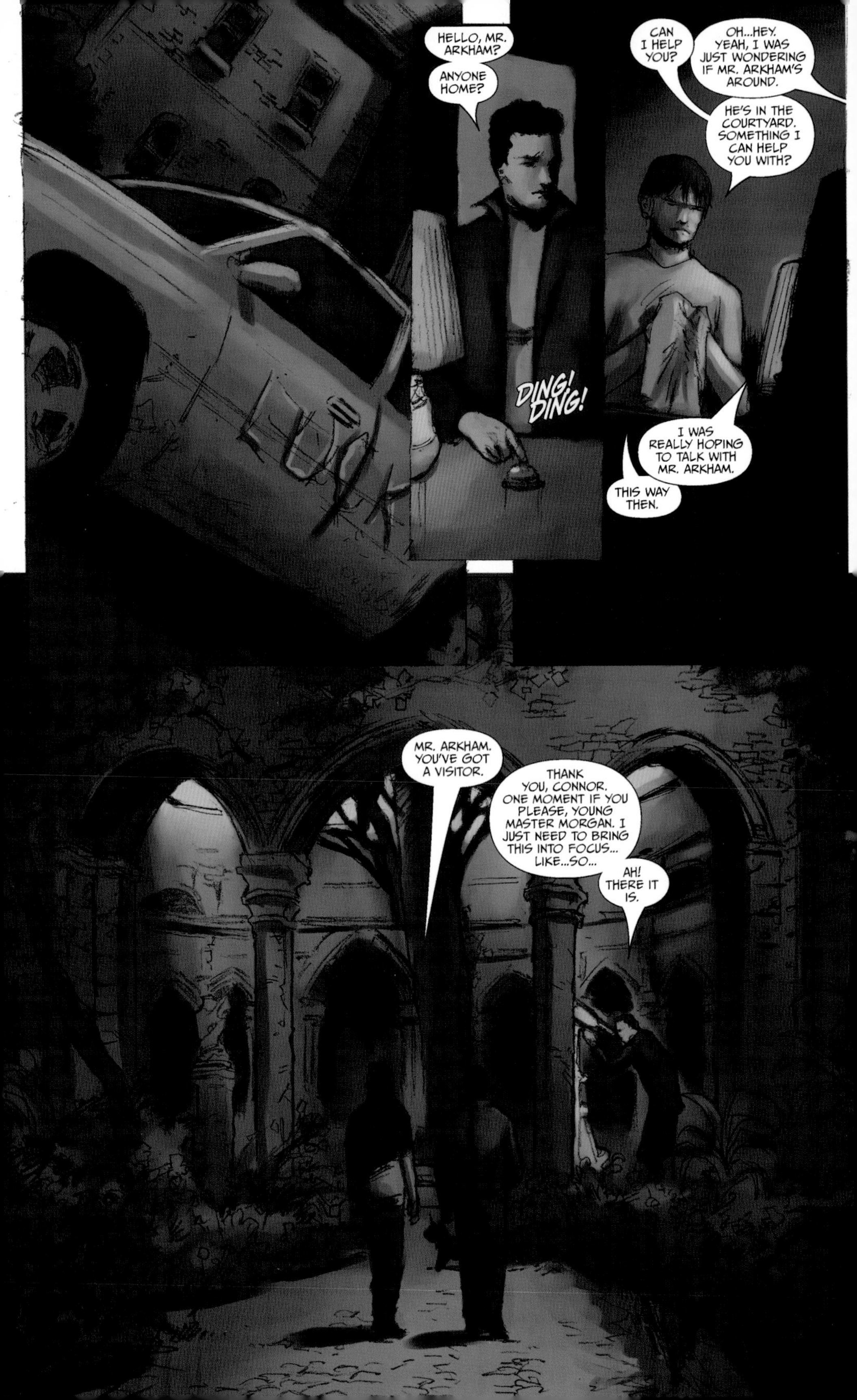
HELLO, MR. ARKHAM?
ANYONE HOME?
DING! DING!
CAN I HELP YOU?
OH...HEY. YEAH, I WAS JUST WONDERING IF MR. ARKHAM'S AROUND.
HE'S IN THE COURTYARD. SOMETHING I CAN HELP YOU WITH?
I WAS REALLY HOPING TO TALK WITH MR. ARKHAM.
THIS WAY THEN.
MR. ARKHAM. YOU'VE GOT A VISITOR.
THANK YOU, CONNOR. ONE MOMENT IF YOU PLEASE, YOUNG MASTER MORGAN. I JUST NEED TO BRING THIS INTO FOCUS... LIKE...SO...
AH! THERE IT IS.

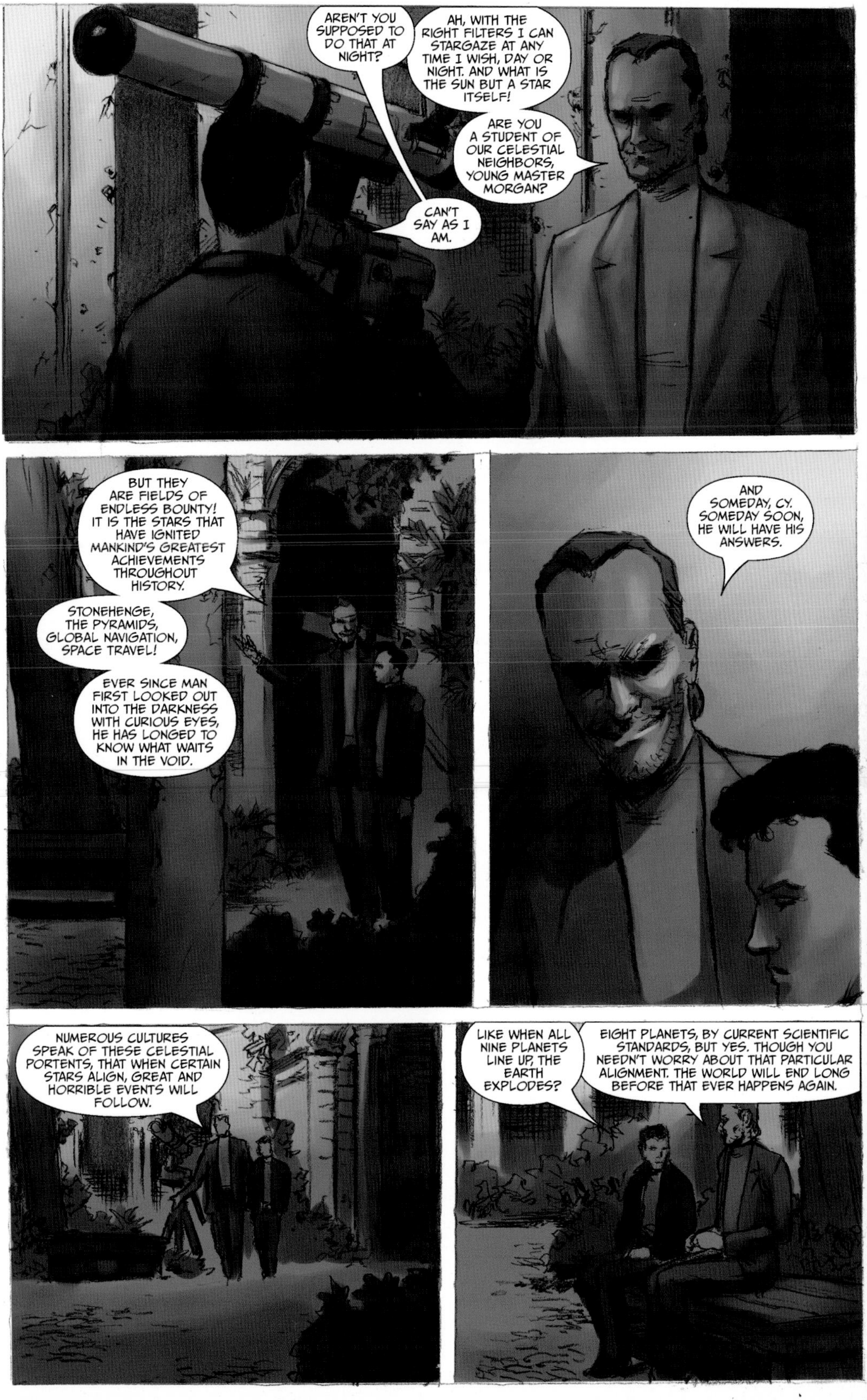
AREN'T YOU SUPPOSED TO DO THAT AT NIGHT?
AH, WITH THE RIGHT FILTERS I CAN STARGAZE AT ANY TIME I WISH, DAY OR NIGHT. AND WHAT IS THE SUN BUT A STAR ITSELF!
ARE YOU A STUDENT OF OUR CELESTIAL NEIGHBORS, YOUNG MASTER MORGAN?
CAN'T SAY AS I AM.
BUT THEY ARE FIELDS OF ENDLESS BOUNTY! IT IS THE STARS THAT HAVE IGNITED MANKIND'S GREATEST ACHIEVEMENTS THROUGHOUT HISTORY.
STONEHENGE, THE PYRAMIDS, GLOBAL NAVIGATION, SPACE TRAVEL!
EVER SINCE MAN FIRST LOOKED OUT INTO THE DARKNESS WITH CURIOUS EYES, HE HAS LONGED TO KNOW WHAT WAITS IN THE VOID.
AND SOMEDAY, CY. SOMEDAY SOON, HE WILL HAVE HIS ANSWERS.
NUMEROUS CULTURES SPEAK OF THESE CELESTIAL PORTENTS, THAT WHEN CERTAIN STARS ALIGN, GREAT AND HORRIBLE EVENTS WILL FOLLOW.
LIKE WHEN ALL NINE PLANETS LINE UP, THE EARTH EXPLODES?
EIGHT PLANETS, BY CURRENT SCIENTIFIC STANDARDS, BUT YES. THOUGH YOU NEEDN'T WORRY ABOUT THAT PARTICULAR ALIGNMENT. THE WORLD WILL END LONG BEFORE THAT EVER HAPPENS AGAIN.

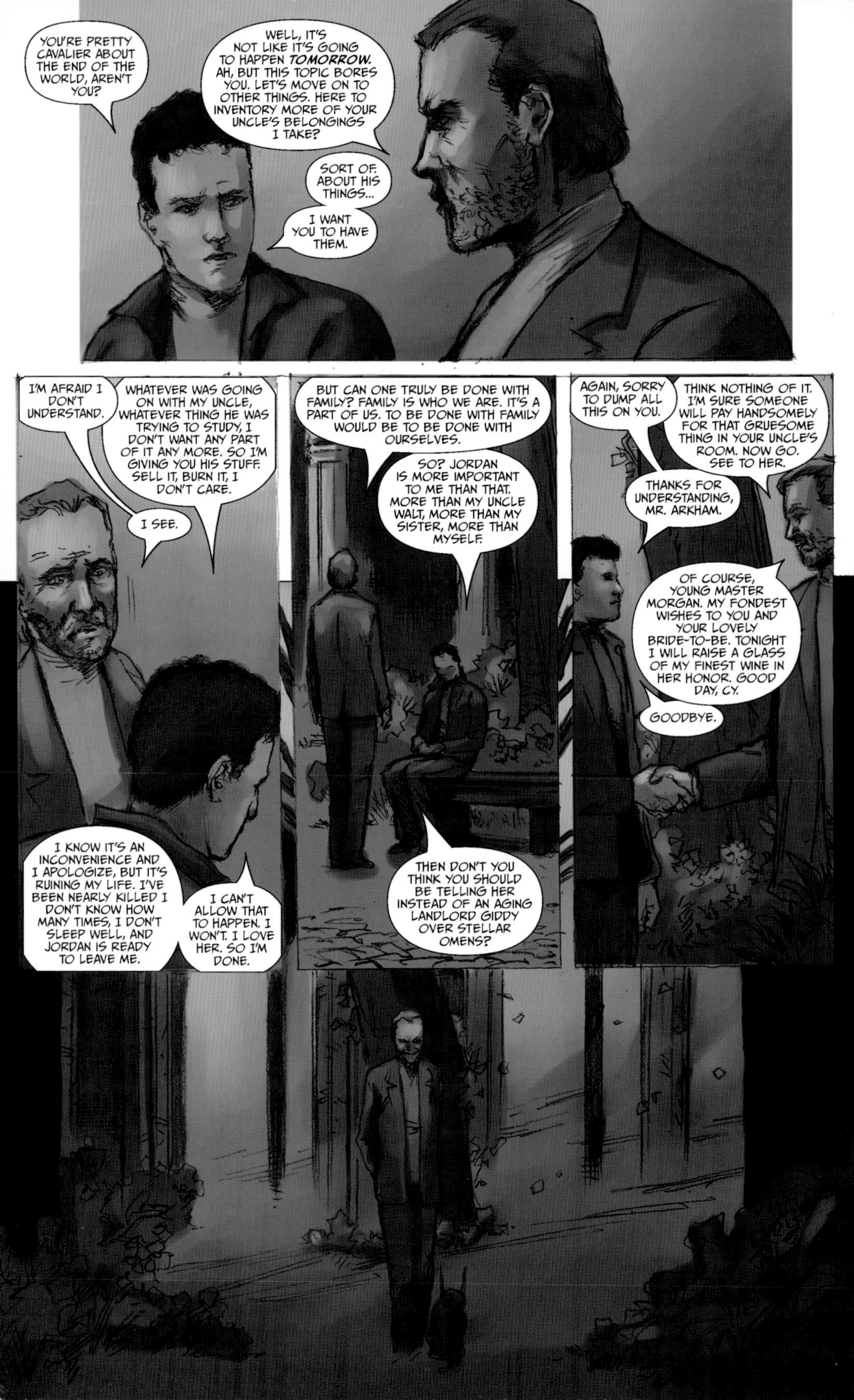
YOU'RE PRETTY CAVALIER ABOUT THE END OF THE WORLD, AREN'T YOU?
WELL, IT'S NOT LIKE IT'S GOING TO HAPPEN *TOMORROW.* AH, BUT THIS TOPIC BORES YOU. LET'S MOVE ON TO OTHER THINGS. HERE TO INVENTORY MORE OF YOUR UNCLE'S BELONGINGS I TAKE?
SORT OF. ABOUT HIS THINGS...
I WANT YOU TO HAVE THEM.
I'M AFRAID I DON'T UNDERSTAND.
WHATEVER WAS GOING ON WITH MY UNCLE, WHATEVER THING HE WAS TRYING TO STUDY, I DON'T WANT ANY PART OF IT ANY MORE. SO I'M GIVING YOU HIS STUFF. SELL IT, BURN IT, I DON'T CARE.
I SEE.
I KNOW IT'S AN INCONVENIENCE AND I APOLOGIZE, BUT IT'S RUINING MY LIFE. I'VE BEEN NEARLY KILLED I DON'T KNOW HOW MANY TIMES, I DON'T SLEEP WELL, AND JORDAN IS READY TO LEAVE ME.
I CAN'T ALLOW THAT TO HAPPEN. I WON'T. I LOVE HER. SO I'M DONE.
BUT CAN ONE TRULY BE DONE WITH FAMILY? FAMILY IS WHO WE ARE. IT'S A PART OF US. TO BE DONE WITH FAMILY WOULD BE TO BE DONE WITH OURSELVES.
SO? JORDAN IS MORE IMPORTANT TO ME THAN THAT. MORE THAN MY UNCLE WALT, MORE THAN MY SISTER, MORE THAN MYSELF.
THEN DON'T YOU THINK YOU SHOULD BE TELLING HER INSTEAD OF AN AGING LANDLORD GIDDY OVER STELLAR OMENS?
AGAIN, SORRY TO DUMP ALL THIS ON YOU.
THINK NOTHING OF IT. I'M SURE SOMEONE WILL PAY HANDSOMELY FOR THAT GRUESOME THING IN YOUR UNCLE'S ROOM. NOW GO. SEE TO HER.
THANKS FOR UNDERSTANDING, MR. ARKHAM.
OF COURSE, YOUNG MASTER MORGAN. MY FONDEST WISHES TO YOU AND YOUR LOVELY BRIDE-TO-BE. TONIGHT I WILL RAISE A GLASS OF MY FINEST WINE IN HER HONOR. GOOD DAY, CY.
GOODBYE.

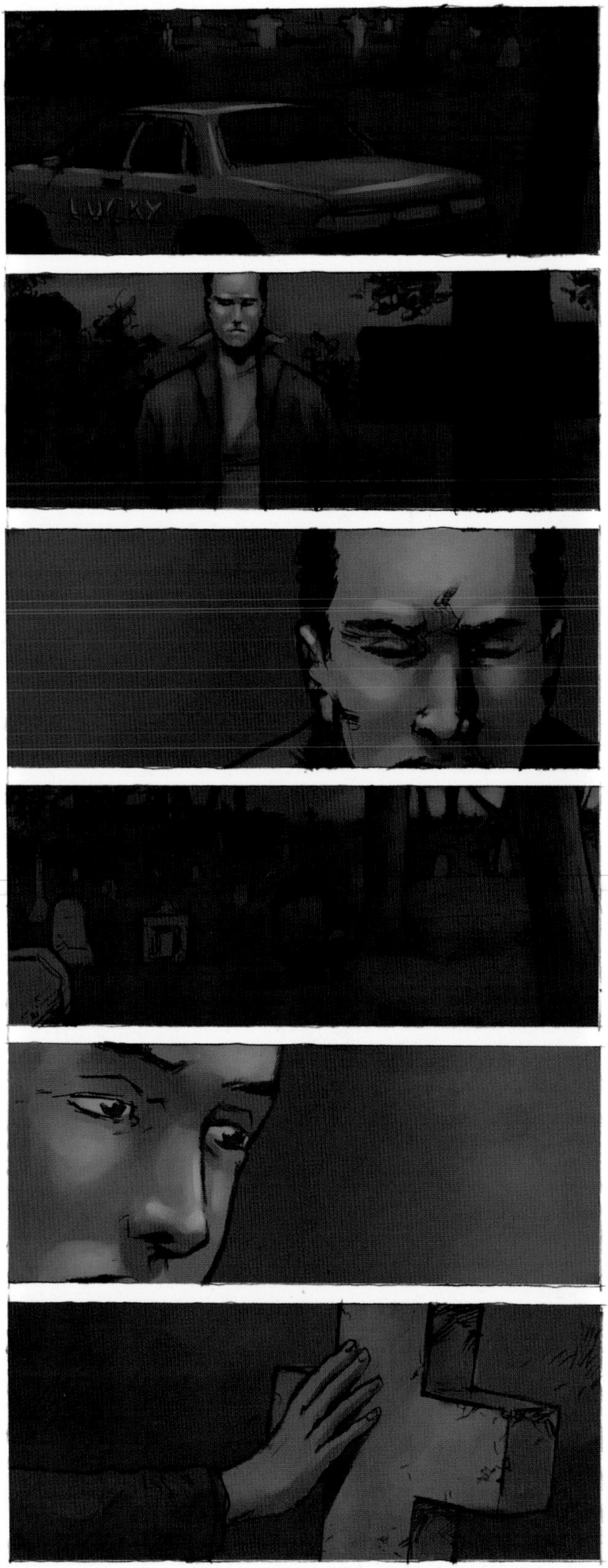

HEY, UNCLE WALT.

NOT REALLY SURE WHAT TO SAY. WHICH IS KIND OF ODD SINCE YOU WERE ALWAYS SO EASY TO TALK TO.

STILL HAVEN'T HEARD ANYTHING FROM SARAH. BUT YOU KNOW HOW SHE IS. SHE'LL CALL WHEN SHE'S READY TO, I GUESS. BUT DON'T WORRY ABOUT HER. SHE'LL DEAL. SIS IS A TOUGH COOKIE.

I MISS YOU. GOD, I MISS YOU LIKE CRAZY. YOUR SANTA CLAUS LAUGH, THE WAY YOU'D ALWAYS STROKE YOUR BEARD WHEN YOU WERE TRYING TO THINK...

I DON'T UNDERSTAND WHY YOU DID WHAT YOU DID. I TRIED TO, I REALLY DID BUT...

I CAN'T DO THIS. I KNOW I PROMISED YOU, BUT IT'S A PROMISE I JUST CAN'T KEEP. NOT IF IT MEANS LOSING JORDAN.

I'M SORRY UNCLE WALT, BUT I'M DONE.

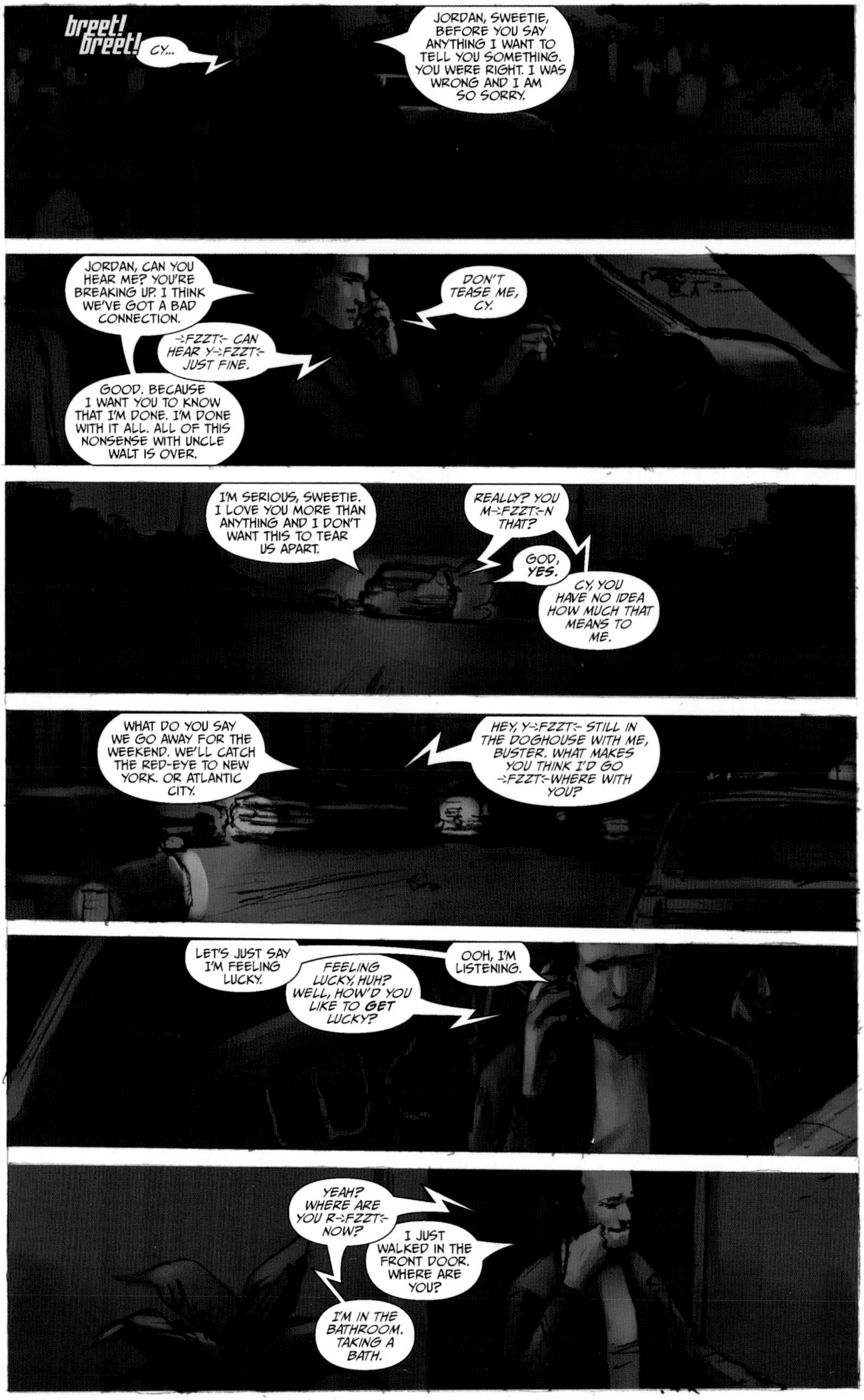
breet! breet!
CY...
JORDAN, SWEETIE, BEFORE YOU SAY ANYTHING I WANT TO TELL YOU SOMETHING. YOU WERE RIGHT. I WAS WRONG AND I AM SO SORRY.
JORDAN, CAN YOU HEAR ME? YOU'RE BREAKING UP. I THINK WE'VE GOT A BAD CONNECTION.
DON'T TEASE ME, CY.
-FZZT- CAN HEAR Y-FZZT- JUST FINE.
GOOD. BECAUSE I WANT YOU TO KNOW THAT I'M DONE. I'M DONE WITH IT ALL. ALL OF THIS NONSENSE WITH UNCLE WALT IS OVER.
I'M SERIOUS, SWEETIE. I LOVE YOU MORE THAN ANYTHING AND I DON'T WANT THIS TO TEAR US APART.
REALLY? YOU M-FZZT-N THAT?
GOD, YES.
CY, YOU HAVE NO IDEA HOW MUCH THAT MEANS TO ME.
WHAT DO YOU SAY WE GO AWAY FOR THE WEEKEND. WE'LL CATCH THE RED-EYE TO NEW YORK. OR ATLANTIC CITY.
HEY, Y-FZZT- STILL IN THE DOGHOUSE WITH ME, BUSTER. WHAT MAKES YOU THINK I'D GO -FZZT-WHERE WITH YOU?
LET'S JUST SAY I'M FEELING LUCKY.
OOH, I'M LISTENING.
FEELING LUCKY, HUH? WELL, HOW'D YOU LIKE TO GET LUCKY?
YEAH? WHERE ARE YOU R-FZZT- NOW?
I JUST WALKED IN THE FRONT DOOR. WHERE ARE YOU?
I'M IN THE BATHROOM. TAKING A BATH.

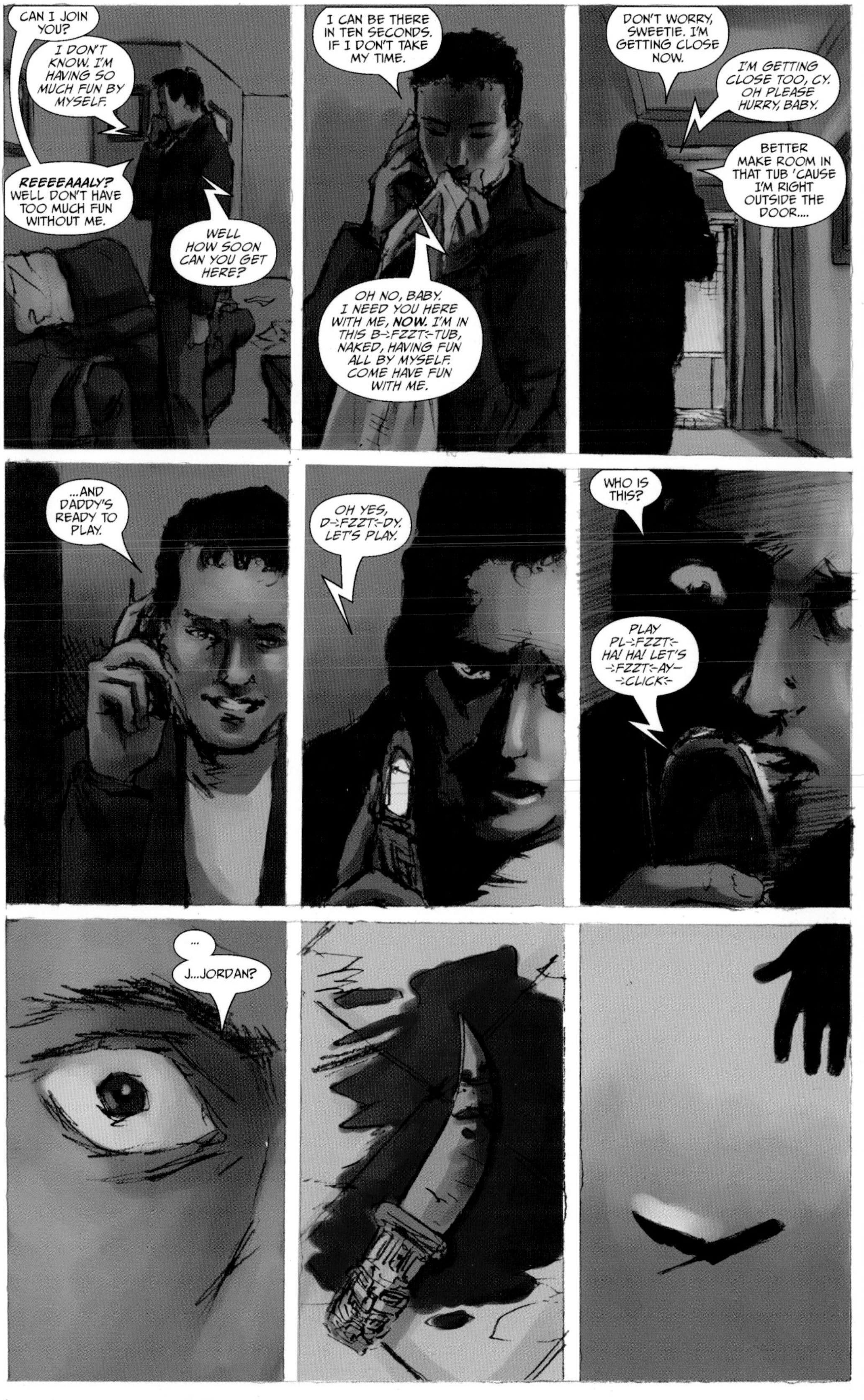
CAN I JOIN YOU?
I DON'T KNOW. I'M HAVING SO MUCH FUN BY MYSELF.
REEEEAAALY? WELL DON'T HAVE TOO MUCH FUN WITHOUT ME.
WELL HOW SOON CAN YOU GET HERE?
I CAN BE THERE IN TEN SECONDS. IF I DON'T TAKE MY TIME.
OH NO, BABY. I NEED YOU HERE WITH ME, NOW. I'M IN THIS B-›FZZT‹-TUB, NAKED, HAVING FUN ALL BY MYSELF. COME HAVE FUN WITH ME.
DON'T WORRY, SWEETIE. I'M GETTING CLOSE NOW.
I'M GETTING CLOSE TOO, CY. OH PLEASE HURRY, BABY.
BETTER MAKE ROOM IN THAT TUB 'CAUSE I'M RIGHT OUTSIDE THE DOOR....
...AND DADDY'S READY TO PLAY.
OH YES, D-›FZZT‹-DY. LET'S PLAY.
WHO IS THIS?
PLAY PL-›FZZT‹- HA! HA! LET'S -›FZZT‹-AY- -›CLICK‹-
...
J...JORDAN?

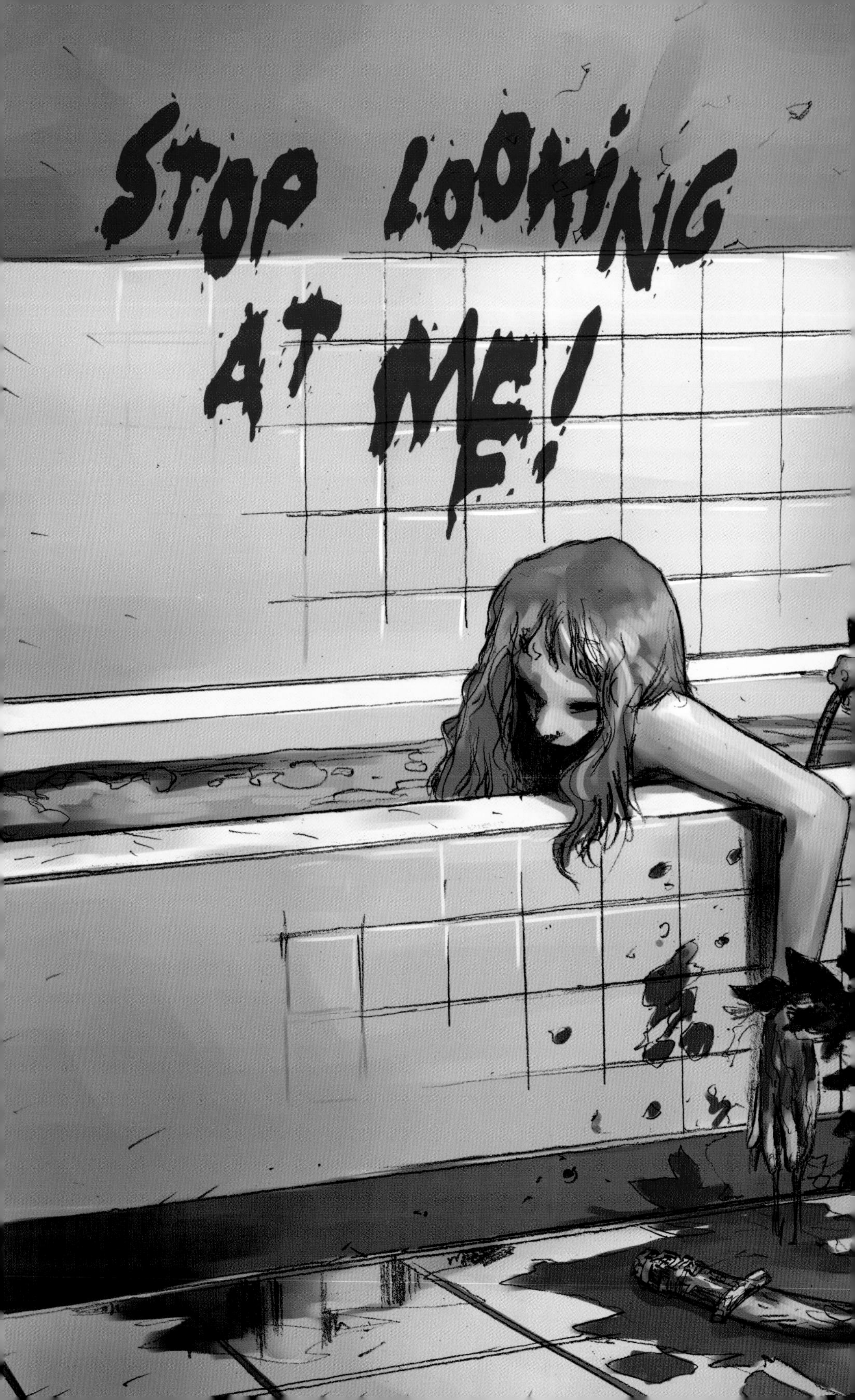
STOP LOOKING AT ME!

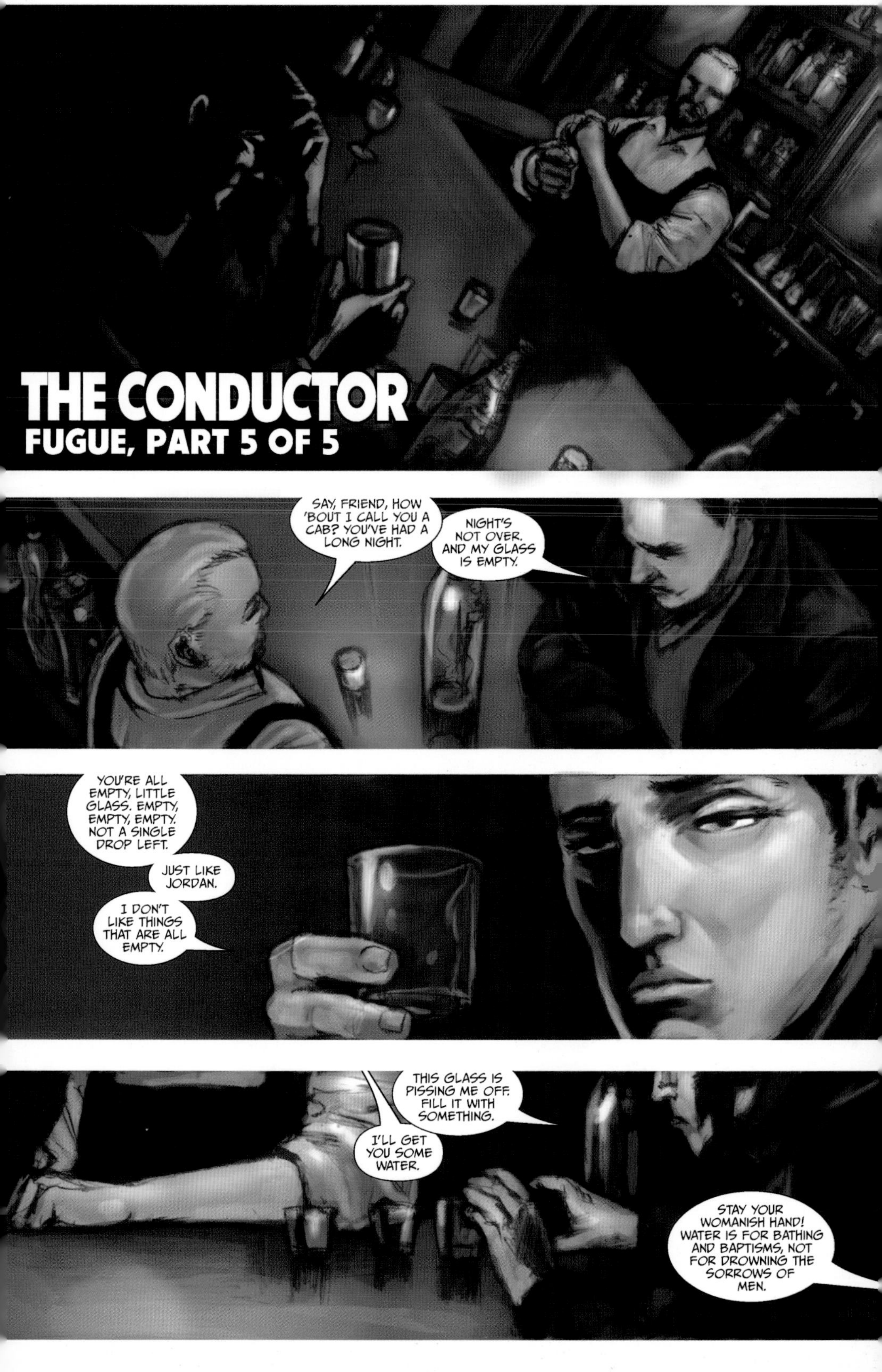
THE CONDUCTOR
FUGUE, PART 5 OF 5
SAY, FRIEND, HOW 'BOUT I CALL YOU A CAB? YOU'VE HAD A LONG NIGHT.
NIGHT'S NOT OVER. AND MY GLASS IS EMPTY.
YOU'RE ALL EMPTY, LITTLE GLASS. EMPTY, EMPTY, EMPTY. NOT A SINGLE DROP LEFT.
JUST LIKE JORDAN.
I DON'T LIKE THINGS THAT ARE ALL EMPTY.
THIS GLASS IS PISSING ME OFF. FILL IT WITH SOMETHING.
I'LL GET YOU SOME WATER.
STAY YOUR WOMANISH HAND! WATER IS FOR BATHING AND BAPTISMS, NOT FOR DROWNING THE SORROWS OF MEN.

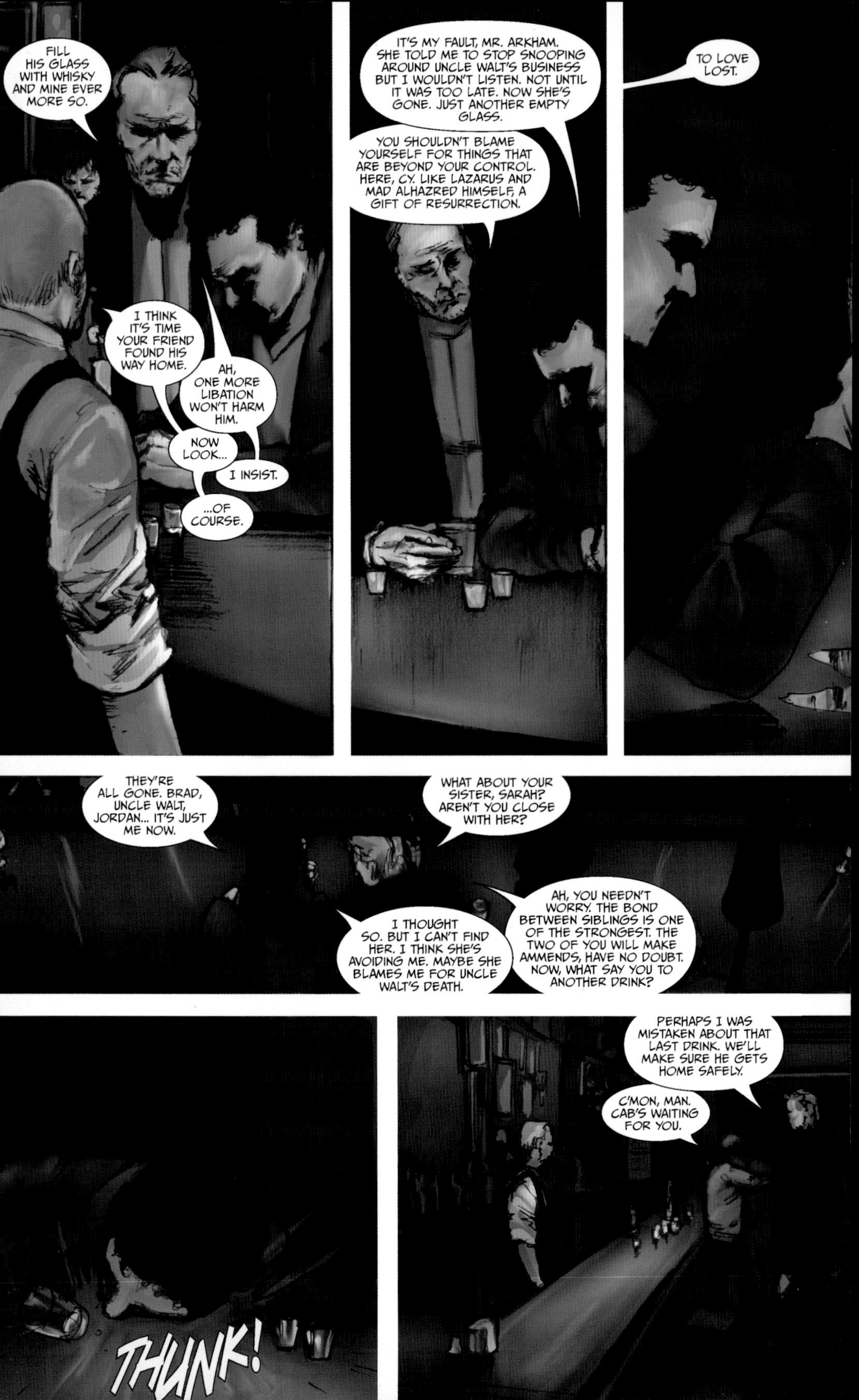
FILL HIS GLASS WITH WHISKY AND MINE EVER MORE SO.
I THINK IT'S TIME YOUR FRIEND FOUND HIS WAY HOME.
AH, ONE MORE LIBATION WON'T HARM HIM.
NOW LOOK...
I INSIST.
...OF COURSE.
IT'S MY FAULT, MR. ARKHAM. SHE TOLD ME TO STOP SNOOPING AROUND UNCLE WALT'S BUSINESS BUT I WOULDN'T LISTEN. NOT UNTIL IT WAS TOO LATE. NOW SHE'S GONE. JUST ANOTHER EMPTY GLASS.
YOU SHOULDN'T BLAME YOURSELF FOR THINGS THAT ARE BEYOND YOUR CONTROL. HERE, CY. LIKE LAZARUS AND MAD ALHAZRED HIMSELF, A GIFT OF RESURRECTION.
TO LOVE LOST.
THEY'RE ALL GONE. BRAD, UNCLE WALT, JORDAN... IT'S JUST ME NOW.
WHAT ABOUT YOUR SISTER, SARAH? AREN'T YOU CLOSE WITH HER?
I THOUGHT SO. BUT I CAN'T FIND HER. I THINK SHE'S AVOIDING ME. MAYBE SHE BLAMES ME FOR UNCLE WALT'S DEATH.
AH, YOU NEEDN'T WORRY. THE BOND BETWEEN SIBLINGS IS ONE OF THE STRONGEST. THE TWO OF YOU WILL MAKE AMMENDS, HAVE NO DOUBT. NOW, WHAT SAY YOU TO ANOTHER DRINK?
THUNK!
PERHAPS I WAS MISTAKEN ABOUT THAT LAST DRINK. WE'LL MAKE SURE HE GETS HOME SAFELY.
C'MON, MAN. CAB'S WAITING FOR YOU.

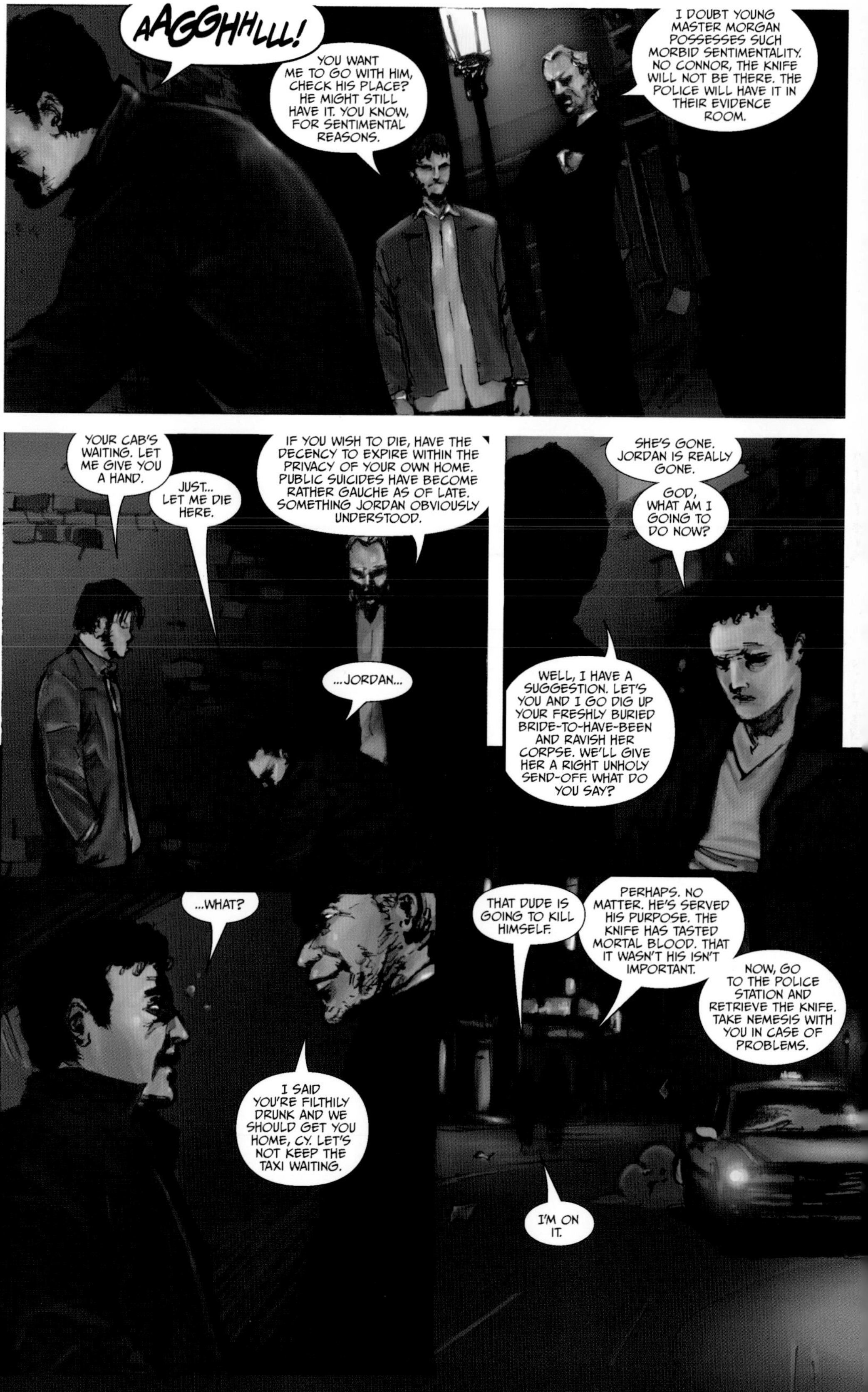
AAGGHHLLL!
YOU WANT ME TO GO WITH HIM, CHECK HIS PLACE? HE MIGHT STILL HAVE IT. YOU KNOW, FOR SENTIMENTAL REASONS.
I DOUBT YOUNG MASTER MORGAN POSSESSES SUCH MORBID SENTIMENTALITY. NO CONNOR, THE KNIFE WILL NOT BE THERE. THE POLICE WILL HAVE IT IN THEIR EVIDENCE ROOM.
YOUR CAB'S WAITING. LET ME GIVE YOU A HAND.
JUST... LET ME DIE HERE.
IF YOU WISH TO DIE, HAVE THE DECENCY TO EXPIRE WITHIN THE PRIVACY OF YOUR OWN HOME. PUBLIC SUICIDES HAVE BECOME RATHER GAUCHE AS OF LATE. SOMETHING JORDAN OBVIOUSLY UNDERSTOOD.
...JORDAN...
SHE'S GONE. JORDAN IS REALLY GONE.
GOD, WHAT AM I GOING TO DO NOW?
WELL, I HAVE A SUGGESTION. LET'S YOU AND I GO DIG UP YOUR FRESHLY BURIED BRIDE-TO-HAVE-BEEN AND RAVISH HER CORPSE. WE'LL GIVE HER A RIGHT UNHOLY SEND-OFF. WHAT DO YOU SAY?
...WHAT?
I SAID YOU'RE FILTHILY DRUNK AND WE SHOULD GET YOU HOME, CY. LET'S NOT KEEP THE TAXI WAITING.
THAT DUDE IS GOING TO KILL HIMSELF.
PERHAPS. NO MATTER. HE'S SERVED HIS PURPOSE. THE KNIFE HAS TASTED MORTAL BLOOD. THAT IT WASN'T HIS ISN'T IMPORTANT.
NOW, GO TO THE POLICE STATION AND RETRIEVE THE KNIFE. TAKE NEMESIS WITH YOU IN CASE OF PROBLEMS.
I'M ON IT.

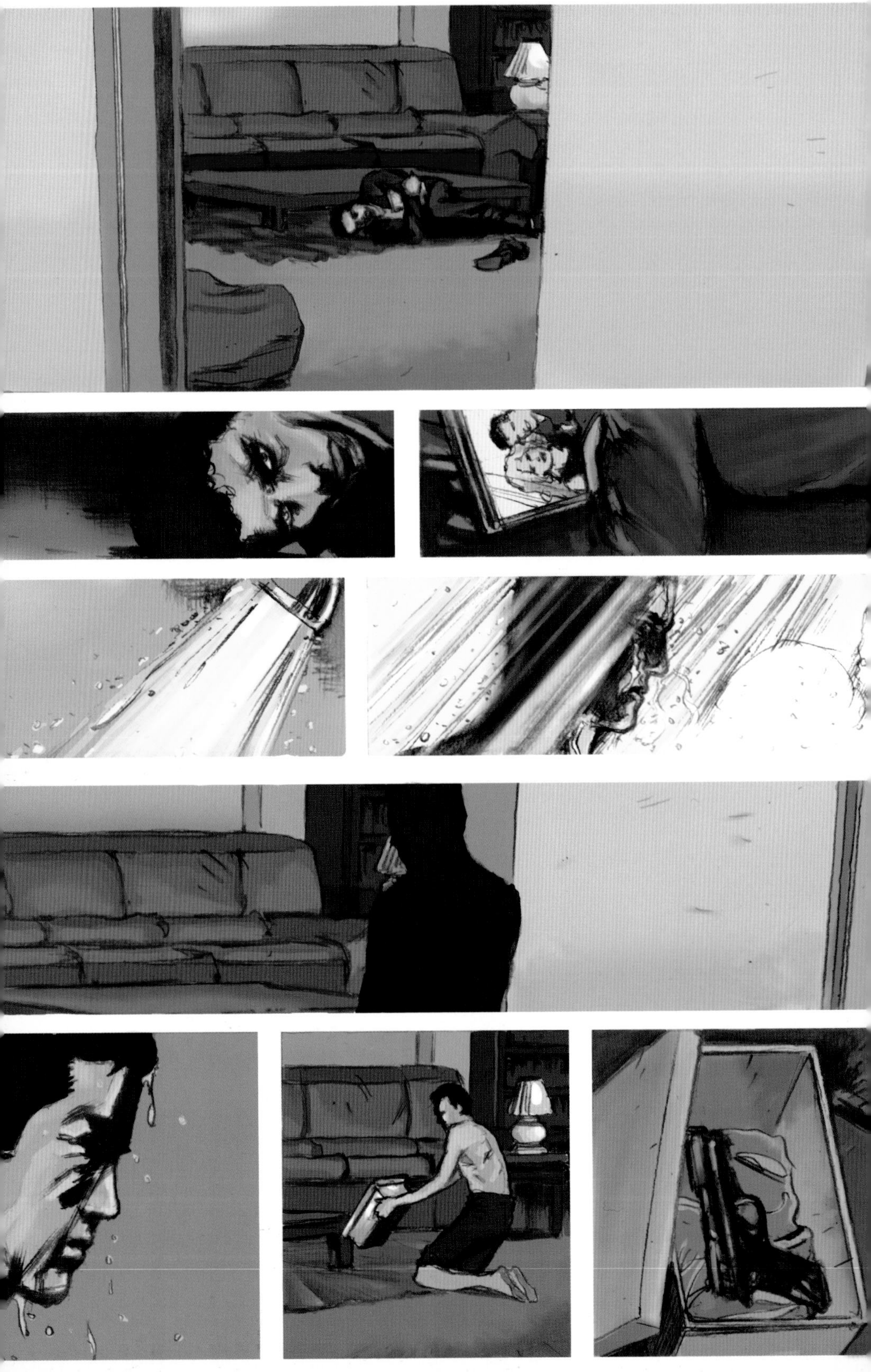

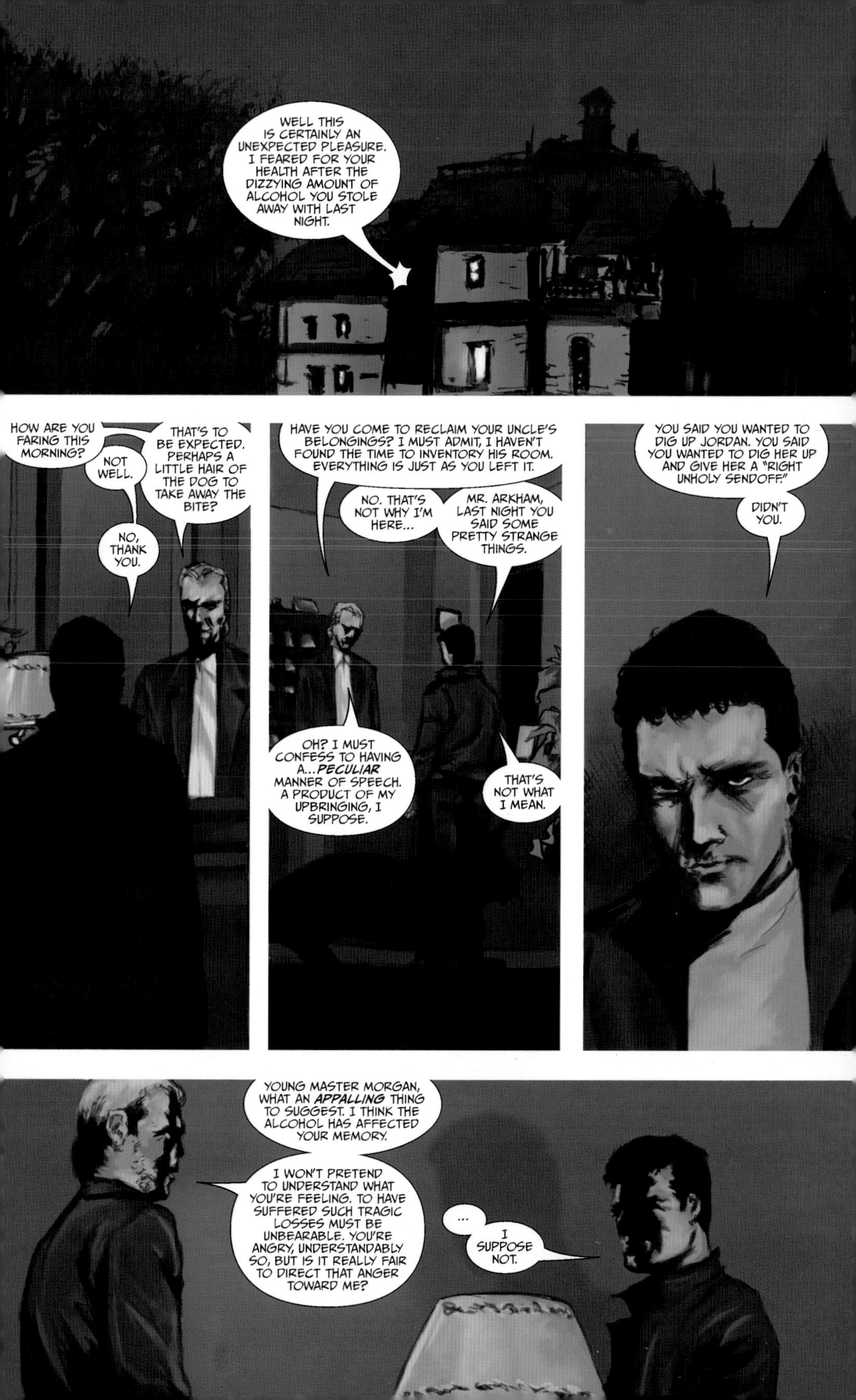
WELL THIS IS CERTAINLY AN UNEXPECTED PLEASURE. I FEARED FOR YOUR HEALTH AFTER THE DIZZYING AMOUNT OF ALCOHOL YOU STOLE AWAY WITH LAST NIGHT.
HOW ARE YOU FARING THIS MORNING?
NOT WELL.
THAT'S TO BE EXPECTED. PERHAPS A LITTLE HAIR OF THE DOG TO TAKE AWAY THE BITE?
NO, THANK YOU.
HAVE YOU COME TO RECLAIM YOUR UNCLE'S BELONGINGS? I MUST ADMIT, I HAVEN'T FOUND THE TIME TO INVENTORY HIS ROOM. EVERYTHING IS JUST AS YOU LEFT IT.
NO. THAT'S NOT WHY I'M HERE...
MR. ARKHAM, LAST NIGHT YOU SAID SOME PRETTY STRANGE THINGS.
OH? I MUST CONFESS TO HAVING A...*PECULIAR* MANNER OF SPEECH. A PRODUCT OF MY UPBRINGING, I SUPPOSE.
THAT'S NOT WHAT I MEAN.
YOU SAID YOU WANTED TO DIG UP JORDAN. YOU SAID YOU WANTED TO DIG HER UP AND GIVE HER A "RIGHT UNHOLY SENDOFF."
DIDN'T YOU.
YOUNG MASTER MORGAN, WHAT AN *APPALLING* THING TO SUGGEST. I THINK THE ALCOHOL HAS AFFECTED YOUR MEMORY.
I WON'T PRETEND TO UNDERSTAND WHAT YOU'RE FEELING. TO HAVE SUFFERED SUCH TRAGIC LOSSES MUST BE UNBEARABLE. YOU'RE ANGRY, UNDERSTANDABLY SO, BUT IS IT REALLY FAIR TO DIRECT THAT ANGER TOWARD ME?
...
I SUPPOSE NOT.

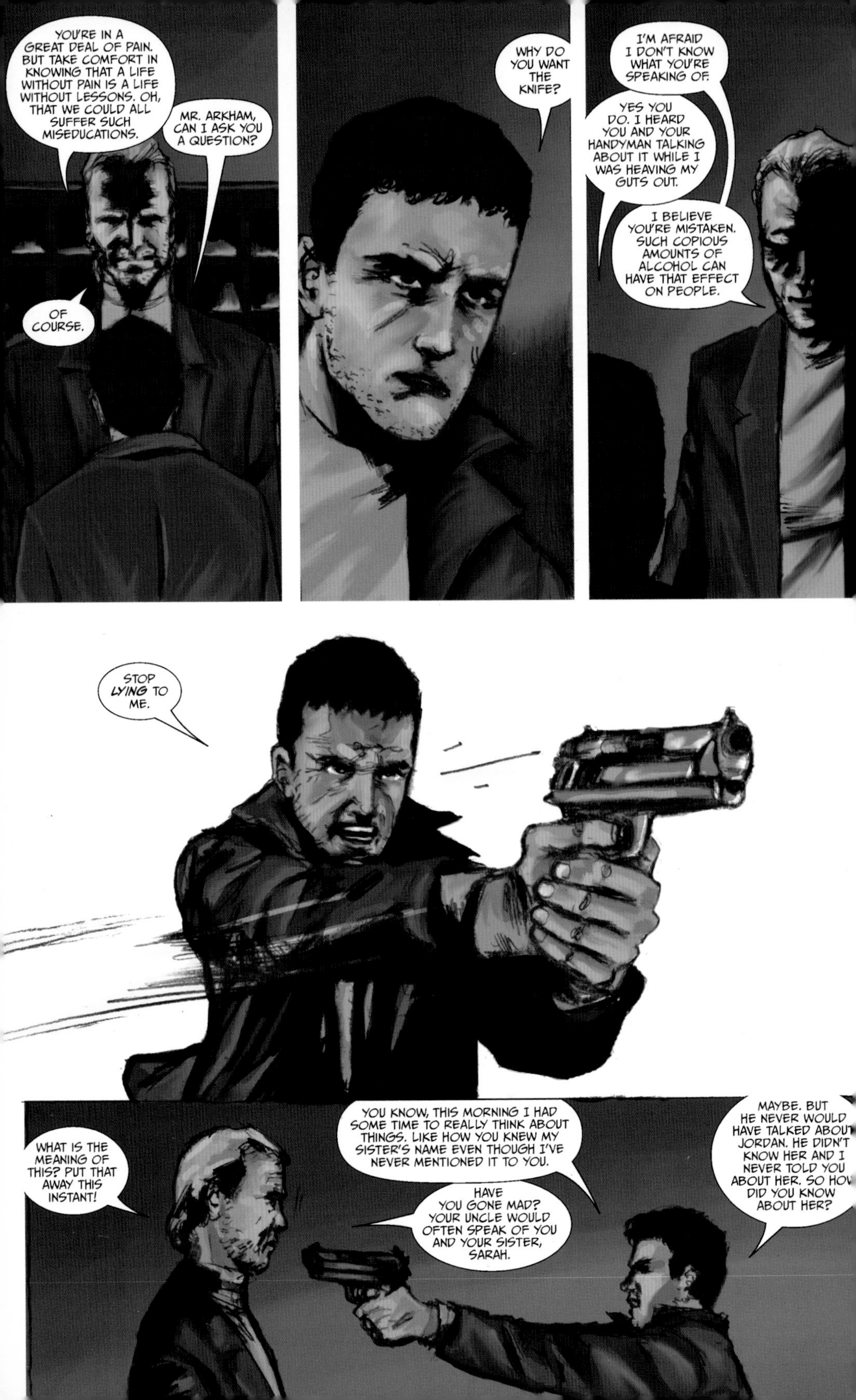
YOU'RE IN A GREAT DEAL OF PAIN. BUT TAKE COMFORT IN KNOWING THAT A LIFE WITHOUT PAIN IS A LIFE WITHOUT LESSONS. OH, THAT WE COULD ALL SUFFER SUCH MISEDUCATIONS.
MR. ARKHAM, CAN I ASK YOU A QUESTION?
OF COURSE.
WHY DO YOU WANT THE KNIFE?
I'M AFRAID I DON'T KNOW WHAT YOU'RE SPEAKING OF.
YES YOU DO. I HEARD YOU AND YOUR HANDYMAN TALKING ABOUT IT WHILE I WAS HEAVING MY GUTS OUT.
I BELIEVE YOU'RE MISTAKEN. SUCH COPIOUS AMOUNTS OF ALCOHOL CAN HAVE THAT EFFECT ON PEOPLE.
STOP *LYING* TO ME.
WHAT IS THE MEANING OF THIS? PUT THAT AWAY THIS INSTANT!
YOU KNOW, THIS MORNING I HAD SOME TIME TO REALLY THINK ABOUT THINGS. LIKE HOW YOU KNEW MY SISTER'S NAME EVEN THOUGH I'VE NEVER MENTIONED IT TO YOU.
HAVE YOU GONE MAD? YOUR UNCLE WOULD OFTEN SPEAK OF YOU AND YOUR SISTER, SARAH.
MAYBE. BUT HE NEVER WOULD HAVE TALKED ABOUT JORDAN. HE DIDN'T KNOW HER AND I NEVER TOLD YOU ABOUT HER. SO HOW DID YOU KNOW ABOUT HER?

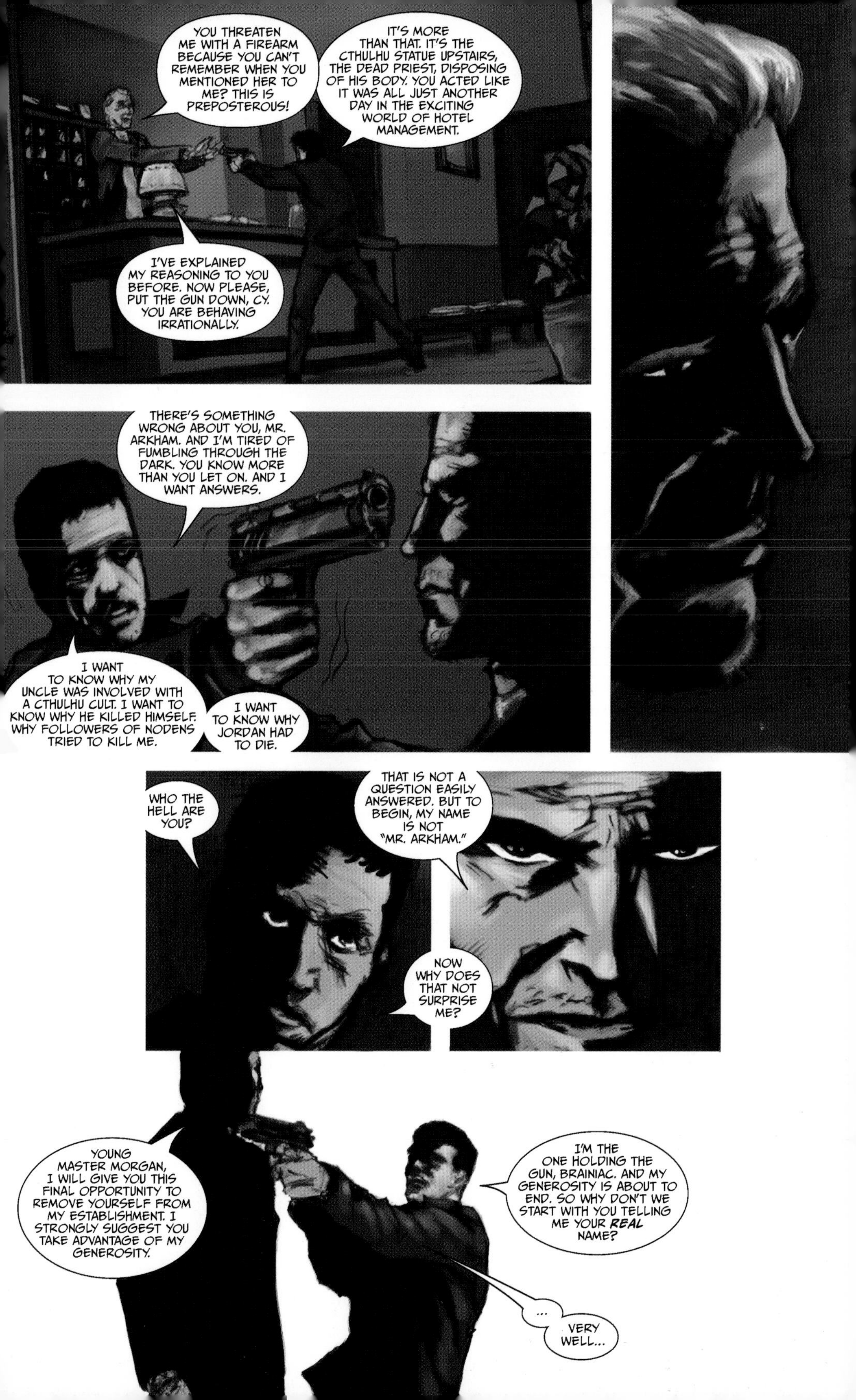
YOU THREATEN ME WITH A FIREARM BECAUSE YOU CAN'T REMEMBER WHEN YOU MENTIONED HER TO ME? THIS IS PREPOSTEROUS!
IT'S MORE THAN THAT. IT'S THE CTHULHU STATUE UPSTAIRS, THE DEAD PRIEST, DISPOSING OF HIS BODY. YOU ACTED LIKE IT WAS ALL JUST ANOTHER DAY IN THE EXCITING WORLD OF HOTEL MANAGEMENT.
I'VE EXPLAINED MY REASONING TO YOU BEFORE. NOW PLEASE, PUT THE GUN DOWN, CY. YOU ARE BEHAVING IRRATIONALLY.
THERE'S SOMETHING WRONG ABOUT YOU, MR. ARKHAM. AND I'M TIRED OF FUMBLING THROUGH THE DARK. YOU KNOW MORE THAN YOU LET ON. AND I WANT ANSWERS.
I WANT TO KNOW WHY MY UNCLE WAS INVOLVED WITH A CTHULHU CULT. I WANT TO KNOW WHY HE KILLED HIMSELF. WHY FOLLOWERS OF NODENS TRIED TO KILL ME.
I WANT TO KNOW WHY JORDAN HAD TO DIE.
WHO THE HELL ARE YOU?
THAT IS NOT A QUESTION EASILY ANSWERED. BUT TO BEGIN, MY NAME IS NOT "MR. ARKHAM."
NOW WHY DOES THAT NOT SURPRISE ME?
YOUNG MASTER MORGAN, I WILL GIVE YOU THIS FINAL OPPORTUNITY TO REMOVE YOURSELF FROM MY ESTABLISHMENT. I STRONGLY SUGGEST YOU TAKE ADVANTAGE OF MY GENEROSITY.
I'M THE ONE HOLDING THE GUN, BRAINIAC. AND MY GENEROSITY IS ABOUT TO END. SO WHY DON'T WE START WITH YOU TELLING ME YOUR REAL NAME?
...
VERY WELL...

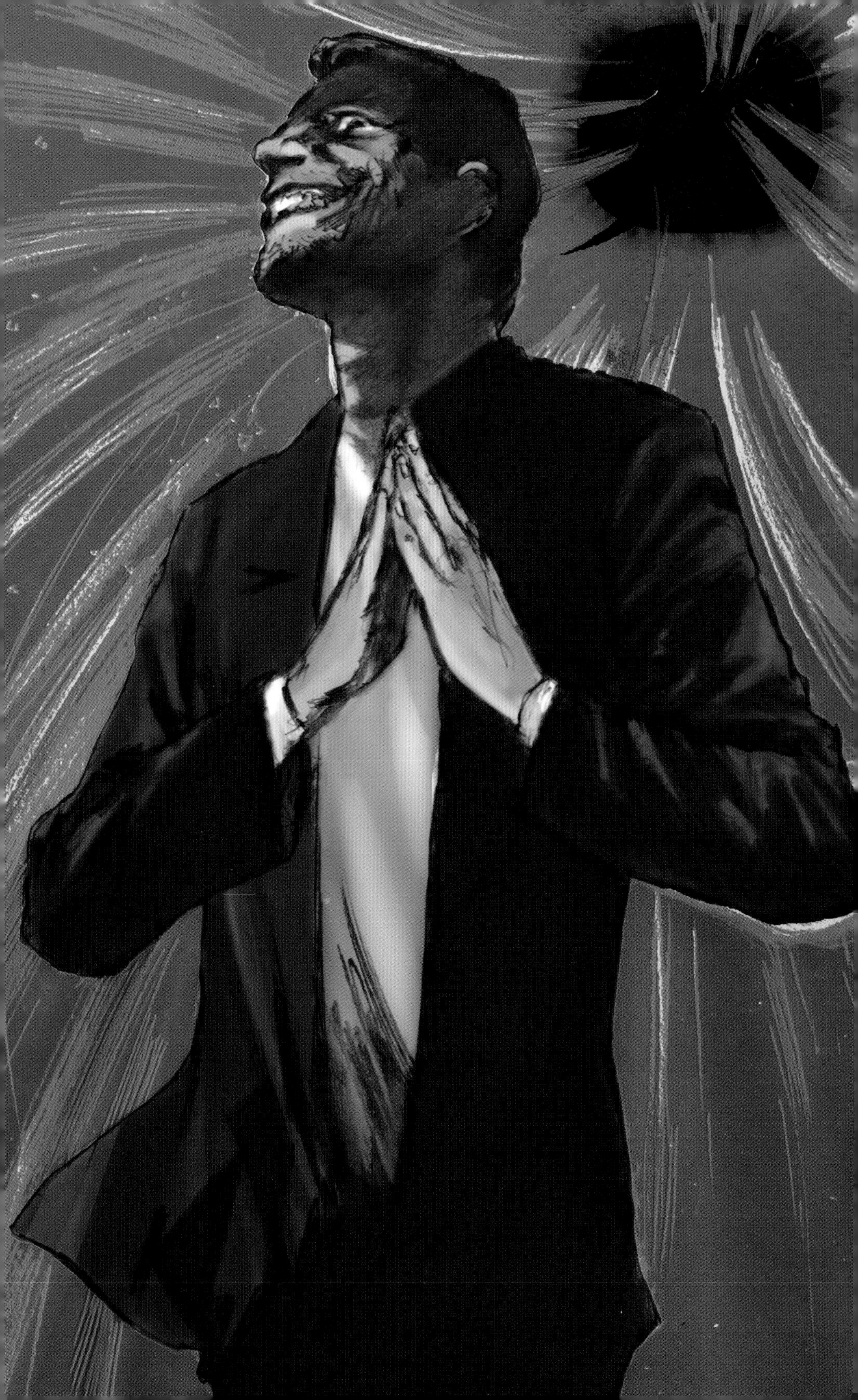

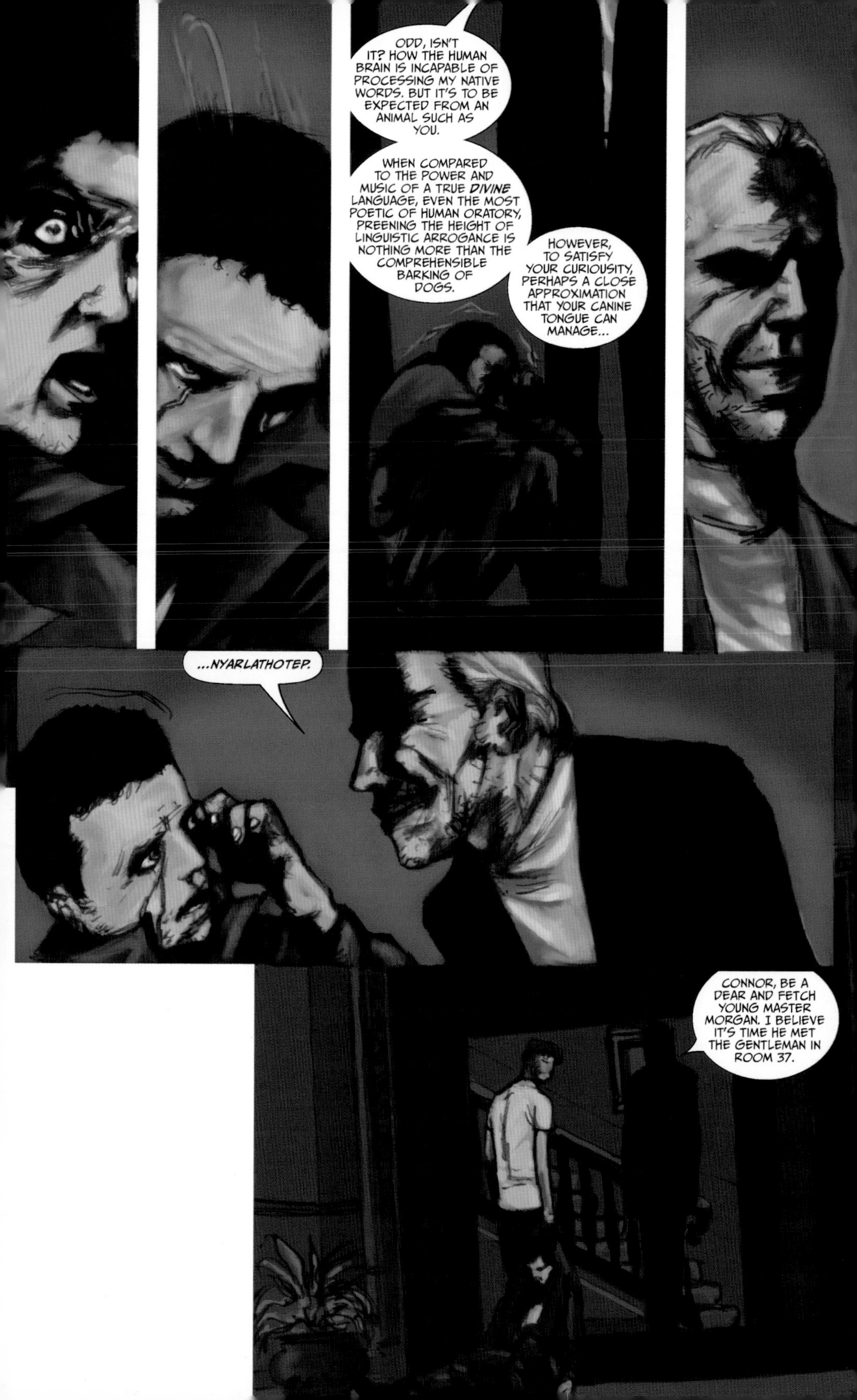
ODD, ISN'T IT? HOW THE HUMAN BRAIN IS INCAPABLE OF PROCESSING MY NATIVE WORDS. BUT IT'S TO BE EXPECTED FROM AN ANIMAL SUCH AS YOU.
WHEN COMPARED TO THE POWER AND MUSIC OF A TRUE *DIVINE* LANGUAGE, EVEN THE MOST POETIC OF HUMAN ORATORY, PREENING THE HEIGHT OF LINGUISTIC ARROGANCE IS NOTHING MORE THAN THE COMPREHENSIBLE BARKING OF DOGS.
HOWEVER, TO SATISFY YOUR CURIOUSITY, PERHAPS A CLOSE APPROXIMATION THAT YOUR CANINE TONGUE CAN MANAGE...
...NYARLATHOTEP.
CONNOR, BE A DEAR AND FETCH YOUNG MASTER MORGAN. I BELIEVE IT'S TIME HE MET THE GENTLEMAN IN ROOM 37.

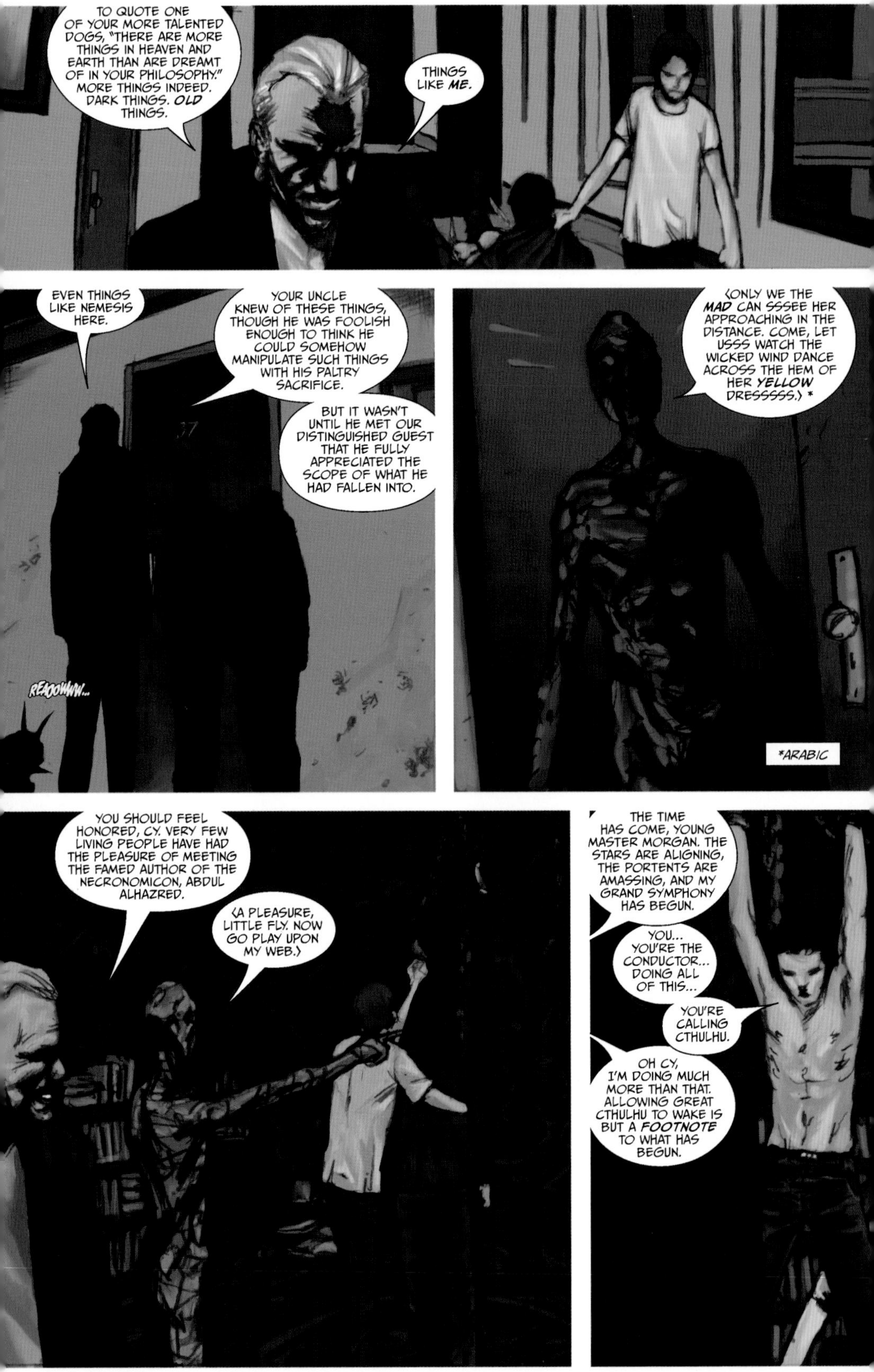
TO QUOTE ONE OF YOUR MORE TALENTED DOGS, "THERE ARE MORE THINGS IN HEAVEN AND EARTH THAN ARE DREAMT OF IN YOUR PHILOSOPHY." MORE THINGS INDEED. DARK THINGS. OLD THINGS.
THINGS LIKE ME.
EVEN THINGS LIKE NEMESIS HERE.
YOUR UNCLE KNEW OF THESE THINGS, THOUGH HE WAS FOOLISH ENOUGH TO THINK HE COULD SOMEHOW MANIPULATE SUCH THINGS WITH HIS PALTRY SACRIFICE.
BUT IT WASN'T UNTIL HE MET OUR DISTINGUISHED GUEST THAT HE FULLY APPRECIATED THE SCOPE OF WHAT HE HAD FALLEN INTO.
REAOOWWW...
<ONLY WE THE MAD CAN SSSEE HER APPROACHING IN THE DISTANCE. COME, LET USSS WATCH THE WICKED WIND DANCE ACROSS THE HEM OF HER YELLOW DRESSSSS.> *
*ARABIC
YOU SHOULD FEEL HONORED, CY. VERY FEW LIVING PEOPLE HAVE HAD THE PLEASURE OF MEETING THE FAMED AUTHOR OF THE NECRONOMICON, ABDUL ALHAZRED.
<A PLEASURE, LITTLE FLY. NOW GO PLAY UPON MY WEB.>
THE TIME HAS COME, YOUNG MASTER MORGAN. THE STARS ARE ALIGNING, THE PORTENTS ARE AMASSING, AND MY GRAND SYMPHONY HAS BEGUN.
YOU... YOU'RE THE CONDUCTOR... DOING ALL OF THIS...
YOU'RE CALLING CTHULHU.
OH CY, I'M DOING MUCH MORE THAN THAT. ALLOWING GREAT CTHULHU TO WAKE IS BUT A FOOTNOTE TO WHAT HAS BEGUN.

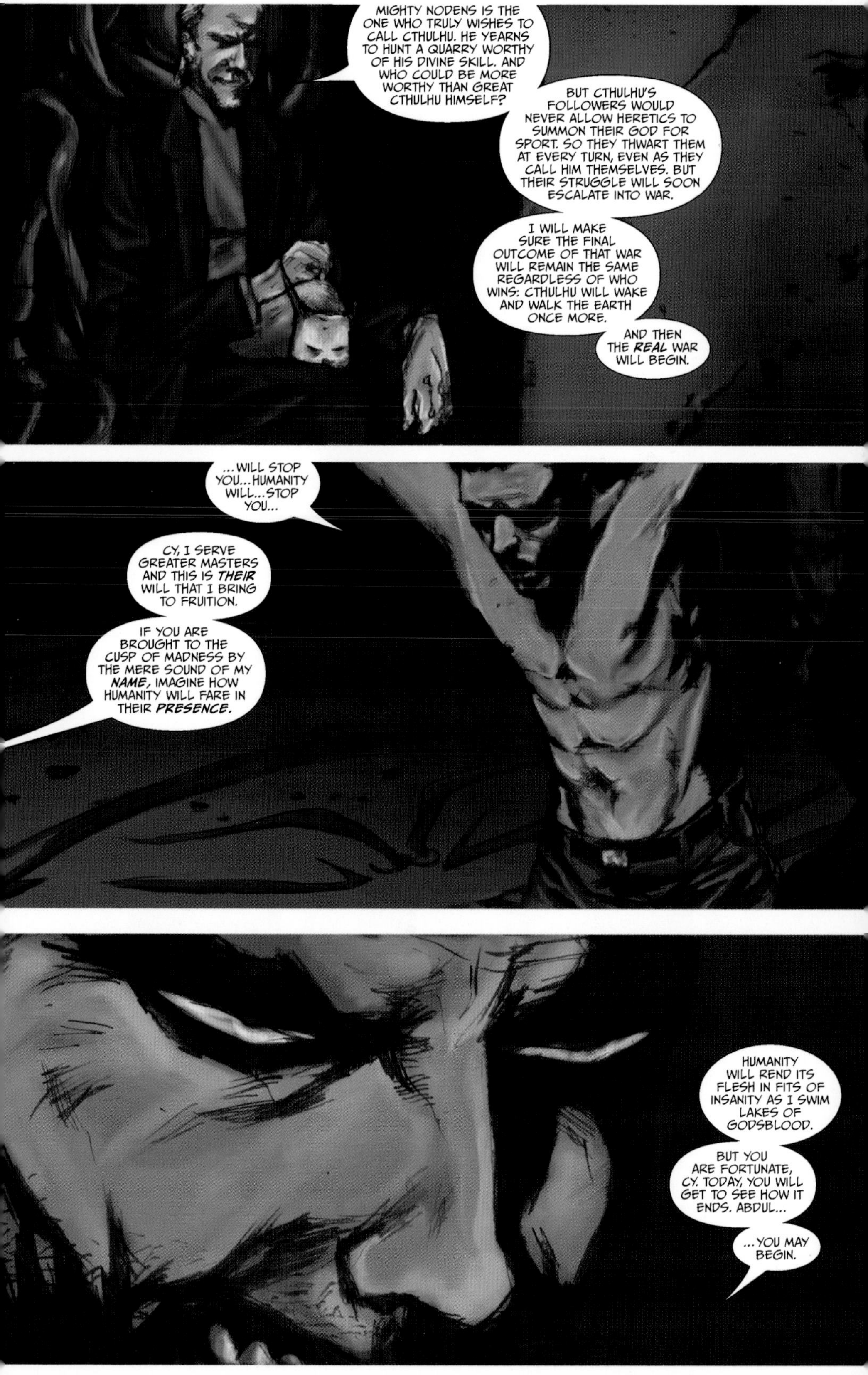
MIGHTY NODENS IS THE ONE WHO TRULY WISHES TO CALL CTHULHU. HE YEARNS TO HUNT A QUARRY WORTHY OF HIS DIVINE SKILL. AND WHO COULD BE MORE WORTHY THAN GREAT CTHULHU HIMSELF?
BUT CTHULHU'S FOLLOWERS WOULD NEVER ALLOW HERETICS TO SUMMON THEIR GOD FOR SPORT. SO THEY THWART THEM AT EVERY TURN, EVEN AS THEY CALL HIM THEMSELVES. BUT THEIR STRUGGLE WILL SOON ESCALATE INTO WAR.
I WILL MAKE SURE THE FINAL OUTCOME OF THAT WAR WILL REMAIN THE SAME REGARDLESS OF WHO WINS: CTHULHU WILL WAKE AND WALK THE EARTH ONCE MORE.
AND THEN THE *REAL* WAR WILL BEGIN.
...WILL STOP YOU...HUMANITY WILL...STOP YOU...
CY, I SERVE GREATER MASTERS AND THIS IS *THEIR* WILL THAT I BRING TO FRUITION.
IF YOU ARE BROUGHT TO THE CUSP OF MADNESS BY THE MERE SOUND OF MY *NAME,* IMAGINE HOW HUMANITY WILL FARE IN THEIR *PRESENCE.*
HUMANITY WILL REND ITS FLESH IN FITS OF INSANITY AS I SWIM LAKES OF GODSBLOOD.
BUT YOU ARE FORTUNATE, CY. TODAY, YOU WILL GET TO SEE HOW IT ENDS. ABDUL...
...YOU MAY BEGIN.

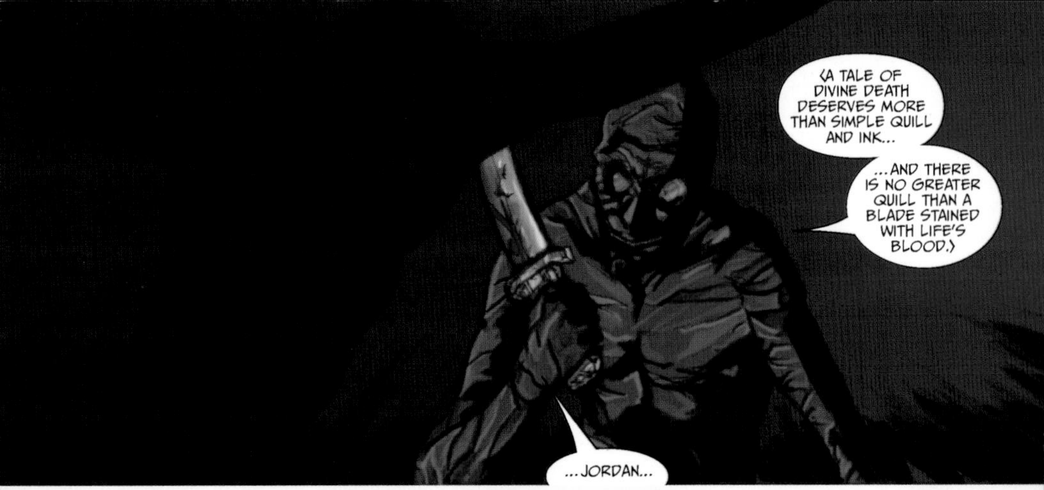
⟨A TALE OF DIVINE DEATH DESERVES MORE THAN SIMPLE QUILL AND INK...
...AND THERE IS NO GREATER QUILL THAN A BLADE STAINED WITH LIFE'S BLOOD.⟩
...JORDAN...

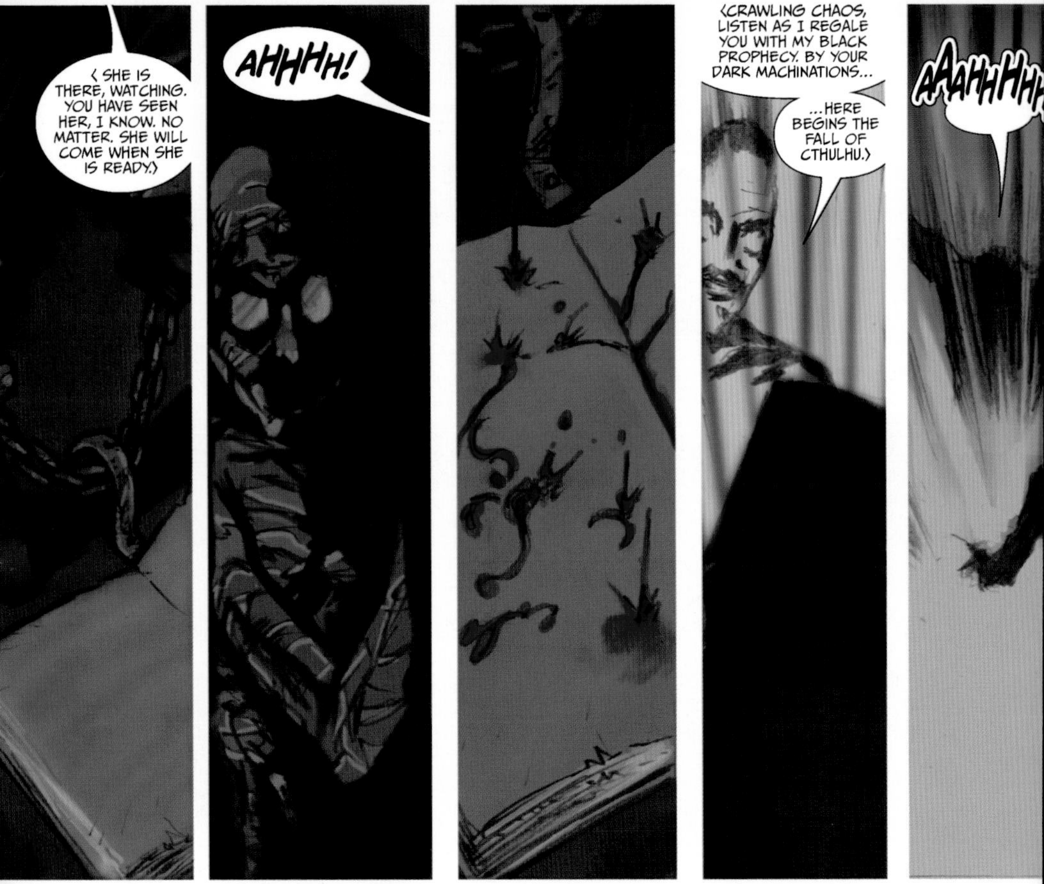
⟨ SHE IS THERE, WATCHING. YOU HAVE SEEN HER, I KNOW. NO MATTER. SHE WILL COME WHEN SHE IS READY.⟩
AHHHH!
⟨CRAWLING CHAOS, LISTEN AS I REGALE YOU WITH MY BLACK PROPHECY. BY YOUR DARK MACHINATIONS...
...HERE BEGINS THE FALL OF CTHULHU.⟩
AAAHHHHH

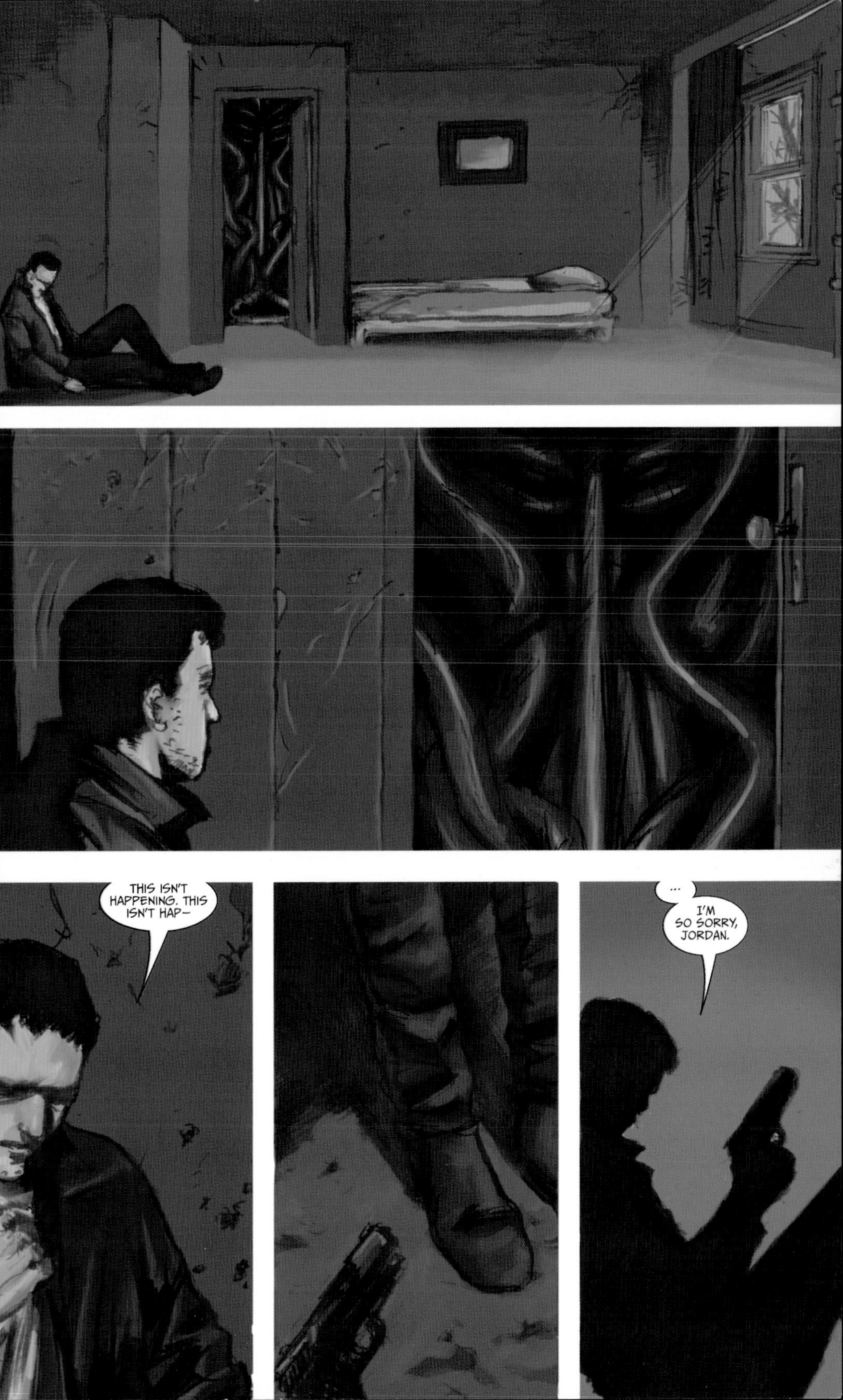
THIS ISN'T HAPPENING. THIS ISN'T HAP—
...
I'M SO SORRY, JORDAN.

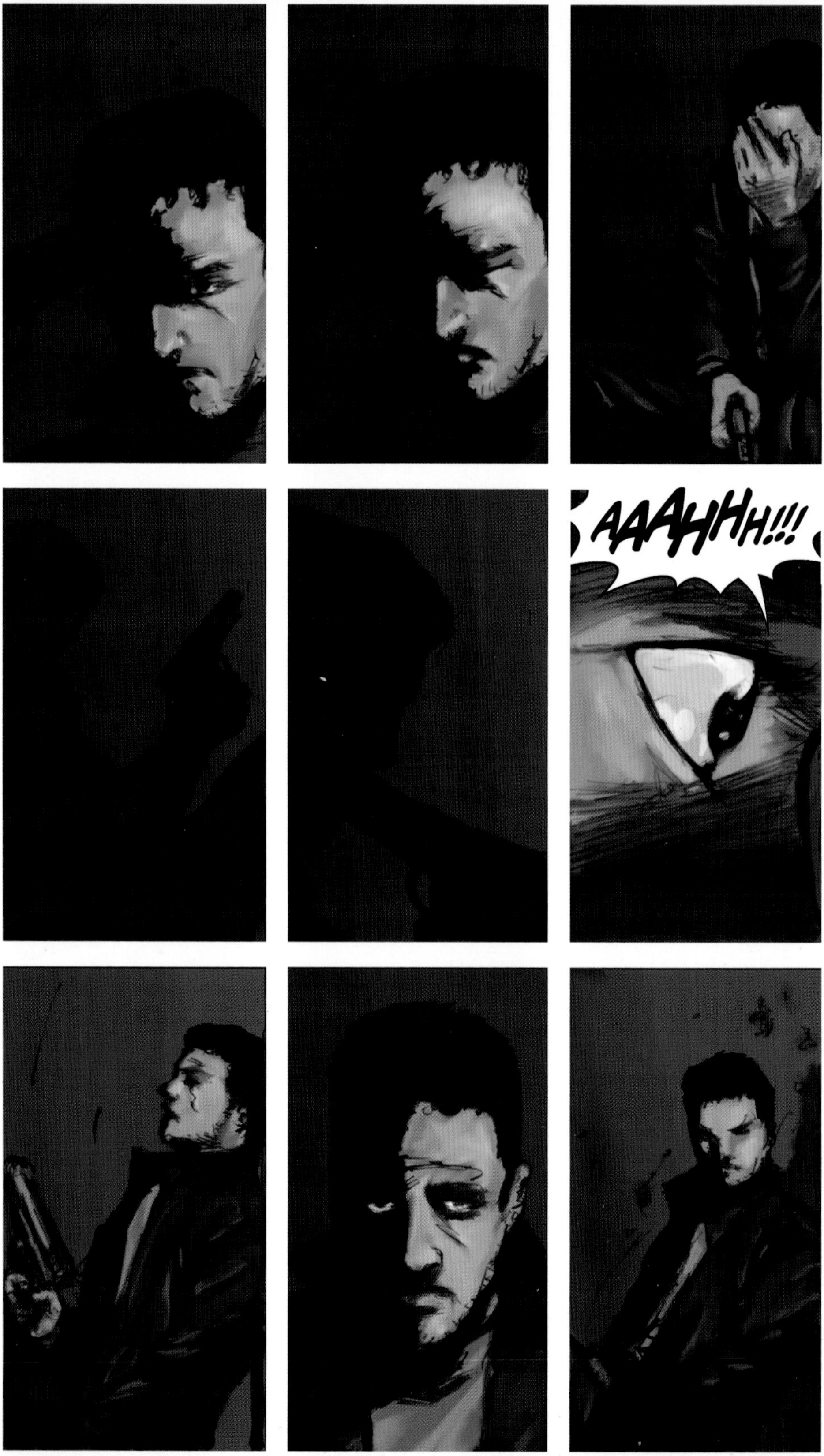
AAAHHH!!!

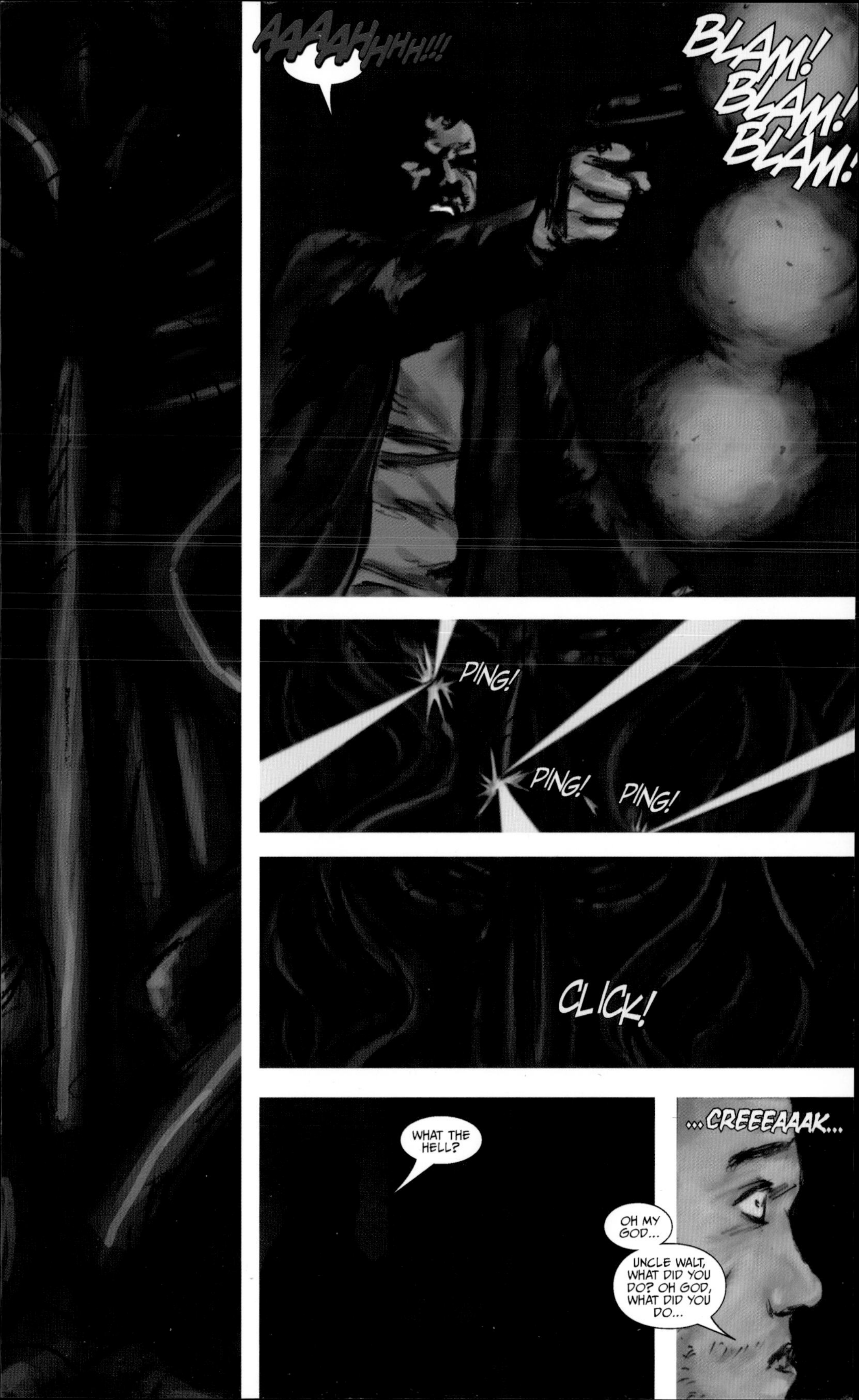
AAAAAHHHH!!!
BLAM! BLAM! BLAM!
PING!
PING!
PING!
CLICK!
WHAT THE HELL?
...CREEEAAAK...
OH MY GOD...
UNCLE WALT, WHAT DID YOU DO? OH GOD, WHAT DID YOU DO...

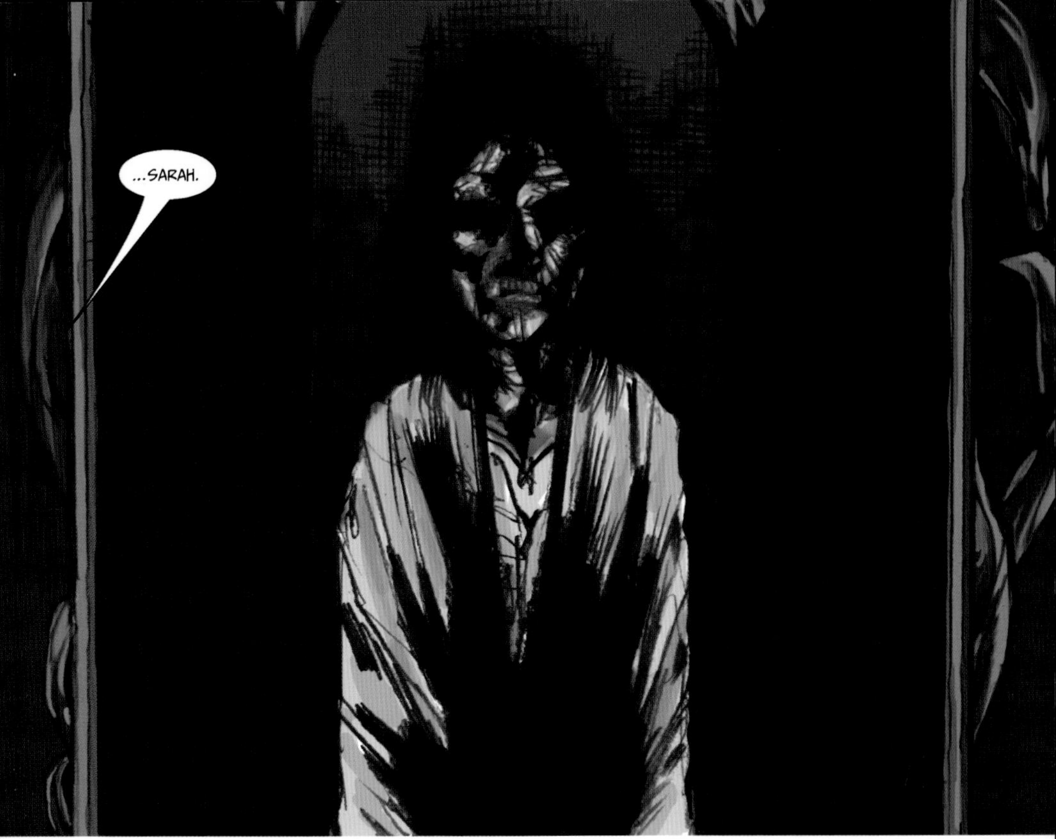
...SARAH.

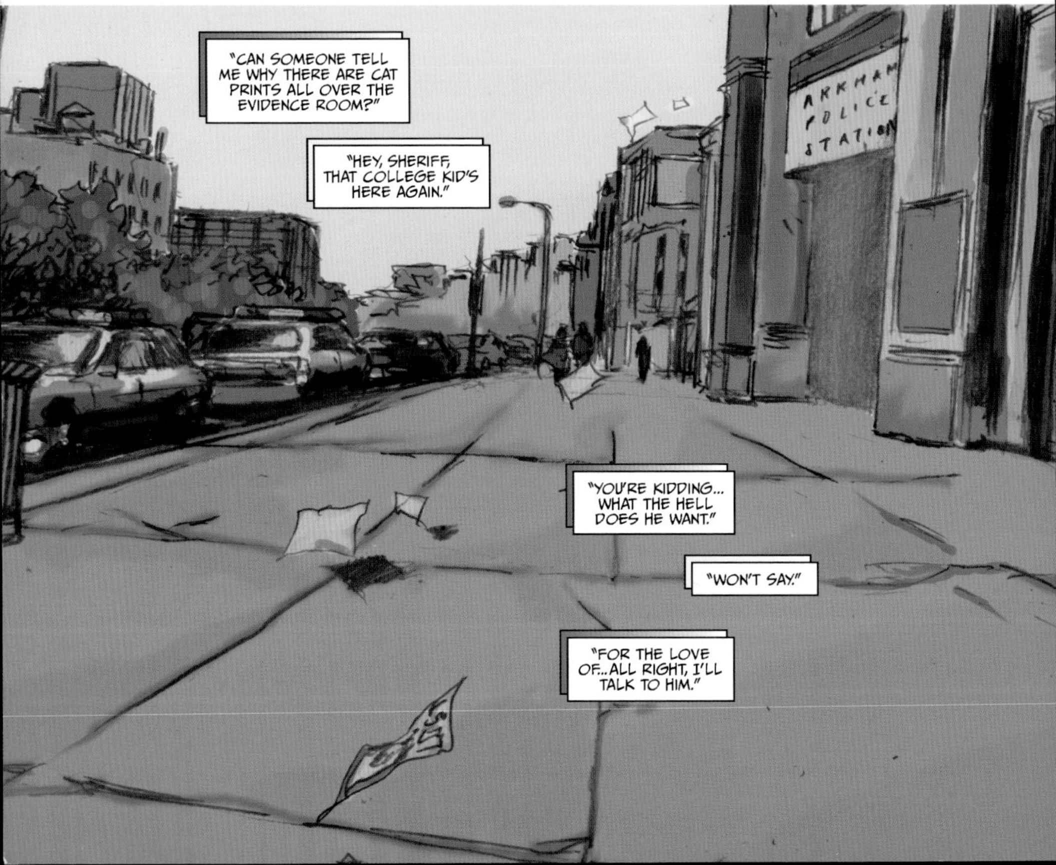
"CAN SOMEONE TELL ME WHY THERE ARE CAT PRINTS ALL OVER THE EVIDENCE ROOM?"
"HEY, SHERIFF, THAT COLLEGE KID'S HERE AGAIN."
ARKHAM POLICE STATION
"YOU'RE KIDDING... WHAT THE HELL DOES HE WANT."
"WON'T SAY."
"FOR THE LOVE OF...ALL RIGHT, I'LL TALK TO HIM."

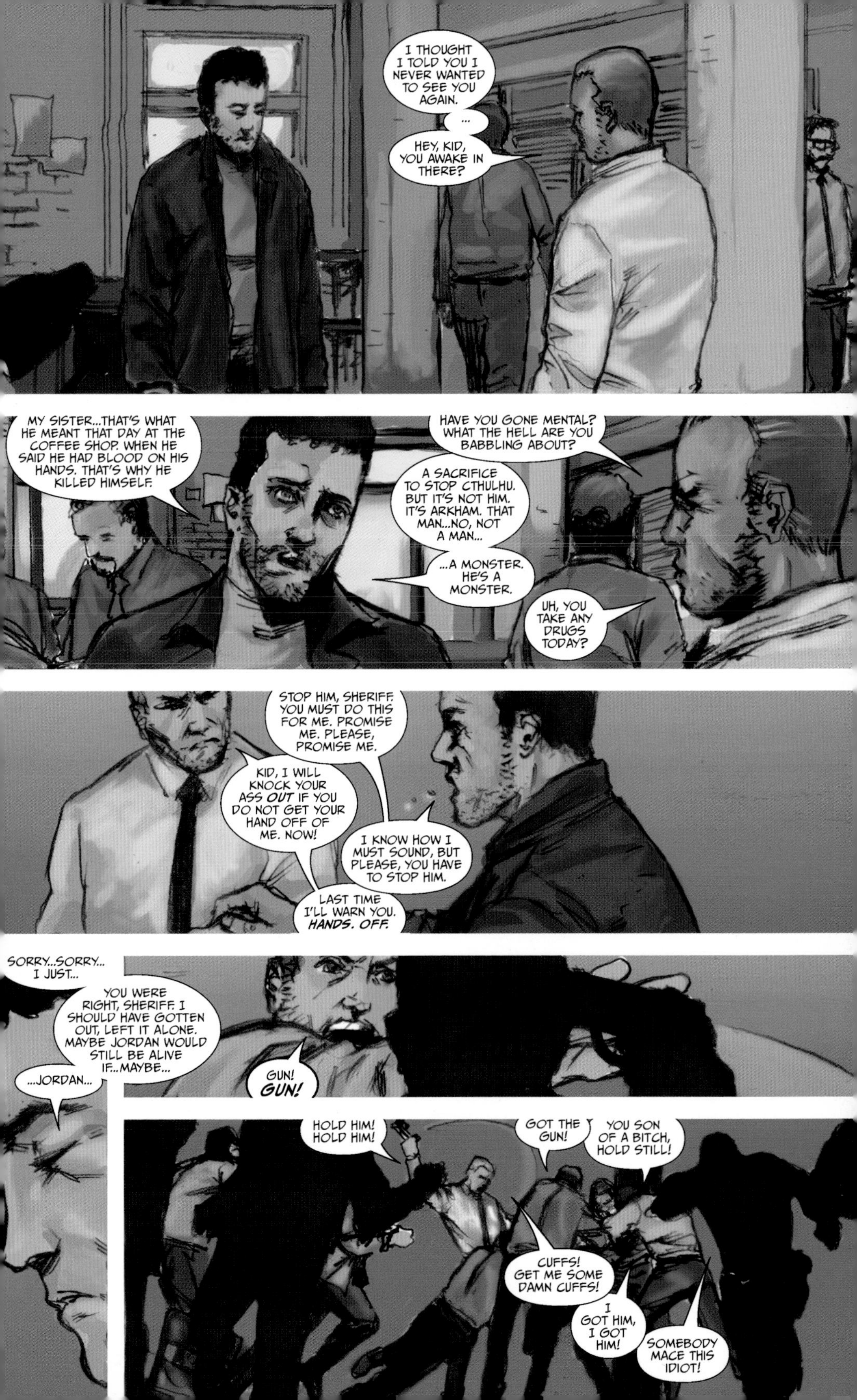
I THOUGHT I TOLD YOU I NEVER WANTED TO SEE YOU AGAIN.
...
HEY, KID, YOU AWAKE IN THERE?
MY SISTER...THAT'S WHAT HE MEANT THAT DAY AT THE COFFEE SHOP. WHEN HE SAID HE HAD BLOOD ON HIS HANDS. THAT'S WHY HE KILLED HIMSELF.
HAVE YOU GONE MENTAL? WHAT THE HELL ARE YOU BABBLING ABOUT?
A SACRIFICE TO STOP CTHULHU. BUT IT'S NOT HIM. IT'S ARKHAM. THAT MAN...NO, NOT A MAN...
...A MONSTER. HE'S A MONSTER.
UH, YOU TAKE ANY DRUGS TODAY?
STOP HIM, SHERIFF. YOU MUST DO THIS FOR ME. PROMISE ME. PLEASE, PROMISE ME.
KID, I WILL KNOCK YOUR ASS *OUT* IF YOU DO NOT GET YOUR HAND OFF OF ME. NOW!
I KNOW HOW I MUST SOUND, BUT PLEASE, YOU HAVE TO STOP HIM.
LAST TIME I'LL WARN YOU. ***HANDS. OFF.***
SORRY...SORRY... I JUST...
YOU WERE RIGHT, SHERIFF. I SHOULD HAVE GOTTEN OUT, LEFT IT ALONE. MAYBE JORDAN WOULD STILL BE ALIVE IF...MAYBE...
...JORDAN...
GUN! ***GUN!***
HOLD HIM! HOLD HIM!
GOT THE GUN!
YOU SON OF A BITCH, HOLD STILL!
CUFFS! GET ME SOME DAMN CUFFS!
I GOT HIM, I GOT HIM!
SOMEBODY MACE THIS IDIOT!

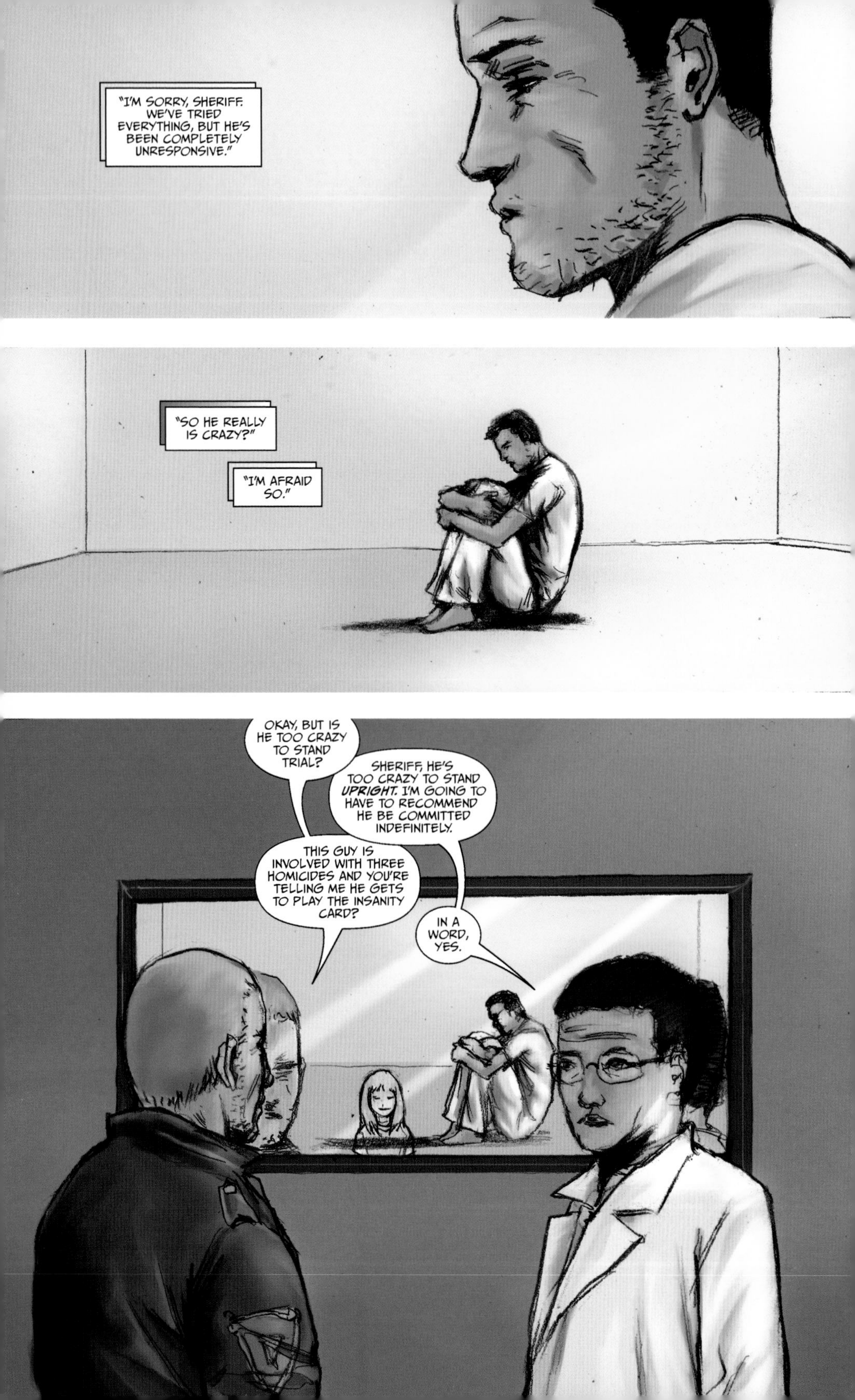
"I'M SORRY, SHERIFF. WE'VE TRIED EVERYTHING, BUT HE'S BEEN COMPLETELY UNRESPONSIVE."
"SO HE REALLY IS CRAZY?"
"I'M AFRAID SO."
OKAY, BUT IS HE TOO CRAZY TO STAND TRIAL?
SHERIFF, HE'S TOO CRAZY TO STAND *UPRIGHT.* I'M GOING TO HAVE TO RECOMMEND HE BE COMMITTED INDEFINITELY.
THIS GUY IS INVOLVED WITH THREE HOMICIDES AND YOU'RE TELLING ME HE GETS TO PLAY THE INSANITY CARD?
IN A WORD, YES.

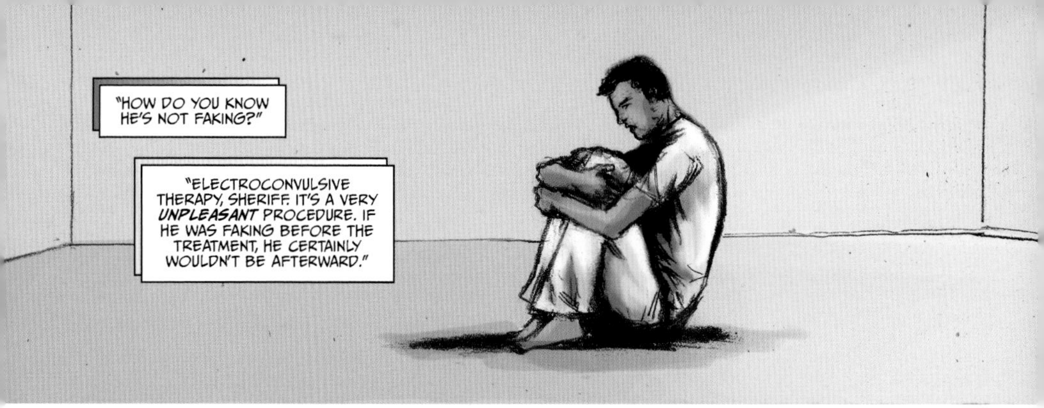
"HOW DO YOU KNOW HE'S NOT FAKING?"
"ELECTROCONVULSIVE THERAPY, SHERIFF. IT'S A VERY *UNPLEASANT* PROCEDURE. IF HE WAS FAKING BEFORE THE TREATMENT, HE CERTAINLY WOULDN'T BE AFTERWARD."

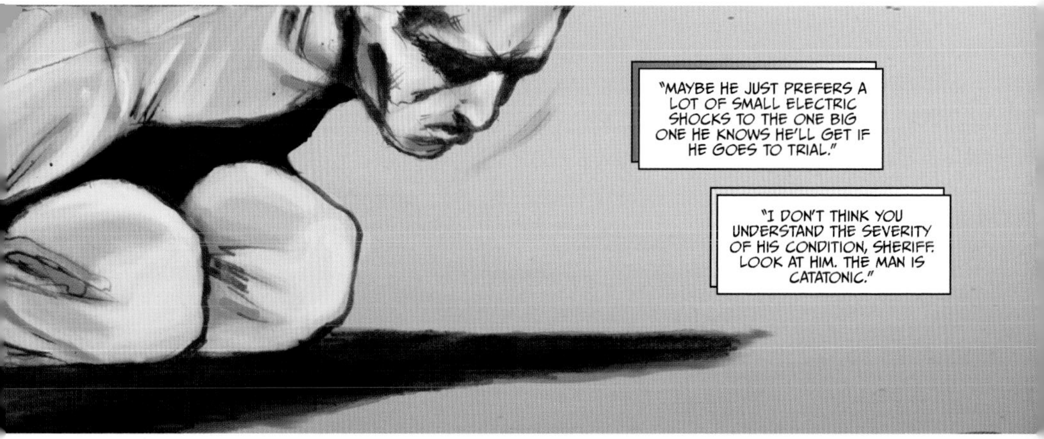
"MAYBE HE JUST PREFERS A LOT OF SMALL ELECTRIC SHOCKS TO THE ONE BIG ONE HE KNOWS HE'LL GET IF HE GOES TO TRIAL."
"I DON'T THINK YOU UNDERSTAND THE SEVERITY OF HIS CONDITION, SHERIFF. LOOK AT HIM. THE MAN IS CATATONIC."

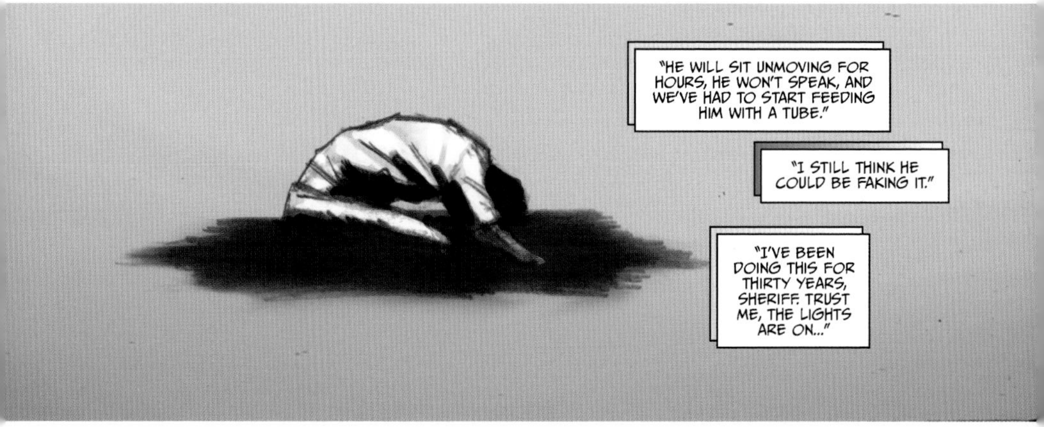
"HE WILL SIT UNMOVING FOR HOURS, HE WON'T SPEAK, AND WE'VE HAD TO START FEEDING HIM WITH A TUBE."
"I STILL THINK HE COULD BE FAKING IT."
"I'VE BEEN DOING THIS FOR THIRTY YEARS, SHERIFF. TRUST ME, THE LIGHTS ARE ON..."

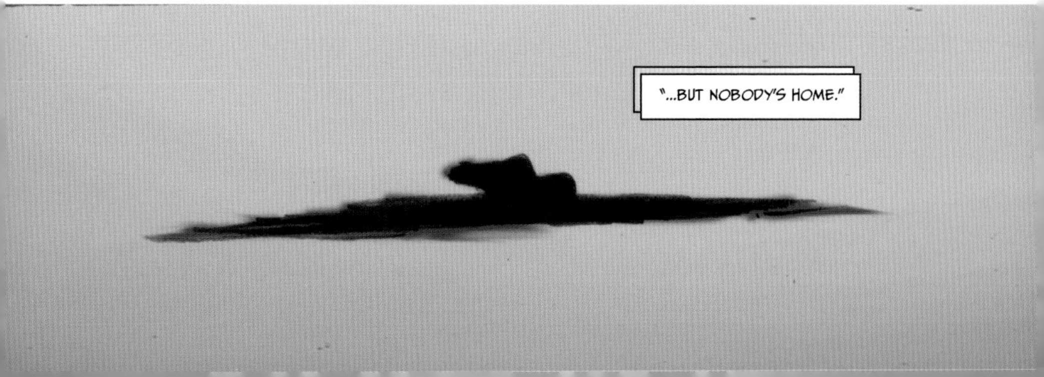
"...BUT NOBODY'S HOME."

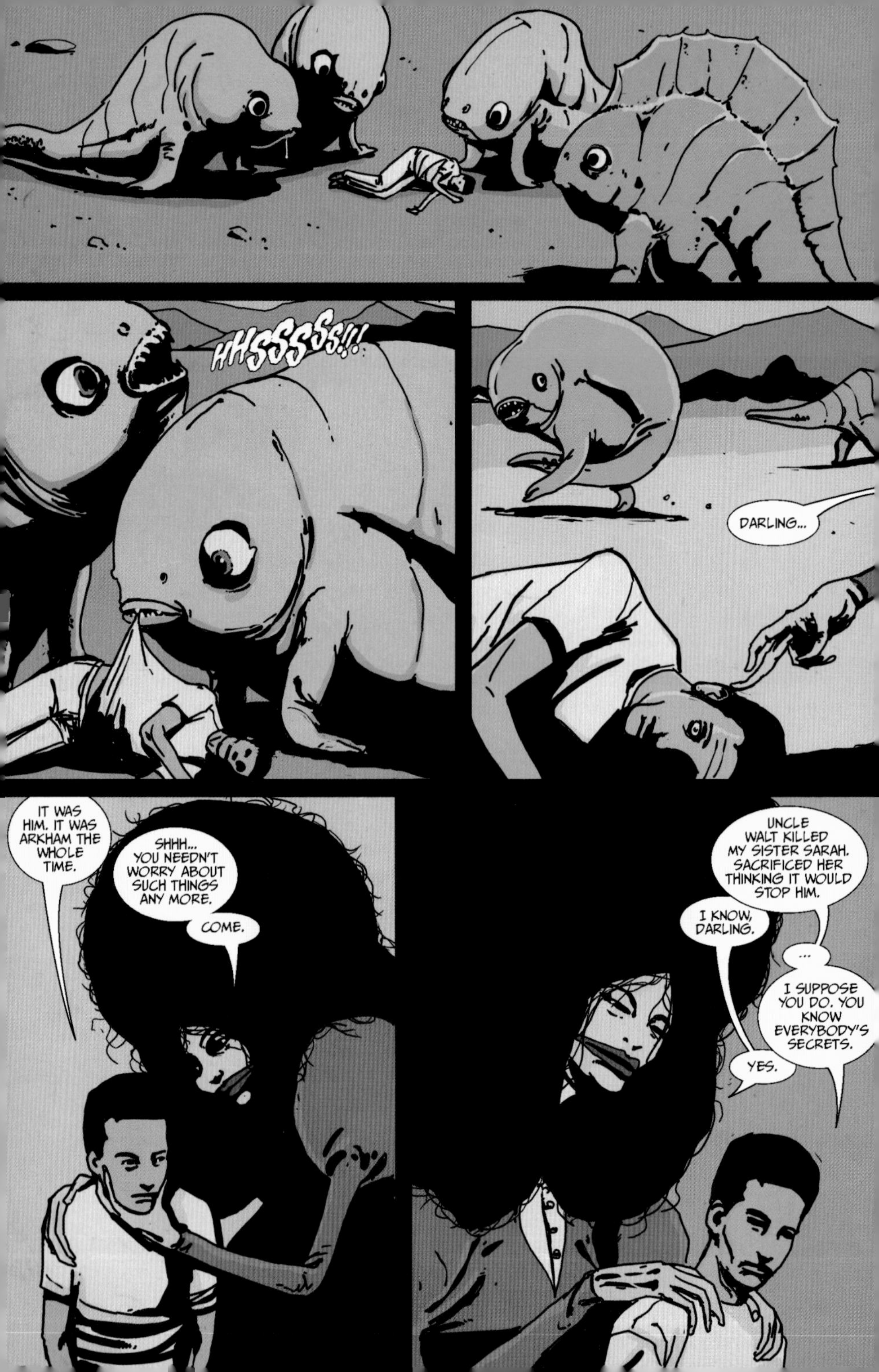
HHSSSSSS!!!
DARLING...
IT WAS HIM. IT WAS ARKHAM THE WHOLE TIME.
SHHH... YOU NEEDN'T WORRY ABOUT SUCH THINGS ANY MORE.
COME.
UNCLE WALT KILLED MY SISTER SARAH. SACRIFICED HER THINKING IT WOULD STOP HIM.
I KNOW, DARLING.
...
I SUPPOSE YOU DO. YOU KNOW EVERYBODY'S SECRETS.
YES.

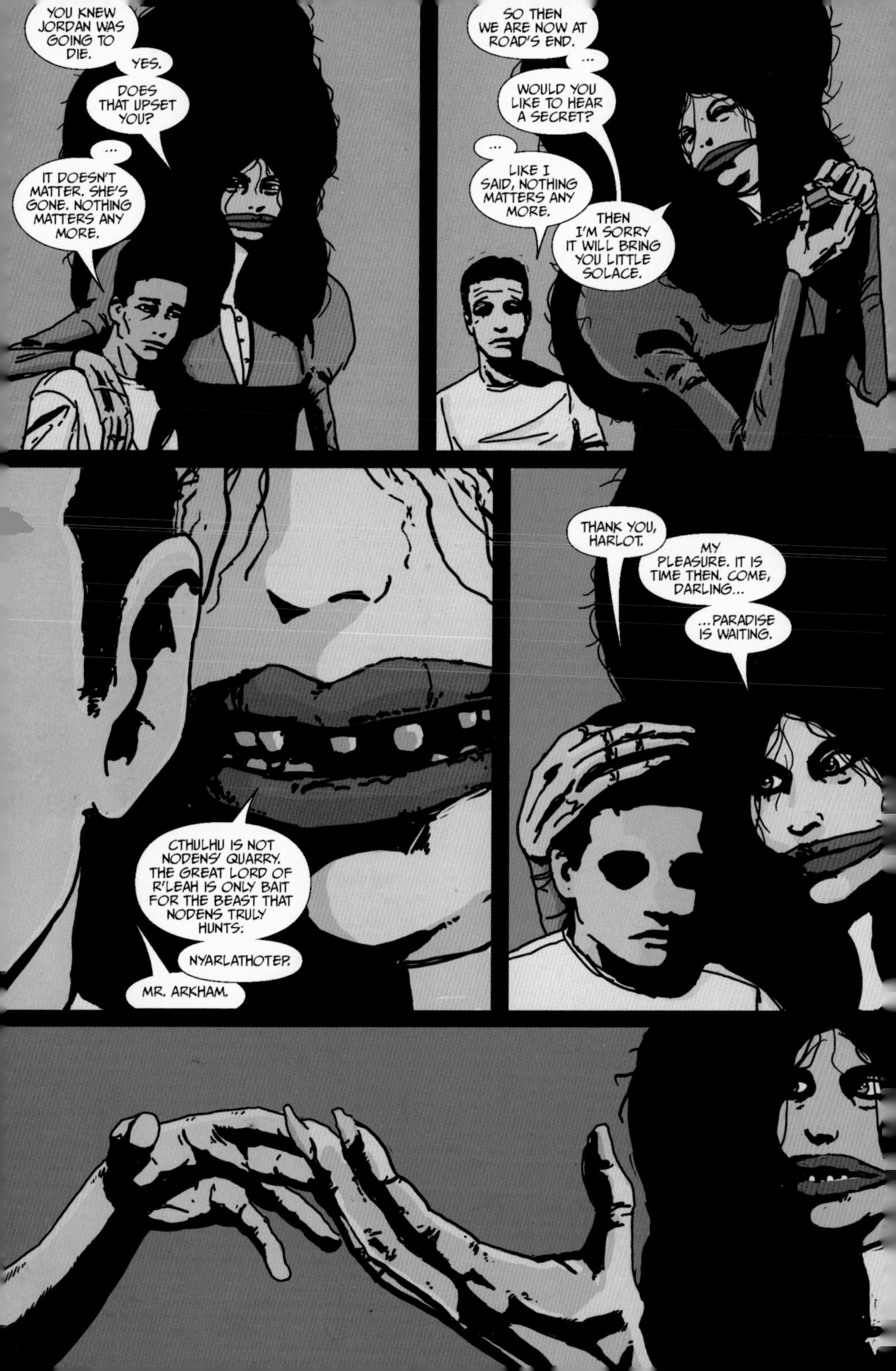
YOU KNEW JORDAN WAS GOING TO DIE.
YES.
DOES THAT UPSET YOU?
...
IT DOESN'T MATTER. SHE'S GONE. NOTHING MATTERS ANY MORE.
SO THEN WE ARE NOW AT ROAD'S END.
...
WOULD YOU LIKE TO HEAR A SECRET?
...
LIKE I SAID, NOTHING MATTERS ANY MORE.
THEN I'M SORRY IT WILL BRING YOU LITTLE SOLACE.
CTHULHU IS NOT NODENS' QUARRY. THE GREAT LORD OF R'LEAH IS ONLY BAIT FOR THE BEAST THAT NODENS TRULY HUNTS:
NYARLATHOTEP.
MR. ARKHAM.
THANK YOU, HARLOT.
MY PLEASURE. IT IS TIME THEN. COME, DARLING...
...PARADISE IS WAITING.

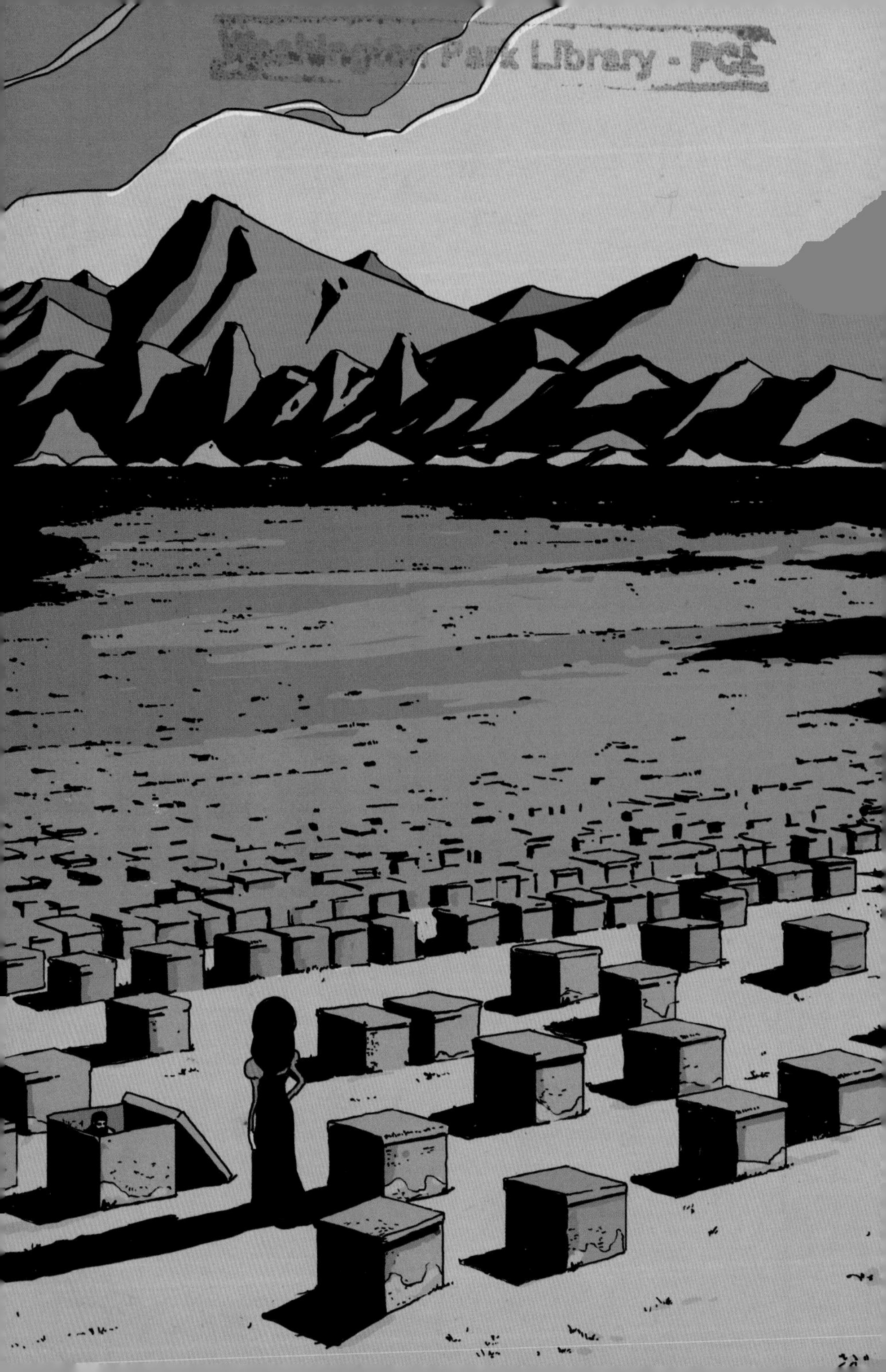